Acclaim for X. QUINN's

Man on Mars: The Wake

"A Martian conflict like no other… Man on Mars is highly recommended for sci-fi readers who like their military battle action tempered by both hard sci-fi and social and psychological inspections."

—D. Donovan, Midwest Book Review

"Valiant humans versus tyrannical aliens… the enjoyable saga is well paced, and the closing battles will hold readers' attention to an ending that deftly opens doors to the sequel."

—Kirkus Reviews

"★★★★★ - As a science nerd, I was super impressed with Man on Mars: The Wake by X. Quinn, and it really does tick all the boxes. …"

—Asher Syed for Readers' Favorite

MAN ON MARS

THE WAKE

X. QUINN

This is a work of fiction. Names, characters, organizations, businesses, events, and incidents are the products of the author's imagination. Any resemblance to actual persons, living or dead, or actual organizations is purely coincidental.

ISBN: 978-1-7378564-1-2

Cover Artwork & Design by Jeff Brown Graphics

Map by X. QUINN, Mars image credit: NASA

To every mind that never gives up hope, love, and truth.

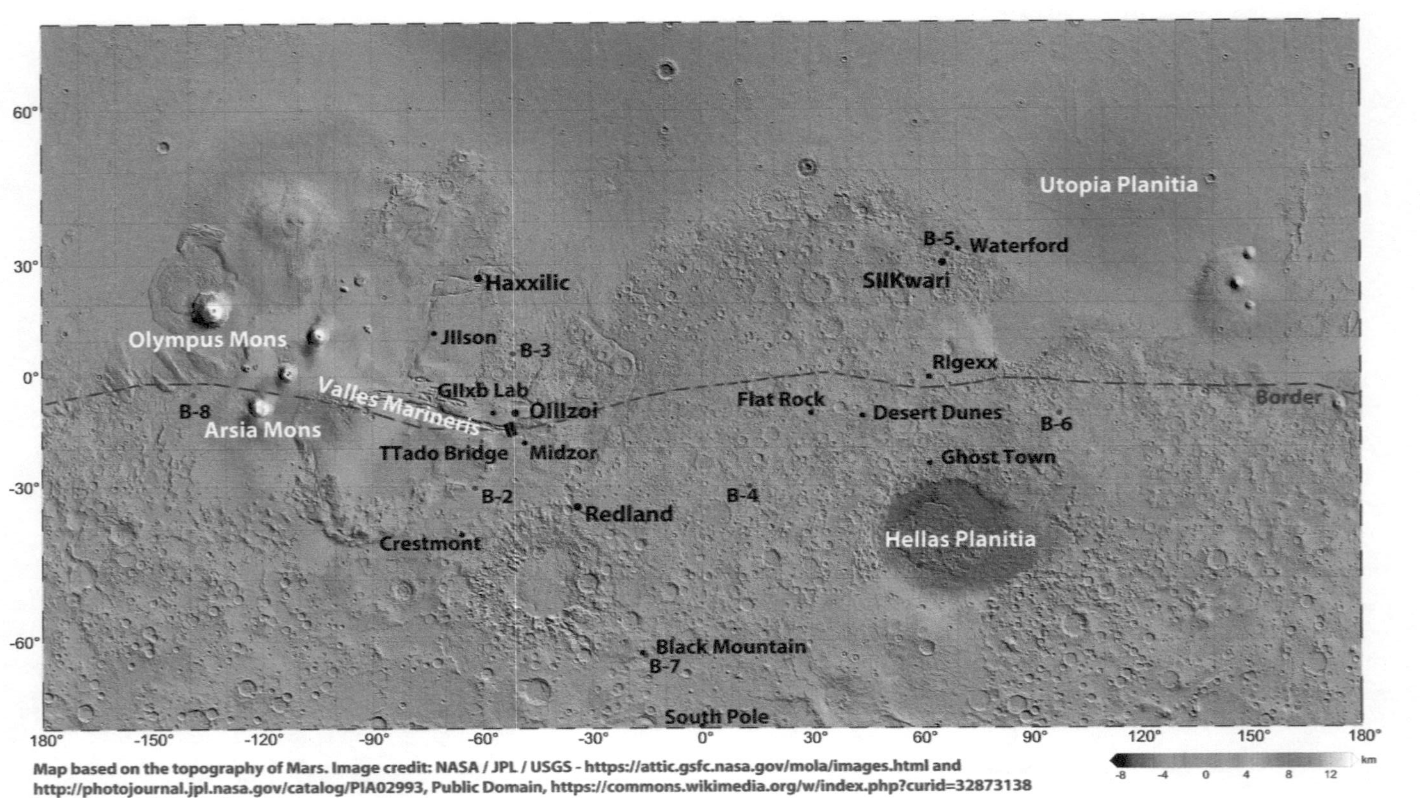

Map based on the topography of Mars. Image credit: NASA / JPL / USGS - https://attic.gsfc.nasa.gov/mola/images.html and http://photojournal.jpl.nasa.gov/catalog/PIA02993, Public Domain, https://commons.wikimedia.org/w/index.php?curid=32873138

Contents

Prologue

The remote sun sank swiftly under the horizon, and the sky dimmed. Yet the sandy wind blew heavily, creating turbulence that swept the tallest mountain on Mars — Olympus Mons.

A deafening boom broke the night's solitude, and a Gatti cruiser appeared abruptly in the distant sky. It pierced the atmosphere, and the rumbling sound shook the very air.

Two more Gatti ships followed.

They swept towards the Communication Tower in the south region of the vast mountain and then decelerated in a fraction of a second. Not far from them, an enormous flat surface carved from the rocks was their intended destination.

The three Gatti ships changed their formation from a triangle to a straight line and landed smoothly, one after the other.

Dvexu jumped out of the first cruiser and dropped to the ground the instant the ship touched down. A dozen guards swarmed out to follow him. Dvexu was all dark, more than two meters tall, and armored. He had a rough, scaly face and round eyes. A deep scar ran beneath his left eye, cutting across older marks. From his lower back, five long tentacles emerged and fell to his feet, and one of them whirled behind him with an extra eye. He didn't wait for the guards and headed straight into a corridor that led to a vertical skylift.

Another Gatti emerged from the second ship. This one was Zullom. He shared Dvexu's rugged features, and his lower teeth looked particularly jagged, jutting upwards like daggers and seemingly preventing his mouth from closing. Unlike Dvexu, however, his silver scales were pale. Zullom hopped off his ship and hurried into the same corridor.

Amosirx was last. He was short by Gatti standards, more like the size of a regular human. By the time he climbed out of his ship, the others were almost gone, and he had to run to catch up. When he reached the end of the corridor, the other two had already taken their places in a skylift capsule. All their guards remained outside, standing by.

Amosirx got to his spot. The door of the capsule closed automatically, and it ascended. Its speed was so astonishing that the surroundings blurred completely. It shot up three kilometers in less than a minute and arrived at the top of the tower.

"Ready the port," Zullom said in Gattish, their language, the moment the three Gattis entered the communication room.

"Yes, coming right up," a robotic voice answered, and the lights on the control panels turned on.

"Zullom, are you so eager to talk to Father?" asked Dvexu, squeezing his face into a peculiar smile, making fun of his brother. "You are so sure he will be pleased, and you will be rewarded?"

"I do not joke in a meeting like this," Zullom answered curtly. He kept his eyes straight ahead and crossed his arms in front of him. "But you are right. He will be pleased to hear the progress I've made, and he will make me System Architect." Zullom then tilted his head to watch Dvexu's expression, his eyes sharp and deep.

Dvexu corrected him at once, "No way! It is not only you. *We* have made progress together."

Zullom hissed from his nostrils and ignored him.

A Gatti operator double-checked the automatic settings and examined the status bars on the control panels. He then confirmed the pre-stored coordinates of the distant star system and pushed the start.

The robotic voice came out again. "Initializing communication… Force field starting up…"

They waited in the center of the room in silence while the machine gave them the sequence.

Soon enough, a tiny dot appeared in midair above them at the right time. The dot grew into a glowing sphere. Patterns of light shifted on the surface of the sphere, and its color changed from black to grey to silver.

Moments later, the sphere stopped growing and was suspended under the high ceiling of the tower. The traversable wormhole had reached its size and stabilized, stretching from the other side of the galaxy to the Communication Tower on Mars.

"Connection made… Communication ready…

"Transmitting Location: Star Chain System Ref: 0779, Planet – 1: Mars.

"Local Time: Mars Year 8, Month 24, Day 27, Time 24 h 39 m 30 s…"

Zullom raised his tentacles in greeting. "Superior, this is Zullom, Acting Architect of System-0779."

Photons brought distorted images of Superior from the other side. The images were then re-projected to become clearly recognizable.

Zullom continued, "I have with me today the Head of NIISS Guard, Dvexu, and the Head of Military Technology and Engineering, Amosirx."

A husky and harsh voice came through. "Amosirx, is it still true that this is the maximum size of any port? And this port can be opened for only twenty minutes, the same as last time?" The voice was from Superior, an elderly Gatti. He sat in the middle on the other side, with his high council members standing behind him.

"Yes, Superior." Amosirx was slightly tremulous as he spoke.

"You do understand our goal is to have a much bigger, stable corridor to transport our ships, army, and supplies? Right now, it is so small that none of us can pass."

"Yes, yes. Our team has been working on increasing its size and stability since we discovered the Exo matter to hold it open. But producing Exo matter in large quantity is still challenging —"

"Find a way!" Superior snapped at Amosirx before he could explain more.

Amosirx shut up immediately, not daring to waste another second of this energy-expensive call.

"Zullom, report." Superior switched to the next topic in no time.

"Yes, Superior. Eight Mars years after we first arrived at the current solar system, I am proud to declare our base planet habitable," said Zullom passionately, his voice loud and steady, and he put emphasis on 'habitable' in his reply.

"You must know that the atmosphere on Mars was thin without oxygen. The temperature was low since it is far away from the sun, so it was very cold at night. And there was no water in liquid form to support life. And then — behold, the most glorious planet-wide engineering and transformation we have completed… In the first phase, we needed an artificial magnetic field that could protect the whole planet from solar wind and radiation. That was the first thing we did when our pioneer fleet arrived. A large magnetic dipole shield has been deployed in orbit. After that, the loss of atmosphere from the solar wind is greatly reduced.

"What's more, we identified a good source of nitrogen on our way here. Several massive ammonia-rich asteroids were blasted off their original trajectory and redirected here. After the frozen ammonia on these asteroids breaks down, we have sufficient nitrogen and hydrogen.

"And in the second phase, we installed orbital mirrors, a total of thirty-two panels. They direct the sunlight onto the surface, increase the light level and raise the planet's surface temperature…"

Superior didn't seem to appreciate the efforts, however. He interrupted Zullom impatiently, "I have seen similar processes applied to other planets. You need to be more concise."

"Yes, sure." Zullom went faster, his voice growing nervous since Father didn't seem to be pleased.

"After the success of the first two phases, it took two Mars years for us to achieve a stable atmosphere. Sufficient air pressure can now maintain liquid water at average surface temperature. In the third phase, we have established food production! About twenty percent of the planet's surface has been covered with solar-powered factories. The factories can produce various nutrients via automatic biosynthesis. Synthesized carbohydrates and proteins serve as the main food source, and oxygen is released in the process of the conversion of carbon dioxide into carbohydrates. Therefore, we reconstitute a nitrogen-oxygen atmosphere."

"Where is the data?" one of the high council members asked.

"As of now, detailed data is being transmitted to you via the port," Zullom replied hastily. "We have also built other infrastructures — cities, transportation, and a hatch lab — anything you would like to have...

"So, long story short, the planet can now sustain us and other lifeforms. Congratulations, Superior! You have now added a base planet, and soon the whole solar system will be added to your system chain. What a great achievement!"

"By other lifeforms, you mean humans?" Superior interjected. "I can recall that from our last communication."

"Yes. We found a few locals when we arrived. They call the planet Mars. At that time, they had merely completed some expeditions and built simple facilities," Zullom replied. "We came in with a small population, and we needed time to settle and grow, so we offered to do the development together. As a result, we have adopted some of their naming conventions and their calendar. At this moment, we are at peace with them."

"The next plan?" Superior sounded demanding.

"A much larger population of them reside on their home planet. They call it Earth, our next target. Now that we have established and expanded, the conquest of both Mars and Earth should be easy, given their technology is behind ours —"

"That is where our army comes in," Dvexu cut in. "Amosirx and I are going to build interplanetary warships and, of course, various cruisers and weaponry. We will be ready in the next one or two years to sail to Earth."

“Estimated resistance from humans?” Superior laid back against his seat, evaluating the information that his two sons had provided him.

“Close to zero?” Dvexu turned to consult Amosirx. “Amosirx has done research on them.”

Amosirx answered quickly at the mention of his name, his voice timid, “Yes. They are at the post-atomic stage. They have comparable technology that we used three hundred to five hundred years ago. We have the absolute advantage over them.”

“Good.” Superior stood up and paced the room on the other side, deep in contemplation. Then he said, “Dvexu, hold off the attack. I know complete obliteration is your specialty, but it hasn’t proved to be the best way to triumph.”

“What?” Dvexu and Zullom couldn’t believe what they were hearing.

Superior then continued, waving his tentacles, “Based on our new experience from conquering other planets, I have another plan.”

“What plan?” asked Dvexu.

“I want to use this Mars as a second location for an experiment,” said Superior. “Icus, one of your brothers, is traveling from your nearest star system-0778. In the next two months or so, he will arrive with his team. I have assigned him System Architect to carry out the experiment. Give him a welcome; help him lead the next stage of transformation.”

Zullom asked in disbelief, “Icus as System Architect? Why? Isn’t he the youngest among our hatches? And he has no track records.”

“I do not think he is better than us,” said Dvexu, who didn’t hide his disagreement.

“Icus is the youngest, but with one proven record,” Superior replied firmly as he shot a sharp look at his sons. “He has succeeded in testing out his ideas in your previous base planet. I have decided to give him a chance.”

“Really? I did not know that,” Dvexu grumbled.

“If he fails?” asked Zullom.

"Either of you can give him a quick death *if* he fails," replied Superior, his voice cold and clear.

Dvexu and Zullom almost shuddered at the cruel response. While they stood speechlessly, Superior dropped his tentacles and left, and the connection was then ended.

The decision was final.

Dvexu was annoyed by the announcement of a newcomer. He rolled his eyes and complained, "Our interstellar ships can only travel at half-light speed. Icus must have boarded years ago, yet Father only tells us now."

Zullom regained his calm after a few minutes. He took a step closer to Dvexu, connected one of their tentacles, and delivered him a secret message:

"You can still have your perfect war and your glory. Father and Icus need not know. Let's act before our little brother comes in and takes it all."

On his rough and marked face, Dvexu issued a horrible smile.

Chapter 1
Back from Earth

Shana woke up just before dawn. Sound waves of explosions were rattling her windows. A purge again? She jumped out of bed and watched closely from her upstairs windows.

There were airstrikes in the distance, and of course, Dark Spiral — the NIISS's Mothership — was hovering above the city of Waterford.

She hated that ship. Shaped like a monstrous pentagon, Dark Spiral had surface grids that appeared to twist and turn inward, converging on its black center like a spiral. And on the grids, Gatti fighters parked in rows, looking like iron birds sitting on branches, ready to strike down their prey. The whole thing was like a vortex that would devour everything.

Shana was fifteen by Earth years. As one of the first generations of humans born on Mars, she had enjoyed a peaceful childhood growing up with Gattis around. Gattis had come from the nearest habitable planet that orbited the star of Proxima Centauri. They said their Star Chain System extended to the other far end of the Milky Way.

Gattis appeared friendly at first, and they brought with them more advanced technologies. In the early years, they completed a planet-wide transformation for Mars together with human pioneers.

However, things changed abruptly two Mars years ago. Gattis tried to conquer human settlements with force, and at the beginning of Mars Year 9, the Alien War broke out. The humans lost in just three days. Since then, Gattis had ruled the planet.

Self-organized resistances grew, though, Shana's father told her, and Gattis nowadays often visited human cities to purge them.

Few people had left Waterford as the NIISS guards poured in. They were reluctant to go away since NIISS's previous purges targeted armed forces only. Everyone hoped that they could just remain concealed in their homes until the day passed.

Suddenly, Shana heard someone screaming.

"Is this a clinic? Help!"

She looked out the window and saw a man running towards her house carrying a child, both covered in blood. She hurried out to help. Mother led them to a temporary bed, and Father examined the man and the child quickly after they sat down.

"Shana, get bandages and my medicine box!" Father called. "We need simple surgical instruments later. Get them ready in the cleanroom."

"No problem. I've got it," said Shana, getting to work at once. Both of her parents were doctors; she learned very early from them and became a good helper.

Her family clinic soon became crowded as more wounded people came in. The floor was full of people, moaning and sobbing. All morning, Shana moved around cleaning wounds, stitching, and wrapping up.

"I can't see anymore," an elderly woman murmured. Unfortunately, she had been blinded by strong beams, a common injury caused by Gatti energy guns.

"I'm so sorry." Shana hugged her, then the others, their pain and suffering searing themselves into her memory.

In the afternoon, dust clouds rose high to a red sky. Smoke from the burning became suffocating, and Shana felt tired. Luckily some people in the neighborhood showed up to help, including Dimitri from next door. Dimitri was a tall and strong young man with tousled dark curly hair, and he always came in to assist her whenever he had free time.

Shana got some much-needed rest. Hours had passed since her last meal, but the smell of blood made her sick. She felt her stomach turning and had no appetite.

"At least have some water," said Dimitri, passing her a cup of water and sitting down with her.

"Thank you," she said as she took the cup. "It's very nice of you."

"You know what, they said the purge might last for a while," said Dimitri gloomily.

"Really? That's dreadful…"

"And I can't believe the resistances have fought for two years since the Alien War," he added, "how I wish all this could end soon so that we can get our normal life back."

"Yeah, me too," replied Shana quietly.

Dimitri gave her a gentle pat on the back, and they sat together, got some rest, and went back to work again.

By nightfall, the glare from the Gattis' energy weapons had not stopped, and the sky lit up. Dimitri had gone back home. Mother came over with some bread and handed pieces to everybody; Shana chewed absentmindedly.

"Shana! Hide! Quick!" Suddenly Father shouted from the front door. He must have seen the NIISS guards coming, and he called out a warning. Mother also urged, "Go now!"

Shana hurried past the bunk beds and paused in front of the back wall.

The wall was painted just like the others, and nothing seemed out of place. But when she looked up to the ceiling, a hidden retina sensor scanned her eyes. Then a part of the wall slid silently aside, revealing a small room.

Shana dashed into the room, and the wall closed tightly behind her. She crouched down and made no sound. Through a few breathing holes scattered on the wall, she could hear the noises outside, and she could make out the silhouette of her mother still attending to the wounded.

Moments later, she heard footsteps approaching and becoming louder. There were different voices outside, a conversation between many Gattis. Then the front door burst open, and a dozen NIISS guards dashed in.

“Here,” one of the guards informed the rest. “They said this is the place. The whole clinic is suspicious. The owner must be hiding the rebels.”

“Search!” A cold, harsh voice made the order. “Kill on the spot. Don’t let anyone escape!”

Shana could make out most of the alien language without a translator. Her heart pounded, her palms slick with sweat.

What were they talking about? She cowered behind the wall, feeling worse than ever, a knot of fear tightening in her chest. Why suspicious? Was Father involved? Was he in danger?

“Who is the owner here?” The harsh voice sounded again.

Shana looked through the holes nervously and saw a Gatti commander circling the floor, and he was the most horrible Gatti she had ever seen. His face was covered in dents and scars. His eyes were round and wholly black as if absorbing all the lights. Coarse and dark scales grew all over his body, but that was not the most disturbing. Tentacles protruding from his lower back rose and fell as he walked. One carried a twitching eye that watched for movement behind him, while another swept the floor as if sniffing the air.

People were forced to stay down and nobody dared to make a sound.

A few NIISS guards examined everywhere for weapons and mumbled a report to their commander. His face twisted as he listened. Then he sniffed everyone again and moved further inside.

Shana saw his scaly face coming toward where she was. For a split second, his mouth twitched into an incomprehensible smile as he stopped right in front of the wall.

Shana shifted back a little, held her breath, and prayed frantically that he’d just go away.

Right at that moment, Father stood up and spoke out calmly, “I am the head of the household and owner of the clinic.”

The Gatti commander turned around, glanced at the room, and set his eyes on Father. “Where did you hide the rebels?” he asked.

“There are no rebels,” Father looked into his eyes and said clearly. “As you can see, all people here are injured civilians. Please. We are not armed.”

“Wrong answer!” he yelled. “I’m asking you *where* you’re hiding them.”

“I’ve told you. Whoever you’re looking for is not here.” Father remained calm. But Shana was paralyzed with fear.

“Wrong again. I’m wasting my breath talking to you,” the commander said with a scornful twist of his mouth. He went over, raised one of his tentacles, and pointed it at Father. The next second, he stabbed the tentacle abruptly into Father’s chest, like a dagger, and then pulled out with a gush of blood.

Father let out a painful cry and crumpled to the floor.

Shana’s mind went blank. She couldn’t think, couldn’t move, couldn’t even scream. She heard Mother crying, “Don’t kill him! Please, don’t kill him!”

Screaming filled the clinic. Blood soaked Father’s clothes and then the floor. Mother rushed over to lay him flat, placed both of her hands on his wound, and pressed hard. She cried faintly, “Stay with me. I’m gonna fix it. Just need to stop the bleeding first. Please stay…”

“Stop this noise for me,” said the commander, looking annoyed. A NIISS guard came up and gave Mother a shot from the back. With a burst of light, her body fell slowly on top of Father’s.

Shana gritted her teeth as a sharp, piercing pain shot through her head. It was happening so fast that she couldn’t accept what she saw. She wanted to cry, but no sound came out of her. A deep sense of despair overwhelmed her.

The screaming and crying became louder out there. People panicked and stampeded for the exit. They got shot down, too.

“Erase this place,” the commander gave the last order and turned around to leave.

The guards raised their guns and blasted everything in sight. The intense energy beams scorched the linens and furniture, and fire instantly jumped up. The burning red flame spared nothing.

"Run! Leave here! You need to stay alive!"

From somewhere behind her, a voice told her to run. But Shana didn't move. Shock, anger, and grief filled her mind; her body was transfixed by pain.

She refused to leave. No, not yet, she thought. There was still something she needed to try first.

"It's too dangerous here. You need to leave now!" the voice urged again as the fire burned more and more vigorously. The heatwave of the flame rushed high, and smoke filled the house.

It became hard to breathe, but it didn't matter. Shana waited the longest minutes of her life until all the guards left, and she opened the wall again.

There was a chance that her parents were still alive. Maybe she could still save them. Mother said to never give up. She must try.

She crawled to their bodies and desperately checked their wounds, then the vital signs, respiration, pulse, and eyes.

They were dead.

Shana called a thousand times, but they were not coming back. She cried. She caressed them and let her tears pour from her eyes.

Everything became distant. The smoke filled her nose, and the flames climbed on her clothes, but she felt nothing but agony.

The voice calling her refused to go away…

"No, no. This is not happening again." Shana twisted and turned.

"No one can take my parents away. I won't allow it. I need to stop it!" she told herself. "This must be a dream. I need to be strong."

"Hey… hey, it's Ok. I'm here." The same voice gave her comfort. "Don't worry. I'm here."

Somebody took her hands…

Shana woke up with a start, sweat all over her forehead. Don was sitting by her and watching her closely.

"Are you Ok?" he asked as he took a towel and gently wiped her face clean. Shana realized she had had the dream again. What happened more than one Mars year ago came back often to haunt her. Each time, her dream was as vivid as that night: the night of the Red Purge.

"You saw your parents?"

"Yeah," said Shana, managing a weak smile. "I'm Ok. Thank you, Don."

Don was the 7th squad leader of a resistance called the Wake, and he brought her out of Waterford that night. Thousands of families were destroyed during the purge, he told her on their way out, and Shana learned that Gattis would not hesitate to use violence against human civilians. The purge was only a start.

Since then, Don had taken her in, and Shana joined the resistance.

* * *

Eighteen hours earlier, Don and Shana had completed their mission on Earth and embarked on a space shuttle back to Mars. The shabby cargo shuttle was operated by Gattis. As it soared and left the ground, deafening noises came at them from all sides, even with the space suits provided.

The dust and smoke flew high and blinded the view out of their small windows, and they could barely see the sign showing the time and location — Earth Year 2057, Cape Canaveral, Earth Station.

Shana knew she must have fallen asleep after they reached space and let her nightmares get her. After she woke up, she and Don just sat closely and got comfortable, like old friends. The sensation of burning agony she had a moment ago gradually subsided.

"Don't worry, you're with me," Don repeated, holding her hands lightly. "We're on our way back home, still got two days left for Mars after tonight. Are you feeling better now?"

"Yes, much better. Thank you." Shana nodded. Since her parents' death, Don was the one by her side. She had grown close to him, and the touch of his warm hands made her feel reassured. "When are we getting there?" she asked moments later.

"Let's see," said Don, pulling out two calendars. Shana leaned lightly against him as they looked at the conversion between the two timekeeping systems together.

"Right now, it's the beginning of Month 11, Mars Year 12," he murmured. "Time flies."

"Yeah. We spent quite a while on Earth," she said.

"We should arrive around midnight on the 2nd," Don said, closing out the calendars. Then he glanced at her. "Want something to eat?"

Shana shook her head, letting her gaze drift across the shuttle cabin instead.

Most of the passengers were families, and among them was a cute little girl. The girl was pressing her nose to the window glass with her eyes wide open, trying to capture every view she could see.

"Look at that," she exclaimed, pointing it out to her father, who was kneeling by her side.

"Amazing," her father said enthusiastically.

By then, Earth had drawn some distance away, and the outlines of oceans and continents were zooming out. Ahead of them, distant stars silently blinked green, yellow, red, or silver.

"Dad, are we really going to Mars?" the girl asked eagerly.

"Yes, Alisa. We're going to have a fantastic journey ahead," he replied, and they kept watching out of the windows until the space shuttle entered deeper into the darkness.

Earth — home for humans for more than two million years — was left behind. Further ahead, the endless starlight was still repeating itself in the same huge void.

Alisa started yawning after an hour and she looked tired.

"Are we going back home soon?" she asked, reaching into her father's arms. "I miss home already."

"Why, sweetheart? We've just passed lots of medical screenings to prove that we're free of the virus," her father said gently but firmly as if also to dispel his own uneasiness.

"We aren't going back there. You don't want to live in quarantine, do you? We'll find a new home on Mars."

"But Mom is still back home," said the girl in disbelief. "Why didn't she come with us?"

Her father hesitated but finally said, "Dear, we've talked about this. You need to understand. We've spent all our money on the fare for us two. When I save enough money again, we'll have her fly to meet us."

"All right," said Alisa. Yet her eyebrows were raised, and her mouth remained slightly open as if she still had all kinds of questions in her mind.

"Why do we have to leave in the first place?" she asked, "I know you've told me before, but could you tell me about the virus one more time?"

"Sure," her father began to explain patiently. "You know a deadly virus is spreading to every corner of the globe, causing a highly contagious pandemic disease. Earth has become a sick place —"

"What will happen if we don't leave?" Alisa asked timidly.

"Well, if we get infected, abnormal limbs will grow out from within us. Some are even said to go mad and tear themselves apart, but doctors offer no prevention or cure so far."

"So, it is true. It isn't a scary bedtime story?" said Alisa in shock. Her face went pale, and her mouth opened wide. "Where is this bad virus from?"

"I don't know. Even scientists are not entirely sure either," replied her father. "Some believe the virus had been trapped in ice since the last ice age, but then the ice caps in the north and south poles melted from global warming, and the virus escaped."

"Can we catch it?"

"It's now everywhere in the oceans and in the air. Hard for us to catch it all."

"What do we do then?" Alisa asked, her voice barely a whisper above the hum of the shuttle.

"When you grow up, you'll learn a lot, and you may find a way, right?" said her father with a weary smile. "Don't worry too much anyway. For now, I assure you, we'll have Mom join us soon enough."

Alisa searched his eyes. "Promise?"

"Promise."

The father and daughter looked at each other, sharing a brief, fragile moment of relief. They didn't notice that, not far away, Don and Shana were watching them quietly.

For their trip, Don and Shana had disguised themselves as farmers. Both had wide-brimmed hats that cast deep shadows over their faces. Don wore a rough plaid shirt and heavy cargo pants with straps; Shana had traces of dry grass clinging to her sleeves. Between them sat several bags of pepper, onions, garlic, potatoes and cheese — supplies meant to mask their true cargo. In the cramped confines of the shuttle, the mixed odor from their baggage thickened the already stifling air, making every breath a labor.

"Don, do you want to take a nap?" said Shana.

"Yeah, just watch our baggage for me," Don replied, then he hid his face in his jacket and tried to get some sleep.

Bam!

Before Shana could get Don a blanket, the cabin door slammed open.

A tall female Gatti appeared at the door.

Alisa almost jumped out of her father's arms when she saw the Gatti's tentacles.

The Gatti stepped into the cabin only as far as she needed, her long face expressionless. When she opened her mouth, a coarse voice came out, and a small translation box around her neck sounded at the same time. "This is the meal you get today."

She threw a dozen meal bags into the cabin. They flew across seats and floated temporarily in the air due to low artificial gravity. Passengers rose to catch their meal bags.

"Anyone got any problems?" asked the Gatti as she turned around. She was ready to shut the door again, her tentacles calmly dropping to her feet like part of a skirt.

"Can I have French fries?" Alisa asked quietly to her father.

Before her father could answer —

"You think this is a restaurant here?" the Gatti snapped. Some rustling noises came from her back.

When Alisa looked up, two tentacles rose and hissed towards her. The yellow and green dots on the tentacles looked like the patterns on a snake. Alisa screamed, trembling all over as if having cold tendrils running down her back.

Don sat up instantly, his sharp black eyes fixed on them.

Shana had a bad feeling that something was going to happen, and she was glad that Don had become fully alert.

Alisa's cry was piercing in the dead silent cabin. Her father, astonished, quickly put his hand over her mouth.

But it was too late. The Gatti muttered a curse and looked really irritated. She moved close abruptly, and one of her tentacles shot out toward Alisa's face. It looked like it was going to slam into the little girl's face, or worse, poke a hole. Many passengers cried out; Shana was astonished, thinking that the girl was going to get hurt.

Just then, Don rose and stepped between them swiftly. He blocked the tentacle with his own body, and it paused, then lowered to point at Don's knees.

"She is just a little girl," Don spoke in Gattish.

Shana knew Don started to learn the Gattis' language not so long ago and had mastered it well. Except for some high-pitched sounds out of the human vocal range, he was almost as good as a Gatti. Their mentor and Chief Commander, the old Jack Huntsman, often said, "Skill is a weapon." At this moment, Don was certainly using it as a weapon. He looked straight at the Gatti, calm and poised; his black eyes blazed with confidence under his light eyebrows.

The Gatti seemed bewildered upon hearing her language from a human. Her anger was replaced by surprise, and she hesitated.

"Please let it go. You must have more important matters to attend to," Don suggested when she lowered her head as if contemplating what to do.

Moments later, she hissed a sound in her nostrils, turned away, and left.

People around them couldn't believe Don had pulled it off just like that, since everybody had heard that it might cost one's life once a Gatti was angered. Some looked at him curiously; others murmured, guessing who he was and how old he was.

But the fact was that Shana didn't know his age, and even Don himself didn't know it, since he came from a homeless shelter and never got to know his parents or his birthday.

"That was close!" Shana whispered to Don, feeling relieved. "I knew you could do it."

Alisa's father gave a weak thankful smile to him. "It's very nice of you to help us out," he said after he peeked at the door, as if making sure it was shut.

"You're welcome," Don replied politely.

The father thanked him again before turning to his daughter still in a state of shock. "I've explained to you before the trip," he said, "Gattis are roughly humanoid figures, and their tentacles have various functions —"

"I know, I've seen them on television, but I've never seen tentacles this close…" Alisa whimpered, her tears still on her face.

Her father let out a sigh and said, "Ali, you do feel hungry, right?" Then he opened a meal bag, the Nutrition Mix, and put a straw inside the bag of liquid. Alisa sipped it and frowned, but she dared not say another word.

"Stay open-minded about the food, and you'll get used to it," her father said quietly. "This'll be the most common food available from now on. Real food is more difficult to produce on Mars and rather unaffordable."

Shana looked at the meal bag in her hand. Nutrition facts were written in at least ten languages; some didn't seem readable to her. But the package contained high calories with all the fat, protein, carbohydrates, fiber, and minerals for sure.

Alisa's father sitting next to her drank it and coughed. "Ah, it tastes like dirt," he grumbled. Then he fell silent and looked disheartened for a while.

Shana could totally understand. It wasn't too hard to tolerate the bad taste of the Nutrition Mix for a short time during space travel. However, on the thought that it would be their main food from then on, most people from Earth would miss homemade bread with a touch of sea-salted butter.

* * *

Three long days passed. Tired people got up and stretched their legs in the final hours of their trip. They gathered their belongings and chatted with each other casually. The cabin became noisy. Shana was simply glad that the stressful space flight was coming to an end. She stood up and looked through the narrow windows. There she saw the red planet clearly. It was surrounded by orbital mirrors, and the mirror panels were directing more sunlight onto its surface.

"Look, Ali," said Alisa's father, pointing down. "They say there're thirty-two of those panels, and the planet becomes warmer because of the extra light. That's one of the important things that make Mars habitable."

Alisa looked at them curiously, her face radiant; she seemed to have put her unpleasant experience behind her.

"We have to admit the Gatti's technology is more advanced," her father continued. "We used to learn a lot from them, but things have changed since the Alien War. Now you need to keep a distance from them. Understood?"

"Yes."

"Good. Let's get ready to go."

An announcement sounded shortly after.

"Attention passengers, we are on time to reach the Mars capital city OIIIzoi. We have been decelerating and will land on Cloud Space Station soon. Local time is eleven in the evening, and the temperature is minus three degrees Celsius…

"Currently, the Martian atmosphere has an average oxygen partial pressure of sixteen kPa, which is lower than what is on Earth. It is not a problem for Gattis, but some humans may experience shortness of breath.

"We offer you Ox-100, an engineered artificial organelle, which can carry one hundred times more oxygen than your red blood cell. It works as a supplement and allows you to breathe easier and feel more comfortable. Consider taking one capsule dose at the exit, free of charge. It is a welcome gift from the Gattis."

The announcement was in Gattish first, then repeated in English, followed by other languages.

The space shuttle soon landed, and within minutes passengers flooded the Cloud Space Station. Alisa ran around quickly, bouncing high, and floated a bit.

"This is so cool," she said.

"You'll get used to the gravity here after a while. Come on now," said her father, taking her hand.

Don and Shana also moved toward the exit with the crowd; they waved goodbye to Alisa.

Just then, another announcement sounded.

"Welcome to OIIIzoi, the capital city of Mars. All must go through a screening for rebels. Look at the images of the most wanted and pay attention to those around you. If you identify suspicious characters, do not delay in reporting them to authorities…

"Provide valuable information, and your reward is one million Pink Cubes."

Don and Shana looked up at the large image projections hanging above. One of them showed an old man of medium build. He had a broad face, grey-white hair, and white whiskers on his stubbled chin. Despite his old age, there was a restlessness in his eyes. In the image, his muscled legs bent slightly, as if he couldn't sit but was ready for action.

It was the image of Jackson Huntsman, Shana recognized, their Chief Commander, and she couldn't help wringing her hands and feeling a little worried.

Don seemed to know what she was thinking. "Honey, I've never seen a rebel in my life," he turned to her and grunted, pretending to be disappointed. "Seems like we have no chance of becoming rich. Wouldn't it be nice if we were bounty hunters?"

“That’s alright. I’ve never experienced the life of the rich anyway,” Shana answered with an amused smile. “What would we even do with one million P-Cubes? Besides, we don’t want to get into any trouble. Let’s go home now.”

Don smiled too as they walked down to the screening station together. Several sensors instantly scanned their biometric signatures.

The strong odor of cheese from their luggage obviously offended the Gatti officer monitoring the process. He curled all his tentacles together to close his sense of smell. Then he asked in annoyance, “What is in your luggage?”

Don went forward with unsteady steps and then muttered something in reply under his breath.

Shana said hastily, “Please forgive my husband — he got sick on the last day of the trip. We are farmers from Earth, just bringing some cheese, onions, and potatoes for ourselves.”

“Stinky,” the Gatti officer sneered. Then he stared at their identifications for a minute and said, “Ok, Ok, just go.”

Don and Shana passed the scan. They pulled up their baggage and headed to ground transportation.

The night sky of OIIIzoi City was clear without clouds outside. Occasionally, Gatti ships passed in their speedways, but the ground was rather dark due to low light.

Gattis were largely diurnal beings, active during daylight hours. They didn’t like large expanses of lights in lines, grids, or massive skyscrapers, so there were only scattered night lights flashing from pointy Gatti structures near and far.

A Rover pulled forward silently to meet them. Shana and Don jumped in, and then it turned around swiftly and left the station. Once the Rover headed into complete darkness and onto a rocky dirt road, Don removed his disguise and revealed his true self. He had black, clean-cut short hair. His sharp, clear eyes hinted at years of rigorous training in the resistance. Even though he wasn’t big-bodied, looking relatively thin instead with his narrow shoulders, he was lean and toned.

“Thanks for coming, Brian,” Don said warmly.

The driver was Brian, a member of Don’s squad team. He was a young guy with fair hair and a clear complexion, and he looked sharp in a graphic T-shirt with the great Fibonacci wave printed on it.

Brian grinned at Don and saluted. "Welcome back, sir." Then he turned to Shana and said, "I've missed you, Shana."

"I missed you too," Shana replied with a smile, then she noticed something. "Hey, your eyeglasses look a little different," she said. "Did you just get a new prescription?"

"I did," he answered. Brian was their computer geek and spent too much time in front of screens.

"Try to remember your 20-20-20 breaks," said Shana. "Your ocular nerves need the rest if you're going to keep our systems running."

"Thanks for the reminder," he replied lightly, his bright eyes shining behind his glasses.

"All is good at home?" asked Don.

Brian straightened his body into an upright posture and reported, "Yes, sir. All is good."

"No trouble on the way here?"

"Nope. We're going home to Redland."

Chapter 2
A Friend from Upper Universe

"Good morning, my fellow Martians. Another cold winter day in the southern hemisphere for most of us living in Redland — the capital city of humans. All sunny with the high temperature slightly below freezing and the low of -35° Celsius…

"Your representative Michael Huard sends his greetings to you and urges everyone to comply with Gatti laws. Do not forget to report any suspicious activity to the authorities immediately.

"Next, we'll turn to System Architect Icus. He'll discuss his plans for the future development of the planet and his desire for peace for all of us."

On the video stream, a program — *What on Mars!* — started its daily routine.

Shana watched the video stream while she was preparing breakfast. She glanced at System Architect Icus when he showed up. Icus had unusually large, cold, and detached eyes, and his impassive face was lumpy and scaly. As he spoke, his tentacles waved behind him, a sight that gave her chills and made her immediately look away.

It was the second day after Shana and Don came back from Earth. The Wake had a major event. More than thirty members had assembled at the campsite north of Redland, including Jack Huntsman and the squad leaders.

It was a large gathering, which also meant over thirty mouths to feed. Shana thought about the potatoes and onions brought back from Earth and decided to cook a real meal.

She reached for the twelve eggs she'd set aside and handled them carefully. It wasn't easy to have a tally of twelve. She had been collecting them from the few chickens she raised, saving them for special occasions.

"A hot meal for a change," Shana murmured as she watched the steam rise from the pan, knowing these were likely the last eggs they would see for months — perhaps until the end of the season.

Once finished, she set the table, put breakfast in the common area, and went out to see if anybody was up.

It was a chilly morning. The sun had just risen from the distant horizon. In the wild, several Wake members' tents were bathed in the pale sunlight, covered in a light frost.

"Good morning, Shana," someone greeted her warmly. It was a familiar voice. "So glad that you're back. It was too different when you weren't here."

Shana turned to where the voice came from and met a pair of large brown eyes. It was Dimitri from her old neighborhood. Kind and helpful, he used to volunteer with her at the Waterford Hospital. Since the Red Purge, he'd joined the Wake as well.

"Hi Dimitri, how have you been?" she asked, walking over at a brisk pace.

"I'm doing great, thank you," he replied with a wide grin.

"I trust the Light-Heat Camouflage is on, right?"

"Yes, Shana. As usual, our camp is under the cover of the camouflage shield," said Dimitri. "We blend in with our environment. Spy beams from Gattis won't detect us easily."

Since Dimitri was in charge of security, it was his duty to take care of safety measures. "I triple-checked the protection myself. No worries," he added to reassure her.

Shana then remembered that Dimitri fell and broke his right arm in his last mission. "How is your arm feeling? Any swelling or pain?" she asked. "Let me see it."

Dimitri stretched out his arm for her to examine like he was going to a clinic for a checkup. "It's been a lot better," he said, "thanks for putting it back together."

She felt his arm lightly, giving it a little pressure while watching his expression for any sign of pain. "Tell me if it hurts," she said.

"It doesn't hurt anymore," he smiled.

Then she lowered her eyes to check the bandage, and Dimitri just watched her quietly.

"I like the blue sweater you're wearing today," he said after a brief silence.

She paused, a little surprised, then glanced down at the sweater. "Oh… thanks," she said. "I just grabbed it without much thought."

Shana was a good-looking girl with green eyes and dark brown hair. Yet she had never cared much for dressing up or adorning herself with finery. Simplicity had always suited her better. Even now, grown older, she still wore mostly black and white, carrying herself with the same practicality and ease as the men around her.

"You're the most beautiful doctor, you know," he added.

"You're making fun of me again," she said, smiling. "I'm not a doctor. My parents were. Most of what I know came from helping them in the clinic."

"Yeah, I miss the old days. You know what, I used to find excuses to pass by your place, but I couldn't get up the nerve to talk to you."

"You did?" she asked.

"Yeah, until years later when I said hi for the first time."

Shana didn't pay attention to his answer. It hurt too much to think of the old place and her parents, so she quickly stopped there. "Your arm is getting much better. Should be Ok to use it after a week or so. Alright then — I'll go check on the others now."

Dimitri nodded.

Then she waved goodbye to him and went towards Don's tent.

As she drew near, she paused and hesitated, wondering if Don was already up or if he was tired from the travel. Don usually slept the minimum hours required; maybe she should let him sleep a little longer, Shana thought.

"Don is done with his Nutrition Mix," Brian called from behind her while she was fumbling her fingers and kicking stones on the ground. "He's already on his way to meet Jack."

"Oh, Brian… good morning," said Shana, turning back with a shy smile.

"Our scientists, Yang, Nelson, and Cohen are also going," Brian added. "I think they're about to start the meeting now."

"Thank you for telling me."

"You're most welcome," he grinned.

* * *

The Wake's regular meeting was held in the commander's tent. Jack was already sitting straight in his chair when Don and the others came in. Jack was wearing his usual grey shirt that'd been worn out threadbare. His face was heavily lined with wrinkles, but his eyes were sharp and bright.

"First, I have good news to share," Jack said after everybody sat down. "As you know, we rely on our members' contributions to cover the cost of our activities. I'm glad that I secured another amount yesterday. On top of that, a local farmer Alan Holcomb and his son Patrick volunteered to supply us with some food whenever available. It really made my day."

"That's great news!" said Don in high spirits. He was delighted to see they got so much support.

Jack smiled and moved on to the next topic. "The mission to Earth is completed," he said as he turned to look at Don directly and gave him a nod of approval. "Why don't you tell us about it?"

"Sure. Shana and I have brought back Thallium," said Don. "And the reason — we've noticed a strange thing since two Mars Years ago. Many NIISS guards have gained the ability to heal very fast, which wasn't the case before. Therefore, even though we have laser guns, the damage we can do to them is limited. They can come back alive and well in about twenty minutes. Fortunately, Dr. Yang has discovered a way to deal with that."

"Yes," Yang said enthusiastically. "Thallium, atomic number 81, is highly toxic in small amounts. I've tested it in vitro. It can block the regeneration of Gatti cells and cause tissue death. I believe this metal can be added to traditional bullets, making the resulting ammunition our secret weapon."

Jack seemed elated to hear that. He leaned forward and smiled at them broadly. "Now we have secured the raw material," he said, his eyes shining. "Andro and Cohen could be the guys to make these death bullets. Don, will you see to it?"

"No problem, Chief," Don confirmed quickly.

Jack turned to Yang and said, "Dr. Yang, soon enough, you'll have some fun analyzing their effects."

"Yes, Chief. I'll need samples once the bullets are used on NIISS guards," Yang replied, looking rather pleased.

Jack then continued, "Another piece of information I got — NIISS has developed a new energy weapon called a Wkeye gun, which is said to be very powerful and energy efficient. I really want to understand their technology behind that."

At these words, Jack rose and paced the floor thoughtfully. "I worry our current way of living will be at the mercy of Gattis if we lag behind," he added. "And in my opinion, peace in the strictest sense can only be achieved between equal powers. It's a race of technological advancement in the long run. Yang, Nelson, and Cohen, we rely on your research to give us a true advantage —"

Cohen interjected, "If I could see this weapon, things would be much easier."

"Then you shall have it," said Jack. "I'll talk to the squad leaders and see who can bring back a Wkeye energy gun."

"I'll do it." Don volunteered at once. He was always eager to do more for the Wake and didn't need to think about it.

Jack nodded with satisfaction and agreed. "Great. This is all I have on my agenda today," he said, wrapping up the meeting when he was done. "Let's use the rest of the time for free discussion."

And they talked until noon when Jack said he had to leave. Brian came to tell Don that Shana was looking for him earlier, and he winked at Yang, Nelson, and Cohen, who took the hint and quickly rose to leave as well.

"Ok, I want to see her too," said Don, getting to his feet.

* * *

Shana was cleaning up the kitchen when Don came by. He raised the tent flap and gave her a smile. A ray of sunshine shone around his silhouette and brightened up his long figure; she was dazed for a moment.

"Did you get a good sleep last night?" she asked, suddenly not knowing where to put her hands. Although they often pretended to be a couple while on missions, she got a little nervous when they were alone.

"I did."

Don looked refreshed. But it seemed that he was thinking through something else, as he always was.

"Can I do anything for you today?" Shana put her stuff away and pulled out two chairs.

"Yeah, I was going to ask you something… I hope you can help me." He came in and walked by the cooking counter, his fingers tapping along its edge.

"What is it?" she asked, looking into his eyes intently. "Something bothering you?"

"Nothing, Shana. I was just thinking… if it's Ok to ask you — " Don paused there and gave a sheepish smile as though not sure where to begin.

What was going on? Shana wondered. Don rarely hesitated to do anything. Her instincts told her that it was not about work. Just then, he came near her, and her heart skipped a beat. Although she knew it was highly unlikely for him, it felt almost like he was going to express his feelings for her.

Don sat down close by her side.

The fact that he was so close to her made her nervous, and her heart started racing. She dared not look into his eyes anymore and only laid her glance on his long neck and sharp jawline, waiting.

"Do you recall seeing a blonde young woman on the space shuttle the other day?" he asked carefully, his eyebrows arching. "I had some visions last night… Strangely, she seems familiar to me."

It was a totally unexpected question that Shana was very disappointed to hear. She looked down at her feet, thought for a minute, and shook her head.

"No. I don't think so. What does she look like?"

Don didn't answer the question right away. He rested his head in his hands and rubbed his temples, and then he closed his eyes as if trying hard to get his mind to focus. After a while, he told Shana what the blonde woman looked like.

"She sat in the corner of the cabin, rather young and beautiful, probably eighteen or nineteen.

"She was traveling by herself and had only light luggage. There were sheets of paper and a pen in her hands… The paper was full of scrawls of music symbols. She kept crossing out and rewriting some sections of the music, trying out different harmonies… she was composing. When she settled on some new notes, her face lit up, and she hummed the tune."

Shana's stomach sank. "I'm sure there was no one like that among the passengers," she slouched and replied in a small voice.

Don raised his eyebrows, looking confused by her clear answer. "How did the images come into my mind then? Did I dream about it? It was so vivid," he murmured. "I may have had this dream because of the Alisa girl we met on the space shuttle."

"Maybe," she said.

But to Shana, the blonde woman sounded like someone important in Don's previous life, which was something she had wanted to ask long ago but never gathered the courage to bring up. She glanced at him, hesitating. "Did you know her before?" she finally asked after a moment of silence, careful to keep her tone casual and composed. "You've never mentioned you know any blonde woman."

Don paused to think harder, then he opened his mouth, trying to say something, but seemed blocked.

Shana knew it was a difficult question for him since he didn't remember anything about his past.

According to Jack, he picked Don up from a homeless shelter — a temporary living place for hundreds of people who fled the Alien War. At that time, Don had just recovered from a severe illness, after spending a month lying in bed unconscious due to a high fever. He couldn't recall his parents, relatives, or even his own name. No memory before the war at all.

Jack gave him the first name Don, without a last name. That was three Mars Years ago, and that was all Jack could tell him. Everyone could only guess that Don was about twenty-five years old, judging by his appearance.

"Perhaps she's your ex-girlfriend?" Shana tried to lighten up — she told herself whatever he was going to say would be Ok. She nudged him like his good buddy and said, "Come on, do tell."

A girlfriend was quite possible for any regular guy. However, Don looked puzzled, as though that thought had never crossed his mind. He frowned for a moment and said frankly at last, "I don't know, she could be. I can't remember anything before the war, you know. I've tried from time to time, but still nothing."

That answer discouraged Shana. But on the bright side, she'd never seen Don with any woman. Sometimes she wished he could remember his past so that she'd know how to deal with it, but at the same time, in contradiction, part of her wished he'd never remember.

Just then, Don raised one hand to press on his forehead. "My head hurts when I try to remember things," he said, frowning.

"Are you Ok?" Shana asked nervously. Her earlier moments of sadness dissipated in an instant. She reached out to feel his head and checked if he had a fever.

"Nothing serious. It'll pass by itself," Don replied, taking her hand off him. "Please don't tell Jack about this."

"Don't worry. I won't bother him with such trifles," she said, knowing Don wouldn't want to show any weakness before the others.

It might be a good idea to try to take things off his mind, Shana thought, and she suggested, "It's noon. You missed my homemade breakfast. Let's go get lunch now."

When Don seemed to have gotten over it, she held his arm, and they headed out.

* * *

The sun had risen high, and the temperature picked up slowly. The common area was already packed with members enjoying their lunch. Earlier in the morning, everybody was excited when they saw real scrambled eggs cooked with potatoes and onions. Each of them got a small portion of it. By the time Don and Shana came in, most of the food was long gone, and only some leftovers were set aside.

"Something Shana and I brought back from Earth. Help yourself," Don said, smiling.

"We enjoyed our breakfast," Brian replied.

"So tasty."

"Thank you."

"Shana's cooking is the best," Yang added.

"Right, smells like heaven," said Don, taking a deep breath. "I wish we could have eggs every day."

"So much better than our daily dose of Nutrition Mix," Dimitri said. "Seriously, have you guys seen those slimy blue-green algae in their swamp? Isn't it gross? I hate to think the Mix comes from there."

"Don't always complain. Just get used to it," said Terence, the leader of the 4th squad.

While the chatter continued, *Opinion* followed *What on Mars!* on the video stream. A Gatti host invited a famous Gatti scientist, Mu Arae, to talk about his big idea: Gene Pool.

Jack was the last one to come in. He sat down with the others to watch the *Opinion* show.

"… We all know that human science and technology are more than six hundred years behind us. So, there's this intense debate about our relationship with humans," said the host, looking excited. "Here, we've been receiving different views from our audience… Mu Arae, would you like to share your thoughts on this? Why do you think putting humans in a Gene Pool is a big idea?"

"Well," said Mu Arae, "I am not the only one who believes in this. I am just the one who says it out loud.

"From the evolution point of view, I believe Gattis have total superiority over the human race. Physically, they are weaker, and their life span is shorter. Mentally, they are also weaker, and their decisions are often emotional rather than rational…

"Their existence has become meaningless since our civilization, which is far more advanced, has come to them. The stronger and better will replace the weak and useless. That is the whole essence of competition.

"Of course, for the sake of biological diversity, we can consider keeping their existence at the gene level."

"You mean we could just store their genome sequences in our gene library," said the host, nodding and raving about the brilliant idea. "… But your opinion is not supported by the current System Architect Icus, not to mention putting it into action."

"Icus is too kind. However, it is only a matter of time before he will listen to the majority and agree with what I said…"

Terence frowned at the horrendous comments. "Why do we watch a Gatti channel like this?" he said. "Are you guys trying to find unhappiness in life?"

"Know your enemy — hundreds of battles can be won," Jack replied with an undisturbed look on his face.

"I can't agree more with that," said Don supportively. "We're going to find out what the Gattis are up to and beat them at their own game."

"Exactly," said Jack, beaming at everybody.

In the meanwhile, Don had gathered the rest of the food and sat down by Jack. But when he looked at his plate, he found one of his potatoes half-bitten.

"Hey! Guys, you didn't even leave me a whole potato," said Don.

"There's another plate. We saved you a big portion," Dimitri replied, pointing to a corner table in the tent. But when he looked towards it, there was just an empty serving tray. "What the hell? The food is gone?" Dimitri grunted and looked around dubiously.

Don grew cautious as he got closer to investigate. He noticed spilled food on the table and a trail of potato bits on the floor leading outside. He called out at once, "Somebody paid us a visit!"

The next second, he heard a sound and dashed outside with Jack.

"Who's there?" Jack demanded as he quickly glanced around.

Nothing was out there except pale red rocks, sand, and some tiny lichens crawling within the cracks of stones.

Then Don saw something lying in his shadow on the ground. It looked almost entirely transparent.

An alien being!

Don didn't notice him earlier because he blended well with his surroundings. The only thing that told him apart from thin air were some tiny black dots all over him, giving him an outline of his body parts.

"Not sure what he is. Doesn't look aggressive," said Don, turning back to signal Jack to relax.

"Hmmm, not a G-man?" Jack said as he came up and nudged the alien's head. "Can this thing talk or not?"

The alien remained silent.

More people closed around him, staring and talking with great interest.

When the alien realized there was no escape, he straightened up. Don saw that he was only half the height of a regular human, and he had to tilt his head to stare back at a dozen pairs of eyes. He had an oversized head fused with his body, slender arms, and diminutive legs. More interestingly, he had only eyes and a mouth, with no ears or nose.

But what made him the most remarkable alien was that he was mostly transparent, and his shape shifted from time to time; different parts of him could go out of view occasionally.

"Who are you?" asked Jack. "Do you need a translator?"

There was a minute of silence.

The alien looked at the movement of Jack's mouth and the ears of the people around him, and he seemed to understand that was the way they communicated. Then Don witnessed the most stunning scene.

A pair of ear-like structures grew out from each side of the alien's head, little by little. They appeared small and pointy at the beginning, but when he finished growing, he adjusted them to be rounder, more like human ears.

"What is that?" Dimitri gasped.

The alien repeated, "What is that?" His first words sounded like gibberish.

"Are you the thief who stole our food?"

"Are you the thief who stole our food?" he iterated, this time shockingly close to English. Everyone surrounding him was amused, and they talked about him excitedly, guessing what he was. The alien listened carefully now that he had ears, turning his head from one person to another.

"Are you dumb?" asked Jack, losing his patience after a while.

"No, I am not!" He deciphered the human language this time and replied with his own clear sentence.

"What's your name?" asked Don curiously.

"Eio," he replied.

"So, it is you?" Brian pointed out that there were still crumbs of scrambled eggs around Eio's mouth.

There was no point denying it after Eio realized what Brian said was true. He wiped his mouth clean and said nothing.

"Hey, answer the question, Pumpkinhead." Dimitri stepped up, knocking on Eio's head, which did look like a pumpkin, round with groves all over and out of proportion to his body.

"Is that my potatoes inside his stomach?" Don came closer and noticed something interesting. Since Eio's body was fairly transparent, one could see through and make out what was in his stomach — if that part was his stomach, as Don believed. It contained some potato pieces that Eio had swallowed.

Everyone was so curious that they formed a small circle to see if they could really make out food inside him.

"Don't be so hard on him. He doesn't seem like a bad guy," said Shana, making her way into the circle to see the little one they'd caught.

"Are we sure it is a *him*?" Yang asked out of professional habit.

The question made everyone scan Eio for any indication of his gender. Some didn't seem convinced.

"There is no him or her in my world!" said Eio, his face shifting with anger.

Still, Yang looked at him curiously and said, "I've seen outlanders, you know, Gattis and the animals they've brought with them here, but none like you."

"Where are you from, and what are you doing here? Alone?" Don wanted to know more.

"Someplace that you don't know of," Eio replied, giving an impatient look.

"We humans have mapped out a lot of galaxies, quasars, white dwarfs, and black holes. Do you mean your home is out of our observable universe?" Nelson finally got his chance to ask, and he was the most curious. "Would you please be specific?"

"Listen. It's impossible to explain everything to you in one breath," Eio complained. "You've got too many questions. I have to conserve energy now… your food has such low efficiency."

Eio's face grimaced, and he looked stressed to Don, a bit dim and not as bright as before.

"It's alright, my friend. Don't be scared," said Shana, lowering to give him a hug. "Are you still hungry now? Would you like more food?"

"Yes," Eio replied frankly. He leaned towards her knees and pleaded, "Please, I haven't been charged in fourteen days. I saw you guys eating food earlier. That seemed to be the way you gain energy. I was just wondering how eating works here."

"Don't worry. All is forgiven," Shana assured him. "But there's not much food left. You can have a bag of Nutrition Mix if you're still starving."

"Here, I can share half of mine," said Don, remembering his hungry days in the homeless shelter. He gathered his portion and put half of it on another plate. Then he handed it to Eio and patted his shoulder. "Eat up. After you finish, you can go."

Eio quickly shoveled everything down and then asked eagerly, "Can I stay?"

"Let's talk about staying — or not — after you've got your energy back and feel better," said Jack. "Shana can take care of you in the meanwhile."

"Alright," Eio agreed.

For the next couple of days, Eio got Nutrition Mix just like everybody else. Whenever Shana got the chance, she read him books, showed him pictures, and explained to him the meanings of words, one by one, using a dictionary.

Eio was a quick learner. He understood and remembered everything Shana told him. His vocabulary expanded so fast that he talked like a human in no time.

When Don came to check on him, he insisted on staying.

"Why? Don't you want to go home?" asked Don.

"I can't go home now. I have no available means…" Eio looked like he might cry if he could. "An accident happened while a group of us were traversing the forest. I'm not sure what happened exactly, but some strange matter hit our vehicle, and it was destroyed. We were forced into your universe. I've lost contact with the others, and here I am. You see, I'm stuck."

Don couldn't fully understand what Eio said happened to him, but he got the part that Eio couldn't go home. Don knew that feeling. Once, he had no home and nowhere to go. But now he was lucky to call the Wake home, a place where he felt he belonged.

He said, "If you want to stay with us, you need to talk to Jack, and he needs to agree."

"Please, I've been out in the wild for two weeks," Eio added hastily. "It isn't convenient at all in this universe when I can't use my telesense to communicate. Now I'm low in energy and out of range to the others. I could be dead soon enough if I can't find a powerful enough energy source or the rest of my kind."

"I see. We'll figure out how you can go home," Don looked into his eyes and said, "and you can look for your friends while traveling with us."

Then Don brought Eio before Jack and the others for a formal enrollment.

"You'll have to join us to stay with us. Do you want to join the Wake?" Jack asked seriously. "I need to hear it loud and clear."

"Yes!" Eio said loudly.

"We fight Gattis for our freedom. It's a deadly business," Jack continued in a firm and solemn voice. "Do you support that?"

"Sure, I love freedom as much as you do," Eio grunted.

"You'll obey our rules, and you must go with our codes. Do you understand?" Jack looked straight into Eio's eyes until he saw a confirmation.

"Your codes come with free food, right?" asked Eio, his face lighting up.

"Yes. Help out whenever you can, then you'll have free food," Shana said, smiling at him. "Don't expect a daily feast like the other day, but yeah, you won't be hungry."

"I'll obey the rules," Eio swore.

"Now you're one of us. You're our 2401st member," Jack announced, and the others clapped to welcome him. Then Jack held onto Eio's shoulders and said, "Let me introduce you.

Don't be frightened. After you get to know us, you'll see we're really nice people.

"My name is Jackson Huntsman — Chief Commander and 1st squad leader of the Wake."

"This is Don, the leader of the 7th squad." Jack pointed at Don.

"And this is Geoffrey Jones, the leader of the 3rd squad." He gestured to a middle-aged man with a trimmed beard.

"Terence Neumann, the leader of the 4th squad. A true athlete, once a swimming world champion, our top guy." Jack indicated a heavily built man on his left, whose muscular upper body looked broad and thick.

Terence waved.

"Dimitri Kolettis, 5th squad. He's responsible for communication and security. Dr. Yang Yu, our life scientist, an expert. Nelson Wagner, a self-made physicist. Cohen Hilbert, the best engineer you can find on this planet. Brian, our computer guru.

"And Shana, our primary medic — the very heart of the Wake."

They all came up to shake Eio's hand when Jack called them one by one. Eio scratched his head awkwardly while shaking their hands. Shana gave him a hug at the end.

"You'll meet more of us when the time comes," said Jack.

"If there's anything you don't understand or need help with, feel free to ask," Don added.

After the introduction, Jack showed Eio a screen of a registration form. "You'll have to fill this out. Every member has one."

Looking at the form, Eio scratched his head again and wrote down,

Name: Eio
From: Upper Universe
Gender: Not applicable
Age: Unknown
Skills: Disabled
...

“Doesn’t look like he can do anything to help us with his skinny arms and no skills.” Dimitri couldn’t resist stating the obvious as he watched Brian updating their database with Eio’s information.

However, many others had less of a practical nature than Dimitri. They were fascinated by Eio and couldn’t forget how he grew a pair of ears within minutes. They found him a fun addition to the Wake and loved to play with him when they had free time.

“Hey, Eio, how did you grow your ears in such a short time?” Don asked.

“It should not be called growing — it should be called re-arranging instead. I can simply command my body to change my functional structure as I need it.”

“Amazing. You can do that?”

“Do you want to grow a nose? I think a nose would look good on you,” Shana teased him.

“No, thanks. I have no use for it,” Eio refused flatly.

“We use our noses to smell food. You know, tasty food smells good.”

“Really?” Eio looked tempted, his eyes widened. He hesitated a moment and said, “But it isn’t absolutely necessary, and it’ll cost me a lot of energy.”

Nelson waited patiently for the others to finish their “wows” and “ahs,” and then he plowed on. “I’m really curious where you’re from,” he asked Eio again, “is your Upper Universe part of our observable universe?”

However, Eio rolled his eyes and seemed to have lost interest in answering questions. “I’ve never noticed the existence of your universe before. I bet your observable universe is too small,” he said, ready to head out. “Don is going to show me around. Bye now.” Then he ran out of the door.

Poor Nelson looked crestfallen as he was left there with his mouth half open.

Chapter 3
In a World of Gattis

It was near the end of the twelfth month, the middle of a Mars Year, and summer in the north. The sky was clear without a cloud. Liquid water could exist on the surface, but still, clouds were rare, like in a desert.

Under the bright sky, a brand-new interplanetary warship parked at the Haxxilic Flight Center.

"Look at this, a full upgrade from our last generation," said Amosirx, showing Dvexu his first warship built on Mars. "Eight engines, ten energy cannons, each powered by three Black Cubes. Two cruisers and more fighters can dock on each side. It requires two crew members and can take more than three thousand NIISS guards."

"Impressive," Dvexu replied. He circled it, touched its rough black body, and closed his eyes as if enjoying a thrill of excitement. "My killer machine…"

Amosirx let out his breath in a long exhalation; he was relieved to see that Dvexu was satisfied. He had been worried that Dvexu would shoot holes through it if he didn't like it.

"What is its range?"

"Enough for a round trip to Earth even when Earth and Mars are farthest apart," Amosirx answered quickly. "Do you want to go on a test flight today? I have a place in mind."

"Oh? Where?" Dvexu asked with great interest.

"Our asteroid mining platform. I can set a course to visit it."

"We are going to the Asteroid Belt? Excellent," Dvexu said, climbing up the ship at once. "You know what? Two weeks ago, Jyvesi, our Head of Resources and Mining, informed me that the platform had been put into mass production. There is no better time for a visit."

"Right, let's go," Amosirx replied.

With that, Dvexu, Amosirx, and a dozen NIISS guards stepped on board. It didn't take the ship too much effort to fly out into the dark space due to the relatively low escape velocity on Mars. The warship's engines hummed quietly as it went towards the outer planets.

Initially, there was nothing in front of them other than the distant stars. Hours later, their deep space probe brought back live images of the Belt ahead. It looked like a massive spread of rocks and debris at first, and then the fragments of rocks appeared clearer as they came closer. Some were small and irregularly shaped, while others were massive and spherical, and many were pockmarked with craters.

Their ship began to swerve wildly as the pilot navigated through a cluster of asteroids, trying to avoid colliding with any of them.

"Make sure you stay on track," Amosirx reminded the pilot while staring at the instrument panel.

"Yes," the pilot replied, "we will be there in a few minutes."

Just then, the ship slowed down to approach the asteroid mining platform located on the inner side of the Belt. As the ship hovered to close in, they saw a sizeable cylinder-shaped space miner moving towards an asteroid from their windows.

There were other asteroids in various shapes and sizes floating around. But the space miner used several miniature maneuvering thrusters to adjust its position precisely and align with its target.

Once the space miner was in position, a circular door at one end of the cylinder opened and swallowed the asteroid completely. The door then sealed itself again, and an extraction and refining process began.

"Incredible," said Amosirx, staring closely.

"Not bad," Dvexu agreed.

Their ship slowly docked at the platform. When the airlocks were lifted, Jyvesi was already on the other side of the double doors to welcome them.

"Have you seen it? What do you think?" Jyvesi asked eagerly as he greeted Dvexu and Amosirx with his tentacles.

"We just saw a cylinder eat an asteroid."

"Ahh, that is a Refiner," Jyvesi said.

"Give me the details," said Dvexu as he strode straight through the doors.

"Sure. This way, please." Jyvesi hurried to catch up and led his guests into a control room. Rows of monitors showed them all the spacecraft at work.

"Look here. We have developed three different types of space miners: the Explorer, the Refiner, and the Transporter. All three can be launched from the platform," Jyvesi said with a self-satisfied smirk on his face.

"As you may know, the first step is to identify valuable asteroids. Based on initial spectrum analysis, we have classified about ninety percent of asteroids in the proximity of the platform. The Explorers are then used to sample, analyze, and confirm whether resources are available in the selected asteroids."

Dvexu and Amosirx noticed those small, winged Explorers were searching for their next targets and trying to land. From where they were, the Explorers looked like insects in large quantities, in and out of the platform for recharge, busy with their tasks.

"The Explorers then give reliable information about asteroids. They send this information to the Refiners you have just seen," Jyvesi pointed and explained, using his hands to indicate a suitable size. "The Refiner harvests those asteroids valuable for mining. It can handle the processing of ore *in situ*; an extraction with high temperature and high pressures can start inside."

Dvexu nodded slightly, and Jyvesi continued to boast, obviously very pleased with his achievement.

"As the last step, the Transporters collect the semi-finished products from the Refiners and bring them back to Mars for further processing. The whole production process is streamlined. This way, we don't have to bring raw asteroids back to Mars for use, saving energy."

While they stood in the middle of the room and watched, Dvexu demanded, "What is your priority regarding what to mine first? You do understand what I need?"

"Definitely. Right now, we are focused on those relatively bright, high albedo asteroids, which indicate high metal contents, the B-type. The Refiner is designed exactly for that."

Jyvesi pointed to piles of labeled metals and said, "Here, we have some product samples that you can examine."

Amosirx took a block of metal intended for the hull of warships and looked at it. "The quality is good," he said.

"Of course, everything here is done according to the highest standard," replied Jyvesi with smugness in his voice. He then showed them a long list of specifications on a screen. "Here I have all the details: grade, type, and class. For subcategories: strength level, thermal properties, surface finish, etc."

Dvexu glanced through the list with a half smile on his face. "Well done." He gave a rare compliment, seemingly pleased with what he saw.

"Perhaps we can showcase our remarkable progress in the upcoming council meeting?" Amosirx suggested tentatively.

"No," Dvexu refused point-blank. "This will remain a secret until we have a fleet."

"Right," Amosirx agreed at once.

Jyvesi asked, "On your way back, can you take a batch of the semi-finished products with you?"

"Of course, just load them to the ship," replied Amosirx, nodding readily.

Dvexu cast a meaningful look at Amosirx and said, "Now you have more raw material. I believe I can trust the rest to you?"

"Yes, yes," Amosirx made a hasty promise. "Since we have the platform up and running, I can start a large production of the warships. Soon you will have everything you want."

* * *

Michael Huard had a busy schedule on the last day of month twelve. As a human representative, he would attend the monthly council meeting with many important Gatti figures.

His personal assistant John Johnson was driving him to OIIIzoi in his Rover. On their way, they were going to cross Valles Marineris, a vast rift zone that ran just below the Martian equator.

TTado Bridge was built across the valley. The two hundred kilometers long bridge was enormous, sturdy, and spectacular. It was a convenient route connecting the southern highlands and the northern plains of relatively low elevation.

After they passed the border checkpoint on TTado Bridge, they saw cluttered Gatti residences. Some of them were low mounds with wide bases; others were caves carved along the hills. Pointy and curved structures extended from the top of those caves, like the big dry branches of a tree. When they got close to OIIIzoi, however, the streets became wide, straight, and well-organized with grand buildings and skyscrapers.

Michael and John arrived early at the Central Hall. Michael was a short, bald man with a tidy mustache. The mustache certainly compensated for the loss of hair elsewhere and added authority. For the meeting, Michael was dressed in his best suit, with an ironed shirt and gold cuffs. His shoes were polished to a shine. Although he was bald, his remaining hair was well-groomed.

John carried Michael's briefcase for him to the door and then John would wait outside until the meeting ended, since only important figures were allowed to enter the Hall.

Michael was always the first to take his seat for the meeting. He sat upright since he took great pride in his role. He did not want other intelligent beings to underestimate him simply because of his height. Then he pulled a tablet from his briefcase and read messages that John had already sent him regarding the day's discussion.

He glanced down — a report on algae productions was well-written and ready to submit. Great, Michael thought.

He was supposed to bring up several issues, though, something John summarized from recent surveys — the six goals of people on Mars:

Autonomy
Access to resources
Open border
Lower taxes
Free trade
Bear arms for self-defense

John added a note at the end, "As mentioned before, many have voiced their desire to negotiate a certain level of autonomy. Therefore, it is the most important of the six goals."

Michael pressed his hand over his forehead as he scanned the wish list and crossed them all out mentally. How naive! he thought, these people assumed the meeting was like Christmas time and the council would be as kind as Santa Clause. They didn't understand the courage it took to just sit among those aliens. Weak minds would have fainted.

Michael peeked at Jyvesi as he came to sit next to him, and surely, Jyvesi didn't seem to have the face of a friend.

The way to survive was to take things as they were and obey the rules, Michael believed. Even if he put forward those suggestions, his opinion wouldn't matter. He was only an observer as a courtesy of System Architect Icus, so that he could deliver the proper message and humans would understand Gatti policies.

While Michael was deep in thought, the door of the Central Hall swung open, and Zullom entered the room grimly. Seeing Zullom made Michael feel sick. His light-colored scales reminded him of poisonous snakes, and his sharp teeth were like a viper's.

Zullom shot Michael a dark look as he walked to the podium. A bad feeling settled over Michael immediately, as if trouble were just around the corner.

From Michael's observation, Dvexu was the mad dog among the three brothers who carried out the order of killing; he might not even care for the NIISS Head title as long as he got his perfect battles.

On the other hand, Zullom, the Architect-wannabe, was a mysterious one. He wore a never-changing white face and rarely talked to anyone below him as if that would be a waste of his breath. Talk about efficiency with Gattis, Michael thought.

In the past months, Zullom had focused on setting up the laws of the planet. He made a new special law, *The Criminal Law of the Current Solar System.*

More than a thousand articles were in that criminal law, providing for more than a hundred kinds of crimes. There was the crime of anti-Gatti superiority, the crime of opposing Gatti courts, the crime of sabotaging military installations, the crime of obstructing a law enforcement NIISS guard, and more.

During that short period — after the Alien War but before Icus came along — Dvexu and Zullom created the Gatti terror. Humans didn't dare to say anything in public. When people passed each other, they would only check the other's facial expression and use their eyes to indicate.

Fortunately, things had improved a lot since Icus's arrival.

Like his brothers, Icus was not blessed with any good-looking features, not by human or Gatti standards. His eyes were so outsized, protruding, and cold that Michael got goosebumps whenever he looked at him.

However, Icus was perhaps the one with a trace of humanity. He ended the Gatti terror and tried to foster peace and development. He gave Michael his job as a human representative to encourage communication.

Michael believed he could keep his head on his neck for a while under Icus's rule.

When all the attendants arrived, Zullom announced, "We are going to change our meeting agenda a little bit today. An informer just let me know that he had a sighting of our most wanted rebel leader. Let us hear it."

Michael didn't want to hear about any rebel trouble around human towns. There had been enough suffering during the Red Purge. He hid his head lower, thinking of the best way out of this.

"Please come on in," Zullom said to a freakish-looking Gatti at the door. He entered the meeting room and walked slowly to the center. He seemed to be wary of his surroundings since he scanned the room cautiously.

It might be his first time in the Central Hall, Michael thought. Then something about the Gatti's appearance caught his attention. The Gatti's arms seemed abnormally reduced, like forelimbs becoming wings that could bear feathers, and his mouth stuck out like a beak.

A weird thought popped into Michael's mind. A bird? But he didn't want to think more about that. The mention of rebels had given him a chill on his back. This was going to be bad.

"Do you have information regarding the rebels we want?" Zullom asked, standing straight at the podium.

Strange sounds of trills came from the informer just when Michael wondered if he could speak, and a translation box he was carrying sent out a mechanical voice.

"When I was hunting for my dinner one night, I saw rebels camping on the outskirts of Redland. At least twenty of them. I'm sure they're up to something. One of them looked just like the old man here," he said, pointing to one of the images Zullom displayed.

"Are you sure?" asked Zullom.

"Yes, I'm positive. I watched them for a long while," said the Gatti in excitement.

"Tell us when and where exactly." Zullom pressed on. "It will be a waste of everybody's time if you provide false information."

"Three days ago, after dark. I believe it was half past seven. Over the hills, north of Redland."

“Three days ago? Why didn’t you come in earlier?” Icus moved his prominent, sharp jaw to question. He had not said a word until then.

“I have no means of transportation to come here from Redland. I had to ask for a ride. I need Cubes. Give me the million Cubes you promised.”

“Kyinn, bring up the orbital recording for the area,” said Icus. “We want multi-dimensional information around Redland — image, sound, and radiation records — three days ago from 00:00 to 24:37.”

Icus’s assistant Kyinn brought up the records and started an auto-analysis.

Zullom quickly went through the full time-lapse, and there were just plain rocks, sand, and dust. “Nothing unusual on the images,” he claimed.

Kyinn confirmed minutes later, “I’ve finished analyzing the records from before dawn to midnight in the radius of five hundred kilometers of Redland. I do not see anything.”

“This is the place you have told us about, at the foot of the hill in the shape of an arrowhead,” Zullom pointed out. “Nothing.”

“Impossible!” the Gatti yelled in disbelief. “I saw them, at least a dozen tents and Rovers. There must be something wrong!”

“Thermal radiation readings also showed no human life signs there,” Kyinn added.

“You are dismissed. Do not lie next time,” Icus said to the Gatti, closing the discussion upon hearing Zullom and Kyinn. Although there was no expression on Icus’s face, his voice was harsh.

“No! I was telling the truth. I didn’t lie. I swear, I don’t know why…” The Gatti refused to leave.

“Take him out,” Icus gave the order and looked away, obviously not willing to say another word or waste another second.

Yet the Gatti still tried to explain. He remained rooted to his spot, his eyes fixed on the guards coming through the door, and he waved his arms as if he was going to attack.

A white flash streaked across the room. Dvexu had surged to his feet and thrown a dagger at the Gatti.

The Gatti screamed wildly in pain as the blade cut deeply into his head, and slimy green fluid splashed on the floor. Stunned and enraged, he locked his gaze on Dvexu and charged.

Dvexu stepped out from behind his seat and drew a Wkeye energy gun. Short, high-frequency emissions blasted from the weapon, sending intense flashes of light toward the Gatti. A second later, he fell to the floor, motionless.

The attendants were all in shock — they looked at the dead Gatti and then back at Dvexu.

Michael dared not to draw a breath.

Icus fretted over the scene; he turned to Dvexu and gave him a stern look. "I did not say kill him!"

"Our brother could use better discipline," said Zullom, shooting a look at Dvexu as well. "What is the point of having laws in our ruling?"

"We do have laws and orders," Icus agreed.

"Sorry, I was just testing out the dagger I obtained from humans," Dvexu said with a horrible smile. "I will ask the guards to do some clean-up here." Then he returned to his seat, untroubled.

"Nevertheless, there could be rebel activities in Redland," Zullom said, turning to stare at Michael, his expression tightening with clear displeasure.

"Right," Dvexu agreed. He played with the energy gun in his hand, observing its glint, then turned his attention to Michael as well. "Only one Mars Year after the Red Purge, the rebels have bounced back. What do you have to say on this?"

Michael felt he was already threatened with death. He panicked and almost cowered under the table. "No, no, no. It must be false information," he said shakily. "I haven't seen a single rebel. I swear."

"Dvexu, send some ground scouts to Redland and check it out," Icus said thoughtfully.

"Sure," Dvexu replied.

"That's not a long-term solution, though," Zullom commented in a lofty manner. "I propose a simple measure to safeguard our environment and ensure order. We can have NIISS guards deployed to Redland. In addition to that, we can set up at least ten NIISS stations in the southern hemisphere."

"No problem with me," Dvexu replied lightly. "I can work on it right away."

"Michael, prepare for a tax hike," Zullom said as he turned to look at Michael again. "Humans will be responsible for covering the cost of this measure. Do you agree?"

"Certainly, certainly." Michael forced a hollow laugh, knowing that he would agree to anything at that moment.

Zullom then went on with the usual meeting agenda as if nothing had happened. But Michael couldn't hear anything else. He signed all the Gattis' proposals, and he just wanted the suffering to end so that he could leave as soon as possible.

When it was finally over, Michael hurried out of the Central Hall and was glad to find John waiting for him in the Rover. He jumped into the vehicle quickly and began to vent.

"Can you believe what happened at today's meeting?" Michael grumbled. "A Gatti reported sightings of some damn rebels near Redland! I haven't heard about any activities since the Red Purge, but I was almost grilled for that!"

"Really?" John gasped in astonishment at the news. "It must have been a tough situation for you."

"It sure was." Michael sat back and exhaled deeply. Then he went on to describe how bizarre the bird-like Gatti was and his terrible fate; John just listened and kept nodding.

"And there's going to be a tax hike," Michael said at the end, "I hate to admit I've signed it."

"I know… No one else could have done it better than you," John assured him. "You know what? I admire your calmness under pressure."

Michael felt much better after hearing that. John always made supportive comments, and he chose him as his assistant exactly for that reason. Besides, John had a short stature, an average look, and a forgettable face. So, Michael was the taller, smarter one in front of him, with unquestionable leadership.

"Did the council get any useful information from the Gatti?" asked John.

"No. Their recording showed nothing, but they did order a ground search," Michael replied, feeling exhausted. "Let's go now."

Without any delay, they rushed back to Redland.

* * *

"There is a hatching ceremony this afternoon," Kyinn carefully reminded Icus as he headed out of the meeting room. "You have it on your schedule."

"I know. I never forget," Icus replied curtly.

"Do you want me to drive?"

"No. It is a short distance. I will take a walk there."

Icus went down the stairs as they spoke, and Kyinn hurried behind him to catch up. As they walked along the busy streets in silence, Icus took time to enjoy the best landscape of OIIIzoi.

Most Gattis didn't care for any view. Their settlements typically mirrored their natural habitat. Rather than streets and building blocks, their places often featured simple trails leading to small and large caves.

But Icus had designed OIIIzoi with a sense of magnificence, taking up the concept of beauty in forms of symmetry and proportion, so it was more like a large capital city of humans.

To truly appreciate the vista, Icus walked a few more blocks, then turned onto the scenic walk. To his right was TTado Bridge. There was a constant stream of traffic on it; Gatti and human vehicles roared past. To his left stood his private residence. It was an immense mansion standing on the south hill, overlooking the grand valley of Valles Marineris.

The center part of the mansion was an upright oval structure with a sphere in the middle. It was dark blue during the daytime, absorbing sunlight as much as possible. But at night, it gave out white fluorescence, defining the skyline.

Humans called it "The Eye," and Icus actually liked that name, because from the Central Hall, it looked like a standing eye on the hill, dark blue and blinking.

Like the eyelids of the standing eye, two water channels were built on each side of the mansion, where grand waterfalls of three thousand meters high ran down into the valley. The waterfalls became merely a trickle of water when they reached the bottom of the valley. But since water in any form was precious on Mars, the small creek flowing to the east was still admired as the OIIIzoi River.

Soon Icus and Kyinn reached their destination — the hatch lab. A group of Gatti scientists were already waiting for them at the gate.

"The arena has been prepared," one of the scientists said. "Please follow me."

Icus marched through the entrance. The lab was an arched structure built along the cliff of Valles Marineris. The arena, a large cave carved out of the cliff, sat at one end of the arch.

Icus entered a viewing room at the other end of the arch, where he could see what was happening in the arena on multiple screens. There was also a balcony facing the open valley, where he could go out to watch the live action.

There was already movement inside the arena. A gate slid open, twelve artificial incubators were thrown into the cave, and then the gate was closed again.

The duels were about to begin.

For many offspring of the Gattis, there was only one way to come into the world: to kill all the others from the same hatch, or be killed, end of everything.

The reproduction of Superior's sons was carried out on a much larger scale than that of common Gattis. One hatch lab would be built on each of their base planets, and a hatching ceremony would be held annually.

Of course, Icus killed the rest of his hatch, and so did his older brothers Zullom and Dvexu when they were born. The process was cruel but effective. Only the strongest and smartest needed to live on, Superior once said. And his breeding factory would guarantee he had plenty of sons to rule the many solar systems for him.

Soon Icus could have another newborn brother in this solar system.

Shrill screeches now sounded as the newborns tore away the fluid-filled sacs and struggled to crawl out of the incubators. Within minutes they ran on their four limbs wildly, trying to comprehend their surroundings.

"There are four groups in this hatch. Each group has three newborns," said Kyinn as he showed a screen to Icus. "The first group of three are the controls. They are modeled after you."

Icus glanced at the looks of the three; one of them closely resembled him when he was young.

"Little Icus —" Kyinn made a quick comment.

That name caused Icus a prickle of pain. Kyinn had said something he shouldn't, so Icus silenced him with a glare.

For the Gattis, everything was about competition and survival. Icus hated the possibility of failure now that a version of him was going to be put to the test. "Do they have my signature sequences?" he asked coldly, his gaze flickering to Little Icus for a second.

"Yes, a total of more than three hundred genes," Kyinn replied uneasily, then he continued to provide more information.

"The second group of three have the growth factor enhancer labeled as this — . Their bodies appear bigger from the extra muscles. The third group has the neuron stimulator labeled as . Their brains generally weigh more at birth. Look here, bigger heads —"

Icus looked at the newborns with the enhanced genes and asked himself if they were really going to be better than him.

"The fourth group has the two test genes combined, + ."

Icus studied the fourth group but didn't find anything special in their appearance. No big bodies nor big brains. In theory, the combined group should have an absolute advantage, but nature didn't always play out as simple addition.

From the reports on previous hatches, Icus had seen conflicts and competitions in gene expression, something that GIIxb Lab was still figuring out.

Who would win? The old model may not have any chance against the muscles and the brains. Icus suddenly felt sorry for Little Icus and himself.

The kill switch was triggered by a burst of high-pitched cries. Muscular newborns were already at the others' throats with their stronger forelimbs. They snapped the necks of two controls and two brainers in no time.

Luckily, Little Icus saw his chance when no one else noticed. He snuck back into an incubator, then rolled into a corner to hide out.

The remaining one brainer and three combines quickly understood the circumstance and used teamwork. They formed a circle to push out the barking muscles. The three muscles ran fast around them in a larger circle, charging them at any sign of weakness.

It was a thrilling test of stamina. After thirty minutes, the brainer peeled off, and then a combine. The muscles chased off and killed them. But at the same time, the process also tired out the muscles.

In a final madness, the last five left became driven by crazed bloodlust, and they took out each other. In the end, only one combine stood from the pile of dead.

There was a long period of silence.

Icus grew excited… and anxious. Unexpectedly, Little Icus had a chance of survival.

Icus moved to the balcony and grasped the rail tightly. He took a deep breath, catching the strong smell of blood on the gusting wind. He lost himself for a moment, remembering his own hatching ceremony…

Father would lose no sleep over the killing of his sons. He had many of them, anyway.

Little Icus peeked to the outside as the last combine fell quiet. The massacre seemed to be over. He crawled out of the incubator and tiptoed to search for an exit from the cave, but the gate was hidden, and there was only a wide opening leading down to the steep slopes of the gully.

The moment Little Icus drew back from the cliff, he met the gaze of the last combine.

The stakes could not have been higher. For both, it was a matter of life and death in that ultimate moment.

The combine pounced, bit, and pulled on Little Icus's hindlimb. Little Icus kicked hard with his other leg and tried to break away. The combine was tired but still stronger, and he didn't let go. Little Icus let out a loud cry as his leg was being torn off. There was nothing left. He threw his forelimbs at the combine's neck with all his strength.

The two wrestled together. Suddenly, Little Icus pushed himself aside and rolled off the edge of the cliff together with the combine.

Icus watched as both of them fell. It was too steep a valley to hear anything afterward; there was only the howling of the wind. So, no winner from the hatch; Icus lowered his head.

Success was never guaranteed. Yet in another year, a fresh hatch would come again.

Icus let out a long whistle before he left the balcony. It was a fierce scream and a monstrous mourning that echoed in the whole grand valley.

Chapter 4
A Field Member

In less than a week, Shana and Don provided Eio with a wide range of knowledge, and Eio mastered the basics of living among humans. He could understand what everybody was talking about. He could communicate his needs and ideas. He had learned human facial expressions and body gestures to tell if somebody, but particularly Shana, was happy or not.

He had made friends. The Wake members greeted him warmly everywhere he went; they were happy to show him around and explain to him how things worked.

Life was much better for him.

Meanwhile, after the campsite gathering, most Wake members had returned to Base-H — their home base in downtown Redland. Base-H included many locations, such as members' own homes, interconnected basements, underground shelters, and tunnels. It was usual for the Wake to keep moving around to different places so that the risk of being discovered was lower.

Dr. Yang had returned to work since his public identity was a researcher at the Redland Institute. Before Yang moved to Mars, he had been a top life scientist on Earth.

That day, Yang invited Shana and Eio to visit his newly expanded greenhouse. Early in the morning, Shana was busy in the kitchen preparing food for the trip. She took out two bags of Nutrition Mix and a bowl of roasted peanuts, setting them on the table before turning to the cabinet in search of a container. It was just her there, and she didn't hear any footsteps coming. But when she finally found one and turned back, half the peanuts were gone.

“What?” she blurted. She was sure the bowl had been full only moments ago.

Just then, two thin strings of highly transparent ‘hands’ extended from below the table to reach for the bowl, snatching up another peanut.

“Eio, is that you?” Shana called out. “What are you doing? Have you eaten all the peanuts?”

“No, madam,” said Eio, who was shorter than the table, now coming out from under it. “I ate only half. I haven’t eaten all of them.” He shook his head, a human gesture he had recently learned, and while he did that, he was still eyeing the rest of the peanuts in the bowl.

“Since when can you extend your hands like that? Shouldn’t you conserve energy?” She frowned.

“Since just now,” Eio said, retracting his hands at once and putting them behind him.

Shana exhaled slowly, unsure whether she should be more concerned about the missing peanuts or the fact that Eio used his ability carelessly. “You need to ask first. Can you do that?” she added. Apparently, she must teach him manners as well.

“O… K… I’m just experimenting,” Eio replied reluctantly. “You know, find out what food is the most energy efficient for me.”

“Next time, experiment with a smaller size, please?” Shana told herself to be patient with the naughty alien. “You don’t know if it’s good for you. Some people are allergic to peanuts.”

“I’ll keep that in mind,” said Eio, nodding quickly. “But I’m not human.”

“Fine! Let’s go to the greenhouse now.” Shana ushered Eio out of the base, and they drove off in her Rover.

Rovers were the most common means of transportation on Mars. They were designed for performance over rough terrain. Many were electric with solar panels all over the vehicle, and the on-board AI pilot was very helpful for navigation in the wild.

On their way, Shana drove past the city center and showed Eio Redland's landmark, a group of five towering skyscrapers that looked like standing prisms, each of which had a sky garden on its roof and solar panels on its wall. The buildings were connected by arching walkways and elegant bridges, all glittering in the sun.

"Impressive," said Eio.

Shana gave a small nod, her eyes still on the road. "It looks better at night," she replied.

Soon they arrived at the Redland Institute on the other side of the city center.

Dr. Yang greeted them at the gate. He wore a white lab coat and square glasses, looking very approachable with his round, smiling face and friendly eyes.

"Welcome, come on in," he said as he walked them through the campus and showed them his greenhouse. It was divided into two sections: Earth plants on the left and Gatti plants on the right. Yang led them into the Earth plant section first, and Shana saw hundreds of different plants growing in neat rows.

Like everyone else who got used to the dull and barren landscape of Mars, Shana found the greenhouse like a hidden oasis in a desert. It was comforting to stroll among the green, red, pink, and yellow colors.

"It's so beautiful here," she murmured. "I love those flowers."

"Yeah, I feel like I'm on Earth whenever I come here," said Yang. "I'm studying how things grow in Martian soil after toxic substances are removed."

"Everything here is for research?" Shana asked, glancing around.

"One exception —" he then pointed to a potted bush lily and added, "this one is my personal favorite, the only one here not for research."

"Nice," said Shana, moving closer to admire its strap-like green leaves and orange bell-shaped flowers.

Eio, on the other hand, was most interested in the crops once he learned that they would yield something edible. Yang showed him wheat, sweet potatoes, and soybeans. Eio recognized them quickly.

"Do you do all the work by yourself?" asked Eio.

"No. I have a large team," said Yang, "including researchers, post-docs, students, and technicians in my lab to help me with various projects."

Shana was impressed. "You're going to accomplish a lot in your life," she said.

"I hope so," Yang smiled.

Then they went to the right section to look at some Gatti plants. It was quite remarkable that Yang had collected them one by one from the wild and then grown them in his lab.

"What is this one over here?" asked Eio, pointing to a row of shallow trays.

Shana leaned forward for a better look.

"Don't touch anything!" Yang warned them immediately. "A lot of these are allergens. I've identified at least seventeen alien contact reactions while growing all these plants. Each time I touched them accidently, I spent a week in bed."

Shana withdrew herself at once and said, "Thanks for the warning."

"Please tell us about it," said Eio with great interest, "I want to hear about the allergy reactions."

"Well, the most frightening incident happened when I first came into contact with Saxlic," Yang said. A brief flicker of unease crossed his face, as though the memory still unsettled him. "Saxlic is more than just allergenic. It produces a toxin harmful to humans."

"This waving one here?" Eio asked curiously.

"Yes. One of its branches bit me when I found it in the north," said Yang, sticking out his right hand and showing them a dark mark. "It's half-animal, half-plant. But I didn't know that at the time. It was a sharp pain. I swear it was like being bitten by a rattlesnake or scorpion."

"Did you need to see a doctor?" asked Shana sympathetically.

"Yes, I did. First, my hand went numb, then my whole arm. My mouth was numb twelve hours later. The Saxlic must have released some sort of toxin into my system, and I couldn't feel anything for a while. I panicked and went to see my doctor friend at the Redland hospital, but he had no way to help me except to monitor my condition."

Yang cringed as he said that.

"I recovered three days later. The symptoms went away on their own. The doctor warned me not to get bitten again within a month. If it happens a second time, my immune system could overreact and trigger a cytokine storm, which could kill me very quickly."

"That's what I was afraid of," said Shana. "You need to be more careful."

"Yeah, luckily, the Saxlic that bit me was small," replied Yang.

"What an experience," Eio said, his eyes wide. "Most likely, it'll have no effect on me, though."

Yang let out a short laugh. "You're probably right. Your biology is completely different from ours." He then gestured for them to follow and continued showing them the rest of his collection, and they looked carefully at everything they saw.

At the end of the trip, Shana thanked Yang for his hospitality, and they headed back. Eio was very talkative on the way home. He told Shana what he liked best. "Yang's colorful greenhouse is much more interesting than the campsites and the underground basements," he said with delight. "Can we visit again?"

"Sure, we can go another day," Shana smiled.

That was when Eio hiccupped, one after another.

"Are you Ok? Maybe the road is a bit bumpy here," Shana asked, looking back at him in the rear seat to see how he was doing.

"I don't feel so well. My stomach hurts," Eio complained, folding in on himself with a wince.

"Must be the peanuts you ate earlier." Shana suddenly remembered. "Told you. Peanuts contain specific proteins that can trigger severe immune responses in humans."

"Guess that explains it," Eio replied in low spirits.

"You'll feel better once your system works through it," said Shana, trying to comfort him.

"Right, why didn't I think of that?" Eio said, sitting straight again. "I just need to adjust the chemical solutions in my stomach for better digestion."

Shana's eyes widened, and then she shook her head and continued the drive home.

* * *

In the meanwhile, Don had finished up his tasks for the day and was on his way back to Base-H. The day was almost gone, and it was already dark outside.

Jack had sent him an important message to meet up in the training room, so he didn't take a rest and headed straight there.

Every Friday, the Wake members would have training sessions with Jack. He taught them close combat, how to use firearms and laser guns, how to survive in the field, and most importantly, how to fight Gattis. Jack challenged them physically and mentally to their limit, passing on his thirty years of experience in NATO.

But that day was not Friday. Don wondered what it was about.

The lights in the training room were off. Don thought he must be early. The moment he opened the door, however, he sensed a movement behind him. Someone struck down on his shoulder.

What was that? Don dropped his body low, rapidly spun, jumped backward, and drew some distance from the attacker.

It was a familiar figure, strong and agile.

"Jack!" Don called.

Don knew Jack liked to test them with an ambush, an old habit from his military years.

Jack didn't answer. He pressed on with big strides and threw a fist at Don's face.

Don was not going to avoid it. Instead, he closed in head-on and blocked Jack's coming fist with his left arm. His right arm swung behind Jack and hit the back of his lower neck. That spot would be a weak point on the Gattis, a central part of their nerve system, where Don should aim in a real fight with a Gatti. Jack had told him that on day one.

Don had struck hard. Jack grimaced and stumbled a few steps. If Jack were a Gatti, he would have lost control of his body and dropped to the floor.

"Did I use too much strength?" Don asked at once, stepping up to give him a hand.

"No, no." Jack waved his hands after he got his footing.

After Jack pulled himself straight, his wrinkled face smoothed out, and he said, "Good, very good. You've beaten this old man." He kept nodding in approval as he walked into the firing range in the next room.

Don followed Jack into the room where the members learned how to shoot.

On a table in front of them laid the components of an FN FIVE-SEVEN 5.7x28mm semi-auto pistol. The handgun was an old-time favorite of Jack, with low recoil and excellent penetration potential. "I cleaned it yesterday," said Jack, "I know we have more advanced laser guns now, but this one has personal value to me."

"Time it," Jack told Don after he blindfolded himself.

Don took a timer on the table and held it by Jack's side. He said, "Ready? Go!"

On the mark, Jack pushed the recoil spring into the slide, attached the slide to the frame along the slide rails, pushed in a full magazine all the way, heard it click, and racked the slide to chamber a round. When done, he released and reloaded a fresh mag.

"Twenty seconds for the assembly, point five sec for the reload," Don read the results.

"Two seconds slower than before. I'm getting old," said Jack, who seemed not quite happy with himself. He let out a sigh and walked to the side.

"You're still faster than most of us," said Don.

Jack shook his head and said, "No, an old man is an old man. I'm sixty-five this year. In another Mars Year, I'll be sixty-seven. I need to be prepared. We need to find someone else to lead the Wake when I'm no longer able to."

"Why? What gets you into thinking like that?" asked Don. He realized this was the reason Jack had asked to meet.

"I've already retired once," Jack replied, "I'd very much like to spend the rest of my years in a rocking chair, bathing in the sun and looking at my medals."

Don smiled at those words and said, "That sounds like a good plan."

But to him, Jack was not a man who knew how to enjoy life, nor did he know how to retire. Jack was a colonel in the NATO military forces. For years, he served in the Allied Rapid Reaction Corps. He led many overseas operations and deployed as the commander of Counter Terrorism Forces multiple times. He did receive many honors during his military career, for each of which he could tell a thrilling story.

After his retirement, Jack moved to Mars. He taught people self-defense as an instructor before he founded the Wake.

Don wished he could spend his life like that. "You can lead us even when you're seventy," he said. "What was Yang saying? Sixty is the new middle age."

"The pain from my old wounds wakes me up in the middle of the night," said Jack, giving a bitter smile. "I'm serious. Now listen, you saw it yourself, the Gattis want my head everywhere. One second slower means life and death in a battle… I'll let everybody know that the Chief position is open. Do you want to be considered?"

"Yes, of course, I'd like to be the next commander," Don replied firmly. It had been his goal since he joined the Wake, and he was eager to prove himself.

"Excellent," said Jack, a wide smile spreading across his face and his eyes gleaming with joy. "I know you're very driven, determined, and methodical, though sometimes you can be too eager for success and become impatient. But you're still young. You'll become mature after more experience."

Don hesitated a moment but spoke his mind, "What do I need to do to succeed? How do I earn people's support and the other squad leaders' respect? Like you said, many of them came in before me and have more experience than I do."

"Desire is a good first step," said Jack. "Success will come from your hard work and your achievement. True, Geoffrey is a seasoned warrior. He has more experience than you. On the other hand, Terence looks more muscular."

Then Jack patted his shoulders and continued half-jokingly, "Your narrow shoulders certainly give the impression of a small bone structure. I once wished my training could help you build up your body more. But you know, it is never about the order you came in, or how much muscle you have."

Jack pointed a finger to his own head and said, "What really matters is in here. What I've always seen in you — your ability to go beyond and your willingness to give it all." He then picked up the FN FIVE-SEVEN he was working on and said, "This sidearm has been with me since I joined the army thirty years ago. It is well-maintained and has thousands of rounds left in it. We have newer weapons now, but this can still do serious damage to the NIISS guards."

Jack took a last look at his pistol and placed it in Don's hand. "It is now yours. Don't disappoint me."

Don knew what that meant. "You won't be disappointed," he swore.

"Great! We'll hold an election when the time is right. The best one out of the seven squads will be chosen, and you can start to get yourself prepared."

Don nodded. Then he went back to his compartment with the pistol Jack gave him and a lot on his mind. He thought about his past contributions to the Wake and how he could do more.

But it wasn't too long before he was interrupted by a sharp high-frequency alarm. At the same time, he got an order directly from Jack. In the message, Jack told the squad leaders he had received intel that the campsite north of Redland was exposed. They should abandon that campsite permanently, and they needed to exit all the bases as a precaution.

Don jumped to his feet immediately, grabbed an emergency package, and rushed toward Shana's compartment.

It was past ten at night. Eio and Shana must have gone to bed, Don thought, although he knew Eio wouldn't really fall asleep. Eio once told Don that he didn't need it. Strictly speaking, he would just reduce his energy level and rest.

When Don burst in, Shana had been woken up by the same loud and piercing alarm, and she was already dressed while Eio was still lying back in his energy conservation state. Don gently patted his back and said, "Eio, we need to move!"

"What is going on?"

"There's a potential enemy threat. We're going to exit the base now," Don said seriously. "We'll break into small groups. You're coming with me, Shana, Jack, and Brian."

"A threat?"

"Yes. The alarm is a mandatory evacuation."

Unlike Eio, Shana knew what the alarm meant. She had gathered her stuff in the meantime. "I'm ready," she said.

Eio got up quickly and climbed down the bunk bed.

"Come on now!" Don urged as the alarm sounded again.

"Ok!" Eio had no trouble leaving since he didn't have any belongings. He hurried up and took Don and Shana's hands cooperatively, and they joined the evacuation down some tunnels.

They met Jack and Brian at the end of the tunnel, who were already waiting inside a Rover. Brian started the Rover, and they drove off down the bumpy, dusty road. Everybody kept their silence on the way.

The Wake had good plans to avoid Gatti detection, and they moved quite often. Everybody had gotten used to it except Eio.

"Where are we going? Are we there yet?" Eio asked after they got far enough.

Eio knew nothing of the different locations on Mars. Don supposed he just asked out of curiosity. "We're heading north, towards the border," said Don. "Jack knows the place where we're going to stay. You'll see for yourself when we get there."

An hour later, the dust and sand around them settled. They started to see some streets.

"Is this the border?" asked Eio, his eyes wheeling.

"No," Don replied. "The Human-Gatti border is further north, winding along the equator. Gattis mostly live in the northern hemisphere, and humans, in the south. Here's a map if you want to take a look."

Eio checked on the Mars map. Don noticed Eio's brain was like a supercomputer, for he mastered everything he'd seen with only a few glances.

"Right now, we're in a village between Redland and Midzor," Don added, pointing out their location to Eio. "Midzor is a colorful town on the border, located southeast of TTado Bridge."

Soon they arrived at a cheap long stay lodging in a backstreet. After Brian parked the Rover, they went to the front of the lodge, and Jack fed a Blue Cube to a Cube Operated Machine.

"What is Jack doing?" asked Eio, eyeing the Cube with great interest.

"Paying for our stay," Don explained patiently. "Energy-charged Cubes are the official currency here." He reached into his pocket and took out several more Cubes for Eio to see. All of them were the size of a cubic centimeter.

Eio picked one up and examined it carefully. "Is there any difference between Cubes of different colors?" he asked curiously, his eyes wide open.

Don lined up the Cubes in his hand. "Here, I have a pink one as well as yellow, green, blue, and black ones," he said, "in this order, each of the latter contained ten times the energy of the former."

"They can be used as payment, or they can be easily converted to other energy forms," Jack added, looking at Don and Eio with a smile on his face. "You can use it to power home appliances or Rovers, for example, using a Gatti Cube-Energy Exchanger."

"Understood," said Eio.

"Now you know," Don said, patting Eio on the head. "We'll settle here for a couple of nights."

* * *

The next day, Don went out early to get them some daily essentials since they expected to stay there until the imminent danger was over.

"Will be back in an hour," he told Shana before heading out.

But two hours passed, and he still hadn't returned. Nor did he respond to her messages.

"What happened, Don?" Shana tried again, only to be met with silence.

It wasn't the first time Don was out of contact, but each time, Shana dreaded thinking something terrible might have happened to him.

While Shana waited, she organized their belongings and put the rooms in order. Then she went down to the streets to check things out.

It was close to lunchtime. The streets were full of people coming and going, but Don's face wasn't among them. A few shady-looking Gattis lurked in the shadows; their presence made her even more anxious.

Time went on, and Shana waited for another hour. She felt restless and unable to do anything else. She went back upstairs, stood by the window, and stared out into the streets. It was getting late, and gradually, there were fewer pedestrians in sight.

Don was a punctual man, and he did everything with a purpose and a plan. Shana knew he wouldn't be wandering around in their current situation. Something must have happened to him. She decided to ask for help from Jack and Brian. Brian could check the signal from Don's life sign tracker, and she would know his status at the minimum.

Just when she turned to the door, it burst open, and Don entered the room, his face bruised and his shirt partly torn. He went straight to the water pot on the table.

Shana was startled, but at the same time, felt greatly relieved. At least nothing major had come up, and Don still had his arms and legs. She waited for him to gulp his water before asking him what had happened.

"I ran into four NIISS guards," said Don after he put down the water pot. "They were following me, maybe just because I'm a new face here. I didn't want them to find out where we stay, so I lured them in the opposite direction."

"Did you get into a fight?" Shana asked while examining his bruises.

"Yes, but not with the NIISS guards. I was lucky to find a group of street thugs. I got into an argument with them and then a fight. The NIISS guards thought I was one of them and left me alone."

"That was smart."

"Shana, would you help me look at a cut on my back?" Don said as he took off his dirty shirt and sat by the bed with his back bared. "It needs to be treated. Sorry to bother you so late, but one of the street thugs slipped past my defense."

Luckily, Shana always brought her medical supplies with her. She took out a couple of antiseptic wipes and cleaned out the wound.

"It's not too bad. The cut is not deep. You should be fine without sutures," she said.

When she was done, she couldn't help but look at those old scars and bulging keloids on Don's back. She knew every single one of them; she'd treated many of them herself.

"If you could be more careful next time..." she said, her fingers touching those scars while she put on gauze pads and tapes. It hurt her to see the new and old wounds sprawling across his skin. If only he could take better care of himself when he was out there, she thought.

Then she noticed a new one she didn't think was there before.

“What happened here?” she asked while touching it lightly.

“What?” Don said, puzzled. He seemed to have forgotten all about it. When he remembered moments later, he added, “Oh, that’s nothing. It healed by itself. I didn’t want to bother you.”

Earlier, anxiety had flooded Shana’s mind before Don’s return, and now, his reply almost made her break down.

“Don, please don’t do this,” she cried out, “I want you to bother me. You can’t go and take your chances every day, thinking you have nine lives like a cat. I want to help you.”

Don turned around, looked into her eyes, and said, “You’re already helping a lot. I really appreciate it. Isn’t that enough?”

“Enough? I don’t know!” Shana said frustratedly. “I don’t want to be trapped here, always waiting.” Just then, a bold idea popped into her head. “Take me with you. I want to go with you.”

She had grown up. Why not? Why not go with him on those missions? In that way, she wouldn’t have to wait, worried sick in the bases for him to return. She could treat him right away when injuries happened, and it could make all the difference between life and death.

“You’re a girl. Are you sure? It’s better for you to stay safe. All of us can protect you,” said Don in surprise, his eyebrows raised.

“I can look after myself,” Shana replied. She knew Don would say something like that and quickly added, “I… I can start training with Jack. All you guys do it. I can do it —”

Unexpectedly, Don took her hands and shook his head slightly, his face worried. He opened his mouth again, but before he could say another word, Shana said determinedly, “I’ll talk to Jack tomorrow. I won’t give up until he says yes.”

Don looked at her uncertainly, but she’d made up her mind, and she’d never been so certain. After she said it out loud, she felt good and looked forward to it.

Shana was a girl of her word. The next day she took the chance to ask Jack about becoming a field member. She wanted to start having training lessons like the others.

At first, Jack looked surprised but then seemed to know what she was thinking.

"Are you sure you want this?" Jack said; his expression couldn't be more serious.

"Yes." Shana worried he might have doubts, so she tried to look as determined as she could.

"Are you doing this for yourself or…?" Jack asked, studying Shana's face.

"It's my own decision, and it has nothing to do with others," she said without the slightest hesitation.

"And I assume you want to be on Don's team?"

"Yes."

"Promise me you'll always take care of yourself first, and only then will you be able to take care of others," Jack reminded her.

"I promise."

"I think you already know I'm strict and demanding, and I've made those guys cry," he said, now sounding like a commander. "I won't give you different treatment because you're a girl."

"I understand. Don't worry. I'm tougher than I look," Shana answered as firmly as she could.

"You've certainly grown up. A strong girl with a mind of your own," Jack said, his gaze drifting to the calendars on the wall. Like many of the Old People — those born on Earth before migrating to Mars — he kept two sets of calendars and had grown accustomed to converting the Martian date back to Earth-standard time.

A moment later, he continued, "Shana Schwann, as of today, you are seventeen years and two months old, right?"

"Yes." Shana was surprised that he remembered so clearly. She wasn't sure if Don remembered her birthday like that.

"Very well then. I've decided. You should be allowed to make your own decision," Jack said. "Now you're my trainee." He gave her a warm broad smile, his wrinkles climbing up the corners of his eyes and forehead.

"I need to set you up with a schedule," he added, "I can fit you in with individual sessions every Tuesday when there is no emergency. Also, come join the group training every Friday."

"Yes, Chief!" Shana agreed excitedly.

"When do you want to begin?"

"Today," she said.

Jack laughed, and his eyes widened. "I have no female field member in the Wake. You set a precedent. I'm very proud of you," he said, looking at her gently. "Come on then. I want you to try the virtual Gatti opponent. It's a training simulator designed by Brian and Cohen. Let's start with some basics."

Chapter 5
Midzor

Four days after Jack's evacuation order, Dr. Yang received a request from Michael Huard: he wished to visit Green Rise Farm and hoped Yang would give him a tour.

Green Rise Farm was an algae farm. Growing algae at home, especially spirulina, was a common practice among humans on Mars. Algae could be easily grown in various sizes of containers, some as small as a water bucket, some as big as multi-ponds in family farms. People would send the harvested dry algae to a central factory for processing, which became the main ingredient to make Nutrition Mix.

Yang had helped to set up many of these farms since he got to Mars. Green Rise on the east side of Redland happened to be operated by several Wake members. Yang wasn't sure why Michael would ask for such a visit because he had never shown an interest before. Yang worried that Michael knew something about the Wake.

Yang asked Jack immediately how he would like to deal with it.

"Did he give a reason for the visit?" asked Jack in their video call.

"Michael said, as a human representative, it's his duty to ensure the smooth production of food, and he hoped that I would give him a tour."

Jack was silent for a long moment, his brow furrowed in deep thought. Then he leaned back in his chair, his gaze distant, clearly weighing every angle. In the end, he decided to go ahead with the visit. "Terence's team is currently in

Redland," he said. "I'll get them ready. If this is a trap, we'll do what we have to do."

On the visit day, Yang wore his usual white lab coat with his thick square glasses, and he had a stack of paper full of numbers in his hand, ready to provide his expert opinion.

Yang greeted Michael warmly when he arrived. "We can take a walk around the farm and enjoy the scenery while we talk," he said, stepping forward to show the way.

"Fine," Michael responded curtly, his tone flat.

Yang's internal worry flared, but he pushed it down. To help himself relax, he launched into shop talk, "I love spirulina, the best thing you can have here. But strictly speaking, it is cyanobacteria and not algae."

Michael strode along with both of his hands crossed behind him. He wore a blank expression and didn't show interest in anything.

Still unable to discern Michael's intentions, Yang continued with feigned enthusiasm, "You know, spirulina was discovered on Earth a long time ago. It contains a high percentage of protein when dried, plus other key nutrients like vitamins and minerals. But it only gained popularity on Mars because of the harsh environment here and its super productivity. Look at the green here —"

In front of them, dark green waves rose and fell in the ponds, propelled by multiple circulators. Such intense green was a rarity on Mars, where yellow to dull red sand and dust typically defined the landscape.

However, Michael stared out into the distance and didn't seem to be listening at all. After Yang finished, he said with an air of authority, "Yes, we no longer run on empty stomachs since we have Green Rise and other farms. A huge thank you for that."

Yang forced a smile. He got a few steps closer to the ponds and said, "See there? The white foams that keep coming to the surface? Those are oxygen bubbles produced by the bacteria. Oxygen level must be higher here." He stuck out his head to take a deep breath and exclaimed, "Ah, nice. I like the fresh air. I feel I can breathe better already."

“Fresh air indeed, but I don’t like the smell,” said Michael, remaining at a safe distance. “Listen, the tax for all the algae farms is going to increase by ten percent. I’m here to give you a heads up,” he announced out of the blue. “NIISS will come down to our towns to provide extra security. This increase will help to cover their operating expenses.”

“Really? Starting when?” said Yang in surprise. “You should let the business owners know.”

“Starting next month,” Michael replied, “I’ll let them know, but I want to let you know first. After all, you’re in a good relationship with them. You can talk to them, too. Everybody needs to understand.” Michael then moved on to a lengthy explanation of why the measure would establish a much better social order.

Yang was speechless. For a moment, he only stared blankly at the paper he was holding.

After Michael delivered the message, he looked at his watch and said, “I have an important meeting next. I need to leave now. Nice meeting you, Dr. Yang.”

Yang realized that was the reason why Michael had come for a visit. So, it was true that NIISS guards would be deployed in the south, and humans had to pay for it.

Bad news for the farmers, but the good news — Michael Huard didn’t seem to know of the Wake’s existence.

Yang gave Jack an update on the situation as soon as Michael left. They all breathed a sigh of relief.

For another week, Don and the others continued to stay in the lodge. Jack gave Shana accelerated training lessons, as she wished.

There were no more signs of NIISS guards near them other than the four Don ran into on their first day. Jack communicated with other squad teams. They reported no unusual NIISS movements at their sites either, so Jack believed it should be Ok to resume their normal activities.

One morning, Don watched Brian perform system maintenance on their computer servers remotely. Brian had built several computer clusters single-handedly for the Wake. Their training simulators ran well on them.

"I also have some new electronic devices I need to setup," Brian said as he tapped away.

"Interesting," Don said, looking at the new gadgets Brian had bought. Then Don noticed the keyboard Brian was using was completely blank, without any letters or numbers on it. All the keys were so black and shiny that they almost reflected lights. Yet Brian's fingers flew over them so quickly; he didn't need to find the symbols at all while he typed.

At first, Don thought it must be Brian's new special keyboard, but he realized it soon enough before he asked. It was a worn-out keyboard; the original letters printed on it were entirely gone due to frequent use.

"Brian, have you had this for years?" asked Don.

"Yes. I always pack it in my emergency baggage. Why?"

"I thought you should've got a new virtual keyboard during this upgrade," said Don, puzzled. "This one is so out-of-date. Don't you guys love new things?"

"Yeah, I tried the virtual keyboard, and I love it," Brian answered sheepishly. "But I've given mine to Shana already. Not everyone can get an upgrade this time."

Don understood instantly. Brian was on the priority list since he was the computer guy, but he let Shana have it, knowing that Jack was frugal with their funds and there wouldn't be another upgrade anytime soon.

"I've heard Shana's training with Jack. She'll be on our team and fight alongside us," Brian added. "The virtual keyboard will be more useful for her since it's more portable. She won't have to carry the extra weight in case she needs it. My old keyboard works just fine; I can do my job all the same."

"I see," Don replied. "You're very thoughtful."

It looked like words had gotten out fast, so everyone knew Shana was working hard to become a field member. She meant it, and she was determined, Don realized then. There was no holding her back.

* * *

Meanwhile, Eio complained that he was bored, so Don gave him many books to read, such as *Mars Atlas* and *Encyclopedia of Gattis*. Eio quickly finished all of them, and he learned that the Martian year was almost twice as long as the Earth year, as were the seasons and months. He also learned that Gattis dominated the planet's northern hemisphere. This region's low altitude made it easy for water to flow and form small lakes and rivers, a key reason for their settlement there.

There were three major Gatti cities. They took the shape of a great inverted triangle: SIIKwari in the east, Haxxilic in the west, and in the middle, close to the equator, was the brightest and most structured one, Gatti's capital city OIIIzoi.

"I've learned a lot," Eio told Don, his eyes flickering. "I want to go out and look for my friends. Together, we may find a way home."

Don was very supportive of that. He found the time for Shana and Brian to sit down with Eio and see how they could help.

"I'll ask all our members to watch for relevant information while on their tasks," Don offered. "It may be easier to start from a certain location. Eio, do you remember where you landed after your accident?"

"No. I hardly remember anything," said Eio, lowering his head. "There was a crater nearby? I don't know the name of the place, though."

"There're so many craters around the globe, that's going to be hard," said Don, "and can you tell us what your friends look like?"

"They all look the same as me. There should be fourteen other versions of me."

"Other Eios?" Brian asked curiously. "Are you saying that in your universe, all your people look exactly like you?"

Eio nodded.

"So, there are just millions of Eios wandering around?" Shana blurted out. "Is it going to be a disaster since you're a naughty kid?"

"Millions of me, yes. Disaster, no," replied Eio matter-of-factly. "We look the same, function the same, and act the same. Our interactions with the environment are constantly shared. One's experience is everyone's experience. One's learning becomes everyone's learning. So, the individual has the same information as the population."

"What a world," said Brian, who lowered his head and felt his chin as if thinking hard to visualize Eio's description. Moments later, he slapped on the table and said, "Aha! I know. Your information sharing could utilize something like quantum entanglement. We have computers built on that."

However, Eio didn't seem to understand what Brian meant by quantum entanglement, which was beyond his reading levels. He looked at Brian uncertainly and said, "We call it telesense — we can use it when we are in range of each other."

"You have no parents, brothers, sisters, or family relationships in that sense?" Shana asked.

Eio nodded again and became gloomy. He said, "You're right. We don't have personal interests, only population interests. Without me, the others continue to live, learn, grow, and advance. Another Eio can replace the old and gone. Nobody misses me."

"Oh, poor Eio. I'll miss you after you go home," said Shana, coming over and giving him a warm hug.

Eio leaned into the embrace. "Your warmth is so comforting," he said, and his eyes softened slightly. "Anyway, the problem is, I may not be able to stay here for a long time," he continued after a moment. "I worry I'll lose my transparency gradually and become more like you. That could be the end of me."

"How much time do you think you have?" Don asked, trying to make sense of the situation.

"I don't know." Eio thought for a while and said, "My turning rate used to be slow. I don't see a difference on a daily basis in the first couple of weeks. But today, I lost another tiny view of my stomach. It could still be years, or it could happen very fast at the end."

"Is that so?" Shana said, looking concerned.

"Nevertheless, don't worry too much," said Don encouragingly. "We'll think of a way. There is always a way."

"Right, we'll help you. You won't be alone," Shana added.

While they were talking, Brian invited their physicist Nelson via a video call. Brian filled him in on Eio's situation and asked for his opinion, "Nelson, what do you think?"

Nelson scratched his chin on the other side, in his lab, and said, "Since Eio came here by a vehicle, I'm optimistic we could recreate the vehicle for him with his help… and Eio could return to the Upper Universe."

"How? Do you have an idea already?" Shana asked hopefully.

"I don't know yet. I need to think about it." Nelson opened his palms and shook his head. "It's beyond human's current technology level."

"Oh," Eio mumbled, his voice held a noticeable note of disappointment.

"At least Nelson is optimistic. We can start by looking for your friends," said Don.

"All right," Eio agreed.

* * *

Two days later, while Shana and Eio were eating their breakfast in the dining room, Don came in and sat down in a chair across the table. "Hi, Shana," he said simply, "want to come with me today? I'm going to Midzor to find Andro. No danger involved."

"Sure," Shana replied, unable to hide the small lift in her voice. She'd love to go anywhere with him.

Don nodded with a smile. "Eio, how about you? You want to go out for a change?" he then turned to Eio and asked him. "You may run into your lost friends, you know."

"I can go, too?" Eio's eyes lit up. "Excellent. Who else is going?"

Just then, Yang pushed the door of the dining room open and looked towards their table. "Am I late?" he asked as he came over in light steps and sat down by Don's side.

"You're right on time," replied Don, smiling.

"Dr. Yang, did you just come from Redland to join us?" asked Shana.

"Yes, I'm on my way to visit our Blue Breeze algae farm near Midzor," Yang replied pleasantly. "I need to spend a couple days there to look at the algae growth. Don said I could get a ride. Save energy, you know."

"I see." Shana nodded. Then she remembered something important and said, "Eio, this is our first time going to Midzor. You need to be careful and follow my instructions."

"What else?" asked Eio, looking towards her.

Shana became serious and said, "And remember this — no matter what happens, never give up any chance of survival."

"Right," Don agreed. "I'm glad Shana brought it up. Almost forgot to tell Eio the slogan of our resistance —"

"Stay alive!" everyone except Eio joined in and said solemnly.

"Great. Now you know," Don said with a nod. "Get ready, and let's head out in ten."

The four of them hopped on a rover shortly after. Don entered their destination into the AI driving system and chose a route that cut across the open terrain. There were no paved roads ahead of them, only red sand and scattered rocks stretching into the horizon. Soon, they traveled in a cloud of butterscotch-colored dust.

From the village to Midzor and further north, wild Gatti plants became more common along the barren plains. Yang was thrilled to see such alien things and asked to stop here and there to explore them. "I'm working on multiple projects simultaneously," he said. "One of them is how Gatti plants grow under Martian conditions."

Shana knew Yang never missed an opportunity to study them. Whenever he came across something interesting, he would slip into long explanations while the rest of them stood around, listening intently.

"Look, that's Black FrIx," Yang asked to stop again and told them what he saw, "that short dry bush, the dominant species here."

Shana, Don and Eio got off the Rover to take a look. As its name indicated, the whole plant was entirely black.

"There are black plants on Earth as well," said Yang. "But Black FrIx adapts very well to the low light levels on Mars. It has developed complex pigments that can absorb the sun's entire light spectrum. This allows it to gain more energy than other plants."

"Is it right that Earth plants have green pigment?" Eio asked, his eyes whirling. He seemed to recall what Yang had shown him in the greenhouse.

"Yes," replied Yang. "But Black FrIx has a range of pigments, and it utilizes visible light as well as infrared and microwave frequencies. These lower frequency bands provide thermal energy, and the plant uses that to keep warm, very useful in cold temperatures."

Don asked curiously, "That is why it has the advantage to out-compete other plants?"

"Yes, you're right," Yang replied. "It produces more stems and accumulates biomass more quickly. For that reason, it's dominant."

"Is that so?" Shana said thoughtfully as she studied the Gatti plant. Then she glanced at Yang and added, "There's always something new to learn from you. I wish we could stay here longer."

"Not today. We need to go now," Don reminded them gently.

"Right," Shana replied, getting back to the Rover.

And they continued north. When they were close to Midzor, they saw some simple underground homes. Shana was familiar with that type of human dwelling. Those homes had enclosed upper corridors or domes as entrances, and the main structures were built underground to conserve heating energy. The door was often a round lid on the floor of the dome. One would open the lid-door and climb down a tunnel into their home.

"Is this the place?" she asked.

"Yep. Blue Breeze is right behind the neighborhood," Yang said, pointing ahead.

Minutes later, Don dropped him off at the algae farm, and Yang gave them a brief nod before stepping out. “It was good traveling with you,” he said. “Take care.”

“You too,” Shana replied, waving her hand. “We’re going to look for Andro and the other Eios now.”

Andro was Don’s friend, a man named Alessandro Dyne. Shana knew him as well since he was an old colleague of Jack’s and had visited the bases a few times. But Andro didn’t join the Wake; he had declined Jack’s invitation multiple times.

Once, Brian offered Andro a Senset that the Wake members used to communicate among themselves. He refused again politely. “Too much trouble,” he said.

Nevertheless, Andro helped them out on many occasions. So, if they wanted to see Andro, they would have to check out all his favorite places.

Don, Shana, and Eio arrived at Midzor in the late afternoon. It was a border town and only half an hour to TTado Bridge. Wine was not taxed there, and law enforcement didn’t maintain control all the time.

The streets were a favorite hangout place of a lot of humans and Gattis. “Take your own risk.” That’s what people said, and most people felt safe enough as long as the NIISS guards didn’t come.

In two hours, Shana and Don had checked out many places but didn’t see Andro.

Eio didn’t see any sign of his friends either. Nor did his telesense pick up any signal along the way.

They decided to go to Last Lamp Tavern to wait for Andro as they had planned.

It was past six when they passed the town center of Midzor and parked. It was getting dark, and the air had cooled down quickly. Phobos, the irregularly shaped Mars moon, rose in the west. It hung dimly in the sky, together with the even smaller moon, Deimos.

Two or three pale solar-panel streetlights flickered and came on. They shed light shadows on the alleyways.

Don headed out first; Shana and Eio left the Rover later. This time, they disguised themselves as ordinary people and pretended to be strangers to each other, so that the NIISS guards wouldn't easily identify them.

"Stay close to me," Shana told Eio as she held his shoulders and looked into his eyes. "Understand?"

"I knoooow..." Eio replied, and he seemed very impatient since he'd grown comfortable navigating the lower universe. "You said it many times already. I find it more productive to scan cooking recipes."

"Fine!" said Shana, annoyed, "but I have to make sure you know the safety precautions."

Then she took Eio's long thin hand to keep him close as they walked.

"I'm not a three-year-old," Eio grumbled, but he held on.

Midzor was much busier than the village they had stayed in. There were still a lot of people wandering outside after dark. Several drunkards stood lazily in the corner of an alley. Shana grew a little worried as they walked deeper into the crisscrossed back streets; she wasn't sure if she was heading in the correct direction. As they made another turn, someone from the darkness called out to her, "Hey pretty, what brings you here?"

Shana ignored him and hurried away, but Eio turned to eye him angrily as they passed.

Not far ahead, Last Lamp Tavern's sign cut through the gloom. Old-fashioned neon lights flashed on its rooftop, giving an illusion of the good old Earth days. It read:

Wine a bit; everything will be better.

At the sight of that, Shana felt quite relieved. It was never good to linger in the border town for too long, looking lost.

Although she was sure Don knew the way, there would be situations where she needed to act alone. Jack had told her to be independent and look out for herself since her training started, and she wanted to do her best.

At that moment, Don emerged from the other side of the tavern. He looked her way and signaled that he would go around and check out the surroundings. She nodded and walked into the tavern with Eio.

Inside, an enchanting and mesmerizing tune floated around the room lit by dim spotlights. The scent of ale and cigarettes filled the air, and the chatter of patrons was loud. Shana glanced over the crowd but didn't see Andro.

Eio found some game machines by the entrance and insisted he wanted to play. Shana had to give him ten Pink Cubes.

"Just ten minutes, Ok? Come find me when you're done," she told him.

Eio mumbled a "Yes" and ran off.

Shana found a table and sat down by herself. According to Don, this was the place where Andro came most often. They might have to wait a while and see if he would show up.

Andro hadn't given them his contact information. Shana remembered he once said, "I'll come to you guys whenever I feel like it. But don't call me. I don't want to be disturbed." He wore a peculiar expression when he said that, as if worrying he would be interrupted while with a lady.

Just then, a woman in a bright red dress caught Shana's attention. She was standing in the middle of the floor, her dark blonde hair tumbling over her bare shoulders. She moved her body slightly to the beat of the music and seemed to be enjoying her night. When she walked through the room to greet the guests, they all looked up from their drinking cups and laid eyes on her, as if she was the most beautiful woman they'd ever seen.

"Darling, you're glowing!" a young man complimented her, eyeing her sculpted figure.

"Thank you," she replied, her face smiling, her eyes alluring.

"I have a gift for you..." It was only seconds before another guest thought of something to please her.

Shana heard them call her Laurelynn Lovelace, the tavern keeper.

"Good evening, mademoiselle." Minutes later, Laurelynn came over to Shana's table. Unexpectedly, she lowered her head and said in a small voice, "I haven't seen you here before. In case you don't know, you shouldn't come here alone. Go home and come another night with your boyfriend."

"My friends are coming," said Shana.

"Oh, I see." Laurelynn then went back to her dreamy voice and asked, "Something to drink?"

"Just water."

"Five Pink Cubes, please."

Water was never free on Mars. Shana found a Yellow Cube in her purse and handed it to Laurelynn. "Here you are. Keep the change," she said.

"You don't have to do this." Laurelynn found five Pink Cubes and gave the change back to Shana. Then she winked at her and said, "You're old enough to drink, right? Try a little red wine next time. You know, it adds to your feminine charms."

"No. Thank you," replied Shana.

While Laurelynn went to fetch water, Shana couldn't help but admire her extraordinary beauty. Had she taken a beauty package from GIIxb Lab? Shana wondered.

GIIxb Lab, a Gatti business, was rumored to offer humans beauty and longevity packages. Ever since Icus became the System Architect, its popularity had surged among humans seeking Gatti technology.

Icus was an advocate of technology sharing. He created the free Ox-100 program. Many people took it to increase their blood oxygen levels and breathe easier, so it wouldn't be surprising if some early adopters also tried other offerings.

Shana then noticed some photos on the wall to her left: images of happy customers, both humans and Gattis, drinking away. Some Gattis had even brought their own beverages along with them. It was amazing how everyone, regardless of northern or southern origin, could enjoy drinking together.

A large print of Laurelynn and a Gatti officer hung in the center of the wall, hard to miss. In Shana's opinion, the officer was tall, dark, and hideous. From the insignia on his suit, he was likely a high-ranking official, and at the bottom of the photo, a signature, "Jyvesi," was barely legible.

In the photo, Laurelynn leaned against Jyvesi's chest. Although Laurelynn herself was a tall lady, probably five foot eight, Jyvesi towered over her by more than a foot. He held Laurelynn's face with both hands, while four of his tentacles came from behind his body, wrapping around her waist.

When Shana saw the shiny scales on those tentacles, she felt a wave of discomfort, as if her stomach were churning. Shana could never forget what the NIISS guards had done during the Red Purge, yet she also understood that some people who had been spared such pain could become friends with Gattis.

Still, only an open-minded person like Laurelynn could handle this, Shana thought. It was visually challenging and definitely not her thing.

There were stories of people marrying Gattis, Shana recalled, though she had never seen such couples herself. Some couples were even said to order hybrid babies from GIIxb Lab, as Gattis and humans couldn't conceive naturally due to reproductive isolation — a mechanism Dr. Yang could explain very well.

As Shana was lost in thought, Laurelynn returned with a pitcher. She poured Shana a glass of water and said, "Your friend, how can he make you wait? Ditch him if he's your boyfriend."

"Don't tease me," said Shana, feeling a bit shy. "He is not my boyfriend." She knew her situation with Don was a little complicated; though they'd often pretended to be husband and wife, she couldn't explain it to Laurelynn. Shana stopped there and said, "He's just a little behind. He'll come."

"Oh, not your boyfriend?" Laurelynn said to herself quietly. "But you like him?"

Shana didn't know why Laurelynn's train of thought had gone in such a wild direction. She got a little uneasy, but she nodded. Although she barely knew Laurelynn, the woman felt like a big sister to her, pleasant and approachable.

Since Shana had no one in the Wake to talk to about girl's stuff, she told Laurelynn honestly, "I've liked him ever since I got to know him… that was… more than one Mars Year ago."

"Wait, you've known him for such a long time, and you haven't said anything, not even asked him out?" said Laurelynn, the corners of her mouth dropping slightly, and she looked disappointed with Shana's cowardice.

Shana shook her head. Laurelynn wouldn't know. Every day was like life and death to them in the Wake. All Don ever thought about was how to survive and how to win. It never felt like the right time to do anything romantic.

"Oh dear, you need to do something," said Laurelynn. "If you don't know what to do, I can tell you a few tricks."

"We trust each other with our lives, though," Shana said.

"What?" Laurelynn drew a deep breath. "Even worse, you two are like buddies?"

"That's supposed to be a bad thing?" Shana was puzzled by Laurelynn's response.

"Bad. Real bad. How did you become such friends? The hardest type to turn into love, for sure," Laurelynn said in disbelief. "Don't tell me he thinks of you as one of his teammates, and you would use your body to stop a bullet for him?"

Laurelynn's words struck Shana unexpectedly. She had never considered their relationship in that light. Now she was rather confused. But before she could ask Laurelynn for advice, there was a loud bang.

It was the sound of the heavy door slamming open. Three Gatti males had just entered the tavern.

Laurelynn stopped talking when she saw the Gattis stride in.

"What's wrong?" Shana noticed Laurelynn's face shift to a sullen expression and asked.

"I know the trio," Laurelynn whispered. "They've been coming to my shop for weeks, and they're nasty customers."

"How?" asked Shana.

"Look there, the one in the yellow-green shirt is named Trinn, a drunkard," said Laurelynn. "He'll keep ordering drinks until he passes out by midnight. I had to ask for help to drag him out a couple of times, and he didn't pay his bills on two occasions.

"But he is not the worst. The other two are brothers. The tall and muscular one is Inoff. He leads the pack, and he constantly seeks a fight to test out his muscles, the most troublesome. The fat and shorter one is Gimwu. He likes to harass women."

"What are you going to do?" asked Shana.

"I'll just walk back to the kitchen and pretend I haven't seen them," Laurelynn replied. "But you, you need to leave *now*, quietly." She grabbed Shana's hand and showed her the back door.

"I need to get Eio first," said Shana.

"Who?"

Before Shana could answer, the three Gattis had come up fast and surrounded them.

Chapter 6
The Frequent Guest to Last Lamp Tavern

"My friends, how can I help you?" Laurelynn turned around and asked the three Gattis with her usual sweet smile.

"Two beautiful girls on a beautiful night," Inoff spoke as he towered over them. "Care to join us for a drink?"

"No, thanks," Shana answered plainly.

"No? That is not polite. Nobody says no to me," Inoff said as he moved closer to Shana, grinning. "I don't think I've seen you here. I like you; I always like new girls."

Shana didn't back down. "Please get out of my way," she said, her eyes shooting to Inoff's face with an unflinching determination.

"What if I don't?" He squinted his eyes and straightened his arms.

Abruptly, the young brother Gimwu stepped behind Shana and grabbed her waist. At the same time, Trinn seized Laurelynn's arm with his right hand and clamped his left arm around her neck. Shana gasped and quickly pushed Gimwu away with all her strength while Laurelynn drew herself back, trying to brush off those hands.

Inoff looked at Shana with increased interest and said, "Feisty. Pretty girl with a temper, even better, is it not?" The two brothers laughed.

"Don't be afraid. Many of you turn out to like us," said Gimwu. "You know, we pay good Cubes if you can entertain us." Then he fixed his eyes on Laurelynn and said, "Laulin, is it? I'm sure it'll be fun. I like beautiful outlandish women like you."

Laurelynn remained calm and said, “Hey, don’t get the wrong idea. We only serve food and alcohol here, Ok? How about I give you guys a round of free drinks tonight?”

Upon hearing that, the three Gattis laughed, and they seemed happy about their special treatment. Trinn let go of Laurelynn, swaggered forward, and made a display of sitting down. Inoff forced Shana and Laurelynn to sit down among them.

Shana supposed Laurelynn tried to ease the tension before it was too late, but still, she grew anxious. Don should be here any minute, but where was he?

Laurelynn signaled Jamie, the bartender, to bring a large jar of wine and poured each of them a generous cup. Inoff raised his cup and dumped the wine down his throat, then, after smacking his mouth a few times, he said, “More!”

Shana hoped very much that the wine would work fast on the Gattis. After a few rounds of drinks, she thought it might be a good time to sneak out, since the alcohol might have taken control.

“Excuse me, I need to make a phone call,” she said.

When she stood up, however, Inoff grabbed her arm and pulled her back to her seat.

“Do not play any tricks on me. You are not leaving tonight,” he sneered.

Shana bit her lips. She was outraged but wasn’t scared because she knew Don was around.

It seemed like the Gattis wouldn’t back off easily. How could she get out of it? Jack had taught her to look for the details. These Gattis looked like ordinary scum and most likely didn’t have any combat skills.

If she was right, with the training from Jack, she had a good chance of dealing with one of them, even though Gattis were generally stronger.

Or, she might be able to give them a few kicks and leave fast. But what about Laurelynn? Shana didn’t want her to get hurt.

Or she could try bluffing… An idea popped into her mind.

Just then, Gimwu and Trinn surrounded Laurelynn again; one held her head by her hair while the other brushed her cheeks.

"Take your hands off her!" Shana hollered. "If you don't know, Laurelynn is protected by Jyvesi, a senior official. You've really got some nerve to offend her."

It worked. Inoff winced; Trinn shuddered upon hearing the word 'senior.'

"That's who Jyvesi is," Shana added, pointing to the wall where the photo was, the one she'd seen earlier. "I saw him in this area only an hour ago."

Laurelynn winked at Shana and seemed to understand. "Right. That's him," she said quickly, "he'll be really upset if I get hurt. He's promised me that everything will be Ok while he's in office."

Shana had just made up the story, but she was still surprised to hear it from Laurelynn, who seemed to deal with these situations often. Was it true? That was how Laurelynn had survived all these years? Shana wondered. What was her relationship with Jyvesi?

But she had no time to think more about that. She glanced around the room anxiously for Don. Where was he?

"Should we go now?" asked Gimwu to his brother.

Inoff hesitated, but then he looked at Shana and said, "Don't fool me. Who are you looking for? To see if your senior official is here? I can tell you, I've received an enhancement package and I'm joining NIISS. Their team lead, Taenc, has come many times to test me out."

Inoff looked very smug after these words, and he laughed so hard that his tentacles waved uncontrollably. "You know, I've got the physical aspect of it. I'm sure this Jyvesi wouldn't mind gifting me a woman or two?"

At that moment, Shana saw Don enter the tavern through a side door. Apparently, he hadn't found Andro.

Don caught Shana's eyes when looking toward her table. He frowned at the three Gattis and seemed to comprehend the situation immediately. He signaled Shana to move outside to avoid the crowd.

Shana was greatly relieved. She looked at Laurelynn and then towards the back door.

Laurelynn seemed to read her mind and responded with a nod. Then she turned to Inoff with a smile and said, "Well, what entertainment do you have in mind? There're lots of people here, though. It's not very convenient. Why don't we go somewhere else with more privacy?"

Laurelynn's voice was low but pleasant and suggestive. Shana felt her face would turn red if she had to say that. The younger brother, Gimwu, was dazed for a second.

"How I look forward to it," Inoff said, and the muscles in his face twisted. A winning grin, Shana interpreted.

"Shall we get moving?" Gimwu stood up.

Laurelynn led them out of the tavern and went past a warehouse. She remained silent on their way. The clicking of her heels was the only sound in the dark night.

Shana walked slowly at the rear.

"There's a private room in the back," Laurelynn said. "I apologize for the walk. Let's go just a little further, and that'll be it."

The three Gattis followed her with pleased anticipation until they saw nothing behind the warehouse. There were only dim lights and a bare sandy backyard with a steep slope on the edge.

Laurelynn continued to smile when she stopped. "Here we are," she said, though she withdrew herself to a safe distance on the sly.

The three turned around and scanned their surroundings, looking confused. Inoff asked suspiciously, "Here? Is this it?"

Not far behind, Don followed them quietly. He had picked up Eio from the game machines, and the little creature walked by his side.

"It looks like Shana and her friend are in trouble. I may have to fight the three Gattis," Don told Eio clearly. "Now, in the worst case, are you able to get back to the Rover by yourself? You remember where we parked?"

"Certainly," replied Eio.

"Good," said Don. He gave Eio a pat on his head and nudged him to the corner of the warehouse. "Hide here and wait for me. If I'm losing, make a run for it." Don then took off the Senset from his ear and said, "Use this comm device and press this button here, then you can send Jack or Brian a message. Ask for help." He put it into Eio's hand and hurried forward.

Don had his pistol fastened to his waist, the gift from Jack, but he didn't want to draw too much attention with a gunshot. It would be best if he could just drive the Gattis away, and hopefully, they wouldn't dare to come back again.

Don hid in the dark. He pulled out a sharp, single-edged blade from his leg strap and held it tight in his hand. Once Laurelynn finished talking, and the group slowed down, he ran up to Gimwu, the last one of the three, and kicked him hard in the back of his knees.

Don's movement was quick, and the blow was strong. Gimwu didn't even seem to notice Don was coming at him; he collapsed to the ground with a thud and hit his head heavily on a piece of rock. Then he lay flat, motionless.

Inoff turned back sharply, trying to see what had happened. "Who is there?" he shouted, his eyes on his brother lying on the ground.

Don came out from the dark and stared at Inoff grimly.

"Are we ambushed?" cried Trinn, fear on his face. Shana wasted no time in giving him a strike to his head. "Aaargh…" Trinn let out a loud cry and crouched down to protect his head. "Don't beat me. It's not my idea… please…"

"This is a trap. We have been fooled!" Inoff yelled to Trinn madly.

"How dare you!" Inoff then took a great leap towards Don, his jaw opened wide as if he was going to bite Don on the neck.

"Don! He'll jump on you in a sec!" Shana cried out. Laurelynn screamed and looked away.

Don dodged aside swiftly. "Stop now. Take your friends back home," he spoke in Gattish coldly, "and do not harass these ladies again."

Inoff was first shocked to hear him speak their language but soon pulled himself back and retorted, "Don't you think it's too late? You have hurt my brother and my friend."

"It's never too late," Don replied calmly. "He only fell asleep. Take him home, and he'll recover soon."

Inoff blew through his nostrils and said, "Do not tell me what to do."

"Then it's a pity." Don raised the blade, put his left foot forward, and slightly bent his knees, taking a strong stance.

Inoff roared and jumped at Don again. Don held the blade high with both hands to block him, then he gave a hard kick to Inoff's lower leg; normal Gattis would crumble.

But surprisingly, Inoff ignored the kick. He grabbed the blade out of Don's hands, bent it, and broke it completely.

Don stepped back, astonished. His blade was specially made by Andro, and it had a high yield strength. While Don had met strong Gattis before, this one seemed to be beyond the average build. Don was not convinced that Gattis could have that kind of strength naturally. He backed away immediately and drew some distance.

Inoff flung the broken blade aside. "Humans are weak and pathetic," he rasped. "You'll break just the same." Then he gathered his strength again, yelled and charged headlong.

Don narrowly escaped. Ignoring Inoff's insults, he concentrated on moving around so that he could avoid Inoff jumping at him head-on. He only needed to be more careful and wait for a good chance when Inoff was less guarded. He would then attack once at his weak spot and put him down fast.

Meanwhile, Shana seemed anxious to see that Inoff had the upper hand. She edged closer, her eyes darting back and forth between them as if trying to find a chance to help Don. But before she could make a move, a cold voice came from the corner of the warehouse.

"Bold words, from someone too blind to see his own downfall."

"Who is there?" Inoff startled and turned in the direction of the sound. He squinted his eyes, but probably couldn't see who was hiding in the dark, so he paused to assess the potential threat.

It was Eio's voice.

"Didn't I tell him to hide?" Don thought. He grew a little worried, but that didn't slow him down from taking advantage of Inoff, who was now looking away.

Don took out his pocket knife and ran forward. He leaped, landing on Inoff, then stabbed through the scales to the back of Inoff's lower neck. That was supposed to disrupt the nerves in that weak spot and paralyze his limbs.

"Argh!" Inoff shook madly.

Don's knife went in but missed by an inch.

Inoff was too strong; he grabbed Don's arm and threw him down. They rolled to the ground, wrestled with each other, and struggled to fight. Seconds later, Inoff came from behind; he wrapped an arm around Don's neck, tightening his grip. Don tried to block the chokehold with his left arm.

Suddenly there was a low cracking sound; something was broken. Don felt a sharp pain and realized his left arm had fractured from Inoff's squeeze. Inoff had broken a blade, and he could easily crush him in the next second.

"Don!" Shana cried in fear as she rushed forward and got behind Inoff. Without any hesitation, she grabbed the knife and drove it all the way into Inoff's lower neck. The knife finally took a toll on him. His limbs gave out gradually. But Inoff was heavy, and his arm was still clamping around Don.

"Let go!" Shana grasped Inoff's arm with both hands, trying to move it away. Unexpectedly, one of his tentacles shot up, seized her leg and pulled hard. She groaned in pain and fell to the ground. After that, the tentacle finally dropped flat, motionless.

Don used his good arm to break free. "Are you Ok?" he asked as he struggled to get up and then gave Shana a hand.

"I'm Ok." She took his hand and got to her feet. Then both of them took a deep breath.

Don felt greatly relieved. Just then, he noticed that the tentacle's spikes had stung Shana's lower leg; blood was oozing out of the wound. His heart sank immediately, and his mind was filled with worry. However, before he could check her leg, he heard a rustling sound. Someone was coming towards them. Don turned around and saw Gimwu, who had woken up while nobody noticed, now eyeing them angrily.

"Every one of you will pay for all this!" he shrieked.

"Gimwu! Help!" Trinn rushed out at the same time, holding his bloody nose on his swollen face. He'd been curled up all the time and now became excited at the sight of Gimwu. He pointed to Don and yelled, "This guy killed your brother. Get him!"

Just then, Shana almost jumped. "My leg is going numb," she muttered. "Those tentacle spikes must be poisonous!" Then she sat down and quickly tore up her pants into an opening. "Give me a second," she called out to Don. After that, she squeezed hard around the sting site until blood rushed out of the darkened and swollen wound.

"This is no good," Don murmured, reaching for his pistol at the small of his back while keeping his eyes on the enemy. Normally, he could fight off a few Gattis, but now his left arm was badly injured. He didn't want to risk taking too long. It would be best for him to hold them off and let Shana go first.

"Laurelynn, Eio," he called out, "I'll take care of the two Gattis. Please help Shana to leave here!"

Laurelynn had been hiding behind the warehouse door. She came out to see what had happened and gasped at the sight.

"I'm Ok. Don't make me go," Shana said to Don firmly. "I want to stick with you till the end." She tied up her wound with a piece of cloth, straightened up, and stood by him.

"Trinn, let's get them together! They are wounded," Gimwu growled. Then Trinn came slowly from the other side. They looked to Shana and then to Don, hesitating, as if unsure which one would be easier to attack.

Swoosh!

Right at that moment, something flew over and struck Gimwu's leg. With a crash, Gimwu knelt to the ground. "What's going on?" he cried in panic.

"Gotcha." A man's voice rose from behind the warehouse. He then walked out, a blonde guy in his thirties, muscular and strong. He came over and picked up a hammer from the ground.

Gimwu turned to look at what had struck him. After he saw it was only a hammer, he cursed.

The man ran up to Gimwu swiftly. He grabbed his neck in one hand, raised the hammer high in the other, and smashed it down.

Gimwu collapsed right away. It looked like his head was going to be crushed. But the hammer only landed on the ground, inches from his eyes. Sand and gravel shot in all directions.

Before Gimwu was able to gather himself, the man pressed his head to the dirt and asked, "Still want more?"

"No, please, no," Gimwu replied, curling his tentacles together, "no more."

"Is it a good time to go home and *never* come back?" the man pressed further.

"Yes, yes," Gimwu agreed hastily.

"If I see you again here in this tavern, you won't have a second chance to go home."

"You won't see us. You won't see us…" Gimwu repeated.

The man then let go of Gimwu's head.

Gimwu limped slightly to get Trinn. The two carried Inoff's body and hurried away, not daring to look back.

The man clapped to brush off the dirt from his hands, his long blond hair swaying carelessly in the evening breeze, and he was the very person they had come looking for: Andro.

Andro was tall, heavily built, and definitely a handsome guy. He looked at Don and Shana, shook his head, and said, "What would you do without me?"

He then gave a thoughtful glance at the broken blade left on the ground and the blood on Shana's leg.

"How come you two took such a beating from three Gattis?"

"One of them is no ordinary Gatti," Don replied, "we can talk about that later. Thank you for helping out, man." He greeted Andro, and then turned to ask Shana anxiously, "How do you feel? Is it bad?"

Shana opened the cloth again to check the wound. Luckily the dark area hadn't grown bigger. "The pain isn't that bad. I don't think the toxin's gone too far. The wound will heal in a day or two," she said. "Worry about your own broken arm. It may take four to six weeks."

"Do you want water?" asked Eio. He and Laurelynn had helped to fetch some water and a first aid kit so that Shana could rinse the wound better.

"Exactly what I need. Thank you so much," said Shana gladly. "I really appreciate you guys being so helpful."

Eio looked at her with concern while she cleaned up the wound and applied gauze pads and bandages.

That was when Andro finally noticed that Eio was following along.

"Hey, here's a pumpkinhead," said Andro, studying Eio in amusement. "Is he an adopted kid of you two?" he asked while looking at Don and Shana.

Andro's question was so out of the blue that Shana almost dropped the first aid kit she was holding.

"Not again," Eio grunted. "I don't like that name."

"No, he's not a kid," Don replied simply. "Let me introduce him. Eio is a new member in training with us, and he's done great today.

"And this is Andro. He's an ex-NATO fighter jet pilot, the best pilot I've ever met. An expert in weapons, too. More importantly, he's a loyal and trusted friend."

Andro smiled, clearly pleased with the introduction. He ran a hand through his hair, smoothing it neatly back into place, and no one would have guessed he had just come out of a fight. He crossed his arms, looking self-satisfied.

However, Eio shrugged and didn't seem impressed. He protested to Andro, "Don't give me a nickname. I don't like Pumpkinhead. Also, I'm older than you. Show some respect to a senior."

Don smiled, and they all laughed.

"What about Inoff? The strong Gatti," Laurelynn asked moments later. "Is he dead?"

"No. The knife won't kill him," Don replied. "He just passed out. I didn't want to take his life. It's better to teach him a lesson."

"Don, we haven't had time to tell you," Shana put in. "Inoff said he took an enhancement package from NIISS. You should have been more careful if you knew."

"I see… no wonder," said Don. "Now I understand."

"NIISS guards' ability to regrow is strong," Shana explained to Laurelynn. "Inoff will be able to use his limbs again once he's healed."

Don then bent down to pat Eio's shoulders and said, "Thank you for what you did back there. That was very clever of you. You distracted Inoff and gave me a window to strike. Not many can keep calm when facing a strong enemy."

Eio seemed pleased to hear that. A smile spread across his face, and his eyes were sparkling.

"Let's go inside and find a safe place for you guys to rest," said Laurelynn. She welcomed Don, Andro, Shana, and Eio into the back of the kitchen. She showed them hidden stairs leading to a cellar where she stored wine barrels and hid her valuables.

Andro supported Shana by the arm, taking the weight off her wounded leg and guiding her carefully down the narrow stairs. The others followed behind into the cellar. Don sat down at a small table, and all of them got together.

"Let me take a look," Shana said as she inspected Don's left arm and then felt his muscles and bones carefully.

"How is it?" Andro asked.

"Not too bad," she replied. "The radius bone broke into two pieces, but it can grow back. I worried it might have been a comminuted fracture if you had seen the Gatti bend the steel."

Shana's face brightened up. Don knew she had seen much worse on him, and this was not that serious.

"Don," she asked him, "do you need any painkillers?"

“No,” Don replied. He wouldn’t fret about such a minor accident.

Shana then turned to ask Andro nicely, “I have my medical supplies in our Rover. Would you please help me get them?”

“I have something for you, too,” Don added quickly, “there are two pieces of luggage. Could you get both? The supplies are in one of them, and the other one is for you.”

Andro looked at them with a sigh and grumbled, “Of course… I’m at your service.”

When Andro got back shortly after, Shana asked for his help to put a cast on Don.

Andro held Don’s arm in a natural position, and Shana put on a layer of stockinette. She wrapped a web roll bandage with good tension and applied a fiberglass roll on it.

“Amazing. This is how you do it?” said Eio, watching closely. “Shana, you’ve done it in such a skillful way, and you didn’t even blink.”

“Yeah,” Shana replied, smiling. “Don cannot use his arm for a month until the bone grows back together.”

“Man, you are running out of your quota of growing back,” Andro commented. “I’ve seen you like this more than a dozen times. Shana, tell him he’s going to be a cripple if he continues to risk his life.”

“No, you tell him.”

“Since when does Andro worry?” Don replied with a light chuckle. “You’ve always been the cool, playful one.”

Andro was speechless for a second then they laughed together.

In the meantime, Laurelynn found some clean linens and made a bed on a corner bench. Shana ordered Don to lie down.

“Shana, don’t worry too much about me. Take care of yourself,” said Don gently. “Why don’t you rest too?”

After everybody in the room settled, Laurelynn pulled her hair up, leaned back, and exhaled deeply. “What a day!” she said. “I feel like a drink. Anyone?”

“Just water for us,” said Don. “Thank you.”

"Andro, what do you like? Dark beer, the usual?" Laurelynn asked softly, looking at Andro with loving eyes.

"Yep," replied Andro, smiling with his deep ocean-blue eyes. "Laurelynn, you need to be more careful in the next few days. I bet those Gattis won't dare to come back. But just in case, you have my number."

"What?" Shana complained at once, her eyes widened. "Laurelynn has your number, but we don't? Aren't we your friends, too?"

Don tilted his head from his bed and cast a dark glance at Andro.

"Hey, you know, it's different with a lady," said Andro, giving an uneasy grin.

"I knew it!"

"How could you do this to us?"

"Andro, you're bad."

The room erupted with complaints, mutterings, chatter, and laughter until it was time for bed. Laurelynn cleaned out a guestroom for Shana and Eio to rest for the night, so only Don and Andro were left in the cellar.

"Andro, I need to talk to you," said Don, changing to a low voice.

"Can it wait until tomorrow?"

"Better not."

Andro let out a sigh, "You're here for a reason. I knew it." He then checked their weapons and the cellar's door, making sure that they were safe. "No good is gonna happen whenever I see you," he mumbled. "Ok, spill it out."

"I've got you something," said Don. He got up and retrieved the package from the luggage Andro had helped bring back. Using his good arm, he then moved it onto the table.

Andro picked it up, weighed it, and raised his eyebrows. "It's heavier than its size indicates," he said. "Is this what you told me about?"

Don nodded, "This is it."

Andro flipped a corner of the package, revealing a sealed, vacuum container. Inside, pieces of metal shimmered pale gray.

"Thallium. Shana and I brought it back from an abandoned chemical factory on earth," Don said. "Tested it with a chemist. At least ninety-eight percent purity. According to Dr. Yang, it should inhibit the Gattis' regeneration factors and block their fast healing."

"Great," Andro said, his eyes flashing with a sparkle of excitement. "We can do serious damage with this."

"How much ammo do you think you can make out of it?" Don asked eagerly.

Andro weighed the package in his hand again and estimated, "About five kilograms… Depends on the types of bullets you want. Thallium itself is soft. I need to add harder materials to have enough penetration. I'll try to mix it with other metals, such as lead…"

"I want a small batch of the FN 5.7×28mm cartridges first," said Don.

"Sure. In that case, I'll use a tenth of it in my first trial, and that'll probably get you… sixteen hundred rounds."

"That's a lot." Don let out a cry of amazement. "Excellent."

"And then, the most important thing," Andro said, "you'll want to do some tests on the NIISS guards. Let's see if it works before I make more."

"Sure. Makes sense," Don replied. "I'm sure it'll work."

"Do you plan to use it on a large scale, like cartridges for machine guns?" Andro asked a moment later.

Don had already thought about that before he came. He closed his eyes to give it a more careful consideration and said, "If we use it too often, the Gattis may discover our secret weapon and find a countermeasure for it. I think I want those but will save them for the time that matters the most."

"Understood. It's meant to be a surprise. You'll kick some asses." Andro replied as he wrapped up the package safely and put it away.

"Will it cost you a lot?" Don asked with concern. "You can give me a number, and the Wake can pay you back."

"Not a lot. You don't have to pay," said Andro, sitting back and drinking the dark beer Laurelynn gave him. "I'm too lazy to keep track of the materials and tools I need to use."

Don felt a swell of gratitude. He had grown accustomed to being mindful of the means and cost of everything, since he was an orphan and on his own. Andro, however, came from a wealthy family. Unlike him, Andro never had to concern himself with money; he simply pursued whatever he found interesting. Such freedom was something Don could barely imagine.

"Thanks," he said, then he asked hopefully, "Do you think you can make me a new blade as well? The one you gave me was a work of art. I'm sorry to see it broken."

"Now you're getting too greedy!" Andro grumbled. "I don't like the idea of repeating an art."

"Thank you, Andro. I owe you a lot," Don said honestly.

"Yep. I know," Andro replied casually, taking another sip of his beer.

Don gave him a smile. The Wake was in great need of everything: food, equipment, vehicles, and weapons. And he was grateful that Andro helped them whenever he was able to, with his own money.

"By the way, Thallium is toxic for humans, too," he reminded Andro. "Just remember to handle it carefully. Always be safe, will you?"

"No problem with me. Cohen and I have a workstation. It's top-notch. You and Shana should go visit."

"I have no doubt it's state-of-the-art," said Don, patting Andro's back. "I'll go to admire your work someday."

Chapter 7
Inside GIIxb Lab

That night, Don briefed Jack on what had happened at Last Lamp Tavern over the comm. The next day, Don, Shana, and Eio went back to their temporary accommodations in the village, and Andro accompanied them along the way like a perfect gentleman.

Jack's face lit up with delight when he saw them return, and he was overjoyed to see Andro. "It's so good to see you!" Jack said, giving Andro a tight handshake and then a big hug.

"How are you doing, Old J?" asked Andro, smiling broadly.

"I'm doing great," Jack gave a warm reply.

"Are you still capable of finishing up five bags of the Mix at a time?" asked Andro, a grin tugging at his mouth.

"Why not?" Jack said, looking as strong as ever. "Food is a weapon. It gives you good energy."

"I was worried that you might need pills for your joints already," said Andro.

"Don't laugh at an old man. Anyway, thank you for helping out," Jack said. Then he looked at Andro hopefully and said, "We're going back to our home base in Redland tomorrow. Would you like to come with us?"

"No, thanks. I just came by to say hi. I have a lady waiting for me."

Jack raised his eyebrows and opened his mouth to say something but then closed it. Don supposed Jack wanted to ask who the lady was but thought better of it. There were always women around Andro, a constant parade of fleeting interests, so it was rarely worth asking for details.

Yet Jack didn't seem to be discouraged. He said, "If you change your mind, you know where to find us."

"Sure. I'll see you around," said Andro, turning to leave.

Don walked after him and said in a small voice, "Before you go, can I ask you something?" Andro nodded, and they stepped into Don's room.

Don went to the window, tapping his foot, his mind racing. He was still thinking about the fight last night, and he wanted to gather more information from Andro.

"What is it?" asked Andro curiously. "I know that look. Are you planning something risky again?"

"Have you heard of GIIxb Lab?" Don began.

"Yep. They say it provides biological modifications, enhancements, and so on. Why?"

"Inoff, the Gatti I dealt with, had uncommon strength," said Don thoughtfully. "He broke the blade you gave me easily. I don't think it's an individual case, and Shana mentioned that he took an enhancement treatment from NIISS."

"So?"

"I wonder if GIIxb Lab is involved in this," said Don.

"Wait, you think the Lab is behind NIISS?" said Andro, surprised. "You've got to be kidding me."

"It's highly likely. With the help of GIIxb Lab, NIISS is building an army with superpowers," said Don, and he had his reasons. "Many NIISS guards gained the fast heal ability two Mars Years ago, and we've just found a way to deal with it. Now they're getting another ability — becoming stronger. We can't let them keep going like that. I want to know if the Lab is supporting NIISS."

"That's a bold guess," Andro said, his eyes glinting. "GIIxb Lab claims to be a commercial organization. It's headed by a radical Gatti scientist named Olram. But anything is possible. Since Gatti-Human hybrids can be made from there, super guards aren't too far from that."

"Do you know what's in there?" asked Don earnestly. "Have you been to the Lab yourself?"

"No," Andro replied. "What's your plan? Can you at least wait until you can use your arm?"

"I'm going to check it out," Don replied with determination. He must figure out what was going on because he didn't want to put their members in danger unknowingly, especially Shana.

* * *

A month later, Don felt well enough to move his left arm. Now he was energized and anxious to investigate GIIxb Lab.

The Lab was located on the north side of TTado Bridge, west of OIIIzoi. Don drove his Rover and left Redland alone on a quiet afternoon.

The night had fallen when he reached the desolate outskirt of OIIIzoi. He dropped out of the vehicle and headed towards a field full of sand and dust, since he decided to avoid the main road and follow a trail.

The sky was clear, and the wind blew gently. He blended easily into the darkness of the night with his all-black suit, and he walked fast, concentrating on what was ahead of him.

As he went further on the trail, he saw clusters of bushes and scattered trees, mostly dark colored with thorns. These desert-adapted Gatti plants grew denser and denser along his way, and the dim moonlight from Phobos cast obscured shadows of them.

Don looked at the tall, still trees warily. Just then, one of them moved. Its branches waved with a rustling sound, apparently identifying him as food.

Those were Saxlics! Don recognized them at once. He remembered seeing a small one in Yang's greenhouse, but these were much bigger. Saxlics were half-plant, half-animal. They had deep roots in the sand to reach scarce water, but their branches could extend tens of meters, looking for prey.

More Saxlics were aroused now, dozens of writhing, grasping branches swinging wildly. One of them almost hit him while trying to grab his body. Don quickly pulled out his blade — a generic replacement — from his leg strap. He stabbed, chopped, diced, and slashed like a whirlwind, cutting off whatever got close to him.

Then he ran as fast as his legs could carry him, the rustling branches clawing at the air behind him. Luckily, he didn't get tangled in the Saxlics.

He should be close, Don thought as he rushed to the end of the trail.

There was a large open space in front of him, and GIIxb Lab was right there, an enormous ellipsoid jumping out to meet his eyes.

The Lab should be closed at this hour — perfect for an investigation, Don thought. When near, he checked the vicinity and found no guards. There were no Gattis and no humans, either. It was so quiet.

Don slowed his pace, his eyes sweeping across the Lab. Unlike some pointy, towering Gatti structures, it had a unique egg-shaped design. The curves were smooth and uninterrupted, giving it a sense of grace and fluidity. Its shell was a sleek and shining metal, reflecting the surroundings like a mirror.

Don circled the silver-grey building, wondering how he could sneak inside. He wished there was an easy point to break in or something to climb onto. But there were no clear stories nor any windows he could see from outside. The only thing that looked like an entrance was an elliptical recessed panel.

Don gazed at it with intensity. Just then, as if sensing his presence, a billboard he hadn't noticed earlier suddenly lit up. It cast chilling blue light, and it read,

How far will you go?
To become who you want to be?

Then it changed to —

Seek to build a new life or a new self...
What will you choose?

Then a voice speaking English came out of nowhere and said,

"Welcome. Please come in."

He must have been seen. Don turned around vigilantly, but nobody was in sight. Seconds later, he noticed the voice came from a speaker sticking out from a small window of the metal wall. He was sure the window wasn't there before. It had just opened up.

A pale light lit up the entrance. The recessed panel slid to the side and revealed a passage.

Should he go in? Was this a trap? Don wondered. His heart was extremely uneasy.

But Andro said GIIxb Lab was a commercial establishment; it advertised itself as neutral and purely for the good of science. Besides, Jack had asked for an understanding of Gatti technology. Someone had to take the risk, and there was probably no better man than himself.

While Don was hesitating, the panel moved a little as if it was going to close. He felt a sudden irresistible impulse and decided to go for it.

Even if this was a descent into hell, Don thought, he would get to the bottom of it.

After sending Brian a message via his Senset to tell him his decision, Don went in. He held his head high as he walked, calmly as usual, and he followed the passage into a small chamber without haste.

"Is this your first time meeting us?" the voice sounded again, but there was still no one present.

"Yes," Don answered, peering around.

The chamber looked like a reception room. There was simple furniture — an armchair and a table — but no windows. The fact that the entire place was enclosed within walls was disturbing.

"Since you haven't come to us before, let me introduce you to our full services. We offer a wide range of personalized creations and enhancements, such as making a hybrid baby, self-improvement, and disease treatments."

"Tell me more," said Don, looking towards the corners and searching for speakers and cameras.

"Everything you can imagine about improving yourself can be achieved. Choose biological enhancements such as beauty, longevity, or health packages."

Then the tabletop lit up and changed into a screen. Images shuffled in front of him to show each package in greater detail.

"What kind of service are you looking for?" asked the voice.

"I'm looking to increase my physical capabilities, becoming more athletic," Don replied tentatively.

"Yes, that can be done by inserting relevant genes and changing your genome. It's called the performance boost package. You'll see bodybuilding effects: your muscles will grow, and your cardiopulmonary functions will be strengthened."

"Relevant genes… Can I choose between human genes and Gatti genes?" asked Don.

"Of course, you can choose either or a mix of them. Is this what you are looking for?"

"Yes, and I want to choose human genes only," said Don. This was most likely the package that Inoff received. He wanted to see it for himself.

The voice then continued, "Well then. Before we begin, here are our terms that you can choose to accept or reject. If you reject, you may leave as you wish. Remember, what you choose to do in our lab is completely confidential."

Then it read a lengthy document. Don thought he heard that customers would receive the treatment at their own risk. Although rare, unintended side effects might occur, and GIIxb Lab would not guarantee the end results. Customers would only pay when the treatment was successful.

People who had come this far wouldn't be scared off by those terms, Don thought to himself.

Moments later, there was a pause as if leaving him to decide. Upon seeing Don was still there and had no intention of leaving, it asked finally, "Do you agree?"

"I agree," Don replied simply.

"A blood sample will be needed to create a gene key. It'll be used to properly identify you, design your personalized treatment plans, and later confirm whether the genome modifications have occurred correctly."

"Is that absolutely necessary?" Don objected.

"Yes. It's the only thing required and the foundation for us to find the best option for your treatment."

"And what does it mean? A gene key?" he asked.

"We'll run human DNA sequencing on your blood sample. Your DNA sequence is unique, hence the gene key. And you'll access your profile and treatment history via this key later. Once more, you can refuse and exit anytime."

There was a long pause as Don weighed the risk of leaving his biometrics with them. It would be bad if he was found out to be in the resistance. But unlike Jack, he was not on the NIISS's wanted list.

He was a nobody. NIISS couldn't have known of his existence, and he didn't have a lot to lose. Even if they got his image and DNA, it was probably Ok.

Most importantly, he didn't want to leave without any valuable information.

"And your choice is?"

Finally, Don said determinedly, "Go ahead."

"We can start now. Please sit down and place your arm on the side support of the chair." The machine voice sounded again, devoid of sentiment.

A panel on the arm support slid open, and a robotic probe stuck out and took an image of Don's arm for blood vessels.

"Hold still."

A needle on the robot head then rose to poke his forearm and withdraw blood. Don felt a pinch that was no different from Shana's antibiotic shot. It took less than a minute.

"Your blood sample is now being sent for analysis. The DNA sequencing and your treatment synthesis will be ready in just two hours. While you wait, let's review other important information."

Don then read a document about the expected body reactions and changes after receiving the performance boost package.

Above the reception chambers, a group of Gatti technicians monitored the process. Don's blood sample in the vial was drawn into test wells. The wells went through pre-processing and were fed into sequencing machines. With the sound of low humming from the working machines, his gene sequences were recorded into their database.

A very old-looking Gatti scientist was supervising the technicians. He sat in a wheelchair and seemed to only have his head from his original body. His hunched back was fused to a life-support system attached at the neck. The rest of his body had shrunk and couldn't be told apart from the system. The entire wheelchair was covered in tubes for nutrient inflow and waste discharge. Green digits flickered across a monitor beside him, indicating his health status.

The old Gatti scientist asked, "Any update from Xplro Factory? Has our virus finished assembly?"

One of the technicians, Ena, replied, "Yes. For our virus production, we've reserved five poles in Xplro. Another batch will be delivered to us tomorrow."

"Good," said the scientist.

When Don's sample was finished, the database found an existing match to his gene key. At that moment, a red light flashed up, beeping.

"Olram! One of our tracking subjects has returned," Ena called out a notice. "System Architect Icus has put a special tag on this one."

"Oh?"

The wheelchair shifted as Olram thought his instruction, helping him to move forward. He got in front of a screen and said, "Ena, bring me a visual close-up."

The technician did as he said. Olram stared at the gene key sequences and then at Don's image from the reception chamber.

"Hello there," he said as he leaned forward and squinted his eyes, looking fairly interested.

Olram studied Don's appearance for a minute and continued, "You are not what I have expected at all. How fascinating. Ena, why don't you bring him up, and we can have a chat?"

"Yes." Ena did as he asked and went out for Don.

In the reception chamber, Don had just finished reading the documentation presented to him. He had memorized everything; Yang would want the details. Just when he was about to stand up, a door was opened. Don was surprised to see that a Gatti would actually show up. His eyes opened wide.

"Hello, my name is Ena," she spoke rather politely, which was rarely the case when a Gatti talked to a human. "You've been chosen as our special guest. Would you like a tour and get to know more about our technologies?"

Don looked at her; she was young, with mixed features from both human and Gatti, and she even had a name that sounded like Earth origin.

She could be a successful hybrid, Don thought.

He asked, "Why am I chosen as a special guest?"

"It's a random process. Nothing particular."

She didn't seem to be aggressive. Don decided to go for it, so he followed her out into another passage.

The Lab was an elaborate labyrinth. Don's pulse quickened, and he felt uneasy as they walked silently to higher levels. There were no numbers or any signs to indicate where they were. After a while, Ena stopped in front of an unknown section and pressed one of her tentacles on a sensor.

A panel slid open and revealed what looked like a disinfection area inside.

"We cannot bring in any microorganism. All measures will be taken for sterilization," Ena explained as they approached a chamber. "In order to enter the core area of the lab, we must first enter this room, get dressed in a suit, and then pass through a chemical shower."

At her words, the chamber door opened. Inside, there were ultraviolet lights illuminating from all directions. The UV lights turned off before she walked in.

"Follow me and step in," said Ena. "Next, a gown will come down on your head."

A large white gown dropped from above and sealed Don completely and automatically from head to toe, leaving only a window for his face. Ena was dressed in the same.

"Now, we'll enter the next room for a shower."

Unknown gas filled the next room. Antimicrobial fluid spayed down upon them for extra prevention.

After all that, they passed through a buffer zone. Don noticed that airflow was rigorously controlled — the series of airtight doors did not open simultaneously.

Beyond the buffer zone lay a workshop where gas tanks, pumps, and pipelines were chained together with rows of containers. In each container, submerged in some solutions, Don thought he saw various body parts and organs. The scene was bizarre yet strangely familiar. A shudder ran down his spine as he wondered if he had seen a similar setup before.

Don walked in quick strides to take a closer look at the containers. In one row, there were something like living lungs — red lobes hanging on a breathing tube, inflating and then deflating slightly. In another row, some faces seemed to have facial movements from time to time, giving vague expressions. It was so eerie that Don felt nauseous, as well as angry.

"Are these human organs?" he demanded.

"Yes. But it's not what you think," Ena explained at once. "We haven't killed a single creature. On the contrary, we've saved many lives, and we only help those who want to be helped. The organ culture you see here is growing from stem cells and starting tissues provided by our customers."

She led Don to another row, pointed to a container, and said, "For example, in this row, we have cultured hearts. Here, you can see a human heart in this semi-solid nutrient medium. It's almost ready, with all four chambers, veins, arteries, and nerves. It is modeled from a poor kid's remaining heart tissues and his own genes. He needed a heart transplant after he got shot in a fight. So we put him to sleep in our freezing machine to wait for a new heart of his own. Isn't it amazing?"

Don looked at the beating heart in disbelief. Yang once mentioned something like this was possible, but he didn't know GIIxb Lab had actually done it.

"And what is that?" Don went further and arrived at a different section.

"You've come to an area of Gatti organs," replied Ena. "This growing culture is an add-on tentacle for one of our customers. The thin white fiber is a tentacle nerve, which is a bit thicker than human nerves. Tentacles are accessories we can choose when we grow up. Let it be an extra eye, enhanced hearing, or just a decoration. Isn't it wonderful?"

Don had no interest in their decorations, but he gave some thought to the enhanced senses.

"And these are just examples of what we do. You can design your own baby, add all the good things from yourself or your partner and leave out the bad."

Don remembered the hybrids, and he wanted to confirm. So, he asked, "Is it going to work if one parent is human and the other is Gatti?"

"Yes, of course. As you may know, Gattis and humans cannot have babies in a natural way. But we have a workaround. The technology became available three Mars Years ago. You can combine certain genes from both sides, and the newborn will actually look like their parents."

Don's thoughts were racing fast. Different ideas crossed his mind as he connected the dots. If what the Lab claimed was true, he suspected that the NIISS guards would get some kind of new enhancements periodically. He wondered if the production lines for enhanced guards were just on another floor.

At that moment, an old Gatti glided towards them in his wheelchair. Navigation lights flickered along its frame, and liquid gurgled with each movement. He drove straight towards Don and stopped right in front of him. A vision aid camera creaked to check Don out.

"What do you think about the work of my life?" the Gatti then asked with a broad smile that looked unreal on him.

Don studied the old Gatti and realized immediately that he must be Olram, the head Gatti scientist Andro talked about. Olram didn't seem to be able to move most of his body, and Don guessed his wheelchair control system must be connected to his central nervous gateway, just like their tentacles.

"It looks great, but I have questions," said Don. "How long is the physical enhancement going to last?"

"Most people can have it long enough," Ena replied.

"It really depends on your body's reaction to additional genes," Olram elaborated. "Some can keep them for a long time with good body tolerance and utilization. Others may lose them and need a booster shot. In rare cases, one may develop immune responses to them quickly. If that happens, the treatment will fail."

"And if the genes are built into a newborn?" The question suddenly hit Don, and he thought out loud.

"You are smart. You see how things work," said Olram, his eyes fixed on Don. "And yes, it is going to last a lifetime. That is why our infant program is so powerful."

"How many Gattis have gone through this to change themselves?" asked Don. That was something he really wanted to know.

"I would say about thirty to forty percent, but that number is underestimated," replied Olram. "You see, when parents go through the process of genome modifications, their children will inherit the modified genes later. Besides, it is getting increasingly popular around the globe. We even have many human customers."

"What happens if the treatment fails completely?" More and more questions came into Don's mind.

"Well, we did see some failures in our early days," said Olram, hesitating. "Initially, there were some technical difficulties… but it should not concern you because we have fixed that."

"And why are you willing to give humans access to your technologies?"

"Why not? What we do is purely for the greater good of science."

Don stared at Olram sharply and searched his expression for clues of lying, but Olram did look sincere and serious about that.

"Can I ask one last question?" There was another thing Don wanted to know.

"Ask away," said Olram, staring back with great interest.

"Why don't you make yourself a new body and move on to it?"

"So that I don't have to be trapped in this form, and I can continue my great work forever?" asked Olram, meeting Don's gaze while Don glanced at his flesh-machine combination. "What makes you think I haven't?"

Don was quite surprised to hear that.

"Your question is certainly different from most other visitors'," Olram then continued. "This body is my fifth one and probably the last one. My original body died hundreds of years ago in another solar system. Currently, there is a limit to how many times I can replicate myself without major variations, and I haven't found a breakthrough yet.

"But that does not matter because we Gattis have never been keen on immortality. In fact, we find the idea terrifying. I cannot imagine a world full of old consciousnesses. It will become deathly still and stagnant. Changes and evolution should be welcome.

"And as for me, hundreds of years of life are indeed enough."

At the end, Olram closed his eyes and said, "Don't be surprised if you do not see me on your next visit. Ena, see our guest out."

Don wanted to ask more about that, but Ena was already gesturing him toward the door.

"You'll return to the reception area and wait," she said as she walked him out.

Don followed her back to his room, and then she left.

After a short while, Ena was back again with a syringe on a tray.

"Your performance boost treatment is ready in this syringe. You can inject yourself right now. Anywhere is fine."

Don took the syringe in his hand. He struggled inside, and he had doubts. But then he remembered what Jack said about his narrow shoulders and how Jack wished he had a stronger build.

Well, there was a price to pay for everything, he thought, and this was a risk he was willing to take.

Don decided and injected himself in the arm.

"Come back a month from today," Ena said. "Let us know how well it works and how you feel, and we'll see if you need a second shot."

Don felt no difference in the first few minutes. He was still trying to grasp what he'd learned on the day, true or not.

Ena walked him to the exit, and then he left.

From the workshop of GIIxb Lab, Olram and Ena watched Don's retreating figure.

"Did you give him the right thing?" Olram asked seriously. "I want to be sure."

"Yes. I know what to do," replied Ena firmly. "What he took is merely a tube of saline solution. It does nothing. He was created three Mars Years ago. You did it yourself. Now he's coming of age, and soon the trigger for Gatti gene expression will be activated automatically."

"Great," Olram said with satisfaction. "Let's wait for the genetic material to unfold itself."

* * *

On his way back to Redland, Don analyzed what he'd seen and heard. He became preoccupied as he usually was. After a few hours' drive, Don was back at the home base. He parked his Rover, scanned his retina, and went inside as quietly as he could.

It was already past midnight; most people were sleeping. Don hurried across the hallway to his compartment. Then he saw Shana huddling up on the couch in the common area, half-asleep, waiting for him.

Don had helped her find a new place in east Redland after she lost her home. But Shana rarely spent time there; most often, she just stayed at Base-H.

Shana seemed to have heard his footsteps. She opened her eyes and then jumped up to meet him.

"Everything Ok?" she asked, searching his face intently. "You didn't come for dinner, and Brian said you went out this afternoon."

"Everything is fine," said Don, holding her shoulders gently to assure her.

"Really?" asked Shana. "Where have you been?"

"I didn't go anywhere dangerous," said Don. He knew she had been worried, but he didn't want to tell her the details. "It's late. You should go get some sleep."

Shana hesitated but eventually said, "Don't forget to bring me next time if you need help. Jack says I need practical experience."

"I will." Don gave her a smile and then asked, "Is Yang here today? I need to talk to him as soon as possible."

Shana looked towards Yang's compartment. The lights were off. "I don't think he's here at the moment," she said. "But Yang is a night owl. It's not surprising if he's still working somewhere. You can try sending him a message."

"Ok. Thank you, Shana. Good night."

"Good night, Don."

Don went back to his compartment, left Yang a message, and told him what happened.

He went to bed afterwards, thinking he must discuss it with Yang the next day. And then he couldn't sleep for a number of hours. He wasn't sure if it was the slight itch on his arm or the eerie images he saw in GIIxb Lab.

Don didn't know when he drifted off. Strange visions crowded his mind, and the blonde woman from the space shuttle showed herself again.

She came home after a long day at work. The place she rented was a simple home that had a dome on the surface. The clear dome provided natural light during the day, and the rooms were built underground to conserve heating energy.

Just as she stepped inside and kicked off her shoes, the sun set, and the last ray of light disappeared, causing the dome to turn dark. Eager to lie down and relax, she opened the lid-door and climbed down.

She washed up, curled into her bed, and picked up her savings bank. It was a beautiful clear jar with many Pink Cubes, twelve Green Cubes, and one Blue Cube in it. The yellow ribbon around the neck of the jar was from home. For the Mars trip, her mother had helped her pack a few things and slipped a picture of them with the yellow ribbon into her luggage.

"How lovely," she said to herself, smiling.

The one worth the most value in her jar was the Blue Cube. An old gentleman gave it to her after her piano performance at Lule Paradise restaurant, where she worked around dinner times. She clearly remembered how surprised and happy she was. She couldn't help but bow deeply and said, "Thank you, it's so very kind of you, sir." And that kept her happy for more than three months.

While she was admiring the Blue Cube, her roommate, May, came back home and called, "Aria, are you counting your Cubes again?"

"Yes."

"Don't you know exactly how many you have already?"

"Yeah, but looking at them makes me happy," said Aria quietly. "My mother is a single mom back on Earth. She's had a hard life. Every day, she works tirelessly to provide for me —"

At those words, Aria felt a sudden wave of sadness wash over her and broke there. Then she stared hard at the ceiling so that her tears wouldn't fall.

Moments later, she took a deep breath and said with determination, "I want to make it better for her. And the first thing I need to do is to save enough money for one ticket so that she can come join me."

"I see… You're trying hard to save," May said softly as she walked over to Aria.

Aria put down her jar and continued, "Can you believe it, May? It's the biggest change for me since I decided to come to Mars. Before, I never cared much about money. It was just a number in the bank, something that'd come and go. I never wanted more than enough for basic needs, you know, like some food to eat and a bed to sleep in. I couldn't imagine I'd become a money-grubber like I am today."

"Silly you. We're all like that until we need more," May chuckled. "You're just too young."

"No, no, that is not what I meant," Aria explained hastily, "for example, I only want enough money to buy a ticket for my mom. She's by herself back home. You know how expensive those tickets are. I've taken two part-time jobs already, but it seems like I'll never save enough at this rate before my mother gets too old to endure space travel."

"That's exactly what I meant," May replied, becoming serious. "We all have things we hold dear, and we all have our reasons."

"I guess you're right." Aria saw her point and fell into silence.

"Hey, the place I work needs a singer," May said, sitting down beside her and placing a comforting arm around her shoulders. "It isn't something regular, only when there are events. Would you like to try that?"

"I'd love to," said Aria, jumping out of her comforter, her eyes widened. "Thank you so much, May."

"Mind you, there're a lot of Gattis in that place."

"I don't mind. I've learned how to speak Gattish," Aria said happily. Then she snuggled back into her small bed and hummed a tune. A melody popped into the air, and it was as beautiful as fireflies dancing on a summer night.

Chapter 8
A Hyper-V

Don woke up in the middle of the night and pondered over what he had dreamt about. This time he was sure that he and Aria must have some sort of connection.

But he didn't know how much time had passed for her since she traveled to Mars. He remembered her face was a bit chubby, full of the exuberance of youth, and her hair was flowing golden curls down below her shoulders. However, this time her face had thinned out, and her hair was cut short.

"Now I know your name, Aria," he said to himself in the darkness. "Are you trying to tell me something?"

He replayed the fragmented images in his mind, searching for clues, for any deeper meaning. Soon, his eyelids grew heavy, and he drifted back to sleep.

When he woke up again the next morning, his focus was entirely on GIIxb Lab, and he had put his strange dream behind him.

He opened the door of his compartment, eager to seek out Yang for a discussion, only to discover Yang and Nelson already sitting outside, waiting for him. From their long dark faces, Don could tell that they must have talked and didn't approve of his actions.

"Are you out of your mind?" Nelson said. "Yang called me in the middle of the night, and we've been talking about it since."

"Sorry, I shouldn't have bothered you so late," said Don.

"It isn't about that!" Yang complained. "We're stunned by your reckless act!"

“Come with us,” Nelson said, leading Don into another room and closing the door. “I thought about it last night. The first thing we should do is ensure your safety.”

Nelson took out some equipment quickly and performed a full body scan on Don to make sure no tracking device was implanted.

Luckily, nothing was found.

“Still, you should have talked to us,” Nelson said. And then they criticized Don’s decision. They were not happy that he didn’t consult them beforehand.

Yang looked particularly concerned. He said, “You’re the leader of the 7th squad. What if something happens to you?”

“Then someone else can be the leader,” Don replied simply. He really didn’t think it mattered. The sun would still rise without him. By contrast, the first-hand knowledge he gained would be more valuable to them. “I didn’t plan it. I only wanted to do some investigation, but I had to decide then and there,” he explained. He couldn’t have done it differently if he had been presented with the opportunity again. “Nothing ventured, nothing gained.”

“There’re other ways we can do an investigation,” Nelson argued. Then the three of them continued into a heated debate, and in the end, they agreed someone had to take the risk.

“Still, the long-term effect is not yet clear,” Yang said seriously. “I’m worried that in the event of the treatment failure, it’ll change you in a way you don’t want. It could end badly.”

“I’m worried, too,” replied Don. “But I don’t want that to stop us from moving forward.”

Yang and Nelson were speechless for a moment. Finally, Yang said, “Ok then, the only thing we can do right now is to create a reference point of your physical and mental status. A point where you’re presumably still yourself. Go to my lab at the Redland Institute for a full checkup.”

“No problem,” Don agreed.

“I’ll also need a blood sample for your DNA sequence,” Yang suggested. “This way, we save a copy of your status right after your injection. I guess the treatment from GIIxb

Lab uses something like a retrovirus. I hope the retrovirus hasn't spread very far yet."

"Understood," Don replied crisply.

Then Yang continued grimly, "In case something happens to you, this would allow me to reverse your condition in my most optimistic scenario. That is, if I can figure out how to perform an excision of the virus out of your genome and counteract its effect."

"Sounds good. Thank you," Don said. A warm feeling filled his heart, and he was touched by the care and concern they showed him. "I'm grateful you've thought of such a careful plan."

Don then asked them to keep an eye on him, but he didn't want to tell others just yet, especially Shana, since he didn't want to make her worried.

"We won't say anything, but you should tell her at some point," Yang said, his face still etched with concern.

Don breathed deeply and nodded. He felt much better after they talked and understood each other. Without delay, they set off to Yang's lab and got the checkup done.

In the meanwhile, since Shana had her first fight with the Gattis, she put in even more hard work in her training.

Don knew she wanted to become stronger for the next time, and he needed to get her protective gear as soon as possible. Cohen agreed to make some changes to their Ops Tactical Uniform so that it would better suit her build and movement. A week later, when Don and Cohen got her uniform and gadgets ready, they went to Shana's compartment.

"Hey, Shana. We've got you something." Cohen called her and handed her the uniform. "You're about five foot six, right? Don has ordered a uniform for you in size 4. Let's see if it fits you properly."

"Thank you," said Shana excitedly, her eyes shining with gratitude. "You guys are so thoughtful." She took it in her hand to admire it. It was a blue full-body garment, and it certainly looked high-tech.

"It's designed to meet our needs in the field," said Cohen. "The material is a force-deflection polymer, which can reduce physical impact by fifty percent. It's also multi-functional with high thermal performance."

"Try it on," said Don. "I hope I've ordered the right size. We have only black or blue available. I thought you might like blue better."

"I love it," said Shana as she gladly took the uniform to change.

When she was done and came out after, Don was stunned. The uniform suited her unexpectedly well. The good fit outlined her figure; her fair skin stood out against the blue. She looked bright and brave like never before.

"So, it's true," Cohen exclaimed, looking impressed. "I've heard the others talk about your training. They said Jack has made a man out of you. Shana, you really surprise me."

"What did the others say?" asked Shana, looking a bit confused by Cohen's comments. "Do I look ridiculous in this?"

"No, no, you look very… handsome, like a soldier." Don tried to compliment her. But on second thought, he wanted a phrase that suited her better. "Like a blue angel…" he decided a moment later. "It's perfect for you."

"I like that, blue angel," Cohen said, looking at her with appreciative eyes. "And I admire your courage to take on new challenges."

Don smiled. When he took Shana in more than one Mars Year ago, she was a bit slim and delicate. Now she had grown, her frame robust, and she had truly become one of them.

"Come here, let me show you my design," Cohen said, providing more details proudly. "It has thermoregulation. Your body won't be too hot or too cold. For that, it requires one Green Cube to operate per week. Here is where you put in the Cube… So, in case you can't return to the bases at night, you can sleep in it out there."

"Does it have a pocket?" asked Shana.

"Plenty of pockets. You can bring your own survival gear for the wilderness," said Cohen, giving her a manual.

"Complete detailed instructions can be found here. And one more thing, we'd like you to have a Senset. Actually, I've brought two of them. One for you and one for Eio."

"The Senset looks like half a pair of glasses, with an earpiece to secure it and an eyepiece to display information," said Don earnestly. "Let me help you put it on." He came up holding the earpiece. Then he noticed a silky strand of Shana's hair had slipped from her forehead. He took it, tucked it gently behind her ear, and fitted the earpiece and the eyepiece.

The moment Don's hands touched Shana's cheek, she blushed deeply.

Don quickly pulled his hands back.

Cohen didn't seem to notice. He went on enthusiastically, "Senset is all you need to communicate with the bases and other members. The life sign tracker is here. As long as the Senset gets in touch with your skin, we can monitor your temperature and pulse remotely. Very useful."

"It also has other features like location, translation, and a map," Don added. "A built-in camera allows you to do real-time analysis of anything you see. It has both voice control and gesture control. You can wear it like right now, or you can conceal the eyepiece under your collar."

"I really like it," said Shana gratefully, her face radiant. "You guys have put so much thought into it. I'm going to wear it when I go to my training next time."

* * *

A couple of days later, with Shana off at her training, Eio indulged in some light reading on human culture and history. These days Shana went to Jack happily wearing her uniform and came back with bruises and sprained ankles.

Eio strongly disapproved of her decision to become a field member. In his opinion, her strength lay in being a doctor. But humans were a curious species; Don, Shana, and others lived to attempt the impossible, which was something he didn't fully understand.

Eio had been officially assigned to Shana's compartment since other places were all full.

"You can use the upper berth of the bunk bed," Shana said. "We are now bunkmates."

Eio was most happy with the arrangement.

To his annoyance, however, Nelson had been following him recently, trying to get him to talk about his view on physics and cosmology again. At this moment, Nelson was sitting right there in front of him.

Nelson was a short and skinny guy with an oversized head and below-average looks. But a proud intellectual like Nelson didn't seem to care about looks. He told Eio he actually loved his nickname, "Megahead" — an accurate description, it seemed, because his body had supplied all its nutrition to his brain, leaving the rest of him minimally developed.

"I really regret I didn't get to learn from you earlier," said Nelson bitterly, as if worried that something might happen to Eio and he would never have the chance again.

Eio realized it had indeed been a while since their evacuation and his adventure to Midzor. Now that he was back, he bet Nelson wouldn't pass up such an opportunity.

"Is this a good time?" Nelson asked. "There is this project I've spent more than ten years researching…"

Eio wanted to say no, but he kept his mouth shut just to be polite.

Nelson began eagerly, "Do you think there is a unified theory of Quantum Gravity that combines both general relativity and quantum mechanics?"

"Quantum? Sounds like a kind of cookie to me, am I right?" Eio replied carelessly, without raising his head.

"No, not at all. I need to start with something more basic," Nelson muttered, who must believe he was going too specific. Then he asked again, "Did the universe really originate from a Big Bang?"

"What is a Big Bang? Aha, the rhythm of music, isn't it?"

Nelson shook his head and almost rolled his eyes, and then he changed the subject again and asked another question,

"Why is there something instead of nothing? What do you think?"

"What's the difference? Isn't nothing also something?" This time Eio threw a rhetorical question. That answer seemed to take Nelson by surprise, for his eyes opened wide and he paused to think about it.

"Let's try another one," said Nelson after a while.

Eio had lost interest in answering more questions, however. He toyed with Nelson's ideas over the next ten or twenty minutes.

Nelson would soon leave him alone, Eio thought triumphantly, feeling good about his trick.

"Eio, you don't have the proper background knowledge of human science," Nelson said soon enough. "We're not speaking the same language." But he still wouldn't give up. "Let me help you understand my questions —"

"It is *your* pinhead that doesn't understand," Eio cut in impatiently. "I'm not taking your questions anymore."

"Eio, please, I must know if my research has been meaningful —" Nelson pleaded and then shut up reluctantly. But he sat tight and seemed to be determined to wait until Eio's mood improved.

Nelson waited for hours, and it looked like he would wait until the next day if he had to.

Finally, Eio finished the books Shana had given him, and she was not back from her training yet.

"Ok. What should I do now?" Eio said to himself. He then peeked at Nelson and asked, "Do you have something interesting to play with?"

"Let's play with computers," Nelson replied quickly. "I've just come up with a new idea for you to understand me and the science I was talking about."

Nelson pulled out from his backpack a notebook and powered it up. He showed Eio various games, files, and software programs and said, "There are three digital books on my computer: *Fundamentals of Physics*, *A Brief History of Time*, and *The Beautiful Universe*. Try to see if you're interested."

"Let me see…" Eio took the notebook and fiddled around, his eyes wide open. Nelson's computer drew his attention incredibly. "Why didn't you show me this toy earlier?" he asked.

"Because Shana didn't think it was appropriate for you."

Eio re-arranged his hands into ultra-thin extensions, like a group of optical fibers. They went right into the computer ports, and seconds later, his hands lit up in soft blue when the connection was made.

Eio started loading and reading the digital books at once. Nelson's mouth hung open in pure astonishment as he watched. Then they talked excitedly, both thrilled to share their new discovery.

When Shana came back later in the night, Nelson was writing on his notebook as fast as he could to record what had happened earlier. He didn't notice her until she said hi.

"Where is Eio?" Shana asked.

"He became motionless a moment ago," replied Nelson, looking at Eio uncertainly.

Shana found Eio in a chair, holding a lamp in his arms. He looked dim and somehow a little less transparent.

Shana called Eio's name many times and tapped him gently, yet there was no response. "I've never seen Eio like this before," she cried in panic, "Nelson, please send for a doctor."

Nelson gave Shana a look as if she was talking nonsense.

"You're the doctor here," he said. "Besides, chances are human doctors won't be able to help him."

"What happened to Eio?" Shana then asked, frowning.

"He fell asleep while trying to read — or I should say — load three books into his mind." Nelson was overwhelmed by his new discovery and didn't seem to notice the barely suppressed displeasure in Shana's voice.

"Load books? How?"

Nelson scratched his head and said, "I suppose he can initiate a connection from his side to access my computer. After that, he can extract and interpret the binary information directly. You should see it. Eio's hands can extend and work like cables! He was rather excited to discover how to use a computer, too, you know…"

Shana's face grew darker as Nelson went on. "And the lamp?" she asked.

"He might have felt tired in the process and got to the lamp himself, for warmth, I suppose."

"How could you do this? You're wearing him out," said Shana furiously.

Nelson fidgeted in his seat. "I'm so sorry. I didn't know it would be such an energy-expensive thing for him. Eio… he could know all the secrets of the universes. It was a chance I… I couldn't miss," he said.

"I don't need a physics degree to know it's too much for him," Shana said coldly.

"I'm only trying to advance our understanding of science. I… I did it for all of us," said Nelson nervously. He tended to stutter when he was nervous. "Down… down the road, Eio could help us a great deal in beating Gattis."

"I want to beat Gattis as bad as you do. But not at the cost of Eio's life," said Shana, raising her voice. "Don't ever do this again. I won't allow it."

Her order was final.

"Yes, ma'am … Yes," Nelson replied as he quickly gathered his stuff and got out of her way.

The next day when Eio woke up, he found himself in Shana's arms, and he was feeling worse than ever.

"Hey, Eio, how are you feeling?" asked Shana softly while holding his hands.

"Hungry. I feel hungry."

"Here, have some fried eggs." Shana showed him a plate full of food and said, "Let me warm it up for you."

A minute later, while Eio was shoveling down the eggs, she said, "You really scared me yesterday. You looked almost dead."

"I feel better now," Eio replied immediately.

"You do look energized again, but still, I'm not convinced," Shana said seriously. "Why have you turned more solid? You were a bit more transparent the day before."

Eio had to admit Shana was very observant. He didn't know how to tell her initially, but that was exactly what he had been worried about.

"Well… I guess I used too much energy yesterday… but the underlying problem is —"

"What is it?" asked Shana, looking concerned. "Why do I have a bad feeling about this?"

"Remember I told you I'm not from this world? I'm from a higher dimensional universe."

Since Eio had read Nelson's books and found the proper expressions in human language, he could now explain himself better.

He continued, "There, we don't have atoms. In other words, atoms are not the basic building blocks of my world. The element units we use to build our body are not available here, and you cannot see them. That is why I'm transparent to you."

"And now?"

"Remember what I said about losing my transparency gradually and getting some black dots?"

"Yes?"

"That's something interesting. When I try to gain energy by eating, my body has incorporated particles from your universe. These tiny black dots on me are accumulated atoms. They give me an outline and make me visible," said Eio gloomily. "It's surprising to me, too, that atoms are somewhat compatible with me. Therefore, the more I eat, the longer I stay here, the more atoms I have in my body, and the more I become one of you. I may not be able to go back home after that."

"But if you don't ever go back, will you die? Or just live like us?" asked Shana nervously.

"I'm not entirely sure… But I guess that won't be me anymore… I do hope to find other Eios in time. Together we may have a way to go home."

"Don has talked to other squad team leaders," said Shana encouragingly. "So far, there's no sign of your friends, but they'll let us know if they find anything. So, don't give up. We'll find a way."

Eio nodded.

"For the time being, do you think those scientists can help you with your atom incorporation problem? Maybe they have a way to slow down the process," she suggested eagerly.

"That's a good idea," said Eio, his spirits lifting slightly.

"Just don't try any dangerous experiments again, Ok?"

"Ok… I know. Don't nag." Eio stopped Shana quickly there.

Two days later, Nelson came to check on Eio, and Eio was quite happy to see him.

"How are you doing?" Nelson asked carefully. "I feel terrible after Shana got mad at me the other day."

"Not bad. I just finished up a nice lunch Shana made me," said Eio. He knew eating was not good for him, but a delicious meal proved irresistible. He'd decided to ignore the long-term concerns and just enjoy the moment.

"Shana has told me about your trouble," said Nelson sincerely, "and I believe it's necessary for you to answer a few of my questions. It'll really help us to help you."

"Go ahead," said Eio, lying down to listen to some music. He was in a good mood with his stomach full.

"Let's start with some basics. Your home, the Upper Universe you've been talking about, is a four-dimensional multiverse? I mean four space dimensions, not including the time dimension."

"Yeah, I think that is what you call it."

"This is unbelievable." Nelson's eyes widened. He then asked eagerly, "So, you're a 4-D being? And the Eio we see is only a cross-section of the real you?"

"Yes, and yes," replied Eio simply.

"And I suppose you can move in and out of our universe as you wish?"

"Yes, I can. But moving requires energy, and I don't have extra energy to spare right now. Besides, I still can't go home if I just move out of your universe."

"Please tell me again why you're transparent?"

"I've told Shana already; I am not from this universe," Eio answered. "What I'm made of is something your eyes cannot see."

Nelson then wrote down on his notebook:

Eio is not made of any matter known to humans. What kind of particle will it be? What kind of properties will it possess?

"And you can control your body down to the particle level? That is how you grow your ears and extend your hands?"

"Yes, if you want to think of it like that," replied Eio casually. "I also re-arranged my body to have a mouth and a stomach just before I met you guys."

"This is incredible!" Nelson asked Eio to repeat it so that he was sure that he wrote down the correct notes:

Eio has complete control of himself at the particle level... what kind of particle interactions will allow such movement?

"But the parts of you that are tiny black dots? If I heard it correctly —"

Eio replied, "Yes. I take in atoms from your world. Atoms bond together and become molecules, hence the tiny black dots. So, while I'm losing my own — well, particles — to the environment, the black dots fill those empty spots in my body."

"Is that so? I wasn't sure if Shana had told me the right thing," said Nelson, stroking his chin, and he wrote:

Higher dimensional particles may interact with atoms in some way?

Eio continued, "You know, I didn't need a stomach before. But here, it seems everybody has one. You gain energy by eating, and then the energy is released by chemical reactions."

"Speaking of which, I want you to try something," said Nelson suddenly. "I've given it a lot of thought since I went home the other day. I remember you went to a lamp after you got tired, so I wonder if you can utilize electromagnetic radiation as your energy source?"

"Possibly, but the sunlight and the lamp can't give me enough energy," Eio replied with a sigh.

“Still, you may be able to interact with higher energy particles.”

“That’s right. Now I remember,” said Eio, getting up and looking at Nelson excitedly. “From the three books you’ve shown me, I’ve learned that you humans can generate X-rays and gamma radiations. That could be helpful to me.”

“Wait here. I’ll be right back,” said Nelson, then he hurried off.

When Nelson was back an hour later, he showed Eio a device that was in the shape of a tube and had a clear glass envelope.

“What is this?” asked Eio.

“This is an X-ray tube. It can generate X-ray radiation,” Nelson replied after he caught his breath. “The wall of the tube is leaded, and X-ray beams can come out from the window here. The radiation is harmful to humans, but you may give it a try.”

After they plugged the tube into a power supply, Eio got some X-ray exposure. Then he cried, “It works. It gives me energy!”

“Really? That’s great!” Nelson exclaimed, his eyes widening, and he looked more excited than Eio. “The tube itself is not that big, so we can make the whole thing more portable for you.”

“Thank you. I can’t believe you’ve solved my problem,” said Eio gratefully. “Nelson, you’ve proved yourself useful this time.”

“That’s because now we have a better understanding of each other,” Nelson smiled.

Eio and Nelson told everybody about their incredible discovery. In a couple days, Cohen improved the design. He made several portable charging tubes for Eio to carry around and a large, more powerful charging station at the home base.

The X-ray charging tubes and station alleviated Eio’s atom incorporation problem. He didn’t need to eat any longer, he became more optimistic about everything, and he was totally energized.

However, Eio didn't want to give up eating and drinking altogether since he had developed a taste for it. He could keep eating below a threshold, he believed, so that his atom incorporation would be slow enough. In that way, he might have years, even, before he had to face his problem.

A week later, Eio visited Nelson and Cohen in their lab for the first time.

"Eio, you've come at the right time," said Nelson, his spirits high. "I'm excited with what I've got, and I want to celebrate."

"Me too," said Eio, smiling as he clutched his charging tube.

"Listen, I've been thinking long and hard, and I have an idea now, a theory of how you can go home," Nelson exclaimed.

"Really? Let's hear it," said Eio and Cohen together.

"We could recreate your hyper vehicle!"

"How?" asked Cohen in disbelief. "We are confined to our 3-D universe, and we don't even have access to the 4th dimension. How do we build a 4-D vehicle?"

"You're right, we don't have access, but Eio has," replied Nelson.

"I feel like I'm getting there," said Cohen, taking a seat. "Tell me more. I want the details."

Nelson assumed the posture of a professor teaching his students and said, "Recall your geometry lessons in elementary school. How do you make a 3-D cube from a piece of paper? First, you draw a net of six square faces, cut them out, and fold the flaps along the edges. Then whoa! You transform 2-D flat shapes into a 3-D object. Easy, right?

"Now let me put it in another way: if we want to get a square from a line, we move the line in a dimension perpendicular to itself until all four edges are equally sized. Similarly, if we want to get a cube from a square, we move the square perpendicularly to itself until all six faces are equally sized.

"Now, I'll take this approach further into 4-D. In this iteration, if we want to get a hypercube from a cube, we move the cube perpendicularly to itself until all eight faces are equally sized."

"I already know that part," said Cohen. "Your hypercube is also called a tesseract. All its eight faces are cubes."

"Exactly."

"But I still have doubts," Cohen continued as he lowered his head and tapped his feet. "What you've said is done in a geometry sense. How do we do it with real-world engineering? I can't even see the 4th dimension. How do I know if I'm moving perpendicularly into it?"

"Here is where Eio comes into play," Nelson replied, his eyes shining. "We can't see the 4th dimension, but we can see a cross-section of it. Eio, a 4-D being, is right in front of us. You see, Eio has already provided us with some access to aspects of the higher-dimensional space. And we should be able to learn the properties of 4-D space to a certain degree. If we are moving in the right direction, we should get into a space with those properties."

"I see… I see," Cohen said. He sat back, nodding his head and looking relaxed. "Now I'm convinced. In order to build a hyper vehicle, first, we're going to build its eight faces or, say, parts; each part is going to be a 3-D structure in our universe. We can't fold it or, say, assemble it within our universe. But, if Eio can guide these parts perpendicularly into the higher dimension, he can assemble the hyper vehicle there and use it."

"That's exactly what I have in mind. Since the particles from our universe are compatible with Eio, it's likely 3-D materials will continue to work in 4-D space," said Nelson with great excitement. "I'm gonna name this vehicle Hyper-V!"

"Brilliant!" Eio exclaimed. "I think it might work. Then what are we waiting for? Can we start building this Hyper-V?"

However, Nelson scratched his head and became thoughtful at Eio's words. "It's only a simplified theory," he said. "To put the theory into actual engineering, we face two obstacles: first, we need a powerful enough energy source as propulsion. Second, we need to understand the particles, forces, and fields in the 4-D space and their interactions, so that we can make sure the Hyper-V can travel through it and send you back home."

"I can help you with the second part. You'll understand the forces and fields in my world," said Eio eagerly. "That leaves only the first part."

"I don't think we have an energy source for you right now," Nelson said with a sympathetic face. "And we are not going to have one any time soon."

Eio couldn't understand. He asked uncertainly, "How do you fly your spacecraft? Isn't that powerful enough?"

"We use rockets to overcome gravity and get us into space," Cohen replied. "But I'm afraid that is not enough. We're talking about leaving this universe and getting to another. We'll need something capable of interstellar travel at a minimum. Right now, only Gattis can do that."

"I'm sorry," said Nelson.

Eio couldn't believe his hopes were dashed just like that. He was discouraged, but he had learned to be polite, and he said, "An idea is better than no idea. Thank you, Nelson, Cohen. Let's talk again when we have an energy source."

Chapter 9
The Gene Hunters

It was another bright morning. Laurelynn woke up late in her bed. After a good night's sleep, she felt refreshed. She stretched her arms and sat up. Andro had gotten up early. Since the Inoff incident, he'd been staying at her place for more than a month. She enjoyed his company and felt secure with him around. The three Gattis never showed up again.

In the daytime, Andro went out to take care of his own business. At night, they enjoyed good times together. Laurelynn had a feeling he was working on something. She saw how Andro, Don, and Shana fought the Gattis and knew they couldn't be ordinary people, but she was smart enough not to ask.

Soon Andro finished packing his stuff.

"Bye now, dear," he said as he dropped close to Laurelynn's cheek and pressed a kiss on it. The day had come when he said he needed to leave.

Laurelynn looked at Andro's perfectly symmetrical face. He had defined cheekbones, and his nose was elegantly straight, like those on Greek sculptures. It was a face that would stop any woman who came his way. She wouldn't expect to be able to keep him for long.

"Do you know how long you'll be gone?" asked Laurelynn, already missing him.

"I can't know that," he said, his eyes a warm blue.

"Could you fix my Rover before you go? The tires are old, and one of them is really worn out."

"No problem." Andro set to work at once.

Laurelynn put on a cardigan, went down to the garage with him, and watched him from the door.

Andro assembled his gear and opened a tool kit. He then lifted and supported the Rover on all four jack stands. After making sure it was stable, he got down on one knee and loosened up the nuts. His movement was so competent and flowing that it looked like he had been a mechanic all his life.

Laurelynn gazed at him; she couldn't help thinking that he was exactly her type, strong, capable, and confident.

Andro finished up in thirty minutes and put everything back together. "All done," he said, turning to leave. "Now I have to go. Goodbye."

"Come again soon." Laurelynn waved to send a kiss over.

"I will," he replied, turning back with a gentle smile. Then he grabbed his belongings and a well-wrapped package.

Andro's motorcycle Sparky was parked in the corner of the tavern. He secured the package on its back and went out to take a quick glance at the street. There were no NIISS guards out there. He hopped onto Sparky swiftly and kicked off to leave town.

Laurelynn gazed after him until he disappeared in the streets. Only then did she turn toward the distant skyline, lost in thought. It was already Month Sixteen, but since Midzor lay close to the equator, the weather barely changed over the seasons.

Back in her hometown on Earth, however, summer would be ending soon. The next month would mark the beginning of a beautiful fall, and a holiday was approaching, she reminded herself. Most of her friends and family were still there. She should reconnect with them, hear what had happened back home while she remained so far away.

For all the years she'd spent trying to build a life on Mars, she had never truly settled down. Acquaintances came and went, conversations faded, and Midzor still carried the faint feeling of somewhere temporary. Andro had been one of the few people she hoped to keep close. But he never stayed long enough, and probably would not appear again for another two months, Laurelynn thought. She couldn't help but feel a little lonely.

* * *

"Off to fun stuff now. Let's go all cowboy…" Andro hummed an easygoing tune rather excitedly on his way to Flat Rock, where he shared a workstation with Cohen. As he got into the wildness, he sped up, and the engine roared like a beast.

Flat Rock was located southeast of Midzor. As its name suggested, it was a human town full of boulders. Majestic rock formations rose from the ground, and there was a rugged beauty to the landscape.

The workstation was on the outskirts of Flat Rock and hidden away. When Andro got close hours later, he didn't go through the town center. Instead, he bypassed the town and came to the bottom of a cliff.

It was quiet. There wasn't a sound of life except for the swishing of his motorcycle on sand and gravel. Andro waited a moment, making sure no one else was around, then he got off his bike and pressed on the wall of the cliff.

A panel previously under Light-Heat Camouflage was revealed, and a retina sensor scanned his eyes. A voice ID prompt followed.

"Handsome guy," Andro said. His voiceprint was accepted, and then the gate disguised as a piece of rock rose open. He went in the Wake's workstation for engineering, testing, and weapon making.

"Go dock yourself, Sparky," he told his bike, which was fully AI-enabled, and it drove itself inside to a charging station.

Andro had brought the special package Don gave him. During his stay at Midzor, he had managed to acquire all the materials he needed for the death bullets. Now he could finally begin.

"Remember all the necessary precautions," Don reminded him before they parted.

Andro blew his nose at the thought of that. Don could be overprotective sometimes. He himself was obviously the expert in gunmanship. Bullet-making was a hundred-year-old thing that anyone could do in their garage.

Nevertheless, Andro put on a pair of gloves, a face mask with goggles, and a respirator. After looking in a mirror to check his safety gear, he said to himself, "Look who's the professional."

Andro then examined some used wheel weights in the recycling box. The alloy containing lead and tin would be perfect. In a large melting pot, he added the wheel weights and the secret toxic sauce from Don and then moved the pot into a negative pressure hood. Soon the metals melted into liquid on the electric burner.

He dropped in bullet lube. While the fluxing process was on, he pulled out his favorite collection of bullet molds — those for FN 5.7×28mm would be good.

Now that the contents in the pot were a nice silvery color, Andro turned on a machine to pour the melted alloy into the bullet molds. He let the alloy solidify, then opened the mold to shake the bullets out. The newly formed bullets popped out; the metal-clicking sound was like music to him. He picked up a few pieces to inspect them and was quite satisfied with what he got.

The next step would be easy with the ammo-loading machine. He gathered two bags of brass cases of the matching size. He poured the cases into one funnel, the new bullets into another, and checked that he had enough powder and primer.

Machine on.

"The NIISS guards won't know what's coming," he grinned as the machine worked smoothly.

At the end of the day, Andro looked at the finished ammo for a while, feeling smug.

Days later, Don received a message from Andro asking him to pick up his stuff. Don had come back from GIIxb Lab, and he gladly visited Flat Rock.

"Check these out. Your secret weapon. They're perfect," said Andro. "For safety reasons, each bullet has an individual seal, which is designed to be removed during chambering."

"Great!" Don exclaimed as he did a test shot with his pistol. "This's very nice, thank you."

Andro nodded with a smile.

Don then carefully put away the bullets Andro had made. He filled three full magazines, loaded one magazine into his pistol, and slipped the other two in a small bag as spares.

Andro watched Don place the rest of the bullets into a large ammo carrier box. "So, what happened in GIIxb Lab?" he asked suddenly.

"How do you know?" replied Don. His heart thumped at the mention of the Lab.

"I know you too well," Andro said casually, smiling. "You're a doer. You must have been there."

"I took a performance boost package," said Don frankly, "so far, so good." Then he told Andro briefly what happened in the Lab. Andro was not in the Wake. Don knew he could keep a secret, and he wouldn't judge. Therefore, Don never hid anything from him.

"You did that, for real?" Andro chuckled. "I wouldn't do anything like that. I appreciate the perfect way I am. But I do understand your decision."

Don gave a small smile.

"Good for you," Andro added after a moment. He then eyed Don curiously, as if trying to see whether he had become any stronger. "Looks like you still have a long way to go before you have a muscular build like me."

"I know, I know," Don replied. He'd gotten used to Andro's boasting.

"By the way, have you heard of the Wkeye energy gun?" Don then asked hopefully. "They said NIISS put it in service recently."

"What again?" Andro grumbled. "What do you want me to do? I need a vacation before I can do any more work."

It sounded like Andro had already planned a getaway. Don looked at him and said in a small voice, "I'm just asking…"

"Of course, I have," Andro replied, eyeing Don with a displeased expression. "But no, it's impossible. Are you trying to get yourself into trouble again?"

"I know it's categorized for NIISS high-ranking officers only," Don continued, "but if we could get our hands on one of them, Cohen can test it and try to reverse engineer it. In that way, we can better understand their technology —"

"You don't think I'd like one for myself?" Andro cut him off, looking flabbergasted by his words. "So, are you planning to attack an NIISS officer, or a heist in Haxxilic, the heart of their military manufacturing? I bet you'll be blasted into ashes before you can even get a glimpse of it."

Don fell silent; he lowered his head, thinking. He was actually tempted by what Andro just said, but he knew Andro was telling the truth — it was impossible.

"How about an older one?" Don asked, not willing to give up. "Maybe the control over previous models is not as strict? Say, do you know anyone selling it on the black market?"

Andro narrowed his eyes and tapped his foot, and then he said slowly, "I've dealt with arms dealers before to get some light weapons, but never serious stuff like this."

Don was slightly disappointed.

But then, Andro continued after a pause, "Wait a minute, I'm not so sure… I've only heard about it. You may be able to get one from a guy named Ghalf, who is well-known among the black market arms dealers."

"What is special about him?"

"You know, he's the first hybrid manufactured by GIIxb Lab, and he's said to have a human mother and a Gatti father."

"Where does he get weapons from?" asked Don curiously.

"He obtains small arms by defeating other traffickers," Andro replied. "They said he had enormous strength. Once, he merely used his hands to tear a Gatti apart because the latter insulted him in a trade. And he's bold enough to live in Gatti territory, constantly fighting off those who look down on him."

"Where is this Ghalf?"

"In a small town called JIIson, southwest of Haxxilic. You can get to Midzor first, cross TTado Bridge and then go northwest. Be careful though, JIIson is a sketchy area full of scrap yards and shady characters."

"Thanks for the information, Andro," said Don at once. "I'll come up with a plan."

* * *

After Don returned to home base in Redland, he asked Brian to gather everything he could find on Ghalf.

Don then told Jack what he'd learned. "If Ghalf has the gun, I'll persuade him to sell it to us," said Don. "There's a good chance we can get what we want by peaceful means."

Jack nodded and smiled. "That's something worth checking out," he said. "Call your volunteers to join this JIIson mission."

"Yes, Chief."

Following Jack's instruction, Don told the Wake members he needed two groups, a total of five volunteers. In no time, all five spots were filled. Don got four members from his own team: Lei, Steve, Brian, and Shana.

Lei and Steve were among the more seasoned ones. Lei was short and sturdy, with broad shoulders, thick arms, and a square face that always looked slightly annoyed even when he meant well. Steve, on the other hand, was tall and long-limbed. He carried himself with the slow ease of someone careful not to break things by accident. The two worked well together, balancing each other naturally.

Shana insisted on joining her first real mission and argued that she shouldn't be treated differently now she was a field member.

So Don said yes.

The fifth volunteer was Dimitri from the 5th squad. Once Dimitri learned that Shana was going, he was eager to go, too. "I don't want anything to happen to her," he told Don.

Don agreed and put him in charge of getting familiar with JIIson and finding out where Ghalf was.

When Don and the others finished their research on Ghalf, it was already one month after Don's conversation with Andro in Flat Rock.

And it had been more than one month since Don visited GIIxb Lab. Other than the sleepless first night and some mild growing pain later on, Don felt quite normal most of the time. He didn't check back with the Lab as they requested. He did eat more and gain weight, and his muscles were building up. It was almost too good to be true.

Initially, Don was worried that there could be adverse effects. But nothing bad had happened since then. Don felt he'd gotten used to his new body. It was time for him to get out.

It was getting warm in the south, the fair weather of month eighteen marking the arrival of spring. Early in the morning, Don, Shana, Brian, and Dimitri were ready to head out northwest as the first group. Lei and Steve would leave hours later, separately, as the backup group.

Eio squeezed in Don's Rover at the last minute, claiming he was a member too, and he needed to look for his friends.

Don let him stay after he promised to follow their instructions.

"Eio, you've never been to the north before, right?" Brian said, giving Eio a quick pat on the shoulder. "Be careful."

"Understood," Eio replied.

Soon they left home base, and by noon, they had passed the border checkpoint on TTado Bridge. On their way, about eight hundred kilometers north of the border, they saw the largest Gatti factory called XpIro.

"Dr. Yang, here comes the factory you asked to see. It's entirely solar-powered," said Don. He turned on the video stream on his Senset and called Yang on a virtual tour with them.

"Could you please put me closer?" said Yang on the other side. Since Yang couldn't go on missions in the Gatti territory, Brian suggested that he could do it virtually whenever possible.

As Brian drove closer, they saw thousands of large poles standing under the sun on both sides of the road. The poles were as dense as stalks in a field of sugar cane, and they couldn't see the end of it.

Along the poles were layers of discs extending out via nodes, just like leaves arranged nicely on the stem of a plant. There was one disc per connecting node, and the discs extended out alternately in two opposite directions, maximizing the surface area to intercept sunlight.

"Those discs are shallow and filled with organelles and chemical solutions," said Yang. "The ingredients of Nutrition Mix can be synthesized in them."

"Impressive. Each of the discs is like the size of my compartment," said Eio.

"I've read about it, but it's my first time seeing a real one," Yang continued with fascination, his eyes popping behind his glasses. "It is a Cell-Free Bio-Synthesis System — no cultivated organisms needed, just a reconstituted bio environment."

"Do all those discs synthesize the same thing?" asked Shana curiously.

"No. The design is quite clever," replied Yang. "The top layers of discs have light-harvesting complexes. They will collect the sun's energy to produce substrates first. When finished, these substrates will flow through the internal tubes in the poles and enter the bottom layers to synthesize the final products.

"Our essential nutrients — carbohydrates, proteins, fats, and vitamins — can all be produced this way."

Eio asked, "Do Gattis have the same Mix as humans?"

"Gattis have their own version of the Mix, with different nutrients and different proportions," Yang answered quickly. "You know what, the technology itself is not entirely new. I can do it in an Eppendorf tube with cell lysate, but it's not very automatic nor on such a large scale. If you want, I can draw out the flow diagram for you —"

“You can spare me the molecules,” Dimitri cut in irritably, who didn’t seem to be interested at all. He interrupted Yang straight away before he could go into an entire lecture.

Nevertheless, Yang’s enthusiasm wasn’t dampened so easily. He went on to talk about his research to Don, Shana, and Eio.

By the time they arrived at JIlson, it was close to dark. Within a day, they’d reached the northern hemisphere, where it was the beginning of fall. After the sunset, the noise of passing vehicles quickly faded, together with the honking and Gatti yelling.

Unnoticed by the Gattis, their black Rover pulled up at the end of a deserted street. All of them immediately dressed up in their Ops Tactical Uniform and geared up. Such precautions were essential whenever they ventured into Gatti territory, guarding against any potential confrontation.

Don got off first by himself. He checked the surroundings and spotted the self-service roadside inn, their planned stop for the night, picked by Dimitri. It was in a corner far from the main road and only three blocks away from the mechanic shop that Ghalf operated.

“We are here,” said Don as he came back for everyone else. “Be careful, keep quiet, and don’t draw any attention.”

Everybody quickly got out of the Rover and went to the front of the inn.

A sign said two Green Cubes per night. As Don worked on a Cube Operated Machine to check in, the others waited behind him. Soon he opened the door of the inn, which squeaked on its rusty hinges.

However, before they stepped in, Don suddenly sensed that someone was watching them from very close. He looked to his left.

Just then, Shana gasped in horror.

Something was shooting straight toward her! It was like a bullet, but not quite. It came so fast that there wasn’t enough time for her to do anything. She turned her head, trying to dodge it, but it was too late. Just when it got within inches of her face, a pair of arms protected her.

Clink! There came the sound of metal falling, and it hit the ground.

Dimitri had come forward from behind Shana and used his arms to block it. Then he kicked it away swiftly.

Don looked to where the thing had come from and saw a pair of pale grey eyes staring at them.

A short old Gatti was leaning against the wall of a mound next to the inn. He must have been there for a while, but he blended in with the shadow so that Don hadn't noticed him earlier.

Don pulled out his pistol in the next split second and aimed at the attacker. "Don't move, or a bullet will go through your head," he spoke coldly in Gattish.

The Gatti didn't fret over the warning; he even grinned with a twisted face.

Shana was shocked; she froze at the sight of the Gatti. "What's going on?"

"Relax. It isn't a weapon," the Gatti said, giving a mocking smile as he spoke. "It won't hurt you much. It's just a toy."

Don held his pistol tight. He pressed so hard that his knuckles turned white, but he didn't want to just open fire, since he didn't know how many were on the Gatti's side.

"Are you Ok?" Shana looked at Dimitri, who didn't seem to be hurt. His uniform protected him.

"I'm fine," Dimitri replied briefly and pointed his laser gun at the attacker as well.

"Interesting," the Gatti continued viciously, his voice cracking like wood burning in a fire. "Your blood smells interesting. I was just curious. You may be who I'm looking for."

Don was sure he meant Shana. But what was he getting at?

Shana bit her lips and made no sound.

"Have you seen him before?" Don asked the others.

Brian and Dimitri shook their heads.

Don studied the Gatti for a second — broken nose, skinny limbs, and a crooked back. Then he did a real-time analysis of the Gatti using the camera on his Senset. However, he didn't get a match of the image.

"Enjoy your evening," said the Gatti as he retreated into the mound slowly. Dimitri shot him a stern look before he disappeared.

Don went to look at what was shot at Shana and made sure it wouldn't explode. Then he picked it up and examined it carefully.

It was an inch-long needle with a penetrating head and a hollow capillary. Like the Gatti said, it wasn't exactly a weapon.

"Jack may know what it is," Don said as he showed it to the others and then put it away in his pocket. "We're not going to stay in this inn anymore," he added.

"Right, let's switch to a different place just in case the Gatti goes to NIISS," Dimitri agreed. "I know another inn on the other side of the street."

Dimitri then led the way, and they quickly found another place to stay.

This time Don and Dimitri guarded each side of Shana and let her into the inn first; Eio and Brian followed behind. Nobody said anything else.

Once they went into the six-story building, Don and Brian looked around carefully and secured two possible exit routes. After that, they got to their room and settled down.

From their 4th-floor windows, Don scanned the off-color structures scattered out there, and then a facility next to them caught his eye. It seemed out-of-date, for the walls were stained with age, the paint was peeling, and the pipes running along the exterior were all rusty. Faintly illuminated by dim streetlights, some half-recognizable warning labels clung to the walls. According to the labels, the facility might have been used to keep hazardous materials.

Shana came and stood next to him. "What a creepy place," she murmured.

Don saw her pale face and read the uneasiness in her mind. He patted her shoulder and said, "We try not to get into trouble here. But if the Gatti is looking for it, we'll make him regret his actions."

"I'm not afraid of him. I was just caught off guard," Shana replied.

"I know." Don gave her a comforting smile.

"Don't worry. I'm here to protect you," Dimitri added gently. "You'll be Ok with me by your side."

"Let's get some rest," said Don. "We'll see how to get in touch with Ghalf tomorrow."

"I'll watch first tonight," Brian told him.

"I can take the next turn at three o'clock," Don replied. It was their pact whenever he and Brian worked together.

Brian nodded.

Shana climbed into her sleep bag.

Don lay down with his pistol in hand and soon fell asleep.

He woke up before three in the morning. He heard Dimitri talking to Yang. Their voices were so low that Don didn't quite catch what they said. Eio was sitting upright and concentrating, probably searching for his friends with telesense.

Don straightened up, walked across the room, and stopped at the windows. It was rather dark outside. However, the facility next to them remained lit.

Was something going on? He wondered, his gaze sweeping across the facility's windows. On the third floor, a room with a half-open window glowed with a yellow light. Surprisingly, its door was pushed open as Don watched, and a human guy was brought in there by two Gattis. The two Gattis were laughing and talking while they lifted the guy onto a table and fastened a strap around him. The guy looked rather beaten up and unconscious, with cuts and massive bruises all over his arms.

"Where did we get this guy again?" the shorter Gatti asked as he wrote down some notes.

"The city center of OIIIzoi," replied the other Gatti. "We followed him when he was shopping. You hit him on the head as he turned at the corner of Erdao street, then he passed out."

“Ahh… right,” said the shorter Gatti. “Now I remember.” He then placed two large needles into the veins of the human and connected some tubes to several bags.

Minutes later, the human guy woke up and struggled to turn his head. Then he tried to get up, but his arms and legs were strapped to the table.

“The human is still alive,” said the shorter one, sounding impressed. “We’ve got tissue samples and seven bags of blood out of him. That should be enough.”

“What do you think we should do with him?” the other asked. “Just dump him out like this? He couldn’t survive tonight anyway. He can go without pain.”

“I have another idea,” said the shorter one. “Let’s drain his blood and replace it with ours. I’ve never tried this. It should be fun.”

The human guy looked terrified. His face was pale, and he was trembling all over.

Without much ado, the two Gattis turned a pump into suction and fed the guy’s remaining blood into a tank. The guy’s muscles began to tremble so violently that he almost threw the table over. His screams echoed in the room, and the Gattis laughed like savage beasts.

“Don’t worry,” said the shorter one. He patted the guy’s forehead as if to calm him. “We’ll give you pure Gatti blood from the freezer. You know it’s rather expensive. I normally won’t waste it on a human.”

The other opened the valves of a tube to inject Gatti blood directly into the guy’s neck. “This way, you’ll get it faster,” he assured him. The moment the Gatti blood flowed in, the guy let out a final cry and a jerk that seemed to push his inside out of his throat. Then he ceased to move.

Don only caught snippets of the Gattis’ conversation, and he wasn’t sure what was going on initially. Only a minute later, he realized the human was dead, and it was too late for him to do anything.

Those murderers! Don thought furiously.

Just then, the shorter Gatti walked close to the window, and Don finally got a good view of him, the exact attacker who had shot a needle at Shana earlier!

"That's Vgeeht, a gene hunter," said Dimitri, standing beside him.

"A gene hunter?" Don turned sharply and questioned.

"Yes. While you were asleep, I showed Jack the images of the Gatti and the needle, and he shared what he knew," Dimitri informed him quickly. "According to Jack, gene hunters collect genes that they believe may have value. The shorter one who attacked Shana earlier is Vgeeht, and the needle is a gene gun needle that they use to collect samples."

Dimitri then pointed to the other Gatti by Vgeeht's side and said, "The taller one is most likely Lekk, his partner."

"Why? What is the value to them?" asked Don, puzzled.

"For that, I've asked Yang," Dimitri replied. "I sent him images and showed him the gene gun needle."

"What did Yang say?" Don asked.

"Yang mentioned many Gattis believe in accelerated evolution," Dimitri continued grimly, "they think randomly occurring gene mutations and what we call natural selection are too slow. In other words, they have this gene pool idea. They want to study the variation in genes and look for the traits that they want —"

"So that they can add the desired genes to themselves like GIIxb Lab is doing?" asked Don, frowning.

"Right," said Dimitri. "Yang's hypothesis is that humans' million years of evolution and adaption to Earth's environment, including adaption to pathogens, have been reflected in our genes. So, if Gattis can extract the information out of our genes, they can do their accelerated evolution and ensure their success on Earth. That's what they really want."

"You're saying Gattis have been preparing to go to Earth? And Vgeeht hunts humans, selling the genes to illegal research groups?" At that moment, Don fully comprehended the malice behind it.

"Yes. They don't have to kill, though. They could just take some samples," Dimitri replied. "But Vgeeht and Lekk kill their victims to ensure the gene copies they obtain will be the only ones. They must have committed countless crimes against innocent people like that. Their victims suffer the worst pain anyone can endure."

Don fell silent and pondered what he should do. "We'll talk to the others in the morning and definitely Jack when we're back," he said after making up his mind.

Chapter 10
Ghalf

Shana woke up from her restless sleep early in the morning. She had been thinking about the Gatti attacker, and she couldn't shake the image of the needle out of her mind. The most frustrating part was that all the guys had acted quickly except her, and she knew she still had a lot to learn from them.

When Don told her about the gene hunters, a chill of horror ran through her. She hadn't heard of such a terrible thing since the Red Purge, and she was shocked to learn that Vgeeht had done something so cruel.

"What do we do?" Shana asked, taking deep breaths to calm herself down.

Don called everyone together and presented his plan. "Lei and Steve are staying at B-3. They were supposed to meet us later this morning," he said, his voice clear and strong, "Brian, tell them there's been a change of plan. Give them the location of Vgeeht's facility and ask them to check it out in secret. We want to know if there are other humans captured there."

"Will do," said Brian, and he got to it at once.

After a while, Don added, "Tell them to be careful."

"Sure."

Then Don continued, "We are too late to help the poor guy, and we have other plans this time. Let's focus on what we've come to do and see what Lei and Steve can find out."

"Alright." Everyone agreed.

Without delay, they headed out to Ghalf's mechanic shop. There were few pedestrians on the way. Occasionally Shana heard conversations and arguments in the distance. When some vehicles roared past, the sound of screeching was dreadful.

Soon they arrived at the shop. Dimitri pushed open the door. A Gatti sitting inside turned around to look at them.

"Ooh… human guests, how rare," he said as he squinted his eyes and scrutinized them with great interest. "And a girl, the skin looks so soft and silky… I'd really like to touch and feel." He then watched closely for Shana's reactions, obviously thinking that any fear would be enjoyable.

Shana didn't give him the satisfaction. She wasn't scared. Instead, anger rose rapidly inside her, and she stared right back at him.

"Shut your mouth," said Dimitri, raising his fist, ready for a fight.

"Go on. I dare you," the Gatti sneered.

"Who's making so much noise?" Just then, an enormous guy came out. He had a wild, unkempt face, round amber eyes, and long, bushy hair. One tentacle extended from his back and dropped to his feet.

This guy must be Ghalf, Shana thought. Somehow, she had the impression that his hair had never been attended, and his wild appearance reminded her of a lion.

"Get out of here. I've done business with you," Ghalf then yelled at the Gatti angrily, who flinched and left as fast as he could.

In the meantime, Don had led everyone into the shop. Brian gave the shop a quick survey and located the exits. Dimitri moved to stand by the windows.

Ghalf took a careful look at each of his visitors as if sizing them up. In a minute, his eyes had swept across the guys and stopped on Shana.

Shana became self-conscious under his gaze; she was wearing an elegant light blue dress for the day. The dress-up was Brian's idea. A girl could ease up potential tensions, he suggested, and Shana took his advice. She dusted her cheeks with rouge for the first time and tied her hair into a simple knotted updo. The blue dress was a last-minute gift from Dimitri.

Ghalf's eyes lingered on her. Shana felt uneasy and looked away.

"I never want to deal with humans, and I have no plans to change that," Ghalf then said openly as he went back behind his workbench. "You can go back across the border. I should have put a sign on my door, *No Humans*, understand?"

"Please, we've come a long way." Brian didn't give up. "Our lady here is often bothered by impolite Gattis," he improvised instantly. "That's the reason we're here. We only want to get something to protect ourselves, and our lady insisted to see you herself."

"Your lady is beautiful," said Ghalf, "she's like a rose pushing out of a pile of rubble. I feel like my whole place is brightened up by her presence."

Shana felt awkward and didn't know how to respond to that, so she just lowered her eyes.

"What do you want?" Ghalf then asked. "For her, maybe I can make an exception."

Brian's trick worked. Ghalf seemed to have changed his mind.

"Do you happen to have a Wkeye for sale?" Don asked quickly.

Ghalf blinked upon hearing the name. "You can't be ordinary people if you want a Wkeye." He spoke directly. "In fact, I knew it from the moment you walked in. You checked out my shop and secured your exits."

Don ignored his comment, and the others also remained silent.

"None of my business anyway," Ghalf then told them straight out. "I happen to have one."

"I can offer you more than a fair price," Don said readily. "Or anything we can help you with, just name it."

"I don't want Cubes," Ghalf said clearly, now looking toward Shana with a light in his eyes. "I just want to ask her —"

"What do you want from her?" Don cut in, his black eyes flashing with caution.

"I don't like being interrupted," Ghalf responded testily, his eyes fixing on Don. "Is she your woman?"

The question made Shana very uneasy. She peeked at Don, not knowing what he was going to say.

"No. She is not," Don replied without the slightest hesitation.

Somehow Don's *No* hurt Shana, even though it was the truth. The others looked astonished by the unexpected development. There was a moment of silence.

"It's simple then. I only need to ask if that is her wish," said Ghalf with a smile. "Do you want to be my woman?" he turned to Shana and said. "I can give the Wkeye to you as a gift."

"No way!" Shana shouted. She spoke her mind loud and clear, her face heating up. But she regretted losing her composure immediately. She was just shaken by the surprising request. Her response was a bit rude, considering they were there to ask a favor.

Dimitri glared at Ghalf, looking rather irritated by his questions. "Can you stop it?" he said sharply as he clenched his fists, and it looked like he had a strong desire to give Ghalf a punch.

"What was Ghalf talking about?" Eio asked quietly to Shana, "why am I sensing weird vibes?" He looked at Dimitri, Don, and then Ghalf, stroking his head as if trying to understand something.

Shana bit her lips and didn't answer. For a minute, nobody said anything.

Moments later, Eio pulled the corner of Shana's dress and whispered, "Take it easy."

"That's alright." Ghalf remained calm after hearing Eio. He looked at the unknown creature holding onto Shana's hand and said, "Your pet is pretty smart."

"I'm not a pet. Fool," Eio grumbled.

"Is it because of the way I look?" Ghalf raised his eyebrows and muttered. He didn't seem to get upset, though, and his words didn't sound like a question. It was more like a comment he made for himself. He must have gotten used to the fact that people got scared and avoided him.

Shana didn't know how to respond to that, and Ghalf was already turning away from them. They were not going to get the Wkeye for sure, she thought. She glanced at Don, waiting for his signal to leave.

Don's light eyebrows sloped inwards into a serious expression. "Dare to challenge me in an old-fashioned fistfight?" he changed the subject and asked Ghalf. "How about we make a bet? If I can land my fist in your face, I win, and you'll sell us the thing."

Ghalf blew his nose as if it was beneath him to fight someone smaller. "No human guy can last one minute against me," he said. But then he flexed his muscles, glanced at Shana, and seemed to decide to show off his strength.

He walked out from behind his bench and said, "If I knock you down to the floor and you cannot get up, you lose, and you leave."

"Deal."

Don agreed crisply, and that really made Shana worried. Although she knew Don might win with his brain and not with his muscles, she gave a look of clear disapproval.

Don was a lightweight opponent to Ghalf. Ghalf was of a great height, like a Gatti; he had thick, bulging muscles in his arms and legs. Judging from his broken nose, he must have had many fights. Besides, on his body, there were old scars among sparse black scales, adding to his intimidating appearance.

"Ghalf's got hands the size of his face. Is Don out of his mind?" Eio spoke out her worries in a small voice.

Shana cast a side-glance at Brian, looking for support. Brian told her not to worry with his eyes. "I'd trust Don's judgment and leave men's business to men," he said.

Don and Ghalf then walked out of the shop and moved into the backyard for more space.

Don took off his jacket. Shana noticed only then his body had filled out more. Twining cords of muscle had shaped his arms and legs. It was like he had done intense marathon training. She felt better, seeing that Don wasn't as slim as she remembered. But at the same time, she wondered when he gained his weight and why she didn't notice it earlier.

The two guys stood facing each other in the backyard, their eyes locked in a heated stare-down. Suddenly, they grappled with each other, throwing punches. Ghalf soon got a chance, and he struck Don square in the face. Don took the hard blow. It sounded like his jaw was broken, and he spit out blood from his mouth. But he didn't fall.

In the next few exchanges, Don kept his focus and adapted to Ghalf's speed quickly. After that, Ghalf's punches always fell a few inches short, and Don was able to dodge aside every time. For a while, Ghalf could not get him a second time.

Yet Shana couldn't take it any longer. She begged Brian with her eyes to go outside. Brian came to hold her hands and went out with her. When they were out of earshot of the others, Brian whispered, "Don't worry too much. Don actually has a chance."

Upon hearing that, Shana was bewildered. "You mean — how do you know?"

"Weeks ago, when we were preparing for this trip, Don asked me to search for any footage I could find on Ghalf," said Brian. "And to my surprise, I did find a couple videos. Fans filmed him during his fights against his challengers. One of them was even a famous NIISS officer.

"So, we studied Ghalf carefully. Don viewed the videos over and over again, pausing here and there. He watched for shifts in Ghalf's movements, focusing on which part of his body moved first and where he was aiming. Don then told me what clues might be useful, and I built an AI virtual opponent for him."

"You did?"

"Yes. You've trained with Jack, and you know how my stuff works," Brian said with a grin. "This AI opponent is set to have the same height and weight as Ghalf. It mimics Ghalf's body gestures — how he stands, how he turns, and the extent to which he can swing his arms. Using our analysis and predictive model, we can anticipate his next moves. Don then trained with the AI for weeks —"

"I kinda noticed that before we came out here — Don seems to know what's coming," Shana interjected but then waited for Brian to finish.

"Ghalf used to put down his challengers within three blows, but Don is still standing now. After some warm-up with the real person, Don will do well," Brian concluded.

Shana understood in a flash. She exclaimed, "You're good. Thank you so much."

But in the next second, she realized something and complained, "You guys need to tell me these things earlier. I'm your teammate now. Why don't you let me in?"

"My bad. I'll remember to tell you next time," Brian replied with a smile, and they went back, although Shana remained at the side, only peeking in.

For another twenty minutes, Don was playing effective defense is the best form of attack. He ran, jumped, and dodged.

Ghalf went fast after him and landed his fists everywhere. His strength was simply too strong; tables, windows, and walls had been smashed down in his way.

Ghalf furrowed his brow and narrowed his eyes when he saw his backyard was destroyed, and he became extremely impatient and angry when he couldn't get Don. Somehow his breath turned rasping and shallow, and he seemed to have difficulty breathing.

When Don passed in front of a pillar, Ghalf took the opportunity to attack again; he ran quickly forward and struck with both hands.

However, Don was even faster. He dropped his body low to dodge and rapidly spun himself around. Before Ghalf knew it, Don had stepped behind him. The next second, Don kicked right into the back of Ghalf's knees.

Ghalf fell straight to the ground with a loud bang and became motionless.

Don stood at a safe distance for a minute or two, then all of them went for a closer look.

"I can't believe it. Did he just pass out like that?" said Brian. "He is still alive, right?"

"My strength may have increased, but I couldn't have killed in one kick," replied Don.

Shana sensed that something was wrong. She lifted Ghalf's eyelids and saw that his pupils were dilated. She tried to listen to his heartbeat. Nothing. She checked his pulse. Nothing.

"Ghalf may have suffered a cardiac arrest!" she called out to Don. "Help me with CPR!"

She wasn't even sure if Ghalf's heart was in the same place as humans' or if CPR would work for him, but she asked Don to lay him flat, with head and chin raised.

Shana pinched his nose and blew air into his mouth while Don overlapped his palms and straightened his elbows to press hard on Ghalf's chest.

Ghalf's body was thick and hard. If not for Don, Shana didn't think she could make his sternum sink more than a few centimeters.

And she wondered how this could have happened. Had GIIxb Lab made Ghalf a proper heart? His shortness of breath earlier could be an indication of underlying heart problems. Ghalf might have been putting stress on his heart during the fights, but he didn't even realize it since he usually won out in a short time.

Ghalf gave no response in the first few minutes. Just when they almost gave up, he gasped and came back to life.

Shana took his pulse again on his neck. Although it was much faster than that of humans, at least it was regular. She took a deep breath, feeling greatly relieved.

She then went to check on Don. There was bleeding, swelling, and a loosened tooth in his jaw. But other than that, he was fine.

She felt much better and went back to Ghalf to make sure he was doing Ok. She felt sorry for him. He was injured because of them, and it must have been a bad day for him.

Then she saw lots of cuts and scratches on Ghalf and an old open wound on his left leg that didn't seem to be appropriately treated.

She decided she couldn't just leave him like that. She found some gauze pads, antiseptic wipes, and tapes she always brought with her. After cleaning up the wounds, she wrapped them up nicely.

Ghalf had woken up. He lay on the ground, looking disoriented and defeated.

"I'm sorry for what happened to you and your yard," Shana said quietly.

Just then, Ghalf took her hand and sat up.

"You lost consciousness a moment ago," she added. "We did a chest compression, and you're fine now."

Ghalf didn't say anything. He struggled to get up and then went to his house behind the backyard.

Worrying he might fall, Shana followed him to his door and said, "I don't know if there's anything I can do to make it up to you… but I want to let you know that you might have an underlying heart problem. You need to check it out when you get a chance."

"Thank you for telling me," said Ghalf. His face turned slightly red, and he looked embarrassed for a moment but then regained himself. "I could be dead. You saved my life…"

He looked at her sincerely and said, "Come on in and take a seat."

Shana didn't move.

Ghalf let out a sigh, "No one wants to get close to me. The Gattis think I'm some pathetic Gatti wannabe. Humans either fear the way I look or keep their distance, as if my existence disgusts them."

As he spoke, Shana caught a fleeting bitterness on his face. "Surely your parents love you," she said, trying to offer some comfort. She had intended to say a polite goodbye and leave, but somehow felt pity for him and remained where she was.

"My parents?"

Ghalf's mouth twisted into a slight sneer. "My father has never showed his face in my life," he said. "My mother gave me up when I was six. She said I only inherited the bad and ugly from them. You don't know the life of an unloved child. Let's not talk about them."

Then Ghalf went into his bedroom and reached behind his bed into a box underneath, searching for something.

"What are you doing? You should get some rest now," Shana said seriously as she went in and took his arm. When it came to her patients, she was very responsible.

"Just a second," he said, coming out with something in his palm. "A gift for you."

Shana's eyes widened. It was something colorless, and yet it shone with great brilliance. She was certain it had significant value.

"No, I can't take it," she refused.

"This is a C-Cube. I'm sure you'll find it useful."

"A Colorless Cube?" Shana couldn't believe what she'd heard. Although Jack mentioned the existence of C-Cubes before, she had never seen one herself. Nobody in the Wake had.

"You're right," said Ghalf. "It's the most condensed energy form, military-grade. Gattis use it to power their interstellar spaceships. You won't see it for sale anywhere." He took her hand, laid down the Cube in her palm, and closed her fingers gently.

"It's now yours."

Shana knew the Cube would be very useful to them. It would have countless uses even. It could power their aircraft, charge their energy weapons and keep the Light-Heat Camouflage devices running; not to mention that Nelson would be so excited just to have it for science research.

But she shook her head and insisted no. "It must be very important to you. I can't. I shouldn't."

"Yes, you can. A Cube for a life. You don't owe me anything. I know anyone will be lucky to have your company, and I'm just too hideous —"

"That's not true…"

"Please let me finish," said Ghalf. "You're the first one who has been kind to me. I feel I have been warmed here —"

he placed a hand over his heart, and continued, "I won the Cube from a fight. It's just another trophy to me. But I'm sure it can help you."

Ghalf then directed a long, meaningful look at Shana. She almost felt that he knew who they were. Had she blown their cover unknowingly? She fell silent and didn't know what to say.

There was no knowing when Eio had followed her into the room. He seemed fascinated by the Colorless Cube, for he gazed at it in amazement, unable to tear his eyes away.

When Shana caught his eye, he nodded feverishly, silently begging her to take it.

All of a sudden, it occurred to Shana that the Cube could perhaps save Eio's life. Eio did mention he needed a powerful enough energy source to go home. This could be it.

"I'll take it then. It may help my friend here," said Shana. She put the Cube carefully away and thanked Ghalf many times. "I hope I can repay your kindness one day."

"Don't worry, you already did," Ghalf said, a smile spreading across his face. "I'm glad you accept it. It feels good to be accepted. At least now, I've become a little more than nobody to you."

Eio immediately started dancing. He jumped, galloped, and swirled. "Thank you, thank you, thank you!" he yelled.

By then, it was already past noon, and the others followed Shana and Eio to Ghalf's door.

"The Wkeye gun is by the door, just take it," Ghalf said curtly and turned away upon seeing Don and Dimitri, "then get out of my house."

Dimitri wasted no time with social niceties. He went ahead and took the gun without a word. Don laid a bag of cubes on Ghalf's table quietly.

Just when they were about to leave, Lei's voice sounded in their Sensets. "We're trapped!" Lei's voice came through with great anxiety. Seconds later, they all heard a "Help!" from Steve, and then both of them went silent. Strangely, there was a low, continuous humming noise in the background.

Brian quickly checked their life sign location. They were inside Vgeeht's facility, which Don had asked them to investigate earlier.

Lei and Steve must have run into trouble. The guys exchanged a look and hurried off. Shana waved a quick goodbye to Ghalf and said, "Our friends have run into problems with some gene hunters. I must leave now."

They rushed back to their Rover, changed into their uniforms, and drove straight to the facility. They arrived in just ten minutes.

"Eio, you stay here and wait for us," Don said as he jumped off the Rover. "Everyone else, come with me!"

Shana followed the guys, running up fast to the front of the facility. The entrance was not guarded, and heaps of biohazard bags lay around an open gate. Inside, glimmering light lit a corridor that led further. The walls looked thick, solid, and hard to penetrate. There were no windows for the first two floors.

"Get your weapons ready," Don whispered, and then he told Shana specifically, "Stay alive."

"I'm sensing extreme danger," said Dimitri, looking around as they entered. "If Lei and Steve were not trapped inside, I wish to leave this place immediately."

The moment they got in, the gate closed heavily behind them.

"Don't worry. We'll just fight our way out," said Don.

They walked further down the corridor lit by yellow lights.

"Buzz… Buzz…" Before they saw anything unusual, they heard a weird sound.

"A bee colony?" Shana wondered.

The buzzing sound was getting closer as they turned a corner. There! They saw a tall, box structure, like a huge beehive, stretching from the floor to the ceiling. The hive was covered with black vibrating things. However, those black things were not really bees. They were gene gun needles with wings!

Shana had seen the gene gun needle the other day, but obviously, these were more advanced.

This was going to be bad.

Sensing their presence, countless needles took off immediately and waved their wings at the same time. Their black camera eyes searched for their targets, and each inch-long needle pointed its penetrating head toward them.

"Is it…?" Dimitri looked at Don and Brian in disbelief.

"I'm afraid so," Don replied. "Vgeeht is a gene hunter, so those needles must be used for large-scale sampling."

Just at that moment, Vgeeht stepped out from the other end of the dim corridor. There was a creepy smile on his wizened face.

"Look who's here," he hissed, glaring at them like a pack of blood bags he was going to collect. "I was regretting not getting a piece of you yesterday, and you've come back to me yourself. Wonderful."

"I won't let you get away with it," said Don, clenching his teeth hard.

"Lekk, set the main target on the girl. Let them feed!" Vgeeht shouted, wasting no time to attack.

"Sure, right away." Lekk's voice sounded somewhere down the corridor.

"Buzz…" The buzzing sound erupted at once. The vibrating noise from those mechanical wings echoed in the air.

Shana almost turned her head away as the noise shocked her ears. The three guys immediately surrounded her in the middle. Dimitri even took off his jacket and covered her head. They waved their arms ferociously to fend off the needles and shot down many of them in the meantime.

One gene gun needle wasn't terrible since anyone could easily knock it down, but now there were thousands of them. It was hardly to their advantage if they engaged in a fight like this. Shana glanced over her shoulder, and to her fear, she found that Don and Dimitri were not faring well. Blood was all over their faces and necks in minutes.

Vgeeht was howling with laughter, "Isn't this great? It can go on for a day, and there will be no blood left in you tomorrow."

"The humming noise we heard from the Sensets earlier," said Don suddenly, "Lei and Steve must have fought these needles."

"How do we get rid of these things?" Shana thought out loud.

"My guess is they're programmed by some sort of swarm intelligence," said Brian. "I wish we'd brought an EMP bomb to try with."

"They communicate with some platform, right?" asked Don.

"Highly likely, but where is it?" said Brian.

"The control room should be close to him," Don responded as he looked toward Vgeeht automatically.

"Have fun." Vgeeht mocked them and started back. He was about to close another gate to lock them in.

But Don and Brian weren't going to let him. They ignored the needles over their heads and rushed forward.

Vgeeht was old, but he was quick.

Peng! Peng! Peng!

In the life-and-death split second, Don took aim and fired three shots in a row. Vgeeht crouched down before he could reach the gate switch. After a couple of shudders, he dropped and lay motionlessly on the floor.

"Nice shot, Don!" Brian yelled.

Lekk must have heard the gunshot and the loud thud. He sneaked out of the control room and tried to run away. Brian ran fast and caught him up, hurled him to the ground, and finished him off.

Don, Brian, and Shana then burst into the control room. They looked around it and found the control panel.

"Can you figure out how to use it?" Don asked anxiously as he drove away the needles around them.

"I think so," Brian fumbled on the panel and found a homing button. He pressed it.

The needles left them at once. Almost at the same time, Dimitri's voice sounded in their Sensets, "The needles are returning to their hive!"

"Great!"

Quickly, they regrouped with Dimitri.

"Now!" Don shouted, and everyone took their laser guns, turned up the power, and scorched the hive.

Strong beams burnt down the hive, and the place was quiet again.

"What a relief," Shana said as she treated their wounds carefully. It was not surprising to see lots of bumps, bruises, scrapes, and cuts — fortunately, their uniforms saved them some skin.

"We still need to look for Steve and Lei," said Don. "Let's get going."

They walked slowly and carefully down the corridor, moved away boxes that blocked their way, and forced open every door they came across. Finally, Shana found them locked up in a room together with six other humans. All of them went wild with joy when Don smashed down the door. Lei and Steve jumped up to meet them.

"Steve and I didn't expect this at all," Lei recalled. "It was a huge disaster, a living hell!"

"I should have been more careful," said Steve.

Shana noticed that Steve and Lei didn't suffer a lot, but those who were kidnapped earlier weren't so lucky.

"I've been trapped here for ten days," one of them said.

"We thought we were going to die in this slaughterhouse," said another. They thanked them repeatedly for saving their lives.

Two of them were badly injured. Shana rushed to their side and asked anxiously, "Are you guys Ok? Let me see, don't move." She gave straight orders when she was the medic, and they did exactly as she said without a word.

"You're lucky," she murmured as she examined a guy's arm that had turned dark. "It's not necrosis. I was worried that I'd have to cut your arm off."

"Is it a joke?" asked Lei, glancing at Shana.

"No," she replied seriously. "I'm just glad he can keep his arm. I can't do much here. He'll have to wait until we get to a safe place."

"We need to find a way out. The front gate is closed," Dimitri reminded them.

"Brian and I will go in the front," Don said, looking at each of them directly. "All others, follow us."

Shana and Dimitri supported the wounded, and they stumbled through the long dark corridor as Don and Brian scanned for exits.

Just then, they heard rapid footsteps coming their way. Don and Brian raised their guns, ready to fight. Shana stared tensely, her heart pounding in her chest. But to her surprise, it wasn't an enemy. It was Ghalf! He looked around as he ran and stopped abruptly at the sight of them.

Don and Brian exchanged relieved glances and lowered their guns; Shana took a deep breath, knowing that the danger was over.

"Shana," Ghalf called, ignoring a look from Dimitri and heading straight to her. "I was worried after you mentioned the gene hunters, so I came looking for you."

"Thank you," Shana said.

"I'm so glad you're Ok," Ghalf replied, his eyes shining with happiness.

"How did you get in?" she asked eagerly. "We've got injured people. Please help us if you know the way out."

"Sure, I know where the exit is," Ghalf agreed. "You guys need to leave as soon as possible." Then he helped the wounded to move with his strong arms.

"Hurry up, guys. Let's go now," Shana urged. She felt greatly relieved after everybody reached the exit.

Don told Eio to bring their Rover over to meet them.

Before they headed out, Don extended his right hand to Ghalf at the door and said, "Let's make peace. What do you say?"

Ghalf didn't take Don's hand. Instead, he said, "I'll fight you again next time."

"Sure, I look forward to it," Don replied calmly.

Then Don led the way to the Rover after making sure no Gattis were around. Shana and the others hastened out without a sound, while Brian and Dimitri brought up the rear to cover them.

When Shana looked back, she found Ghalf standing by the exit to see them off, and he was half smiling at her.

"Thank you so much for everything," said Shana, smiling back. "I guess I'll see you around."

At first, she just said it out of politeness, but on second thought, she looked at him sincerely and asked, "Would you like to come with us to the south? I'm sure you'll make lots of friends."

Ghalf stared at Shana with a mixture of surprise and joy on his face. He opened his mouth to respond, and it looked like he was tempted to say yes. But he paused there, shook his head in the end, and declined frankly, "No. With humans, I often find disappointment… But I do hope to see you again."

"See you then," said Shana.

And they drove off.

Chapter 11
A Thought Experiment

Once out of JIlson, Shana, Don and the others stopped at Base-3 so that they could recover. A couple days later, they got back to the south safely. Although it had been a rough trip, they gained a lot at the same time. Without delay, they went to report to Jack.

Jack asked Nelson, Cohen, and Yang to join them in the conference room. Shana talked about the gene hunters, and Dimitri described how the flock of needles attacked them.

"I've met Vgeeht once, but I didn't know he'd gone rampant," said Jack, who pondered over it for a while.

"We need to take it seriously," said Yang. He emphasized his hypothesis that Gattis were extracting information from human genes and preparing for adaptation to Earth's environment.

"I've given it a lot of thought," Jack replied. "It isn't an imminent threat, but if you're right, that means Gattis have their aim on Earth. I should notify the United Nations back on Earth. I'll also ask the squad leaders to track down other gene hunters."

After Jack decided, he looked at everybody in Don's team encouragingly, including Eio, and said, "All of you have done great. Would you like to go back to JIlson sometime and see if there're more gene hunters?"

"No problem, Chief," Don replied.

Dimitri then handed the Wkeye energy gun they'd obtained to Jack and Cohen. Shana also took out the Colorless Cube and explained how she'd got it. Nelson and Cohen examined the C-Cube with great interest, while Eio jumped up and down around them, trying to take it back.

"I think it's most useful to Eio. He could even go home," Shana said, voicing her thought aloud, since she worried the others would disagree, and another part of her worried Don might be upset that she'd accepted it from Ghalf.

"Ghalf is smarter and wiser than most. I like him," said Eio. "My first impressions of him are very positive." And he didn't seem to notice that Dimitri's face grew dark as he said it.

Shana looked toward Jack and said, "I know the Wake can make great use of the Cube, but it means life and death to Eio. I want to give it to him. What do you think?"

"You've got the Cube. It's up to you," Jack replied simply and warmly. After Jack was done looking at it, he handed it to Don, and Don handed it to Eio.

"The energy may be enough for me to travel back home!" said Eio, who was as excited as a little kid getting his birthday presents. Again, he spun, danced, and sang something that sounded like babbling to them.

"Think about how you can use the energy," Jack said as he crouched down and stroked Eio's head lightly. "Ask for help from Nelson and Cohen. You may go home earlier than you think. We can't wait to see. Good luck."

Shana was glad that everyone was supportive. They were truly like a family, taking care of each other. She gave Eio a loving hug and said, "We'll be most happy if you can go home."

* * *

Days later, Nelson, Cohen and Eio began their work to design a hyper vehicle.

Since they had obtained a powerful enough energy source, they had only one problem left before they could build a Hyper-V: to understand how fields and forces behaved in a 4-D space.

At this early stage, the workload was mainly on Nelson, and he was elated with the task. He would be the person to reveal the mystery of the Upper Universe, a huge breakthrough for mankind, and his success would win him more than ten Nobel Prizes. No, no, no, the Wagner Prize would be even better. He could totally create a new prize after his own last name.

And Eio was more like a professor supervising his Ph.D. students. He came by Nelson and Cohen's lab once a day for their important discussions. These days he usually came in a good mood, with a sparkling water Shana made him in his hand and a straw in his mouth.

Nelson and Cohen had learned to do their research with Eio when he was energized, so that they wouldn't risk him fainting in the middle of it. Eio's attitude towards them had improved significantly since he got his X-ray charging tubes, which made their collaboration quite enjoyable.

Nelson decided that they might be most productive if they used a top-down approach. He needed to first understand the higher dimensional multiverse and how our own universe fitted into it.

One day, Eio seemed talkative after his refreshment, and Nelson had geared up for a second interview.

"Eio, you say you're from Upper Universe. Then what does the whole multiverse look like?" Nelson began.

Eio replied pleasantly, "Imagine a lake in a forest. The whole multiverse is the forest. Your universe is like a floating leaf of water lilies in the lake, and my Upper Universe is like an ant's nest on the bank."

"That's a fun analogy," Cohen said with great interest. "Water lilies. I love them. You know, I have one of the oil paintings by Monet, a reproduction, of course."

Nelson gave Cohen an impatient look. Cohen was interrupting, and he had no idea of the significance of Eio's description.

"Let's talk about hobbies after work," Nelson said, eager to get back to the point right away. "Eio, are you suggesting

— I can imagine our universe is a two-dimensional brane embedded in a higher dimensional bulk?"

This time, Eio nodded slightly, and he seemed to understand the question after all the human science prep Nelson had given him. "If you'd like to think so," he said.

Nelson was overjoyed to hear that, since it was exactly one of the universe models he was working on. In his model, it would be easier to visualize four space dimensions if our own universe was first treated as a two-dimensional object. So, our universe could be imagined as a flat leaf of water lilies floating in a lake. After our universe was reduced to 2-D, the higher dimensional being — Eio — could be imagined as a 3-D ant.

"And in the forest, there are many other universes, low or high dimensions alike?" asked Nelson, his eyes wide.

"Of course, there are leaves, trees, and animals in the forest," said Eio, who made it sound like a wonderland.

"Are you the animal in this analogy?"

"Yeah, I'm like an ant being trapped on your leaf," Eio replied with a sigh. "I don't like being trapped and helpless."

Cohen suddenly stood up while listening to them. "Nelson, do you think the forest is a good cosmological model?" he asked eagerly, "can it be used to explain those great unsolved problems in physics, such as the accelerating expansion of our universe?"

"That's an interesting idea…" Nelson replied, thinking hard. "You mean our universe begins as a point like a seed, then it germinates and expands, just like a growing leaf?"

"Yeah," Cohen said, winking at Nelson and Eio, as though to show them that he was smart, too. "But if our universe is truly like a floating leaf of water lilies, that means it could age and die someday?" Cohen arrived at a possible outcome of the analogy. "I don't like that prospect," he added.

"That's possible," said Eio. "Everything that has a beginning has an end."

However, Nelson was skeptical about that — the forest model was too complicated, and he liked our universe in continuous expansion much better. He and Cohen were prudent scientists. They wouldn't just take whatever others said to be true.

Sure enough, Cohen spoke in the next second. "But Eio, what you said has no scientific verification, and we cannot test it until we have actual observations from the higher dimension."

"Well, that's something you're going to research and find out yourself," Eio replied simply.

Nelson was partly convinced, though it was hard to believe and hard to digest. And the idea was enough of a start for him. "I'll need to lay out the mathematics for a 4-D multiverse first," he said.

And it took him many days to have something meaningful.

Eio commented on Nelson's equations whenever he came in. Eio's few sketches on Nelson's paper would usually keep him busy for a whole week. At this point, Cohen only listened to their conversations and suggested what kind of engineering might be required.

"Eio, does this make sense to you?" Nelson asked one morning after he believed he had outlined the basics.

"Not at all," Eio replied simply. Then they went on a lengthy discussion again. There was no progress after long hours. Nelson felt his head splitting, and the most frustrating part was that they often talked about entirely different things.

"You need new math," Eio concluded at the end. He drew scratches of equations on a piece of paper and gave it to Nelson. "Here's what I have in mind. Try to see from my perspective."

After that, Eio went home and left Nelson alone.

Nelson studied Eio's symbols and sets of equations closely. He tried to figure out the relations within them but saw only gibberish on the paper.

All of those were meaningless. Every attempt to understand made his headache worse.

No, no, not this, he thought.

That was also impossible.

Ah! Nelson shook his head madly.

After he calmed down, he realized the problem might be far more complex than what he'd initially thought, and he had to abandon his entire framework.

Finally, he called Eio and said, "I'm afraid I have to start over again. Give me some time to work on it."

"Ok. Take your time," said Eio. "I guess I don't need to visit you for a while."

So, Nelson made himself a simple and easy bed in the lab and slept for as few hours as possible. He ate nothing else but Nutrition Mix every day. In fact, he found the Mix so convenient that he could spend the minimum amount of time eating and more time working. As long as his stomach didn't complain about being hungry, his eyes could remain open, and his brain didn't shut down, he was in front of his computers.

He couldn't afford to lose precious time when he was on the brink of such a great discovery. Besides, he never got the formal training to obtain a Ph.D. degree, so he always felt the need to work harder, and his self-made physicist pride wouldn't allow him to fail.

Weeks went by. One night, Nelson found his equations making sense to him. He triple-checked everything. No mistakes. This must be it.

He needed to show it to Eio and gain his approval. An approval meant that they could move on to a second phase soon. Cohen could try a simulation.

Nelson was so excited that he stayed up until daybreak. Then he hurried to Base-H and dashed into Eio and Shana's compartment.

"Here, you have to look at this," Nelson yelled as he climbed up the bunkbed and held his results in front of Eio.

Shana was woken up by the noise and struggled to open her eyes. Nelson looked down to the lower berth and said, "Never mind us, Shana."

"What again?" Eio grunted, "I haven't had my breakfast yet."

Nelson didn't notice Eio was in a bad mood, however, until Eio skimmed through his draft and threw it away.

“This is not it! Are you an idiot?” Eio said sharply, looking extremely unhappy. “What we discussed the other day has vanished from your head completely?”

Nelson felt like he had taken a blow to his chest. Hard to blame Eio’s harsh response, though, he told himself. This was actually the twentieth time in recent weeks that he had modified his theory and showed it to Eio.

“I don’t understand. Look, this equation here —” Nelson said, trying to explain himself, “isn’t it what you described earlier? Of course, what you’ve been talking about is an abstract concept. I need to bridge it with the physical laws of our universe. I think I’ve captured the most important part here… Others are minor adjustments — these parameters here and there, and the last one, I name it Wagner constant.”

“It’s not going to work!” Eio snapped. “Forget your physical laws of this universe. You don’t understand a thing.” Then he looked away with his mouth turning downward. It seemed like Eio had grown impatient with their lack of progress.

“Could you please explain why? This part —”

“I’m not giving more explanations. Your approach has proved useless, and you’re wasting my time,” said Eio, cutting Nelson off without mercy. “I’d rather do it myself if I have access to your lab and all the resources.”

Nelson fell silent.

Eio then asked tentatively, “Do you think Cohen will agree if I want to play with his equipment?”

The rejection hit Nelson hard. He felt hollowed out, the energy draining from him as if a plug had been pulled, and his head was pounding from continuous sleep deprivation.

“Let me think of another way,” Eio said moments later, his face softened. It seemed like he tried to lighten up after glancing at Nelson a few times.

Nelson agreed and left reluctantly. That night, he fell asleep in front of his computers, too tired to go on. Strangely in his dreams, he saw the tensors, symbols, and parameters connecting with his field equations, trying to tell him something… but he couldn't get a good look at it, no matter how hard he tried.

Nelson hadn't gone to Eio's compartment since, nor had they talked to each other after their last conversation ended on a sour note.

Three weeks later, Nelson was still continuing his research in difficulty.

One morning, Eio arrived unannounced, Dr. Yang by his side. The two of them burst into his office and surrounded him. Somehow, Nelson felt an odd suspense in the air when Yang looked so stimulated, totally unlike his usual contemplative demeanor. Eio, on the other hand, behaved like the same old boyish Eio.

"Come over and stick out your head," Eio instructed.

"What?" said Nelson, puzzled, but he did as Eio asked.

"Don't move. You cannot move while I do a test. It won't hurt," Eio said as he felt Nelson's head with his hands. Then an ultra-thin extension, grew out of Eio's hand. It attached itself to Nelson's forehead and kept going.

Nelson couldn't see it, but he imagined it went through the extracellular space between the neighboring cells of his skin, passed his skull, and reached the cortex. He dared not move, and he didn't feel anything on or inside his head, not even a slight tingle.

After a minute or two, Eio said, "I've just sent some electrical inputs into your brain, and your nerve cells responded. Excellent."

Nelson searched his brain but didn't notice any changes. "What did you send me? What's happening in my head?"

"Promise," Eio ignored his questions and said, "promise this will be a secret between you, me, and Yang."

"What?" asked Nelson, looking to Eio and then to Yang, not knowing what Eio was talking about.

"Just promise."

"Ok? I promise."

Eio then went on excitedly, "I've thought of a way to get my knowledge about the multiverse directly implanted into your head. But it'll be an energy-expensive process, and it's somewhat risky for you, too. Shana won't allow it if she finds out, and I'll be grounded. That's why I need you to promise, and we'll keep it a secret."

"Ok… What way?" Nelson was curious about Eio's superpowers, but he was also skeptical since Eio hadn't proved to be capable of anything serious.

"Now listen carefully," said Eio. "There are three critical steps I need to take for the implantation, but we have to put you to sleep first and take your consciousness offline."

"Offline brain manipulation? It's a bad, very bad idea," said Nelson, frowning.

Eio ignored him. He pulled out a map and said, "First, I'll locate the area in your brain that is responsible for intellectual functions. Yang has provided me with this map of the human brain and its functional areas."

Somehow Eio's casual manner made Nelson nervous. He looked at Yang uncertainly.

"He is serious," Yang said.

Yang then pointed to the map and kindly supplied more information, "These are the frontal lobes. They are located behind your forehead and above your eye sockets. Eio needs to focus on the prefrontal cortex region specifically."

Eio then continued smoothly, "During the second stage, I need to wipe clean the corresponding neural circuits in your brain." He made it sound as easy as doing a kid's drawing on a piece of paper, where he could just erase anything he disliked.

Yang quickly interjected as if he was helping, "A neural circuit means a group of interconnected neurons. It's the basic element of your brain function."

"Wiping clean my neural circuits? It means removing my existing knowledge, doesn't it?" asked Nelson. He wasn't sure if he understood it correctly. Eio's plan sounded really dangerous.

But Eio must have done his homework before he came because he said, "Yes. Your understanding of this universe — physics, astronomy, and cosmology — will be gone."

Yang nodded surely and added, "That's what we want. Your knowledge is stored as patterns of interconnected neurons and their electrical activities. On top of that, there are sequences of these patterns characterized by ensembled neuronal responses. All of that forms the neural coding of your cognition."

Yang paused, questioning Nelson with his eyes as if asking whether Nelson was following, and then he went on, "Reinforced learning processes create such coding. Eio has to remove your old neural coding."

"That sounds crazy. This is *not* a joke you two are playing?" Nelson dropped his jaw after Yang's statement — he needed to make sure.

Yang and Eio shook their heads, looking as serious as they could.

"Don't worry too much," said Yang. "Eio actually knows what he's talking about. He spent three weeks in my lab. I've explained to him the electrophysiology of the human brain and shown him my neuron specimens. Oh, we've also looked at a real formalin-fixed brain."

Nelson glanced at Yang, who was now smiling with satisfaction and certainly looked proud of his contributions.

Eio waited for Nelson's astonishment to ebb and continued, "The third step, I'll implant my knowledge into your prefrontal cortex. It should be as clean as a whiteboard by then, and the neurons will be electrically excitable again. There is going to be a training process, during which my hands will act like synapses, sending the stimuli as electrical pulses for your neurons to learn."

Yang added, "In order to trigger action potential in your neurons, stimuli of a certain voltage are required, and this training will be repeated multiple times.

"After that, your ensembled neuronal responses will have the new coding, which means different oscillation patterns."

Yang assured Nelson at the end, "I'll monitor your life signs and make sure you two are Ok during the process."

There was a moment of silence after Eio and Yang finished.

After a while, Nelson's habit of reasoning came back to him, and he asked, "Eio, you said it's energy-consuming. What will happen to you?"

"I could be gone if I use up all my energy," Eio said grimly. "But I'll be gone sooner or later if I can't go home. So, anyway…"

"Is success guaranteed?"

"Of course not!" Eio snapped. "What do you think? This is an experiment. I haven't had a chance to try it out on any humans."

"What will happen to me if you fail? Will I be gone, too, or brain dead?" Nelson asked halfheartedly.

"You won't be gone. The worst case is that you lose all your knowledge about this world and become an idiot," replied Eio, who didn't seem to think that would be a terrible situation.

But to Nelson, becoming an idiot was worse than killing him, since he'd have no more chance to create a Wagner Prize and no reason to live on.

"The experiment could end up badly," said Yang. "You can say no, or you can say you need some time to think about it."

Nelson was grateful that Yang tried to provide an exit for him, so he turned to Yang and asked for more suggestions, "Dr. Yang, what would you do? You're the same type of scientific person as me, and you despise loose thinking."

However, Yang only gave him a grave look, and Nelson knew that meant "this is your decision, not mine."

Nelson struggled inside, but it didn't take him too long to consider the proposal, it turned out. He had researched everything within his capability. He didn't think he would have another breakthrough in his life if he said no.

"When and where do we start?" asked Nelson. After he made up his mind, it became simple and fast-moving.

"Today," Eio and Yang said together.

Yang got excited again and said, "You'll need life support in case anything happens. For that, I've reached out to my doctor friend in Redland Hospital, and he's offered us a ward, basic equipment, and supplies. We can do it there."

Everything had been prepared. There was no reason to back out now. Nelson shut down the lab, and the three of them gathered simple stuff and headed out to Redland Hospital.

Soon they arrived and settled in a quiet ward in a corner of the hospital. Yang made a quick measure of Nelson's head.

"You've got a really big head," said Yang half-jokingly. After he finished, he attached EEG electrodes to Nelson's scalp.

"We're going to put you into a medically induced coma. In that state, your brain activity will be minimal."

"Just do your best," Nelson said firmly after he had prepared to die.

Eio nodded.

"Wait, one last thing…" Nelson suggested eagerly in the next second, "Eio, could you please try on a small section of my brain first and see if it works? If you fail, I only lose part of its functions… better than total oblivion."

"Ok, Ok. I know. Don't talk to me like I haven't thought of it," replied Eio. "I'm smarter than you, you know."

Nelson felt better with the cautious plan. Yang started the IV drip, and he fell asleep. Yang looked at the EEG monitor, turned to Eio, and said, "Go ahead, kid. His Delta wave is slow. He is definitely unconscious."

Eio extended his hands and split them so thin — on the scale of nanometers — that they became millions of fine filaments. He reached inside Nelson's head and started working.

"Are you going through his skin cells like you did in the test?" asked Yang since he couldn't see anything.

"No, I'm going through the 4th dimension so that I don't poke numerous holes in Nelson's head," replied Eio.

Yang watched closely, and Eio murmured to himself while he worked,

"Here… no… Over here… Oh right… there…"

Two days later, when Nelson woke up, he felt like he was floating in a cloud, and his limbs were disconnected from him.

The strange feeling that he had lost control of everything lasted for a while.

In a panic, Nelson initiated a thought process. He tried to think of what had happened and then remembered he had agreed to some experiment.

He asked himself who he was — and yes, he remembered his own name.

I think, therefore, I am. Descartes's philosophy certainly gave him comfort.

When Nelson was able to turn his head around twenty minutes later, he found Eio and Yang by his side. He recognized who they were, and he relaxed a bit.

"Great. Looks like your consciousness has come back online," said Eio, then he lay down on a bed next to Nelson. Eio didn't look so good with a shrunken shape. Most likely, he used too much energy like he had warned.

"Are you Ok?" Nelson asked, trying to sit up.

"Not Ok. But still here," Eio groaned. He looked grumpy and clearly not as energized as he was.

"How did it go?"

"It took me one long day," said Eio. "You know, I had to alter millions of your neurons with precision. Because your neural network is like cotton candy, I've had to send some probes to make sure it was the area I wanted to change…"

Eio paused to take a break before he spoke again. "But it should have gone through, I believe. Now try to think about your physics."

Nelson did as Eio asked upon hearing that. A sharp, piercing pain shocked his head. He felt like he had just come out of surgery and forgotten his oxycodone.

"Ahhh," cried Nelson. He couldn't help but hold his head with both hands, as if in that way, he could prevent it from splitting in half. "What the hell?"

Indeed, it was gone, all gone. The work of his life and his previous discoveries. He only remembered he should have some achievements but couldn't recall any details. All the laws of nature that he was familiar with were erased from his memory.

What took their place was something new… and vague, something he made no sense of. And he couldn't press closer to understand it because his head was going to explode.

Eio studied him carefully and asked, "So, what do you see?"

"I don't know," Nelson replied, feeling blank. "I have no idea at all. Maybe I just need some time." He didn't want to sound too negative. After all, both of them put their lives at risk for this. But at least they were still alive; that part of the experiment should be considered a success.

Nelson's response didn't seem to surprise Eio. "Next, there will be a learning curve for you," he said after a moment's thought. "Don't give up. You'll take a leap of imagination to understand what I want to show you."

"Yeah," Nelson replied, falling back into his bed. Fortunately, he was not a total fool, and that was something worth celebrating.

"I want Shana for my refreshment now," Eio said after seeing that Nelson was Ok. "Come find me when you want to discuss it again." Eio then took the charging tube Yang handed to him and left.

Yang looked eager to stay, though. Quickly, he brought his notebook to Nelson's bedside. His eyes lit up with excitement as he pushed up his square glasses, and he asked all sorts of questions, such as how Nelson felt, any difference he noticed before and after, any side effects…

After Yang wrote down his notes, he said sympathetically in the end, "Some of your neurons may have been damaged in the process. That could be why you're suffering a headache."

Nelson suddenly had this not-so-happy shocking realization: he had become Yang's guinea pig — and that was the reason why Yang had come in the first place.

* * *

While Eio was busy with his Hyper-V project, Shana had been diligently focused on her own training over the past few weeks. One evening, as she headed to the dining room, she noticed Eio wasn't there, so she left him a note with a smiling face on it:

> *Dear Eio,*
> *I'll go train after dinner. Will be back around 9 PM today.*
> *If you are hungry, your snack is in the kitchen, your favorite cookies, and you can have a small scoop of ice cream after that.*
> *Love,*
> *Shana*

She then remembered Eio's casual mention of spending a couple of days at Yang's place. She was glad that Eio managed to get along well with the scientists, and the thought of him finally going home lifted her spirits.

Feeling optimistic, she arrived for another night of training with Jack.

The first thirty minutes were the usual combat against a virtual Gatti opponent. Shana had become more agile recently; she evaded the attacks and struck back many times.

Jack sat on a bench, watching closely. "I'm happy to see the improvements," he said. "You're quite a girl. You've shown progress every single day since we started. This is more promising than I thought."

Shana went to sit down by Jack's side after she finished, grinning. She was delighted to hear praise from Jack, who was hardly known to be generous with it.

Jack smiled, his wrinkled face smoothing out, and he said, "Once, I worried that losing your parents would make you cheerless. Seeing the sunshine in your heart drives that worry away, and the great efforts you put into the training really touch me."

Shana felt a lump form in her throat, as well as a sense of warmth and gratitude.

"You've been in real fights, so you've learned," Jack continued. "Pay attention, anticipate and gain the upper hand… Most of all, follow your instincts."

"Yes, Chief!" Shana answered instantly.

"I believe you can move on to the next level. You can choose a specialty training that plays to your strength," said Jack as he stood up and paced the room. "You know what I have in mind for you?"

"What?"

"A sniper," said Jack, rubbing his hands together excitedly. "By shooting from a concealed position and at long range, you minimize your exposure to the enemy, greatly reducing your risk of getting hurt."

"How does it play to my strength?" Shana asked curiously, her eyes widened.

"Let me ask you this — is your hand going to shake if you take a lancet, cut open a wound, and remove a bullet?"

"No," Shana gave a firm answer after she quickly ran through her mind what she would do.

"That's the reason," Jack said with a smile of satisfaction. "You know what it takes to be a good sniper? Patience and precision. Women tend to be good at that, and you're obviously very good at that."

Shana wasn't sure whether what Jack said was entirely true, but she wanted to take up the challenge.

And they started the first lesson.

Chapter 12
A Devils' Feast

Andro wasn't kidding when he told Don he needed a vacation before he could do more work. After he made the death bullets and a blade for Don, he felt he had accomplished much. After cleaning up the workstation, he was ready to go out for a road trip.

"Time to go," he called Sparky after lunch. His plan was to ride west, cross Valles Marineris and get to Tharsis Montes highland.

Andro got on his bike and stepped on the pedal lightly; Sparky picked up speed. Soon, he left Flat Rock and cruised towards the west.

His destination was Galileo Observatory on top of Arsia Mons, one of the Tharsis Montes' three volcanoes.

Back when Gattis didn't control all the areas of the planet, humans had built an observatory there. Many human pioneers donated large sums for a telescope and a building. Fortunately, the observatory didn't get damaged in the Alien War, and it was a perfect place to study astronomy on Mars. Andro liked to go and admire the stars there. However, most of the time, it was more of a nostalgic place for the Old People to look at Earth.

Andro's thoughts ran as fast as his bike. Just then, before he continued further, a Gatti ship streaked across the sky at an astounding speed, a speed he had never seen, perhaps close to the hypersonic end. Amazingly, the rumbling sound was low.

It must have a military-grade engine, Andro thought as he grew curious. A new warship of Gattis? Something this brilliant could not be owned by an individual… Could this be a military test flight?

"Change course. Follow that," Andro gave Sparky his command. Although he knew his bike couldn't match the speed of a Gatti ship, he still wanted to take a few more looks.

As Andro trailed behind, he gazed at the horizon and noticed that dust and smoke were gathering in the distance. Suddenly he realized something and shouted out, "Bummer. A sandstorm is coming."

The Gatti ship was heading towards Desert Dunes. That place never lacked whirlwinds in spring and summer. While Andro watched, the wind started to blow wildly; it rolled up the yellow sand into billows, racing around the desert. The sky turned dark rapidly as the ship went further, and the ground became murky. It had become a world of sand. There was no place for an aircraft, not even the most advanced machine.

Just as Andro expected, the sand waves surged forward like an invisible giant hand. It slammed the Gatti ship out of control and sent it south, towards the direction of the enormous impact basin, Hellas Planitia.

Andro quickly pulled away and tried to follow the ship from the outer edge of the storm. Yet the ship began rotating wildly and then disappeared out of his sight with one wing lunged downward.

"That ship will get lost," Andro said to himself. However, he had a rough idea of where it or its remnants might be found from his experience. He decided to search for it.

* * *

Hours later, it was already dusk, and the sun had just set near the horizon, leaving the sky a butterscotch color. The ship had broken out of the storm but lost its engines. It was gliding down. Below, there was an abandoned small town close to the edge of a vast basin.

Its screen showed a large flat surface on top of a nine-floor building, which was probably the best place to land. Before the ship went further and crashed, the whole cockpit was ejected as an escape capsule. The capsule went straight up amid blasting gases and intense smoke. Then, as quickly as it ascended, the gases exhausted, and it crashed back down with a loud bang.

A young Gatti female — a Gatta — sat rather frustratedly in the cockpit. She was dressed in a rainbow-draped dress with a wraparound chain belt, and she was fair-colored and quite beautiful.

She realized she was in big trouble. Her father had said the south was not safe and warned her not to go beyond OIIIzoi.

Where was she now? She checked the navigation system but couldn't find the name of the place where she had landed, nor her location on the map. She was quite sure the navigation had been damaged by the crash.

She tried to call her father but couldn't dial out. It looked like the communication device was also broken. She had no way to contact anyone for help.

"Am I going to walk back home from here?" she said to herself. "I need to find someone to send a message."

After several more failed attempts with the instrument panel, she got out of the escape capsule and looked around.

Not far from her, there were broken walls and a utility room. That room seemed to have visitors, since the whole rooftop was covered with a layer of yellow-red sand, but there were footprints in its surrounding areas.

There was no one nearby. The air was filled with an unpleasant scent of dry dust, plus something else… a stench.

As she traced the bad smell, she caught sight of some marks written in blood on the walls. It was hard to tell what had been written, and her heart began to thump wildly with fear. Only then she noticed that pieces of decayed skeletons were scattered in front of the walls.

Her intuition told her it was something worse than the storm. She thought about going back to hide in the cockpit but remembered that the canopy was cracked. It wouldn't offer protection if she was attacked.

However, a weapon would be helpful.

She hurried back and searched in a frenzy. Luckily, she found a Wkeye energy gun in the toolbox and strapped it into the belt around her waist. The gun was a gift from Dvexu. Although her father didn't oppose the idea of carrying a weapon, Dvexu had certainly given her a killer gun. She felt better with a gun and stepped out of the cockpit again hesitantly.

Just then, a voice broke the night's silence.

Apparently, the crash sound had attracted someone. A Gatti came up from the corner staircase — a tall, shabby male.

She heard more footsteps behind him.

The Gatti sniffed with his tentacles and yelled excitedly, "Am I smelling food?" Then he spotted her right away.

She stared at him without a word.

Slowly, the Gatti male made his way to the escape capsule. He then began to circle it, as if estimating its value.

"Who are you?" she demanded.

"Doesn't matter since you'll soon become our dinner tonight," he replied.

Right at that moment, another four Gattis emerged from the stairs and came close, following their leader.

"Get her!" the first Gatti male shouted.

The four of them howled in reply. They didn't seem able to say any recognizable words and just shook their bodies, yelling.

As the attackers closed in, her heart pumped fiercely. Although Gatti females generally had the same strength as their males, she was not a match for five, each of them larger than her. "A true Gatti should face any enemy." She then remembered her father's teaching. "I won't… be afraid."

Together the five Gattis drove her toward the walls.

"Stop! Stop right there!" she cried as she drew the gun, pointing it at the first Gatti and then at the others.

They paused.

She continued loudly, "Do not step further. I'm the daughter of Amosirx, the Head of Military Technology and Engineering. If you touch me, my father will crush you with his super weapons."

The Gatti flinched at the name. Good. He knew it. Usually, when she spoke her father's name, others would know their proper place.

However, seconds later, the Gatti sneered, "You hear that? She said her father has big guns." Then he stared at her with pure malice and continued, "If I kill you right here and now, your father will not know, will he?"

"Well, we can negotiate." She didn't understand why he laughed, but she felt the need to quickly change her tactic. She added, "If you escort me back to my family, you can get a lot of Cubes as a reward."

"No, you're being ridiculous. We do not want a reward. We want revenge," he retorted. "You just gave us one more reason to kill you. What you are looking at are your father's discarded experimental subjects. Thanks to him, my brothers have lost their minds and can no longer speak. They only worry about their empty stomachs right now. I may just become like them tomorrow."

Father's experiments? Why here? She thought desperately. So, they were once normal and now had degenerated?"

But there was no time to think more about it. The four of them were ready to jump at her.

"I'll have to kill you then," she swore under her breath. But she had never used a gun before and wasn't even sure how to use it. She just pulled the trigger in a hurry and fired blindly at them.

The gun gave out intense, deadly flashes, but her aim was bad. In her hundreds of shots, she only wounded one of them.

"It's your death or mine!" she cried. Her words were brave enough, but her trembling voice almost gave her away.

The first Gatti was astounded; his face twisted as he stared at her gun viciously.

The rest of them were less sophisticated, though. They clawed and scratched frantically and then ran off. Seeing his guys gone, the first Gatti reluctantly backed off. He said the foulest curses and turned to leave.

She pretended to stay offensive until they disappeared down the corner stairs and completely out of sight. Her legs then gave out, and she sat down on the floor. Three low beeps came out of the gun, and a flashing light indicated it had run out of power.

What should she do? She worried the attackers might still be there and dared not go down the stairs. But she couldn't just sit and do nothing either.

Just when she went crazy weighing all the possibilities, a soft chuckle came from behind her.

"Who is there?" She jumped and turned around sharply. Someone else had come close quietly. She must have been so overwhelmed in the past few minutes that she didn't notice.

When she saw it was only a human standing on the other side of the roof, she relaxed a bit. She had no problem dealing with one human. She gathered herself and cast a long look at the man.

"Not bad, not bad at all," the man clapped his hands and said. He stared at her gun with wide eyes and seemed to admire what she had done with it. "Your powerful weapon saved your life."

Neither of them knew how to speak the other's language. Thus, the man's translation box was busy doing its job for them.

So, the man had been watching her and knew what had happened, but he didn't show himself earlier. Nevertheless, he didn't seem like an enemy.

"I never thought I'd have the need to speak to a human," she murmured as she dusted off and rearranged her dress. "How long have you been watching?"

"Only the part where you fired the gun," the man replied calmly with his arms crossed. "By the way, I have a name, and my name is Alessandro Dyne. You can call me Andro."

Andro had searched around and spotted the fire and smoke of an explosion. He went to check on the crashed ship.

He had been hoping to get a glimpse of Gatti technology. But unfortunately, it appeared to have initiated a self-destruction program. All he could see was a pile of burned-down wires and a melted metal hull.

Then he rode his motorcycle across town to the building.

Andro looked at the Gatta and noticed that she didn't have tentacles yet, probably still too young for that. She stood at a modest five foot six and could be mistaken for a human girl if not for the Gatti's round eyes and the lack of eyebrows. Then Andro wondered why he thought Gattis were all ugly before. Undoubtedly, she was the most beautiful Gatti female he'd ever met, and her deep violet eyes were particularly fascinating.

"What are you looking at?" asked the Gatta, meeting his gaze directly. The translation that came out of the box was adequately contemptuous to reflect her tone.

"The cockpit behind you," said Andro, tilting his chin. "What a sleek design. I've never seen one of these."

"Of course, you haven't," she replied proudly, holding her head high as if she was the most glamorous princess. "It's a prototype, and there's only one on this planet. My father built it and named it after me."

"Your father?"

"Yes, his name is Amosirx."

Amosirx, the most famous Gatti in spacecraft development. That explained everything. Andro blinked. "A marvelous piece indeed. May I take a look?" he asked, and without waiting for an answer, he went ahead to assess it.

Impressive, Andro thought. Maybe he could come back later to tow it to his garage. He pinned his coordinates on a map. After that, he let out a sigh and said, "What a shame. I could have taken better care of her."

The Gatta tightened her mouth and didn't respond to that.

"I guess you need a ride going back home?" Andro glanced at her, changing the subject.

Her face ran all kinds of colors, from pink to purple and then white. She opened her mouth but then shut it as if she was fighting to keep her silence. Andro knew what was on her mind, something like, "I never thought I'd have the need to ride with a human."

He bowed to her in his graceful manner and said, "Nice meeting you tonight, Princess. Enjoy the rest of your evening." Then he turned away, ready to leave.

"Wait," she cried out. Andro smirked in triumph secretly upon hearing that. He knew she couldn't pass up the last chance to get help, but he kept his face unmoved.

At that precise moment, before Andro could say another word, strange sounds like a faint screech of a vulture alerted them. Some creatures were moving close at an alarming speed. Seconds later, low shrieks kept coming toward them from the northeast. Andro looked up toward the dark and ominous sky, feeling sick to his stomach.

"What is it?" the Gatta asked timidly, turning to him for help. "Do you know this place? You've looked at your map, right?"

"We call it Ghost Town. It's said to be monster-haunted, and people have disappeared here," Andro replied briefly, his eyes seeking the direction of the sounds. He was quite familiar with Desert Dunes and its sandstorms, but Ghost Town was only a collection of tales to him. He'd never been inside, so he grew cautious.

"You better run down and find a place to hide," Andro said, pointing to the corner where he'd concealed himself. "I climbed up there. You can do the same. Find some pipes to grab on and slide down. In that way, you won't risk running into those Gatti scum again."

She hesitated for a second, then did as he said. She rushed towards the edge of the building, trying to see how to get to the ground. "The pipes are thin, rusty, and covered in dirt," she cried, "and there's no place to set my feet."

"Suit yourself," Andro replied, raising his head to look around, gun in his hand.

The strange sounds had started low and somewhat lofty but now became louder, piercing, and intense.

"Let me see what kind of monster you are," he thought out loud.

Another scream reverberated, this time close to Andro's ear. With some flutters, several shadows drew near in the bleak light of the two Mars moons. Three of them came hovering over his head; others lowered to stop on the broken walls of the utility room.

After a quick peek at the creatures now only feet away, Andro was astonished.

Surrounding them were seven giant birds, and they were the strangest birds Andro had ever seen. Their bodies were the average size of most humans. But there were no feathers on the birds' bodies, not even on the wings. Instead, they were covered in fist-sized, pebbly scales. The scales were of a dark green color, which made the birds appear like steel.

The heads of the birds resembled those of the Gattis, but with large, hooked beaks. Small lumps of skin occupied their faces, which gave an odd feeling of a half-mocking expression.

"What are these?" Andro asked but immediately realized he had attracted the birds' attention. Their extremely large eyes fixed their stares on him, and their bone-white talons stretched out, ready to grab his limbs.

These were no doubt birds of prey, Andro thought. He should have run for his life. Why was he always so curious? He should have gone to Galileo Observatory as planned. Now he had to figure out how to escape without losing an arm.

And it was also too late for the Gatta to climb down. It would make her an easy target if the birds attacked while she was halfway down. "Are these gene-mutated humans?" she cried. "Birdmen?"

"Don't know. They look more like mutated Gattis," Andro yelled.

At first, the birds on the walls just strode about on their thick legs, and the three in the sky glided back and forth, rounding up their prey.

Suddenly, a short whistle came from the utility room.

As if getting the signal to attack, one flying bird shot down toward the Gatta, talons extending forward. Its long wings stretched wide, instantly casting a vast shadow that enveloped her.

She totally panicked and looked around desperately for hiding places. However, besides the utility room, the rooftop was rather empty. She chose to run towards Andro.

"What are you looking for, Princess? Find something. A weapon!" he shouted to her.

Before he could worry about the Gatta, the other two flying birds had split up. One dived toward him like an arrow, aiming directly at his head; the other came from behind at a terrifying speed.

Andro was prepared and agile. He raised his gun, fired two shots at the first one, and sent it down. Then he turned swiftly around to shoot the one behind him. But it had become alarmed; it tilted its wings to fly perpendicular to the ground so fast that he missed.

Two more birds came down to join the fight with Andro. Out of reflex, he took cover behind a broken wall and rolled to one side. Almost at the same time, one bird's beak pecked on the wall with a cracking sound. Sand and dirt scattered in all directions.

Immediately, Andro shifted out after the dodge and shot right at the bird's head. It went down with horrible squawks.

"Gotcha!" Andro yelled, thinking how he could have become the bird's meat if he'd been just one second slower.

Other birds spread out and kept their distance after seeing two of them dead.

Not far from him, one hideous bird was still chasing the Gatta. It turned its head back and forth swiftly, with each peck aiming to kill. In a split second, the bird had torn off a piece of flesh from her shoulder; it opened its mouth and swallowed it down. She cried out in pain.

Andro was shocked by the madness of the birds. He directed several shots to keep them away and shouted, "Don't lose your focus. Move over to me and stay close!"

The Gatta rushed to his side. Andro noticed that her bleeding had already stopped. She must have the fast heal ability.

"You may try to use that," he said, pointing to the metal chain belt that she wore as an accessory. Immediately she pulled it off, waved it, and turned it into a whip in her strong arm.

“Nice.” Andro was surprised to see her strength, definitely multiple times that of a regular man. It might work for her.

Meanwhile, three birds started to move again. It seemed like they would resume their attack in a matter of seconds.

When a bird dived toward her again, she extended her arm and swung hard. “Get away from me!” she shouted.

The bird was hit and drew away, squealing. She kept swinging the whip; strong winds rose around her, forming a protective barrier.

“Your strength is incredible. You beat down one bird by yourself. Impressive,” Andro cheered by her side. But she wasn’t pleased; her mouth was set in a tight line, and she looked stressed out.

How long could they last? Andro wondered as he checked the ammo he had left. How could he defeat those birds?

“We’re not gonna come out alive if we play their game,” he whispered in her ear. “Remember the whistle from that room? These birds could have been trained, and their master may be right inside. Let’s keep fighting but move over there.”

Then he fired his gun for cover, and they burst into the utility room when they were near.

It was completely dark inside, and the room was in total disarray, with rubbish strewn all over the floor. When Andro turned on a flashlight on his left arm, he was able to see… leftover bones… and, above them… a pair of watchful eyes glittering in the dark.

A Gatti stared hard as he tried to straighten himself from a slouch. He had a wizened face and dark teeth. His body was more of a skeleton, as if he’d been physically deformed by some disease. Although Andro was prepared and he had seen all kinds of freaks, his stomach roiled.

“I’ve already sized him up,” the Gatta told Andro confidently. “He doesn’t seem to have any strength or even the ability to move.”

“Who are you? What are you doing here?” she then questioned the Gatti coldly.

The Gatti didn't answer initially. He took a look at Andro and turned away, then he fixed his stare on the Gatta, admiring her beauty.

She seemed to be used to that kind of look, for she made a small contemptuous noise through her nostrils. "Stop the birds," she ordered.

The Gatti let out two short whistles from between his teeth, and the birds' flutters halted. They just stood outside on the walls, waiting.

Andro understood in a flash. He had been suspecting that the rooftop was something like a wolf's den or a thief's hideout. A bird's nest was not far from that. However, understanding it wouldn't improve his situation. The Gatti was unlikely to spare him.

"You ordered these birds to kill us? Are you their master?" the Gatta asked again, holding her chin high. "Have you raised them?"

"Their master? Of course not…" the wizened Gatti replied. "Occasionally, the birds bring back their prey, or they fight for food with the street scum. I never pay much attention to the noises out there."

The Gatti's voice was low at first, but he became bolder moments later. "I didn't order them to kill you," he added. "This is our home. You're the intruders. You're just unlucky that they haven't had any food lately, and they're starving."

"So it isn't your fault," the Gatta sneered.

"If you need someone to blame, you should blame GIIxb Lab," the wizened Gatti argued. "When I met the birds three years ago, they said they participated in some experiments and became the victims of trial and error. Later, they were fed to the Saxlics outside the Lab, and only few of them escaped…"

Andro felt a chill run down his spine at the mention of GIIxb Lab. Remembering his conversation with Don, he couldn't help but worry.

"You mean the birds were once Gattis?" she asked in astonishment.

"Yes." The answer was short and certain. The Gatti studied her horror-struck face and continued bitterly, "But they can still ride the wind and glide in the air, at least better than me."

"GIIxb Lab did this?" she said. "I don't believe you."

The wizened Gatti shrugged dismissively and continued, "I was born weak and then abandoned. You know how we treat the weak and useless..."

"The one there —" the Gatti pointed to the largest bird towering above them and said, "he asked me to help them in case they lost their wits completely. So, I guide them to survive, hunt for food and avoid enemies. They protect me in return. That's how we've come together."

"Hunt as you might, but killing isn't right," said the Gatta with a mixture of disbelief and frustration on her face. "We do have law and order."

"Law and order? What else do you think they can hunt?" the Gatti sneered in a highly cynical way. "You and I both know that our law and order mean the law of the jungle."

"At a minimum, ask them to let us go," she said.

"If you want to live, I can tell them to spare you, on one condition..." said the Gatti, his eyes turning greedy suddenly. "I've been losing my health over the past years. I don't have much time left. Keep me company before I die, pretty, and the birds can be your protectors later."

"Company? Are you out of your mind?" said the Gatta. "It's *you* who should beg for your life, not the other way around."

Andro moved his body slightly and got ready for combat while the two were talking. He knew what the Gatti was thinking: kill the weak and useless. Although the Gatti himself didn't like the idea when he was the victim, that wouldn't stop him from doing it to others.

Meanwhile, the birds on the walls had become more and more impatient during the whole conversation.

"No? Do you want to end up like this poor human?" The Gatti looked toward Andro and moved his mouth. Whistles to the birds to kill him were about to emerge. However, Andro was faster than him.

He raised his gun in a fraction of a second, pulled the trigger, and sent a bullet right into the Gatti's mouth. Before the Gatti could make a sound, the bullet had gone through his throat and forced him into silence.

Once blood spilled, the birds jumped down into the room and attacked the Gatti, apparently forgetting everything about their mutual interests. The Gatti became the birds' feast unexpectedly, and they soon tore him into pieces.

"Run *now*!" Andro shouted, grabbing the Gatta's arm and pulling her out. "Too bad for him, but run before the birds finish."

They hastened to the edge of the building again; she looked down toward the ground and hesitated.

"Don't look. Just get down fast," Andro urged. "Use this." He tied her metal chain quickly around her waist and then around a pipe. Before she could complain, he kicked her off to slide down. Dust rose, and sparks flared as the metal chain scratched the pipe while she glided past. Andro followed her.

They hit the ground in no time and started to run, yet two shadows tracked them down and loomed close again behind them. Apparently, the birds had noticed that their prey was running away.

The Gatta stumbled over some rocks and fell. "Come on!" said Andro, pulling her up. "My bike is just around the corner." He placed her arm around his neck and half dragged her forward. "Sparky, come over here," he called, moving as fast as he could. When Sparky came to meet them, Andro lifted her to the back seat and then hopped onto the bike himself.

The closest bird was only a meter away. Andro turned back and shot it right in one of its eyes.

He sped up in the next second. With a roar, Sparky dashed across the abandoned town into the dark night.

The birds gave up chasing them after a while, but Andro kept going with maximum speed. They rode silently north for more than an hour. Andro then peeked at the Gatta, and she was sitting as straight as she could, holding onto him tightly, still in shock.

"We're far away from Ghost Town now. You can relax," Andro said lightly as he continued.

After they fled far enough, he stopped and jumped off his bike for a break. "Does your shoulder still hurt?" he asked her. "If I could get to you earlier…"

"Only a little bit," she replied, looking at her bare shoulder. "Don't worry."

Andro saw the wound had already healed; a layer of uneven scar tissues covered it well. The fast heal ability did come in handy, he thought, taking a deep breath.

They had been through a horrific night. She lost her ship and part of her shoulder, but she seemed to be calm now with a serene expression on her face.

She got off Sparky and came to his side; only then Andro got a good look at her face-to-face. Somehow, she reminded him of the beautiful moon rising from the oceans of Earth. "You're radiant," he said. "What is your name?" He remembered he didn't have a chance to ask her.

She replied with some vibrating sound, and it was hard to tell if it was coming from the movement of her mouth or her throat. Andro tried to imitate it, but the sound had slipped his mind, leaving him totally blank.

Andro knew language was never his strength. A bold idea popped into his mind instead.

"May I call you Dione?" he asked with a smile. "It means a beautiful moon, just like you."

She tilted her head towards him and leaned in slightly as if drawn to the gentle expressions of his voice. "I know you can't pronounce my name," she replied softly. "Well, forget it. It's just a name."

"Right, right…" Andro nodded, trying to sound as agreeable as he could. But to his surprise, after a moment, she said, "Yes, you may."

Andro was happy that she agreed, and they continued north.

When they arrived at the vicinity of RIgexx, Andro stopped his bike and said, "You told me your home is in Haxxilic, right? It's too far for Sparky to get there. We're at the border. It's safe for you now. You can get help from the locals in RIgexx."

He then grabbed Dione's hand and put his satellite phone in her palm. "If you run into any trouble, press this button here and send me a distress signal," he said. "Sparky can receive it, and I'll come to your rescue."

Dione nodded. "Are you going inside RIgexx with me?" she asked, her eyelids fluttering, "if you don't mind…"

"No, my dear," Andro said while holding her hands. "You know, those Gattis in there won't treat me friendly. Just go straight that way, and you'll be fine."

Dione walked away hesitantly. Andro watched her going past the town's entrance sign. When she looked back, he called out, "Are you going to say thank you to someone who saved your life? You do have the word thank you in your dictionary?"

"You want a reward?" she replied. "My father can give you as many Black Cubes as you want."

"I don't want a reward. But I may need you to return a favor later," he smiled broadly.

"What kind of favor?"

"Haven't thought of one yet, but I'll let you know. Wait for my call," Andro replied freely. He waved goodbye, kicked off his bike, and headed back to the south.

Chapter 13
A Date with a Gatta

A week later, Andro got a chance to visit the Redland Institute. He found Dr. Yang in his greenhouse, intently studying a peculiar plant. "Hey, Dr. Yang," Andro said, "I have important information for you."

"What is it?" Yang asked, his eyes fixed on the plant as he carefully counted its flower petals.

Andro sat down on a nearby table, taking a moment to admire Yang's work before beginning his story of Ghost Town.

"This town is located in the east, close to the Hellas Planitia Basin. I've long heard that the place was haunted by demons, and a week ago, I actually met them," Andro said. He omitted any mention of Dione and her ship, focusing instead on his courageous fight against those birds and his triumphant victory. He then provided Yang with a detailed description of the birds' appearance and behavior.

Yang furrowed his brow when he heard that the birds came from GIIxb Lab.

"So, do you believe the Gattis were telling the truth?" asked Andro after he finished.

"Yes, the birds could be failed experiments of the early days," Yang replied, crossing his arms. "It's not surprising, since Gattis keep adding desirable genes into themselves. Failure should be common to them."

"But they've succeeded after all? That's what GIIxb Lab is doing now, customizing yourself?"

"Yeah. It looks like the Lab has succeeded through trial and error," said Yang, becoming mindful. "The idea is getting popular in human communities nowadays. But still, something worries me. We don't know the long-term effects of all this."

"You mean Don?" said Andro, jumping off the table. That was exactly why he had come.

"Right, and other people who took the treatments," Yang replied seriously. "I'll tell Don about this when I see him. We need to keep an eye on him."

Andro didn't say more after that. Both fell into silence for a moment.

"You said two birds were shot down, right?" Yang then asked tentatively. "Do you think you can get me some samples?"

"Sure. I'll see if there're still bones of the birds left," Andro agreed. He was planning to go back for the cockpit anyway.

"Thanks, Andro. Look out for yourself."

"Bye, Yang," Andro said a quick goodbye and went back to the workstation in Flat Rock.

Before going to Ghost Town again, he needed to get his aircraft Rhea ready. The bird-shaped Rhea was Andro's made-to-order jet designed by Cohen Hilbert. At this moment, it was parked in the center of a hidden hangar next to the workstation. The hangar's exit was a round tunnel ascending straight up to a closed gate. This gate, disguised to match the surrounding rocks, opened directly to the sky.

Cohen had a special design for Rhea so that it could take off and land vertically. Therefore, there was no need for runways.

Although the concept of vertical take-off and landing was not new for a jet, it was particularly useful for the Wake to keep their aircraft hidden under covers.

Cohen took advantage of Mars's low gravity and developed an engine that could get the aircraft airborne by directing thrust downwards. For conventional forward flight, it then seamlessly redirected thrust rearwards. The overall brilliant design gave Rhea incredible speed and range.

Andro opened the gate at the end of the tunnel and looked up at the sky. "Let's go for a ride. Time for you to shine," he called Rhea excitedly, rubbing his hands together. Then he climbed up the jet, patted on the cabin, and swung into the cockpit.

The dashboard lit up automatically as an AI co-pilot was being activated. A female voice came out, "Where are we going, darling?"

"Ghost Town," Andro replied as he keyed in the coordinates he had recorded earlier.

"Got it," Rhea answered, rising slowly and straight up. "What is the task today?"

"Something easy," said Andro. "We're going to do a flyby, find a couple of bones, and lift a cockpit back home. We only need to watch out for some birds."

* * *

For a little more than a week, Dione kept the phone Andro gave her in the corner of her chamber. That was the only piece of evidence that she had ever been to Ghost Town other than her scar. Sometimes she went to check if the phone had rung or if any message was left, but there was nothing. It was a dead piece of junk.

"Damn you, Andro. Did you give me something broken?" Dione said to herself. She examined it and wasn't sure if human technology would work in her area.

She had begged her father to give her another ship, and he had agreed in the end. The ship was then parked in the family hangar, but she had no desire to go out alone. When she finally checked on the ship two weeks later, her almost-deadly adventure resurfaced involuntarily.

"What is Andro doing now? He did say to wait for his call." She gazed at the phone again. Somehow Andro's voice and face had stuck in her mind. Even her brother, Tlagiss, noticed that she had been a bit absent-minded since her accident. Dione did tell her family about the crash and the escape but not the part where she encountered a random human. She was sure nothing positive would come out of it if they knew.

But she wanted to see Andro one more time before she came of age, which was two weeks away. By that time, her tentacles would start to grow out gradually. Somehow, she wanted to see him before that.

By the twentieth day, there were still no calls or messages. Dione decided it wouldn't make a beep anymore. "I'll throw you away if you cannot make a sound," she said to the phone. "I'll throw you away today." But she didn't.

Soon it had been a month since the accident. One morning, her father told Tlagiss that they had a new discovery at work, and then both of them left home early.

Dione had lost her patience waiting for Andro. He hadn't called. He had forgotten all about it. "Humans are all liars. No wonder we never like them," she said to herself. She took out the phone, threw it to the ground, and stomped to smash it with her feet.

Right after that, she heard the noises of a jet approaching. Strangely, the sound was not from Gatti engines; she had learned enough from her father to tell the difference. The noises then became louder and louder, and her windows began rattling.

"Is it…? Is it him?" Dione hastened with quick steps to the windows and tried to see for herself.

A human jet had come hovering overhead, right outside her windows.

"Dione, would you like to go out on a date with me?" a voice was calling from above, and Andro dropped down from his jet on a rope as he spoke, with one hand extending to her.

"A what?"

"A date."

For this special day, Andro had put on his favorite loose linen shirt and a black leather overcoat, even though he knew clothes were of little importance to him and he would be handsome in any style.

"What does a date mean?" she asked, her face puzzled. Apparently, there was no such concept in Gatti's world.

"You and I enjoy some time together," replied Andro, smiling, "assuming we don't end up hating each other at the end of the day." It was the first time Andro had to explain what a date was, and he found it interesting.

"Have you been stopped for an inspection when you crossed the border?" asked Dione timidly yet with an eager look on her face.

"Nope. My jet is pretty stealthy."

"How dare you, showing up like that," she said, still hesitating. "And you've been seen by no one? I can't be seen with a human."

"Seen by your family? Nope. They headed out two hours ago."

"And the surveillance at the entrance hasn't caught you? Energy guns could have blasted you with flashes of lights."

"I've taken care of it. Your surveillance cannot stop me," Andro said. He had prepared carefully for his dashing entry, and he felt great about it. "No alarm sounded."

"I need to give you a warning," she said breathlessly, "Father will kill you if he finds out…"

"Let me worry about that," Andro replied confidently. He was never intimidated by anyone or stopped by anything. "Now hurry up. We'll ride to my favorite places on this planet and have some fun. You can trust me on that."

"Alright then." Taking Andro's hand, Dione climbed out of her window and up the rope, and then they set out in Andro's jet.

"Where are we going?"

"The most magnificent places you can imagine. You won't be disappointed," said Andro. He gave his sunny smile, one that had guaranteed success with many ladies. "It's going to be quite an experience."

As they rose higher in the air, Dione said, "Thank you for saving my life from the birds." Her voice was gentle and sincere.

"Too bad the ship that your father gave you crashed," said Andro. "I could have fixed it up if I were there with you." He was still thinking about her ship with that lightning speed. Luckily, he had lifted the escape capsule back to Flat Rock weeks ago without a hitch.

Then he turned to Dione and said, "You know, there're not many who can match my mechanical skills."

"It's not a big deal. Father has given me a new one," said Dione, taking her time to arrange her dress as they talked. Her face glowed, so did the necklace she was wearing. "If you had called me earlier, we could have gone out on my ship."

"I can get a ride in your new ship?" asked Andro, his eyes widening with excitement. Nothing was better than touching and feeling a new machine.

"Maybe next time," Dione replied.

"Really? I'm looking forward to it," said Andro, amazed at her generosity. "Our first stop is Desert Dunes."

They continued south and soon came above the desert. Andro lowered his jet and slowed down to cruising speed. Below them, the vast landscape stretched out as far as the eye could see. There was nothing else but waves of sand and rocky mountains rolling endlessly.

Just then, Dione's eyes grew wide with recognition, and she seemed to remember. "Is this the place where I ran into the sandstorm?"

"Yes. You came across it on a bad day. Should have checked the weather forecast first," Andro said. He smiled with ease, making fluid adjustments to the flying altitude when needed. "If you had come with me, you'd have enjoyed it calm and peaceful like today."

Unlike other monochromatic places on Mars, Desert Dunes was colorful. Large streaks of red, yellow, and off-white flowed across the sandstone in wavy patterns. The red was warm, the white was pure, and the yellow was golden. In the distance, where the sand reflected the sunlight, a shining horizon formed. The scenery was indeed one of a kind.

Andro found a nice flat sandy area among the dunes and lowered his jet. After he put it on auto-hover, he opened the cabin door and said, "Now we jump."

"What?" Dione didn't understand. "Jump?"

"Are you scared?"

"No."

“Then together.” Andro gave her a hand to jump off Rhea with him. They landed softly on the loose sand.

Dione looked around. There was no sign of life nearby.

“What are we going to do here?” she asked with a puzzled face. “No one can do anything productive in this bare land.”

“Race,” Andro said simply.

Without waiting for an answer, Andro took her hand and ran on the sand. She didn’t break away from his grip, so they ran and ran until Andro felt a burning sensation in his chest. He looked at Dione; her face was all red, and her hand in his palm was so hot. Andro laughed as he tried to catch his breath.

“Now lie down,” he said, and he lay flat on the sandy ground and closed his eyes. It was noon, and the sun had risen to its highest point. The sand was slightly warm. There was actually nothing more pleasant to do than just lie down and relax. Dione stood by his side for a while and then did the same.

“This is what you like to do? It’s so silly,” she said, looking at his smiling face. “I don’t quite understand. Why are you so happy? Or do you guys just like to waste time on useless things?”

“Silly? Useless? I find it breathtaking,” said Andro, sitting back up.

He laid his eyes on her face, then on the majestic nature, and said, “Look at those lines of our footprints, coming all the way here. Tonight, the winds will blow and cover them up, leaving no trace. But I’m glad that we’ve been here, you and me.”

She smiled, the corner of her mouth lifting a little, and her eyes sparkled as her face radiated happiness, making her look even more beautiful and charming.

So, this was how they smiled. Had anyone ever seen it? Andro wondered, his thoughts running wild. How did humans and Gattis come to the point of war? Would it be different if everyone began to know each other with a smile?

While they sat, Andro opened his backpack and got ready for a picnic. He had packed nice food for the date, but Dione only took the Nutrition Mix after looking at the human food curiously.

After they were done, she asked, "Where is the second stop? Don't tell me you're going to give me a tour of the North Pole, then do a jump and lie down again."

Andro laughed. "Sweetie, we don't have that kind of time today," he said. "But there's an equally interesting place. I'm planning to ascend to the top of the dormant volcano — Arsia Mons. From the observatory there, you can get a spectacular view of my hometown."

Dione's face lit up as she readily agreed. They climbed up to Rhea again and flew along the equator toward the west.

Arsia Mons was the southernmost of the Tharsis volcanoes, and Galileo Observatory was built on its summit.

Due to the smaller gravity pulls on Mars, lava flows were longer, and volcanoes grew much higher than those on Earth. Arsia Mons, with a peak of twenty kilometers, was certainly one of the most magnificent mountains on the planet.

When the volcano mountain came into view from far away, Rhea climbed the gentle slope and gained altitude slowly. They went forward and up, then decelerated to land on a flat surface.

The night was about to fall. Earth had risen to the sky, silent and distant. Against the vast sky, the observatory stood there alone on the mountaintop.

Andro led Dione to the front of the observatory, a simple white structure with a dome. There was no one else there that day, and it was quiet. They went into the main room and saw an old-fashioned four-meter astronomical telescope in the middle.

Working with the control system, Andro opened the dome panel and adjusted the telescope. Before long, Earth's continents and blue oceans came into vivid, crystal clear view. When he zoomed in on the Alps, the sprawling mountain range system appeared to surge forward, filling the telescope's lens.

"See that? The crescent-shaped mountains," he said, showing it to Dione. "That's where my hometown is. I was born in Switzerland. You can't see a lot of details from here, but among the Alps, there is a mountain called the Matterhorn. It's like a pyramid with four steep sides. I used to ski down its long slopes in the winters."

Andro smiled faintly at the old memory and added, "I often flew in the air for, like… ten seconds? That was before I got my pilot training. You know, I love that feeling of speed."

Dione blinked intently into the telescope, and Andro just stood by her side, watching Earth, now a bright evening star, with his naked eyes.

"I can't believe that was so many years ago," he said after he had gazed long enough, feeling a deep loss. "It's a pity I don't get to do it anymore."

Dione was quiet and just listening to his babblings. "Why? You can still travel back to Earth," she asked a moment later.

"Most of the snow is gone. It's too warm now to have decent snow for skiing," Andro said with regret.

"I can understand…" she murmured.

Andro then showed her other incredible sights on Earth that could be seen from space, including the Nile River and the Grand Canyon.

"It's so beautiful," she exclaimed. "I've heard about Earth from Father but never paid attention before. Now I really like the blue marble covered in white clouds."

"Glad you like it," Andro said as he closed the telescope and the observatory back down. "Let's go to our last stop."

And they flew back along the equator until Rhea crossed over the night sky of OIIIzoi.

"Are we going back south?" asked Dione a bit uneasily as Andro continued south. "Now it's dark."

"Don't worry," Andro replied softly. "We're friendly people, and you have me."

After a while, he checked the pre-recorded coordinates and prepared to land. It was late at night and completely dark outside.

"What is special about this place?" asked Dione, looking out to what seemed to be the middle of nowhere again.

Andro didn't answer her question immediately. Instead, he took her hand and said, "Close your eyes. Just trust me."

Their flight continued for a short while, and then Rhea landed. "Now open your eyes," Andro said enthusiastically. "Do you see it?"

"What?"

"Aurora."

Amazingly, above them, there were large green bands and red bands displayed in the dark sky. "I can't believe what I see!" Dione exclaimed. She leaned forward and raised her head to look around, her eyes shining.

"This is brilliant."

"Yeah, absolutely," Andro said as they got off the jet. "Let's go out for a walk."

Not far away, a crowd had already gathered for the dazzling light show. The air buzzed with excitement, laughter, and chatter as friends and families mingled, and kids ran around.

A nice woman greeted them, "Welcome to the Aurora Festival! This is for your information." She handed Andro a pamphlet, and he took it and thanked her.

The woman smiled sweetly and added, "Did you know? The green and red lights come from oxygen when electrons crash into the atmosphere. But there is also an invisible part to the human eyes — electrons that crash into carbon dioxide will generate ultraviolet flashes. If you take images using ultraviolet wavelengths, you can see blue swirls."

"Really?" said Andro, looking over to the others. "Maybe we can look at someone's camera with a UV bandpass filter."

Dione touched his arm and said, "I can see it. The ultraviolet glow. I don't need a camera or a filter."

Andro searched her face in disbelief. Dione then told him proudly, "Gattis can see ultraviolet light. The planet our ancestors lived on is far away from the sun. We've evolved to utilize any radiation we get."

"UV vision?" replied Andro. "I'm impressed."

"You knew there was going to be an Aurora Festival today?" Dione looked at Andro and asked curiously.

“Right. They say we have major solar flares today and a festival,” Andro said, sounding like an expert. He was glad that he’d consulted Nelson for the activity.

“We’re near the maximum of the solar cycle,” Nelson had told him. “A massive solar storm has started. Radiation levels on the surface will be many times higher than usual. The magnetic dipole shield in orbit won’t be able to block it all.”

And Andro had made plans accordingly.

“I checked out the viewing location and made sure we came at the right time,” he told Dione, “I hope you like it.”

“I like it very much,” she said as they found a quiet spot to sit down.

“I’ve only seen auroras on images. Aren’t they supposed to happen around the poles of a planet?” asked Dione curiously. “But we’re near the equator.”

“Look here. It should be explained in this pamphlet,” said Andro, looking at the sheets he’d got. He then remembered Dione wouldn’t be able to read it, so he read it to her.

“… On planets such as Earth, Jupiter, and Saturn, a global magnetic field can guide charged particles entering the atmosphere. These particles travel down the magnetic field lines at the north and south poles, where they interact with gases, and auroras occur…”

Andro glanced at Dione to see if she was still interested.

“Keep going,” she said, resting her chin upon her hand, “I like the way you read.”

He went on with a grin, “… Auroras can also occur on Mars, but they are not at the poles because Mars has no planetwide magnetic field. Rather, there are multiple patches of strong magnetic fields in the crust. These umbrella-shaped fields are mainly in the southern hemisphere. They are the remnants of a global field that decayed billions of years ago.”

“Interesting, this is new to me,” said Dione. Her face was soft, and there was a trace of a smiling curve around her mouth again. “Thanks for taking me out on a date. I like all of it.”

Andro smiled; he was delighted to hear that.

Dione then looked toward the human families not far away. Most of the time, they met her eyes with ease, and some gave her a friendly nod. "They seem happy," she said. "Humans get married to start a family?"

"Many of us do. Don't you guys get married?" Andro asked. Odd questions popped into his mind. "How do you get to know your mate? Don't you go on dates?"

"No, we don't get married," she replied. "Marriage is a concept we've borrowed from humans. We don't go on dates either; we do matches."

"Aha, I can understand matching," said Andro, thinking he'd found a common ground. "You put all the information about you in a computer system, and then the computer will help you find your mate, is that it? Age, height, all the appearance stuff, plus personal interests, temperament, and so on?"

"No. We do our matches at the gene level," Dione said. "Everything is written in genes; strength and weakness are all on the table. The system will provide us with a candidate of best fit."

"What do you do with your match then?"

"When the time comes, young females will go to a reproduction center, where we'll have our next generations, and most of us work there to raise them," Dione replied.

"Unbelievable, so there's no romance involved?" asked Andro in surprise. "I thought life was about finding romance and happiness? Wait a second... you don't even have to physically meet your males the whole time?"

"Well, no. We don't have to," Dione replied matter-of-factly, "and I find it natural."

But Andro was awed by the coldness in the process. "Geez, I can't believe this. To me, dating is fun. The unknown is fun, and the unexpected is fun," he said, shaking his head. "You guys kill the fun."

"The unknown and unexpected are just a waste of time," she replied. "The Gatti way is always the most efficient."

"That's because you never know any better," said Andro. He felt responsible for showing her other ways of living. "You know what you need to do to get out of your Gatti mindset?"

"What I need to do?" Dione didn't seem to understand what he was trying to say. She tilted her head to look at him and said, "Why do I have a feeling that you're going to talk nonsense again?"

Andro smiled. "What you need to do is easy. Fall in love with a guy, and then you'll know all this matching talk is bullshit," he replied with a hundred percent certainty.

"Fall in love? And where do I find such a guy?" Dione asked, puzzled by the suggestion.

"For example, me here. Try me out and see if I'm your match," Andro pointed to himself and said. Then he moved to sit directly opposite her so that she could see him better.

First, Dione looked surprised by his self-recommendation, her eyes grew wide, and her mouth opened slightly. She was speechless for a moment, and then she laughed, "What is so special about you?"

Andro laughed, too. He said, "Okay, let me tell you all about me…"

He beckoned her to get closer. While Dione was leaning over, he reached out his right hand, held her chin lightly, and gave her a peck on the cheek.

Dione's eyes opened wide; she didn't seem to know what it was. She stared at him for a long while and then smiled. It looked like she had accepted it.

In Andro's experience, traveling together always worked for foreign women. He chuckled at the thought — now he knew it worked for alien females as well.

Moments later, Dione took off her necklace, placed it in Andro's hand, and said, "Again, thank you for saving my life. This is a gift I received from my father after my hatching ceremony. I want to give it to you."

"What ceremony?" Andro wasn't sure if he'd heard it correctly.

"Nothing," she simply said. "It's very important to me. Keep it."

"Thank you."

Andro took the necklace in his hand. It was a special piece of jewelry made of intricately strung beads. The beads were marked with unknown Gatti symbols, and each of them gave out mysterious lights in the dark, like fluorescence. He put the necklace around his neck, feeling fantastic. It had certainly been a wonderful day.

After Dione had expressed her gratitude, she stood up and set her eyes on the vast horizon, ready to leave.

Just then, something caught their attention. Huge flames and smoke rose in the northwest. The orange and yellow lights lit up the sky, and it looked like an enormous fire erupting in the City of OIIIzoi.

What happened? Andro wondered. Intuition told him something was wrong. At the thought of that, he said, "I'm sorry, Dione. I need to leave now. I'll send you back home and give you a call later."

He headed to Rhea at once, Dione hurried to follow him, and they set out on their way.

* * *

It was a usual evening; Todd was driving back south from OIIIzoi. He operated a store in Midzor, and early evening was the time for him to load his vehicle with goods, cross TTado Bridge and go home. When Todd came to a stop, more than ten Gattis suddenly rushed out from the roadside, and without any warning, they surrounded his Rover and beat hard on the windows and doors.

"Get out!" they yelled.

Todd was totally clueless about what was going on. He didn't know any of them. He held on to the door in a panic and only thought of calling for help a few minutes later.

"Who are you calling?" a Gatti said when he saw Todd dialing out.

"Let's get him out!" another Gatti shouted, pushing hard on one side of the vehicle and overturning it with his bare hands. Then the Gattis swarmed and trampled the Rover. The moment its windows shattered, Todd was dragged out. There was no escape for him from their encirclement.

"Beg for your life."

"Please, don't kill me. I'm just a small businessman," Todd begged at once, protecting his head with both of his arms. "Take whatever you like from my Rover…"

"Look at how funny he is," a Gatti said with a rasping sneer. The others hit his head and kicked his body. Todd was soon covered in blood and crashed to the ground. The goods and Cubes in his Rover were all taken away.

Paralyzed by pain, Todd could only watch as the Gattis set fire to his vehicle. The fire jumped high instantly, and a deafening boom of explosion followed.

Todd was left there to die. He lay on the ground until someone pulled him up and gave him a good smack on his face.

"Hey! Don't go to sleep just yet. You need to hang in there!"

Todd struggled to open his eyes to make out the stranger who tried to help him.

"Bad luck today, huh? I need to get you to a doctor," he said. The man was Terence, the 4th squad leader. He and others had taken an order from Jack and started to investigate suspected gene hunters. Fletcher, the 2nd squad leader, was in charge of Midzor, and Terence was in charge of the OIIIzoi area. So, he happened to find Todd on his way.

"Let's see if we can get your stuff back," said Terence, looking toward his team members.

Several guys from the 4th squad were trying to stop the Gattis from running away, and they got into a fight. Soon the street fight turned into a bigger conflict. A lot of bold people joined the 4th squad to fight the Gattis.

"NIISS guards are coming to arrest all of you," one of the Gattis yelled.

Meanwhile, the vehicle fire had unexpectedly spread to the nearby streets, burning with increasing ferocity. Pillars of flame clawed at the sky. The walls of the burning buildings groaned and cracked, while panicked crowds fled in all directions, desperate to escape the chaos.

Hours later, Andro got there after he sent Dione back home. By then, a swarm of NIISS guards had already arrived to put out the fire. They patrolled the streets and dispersed the crowd.

Andro met Terence and learned everything from him.

"So, the smoke I saw earlier was coming from here," Andro said. "No wonder… What can I do?"

"We've already taken care of it," said Terence. "But if you can help to send some wounded people back home, that would be great."

"No problem."

Andro quickly took the wounded and headed south. "Is this the worst of times?" he said to himself on the way, "I can't even have a peaceful date nowadays."

Chapter 14
A Riot

Ever since Jack took the gene hunters seriously, more Wake members were sent to look into other potential threats, and Don's 7th squad went back to JIlson. However, after weeks of investigation, Don hadn't found anything unusual, so he decided to call it off.

"We're heading back this morning. I've notified B-2 we'll be there in the afternoon," Don told his team members as he checked his pistol and hid it in a pocket inside his uniform.

"I can't believe it's already the beginning of month twenty-one," said Lei while he was getting ready. "It gets cold fast. Soon it'll be winter in the north."

"Yeah," Steve put on his jacket and said, "the perfect weather to hide my uniform under my jacket."

Eio closed the book he was reading, *A Handbook of Star Chain System* by Gattis. He had expanded his reading into Gatti literature recently. He groaned, "I haven't found other Eios, not in JIlson, not in Midzor."

"We'll keep trying. Now let's go home," said Shana. After everybody finished packing their things, Shana took Eio's hand, and they headed out.

From the northern Gatti cities back to human settlements, TTado Bridge across the Valles Marineris was the necessary path for many. People who needed to work, trade, and travel usually went north in the early morning and returned home in the late afternoon. The northbound traffic typically became quite heavy from 7 AM until noon. Luckily, Don, Shana, Eio, Lei, and Steve were traveling south in their Rover.

At the border checkpoint, long lines had formed. A great number of people in their Rovers were waiting for permission to cross the border.

When Don got close to the checkpoint, Eio said, "I feel so good. We hardly need to wait to go south."

Just then, an argument erupted in the opposite lane ahead of them. Don looked out of his window and saw a guy fumbling through his pockets and bags. It looked like he had forgotten his pass.

"Please, I can provide my identification instead," the guy begged a NIISS team lead, "and you should be able to look me up in your system. It's been a long wait for my family." The guy's wife was holding a baby in her arms, and the baby was crying.

"Go away. No crossing without a pass," the team lead said.

"I cross the border every week. There must be some records you can check…"

"I said, go away!"

Just when the guy reluctantly turned away, a coarse voice sounded from the border control booth, "Taenc, why so noisy out there?"

Don recognized the voice immediately. It was Dvexu, who must have heard the argument.

Taenc stood straight at once and replied nervously, "I'm sorry. I didn't know you would be here today." Then he quickly explained the situation, stumbling over his words in his haste.

Dvexu walked out of the booth. He squinted his eyes, listening intently as if pondering the best way to solve the problem.

However, Don knew Dvexu was unpredictable and explosive. This was not going to end well, he thought.

A moment later, Dvexu said to the guy pleasantly, "How about I give you a permanent pass so that you don't lose it next time?"

"Oh, that would be great. That's very nice of you," the guy replied joyfully, knowing nothing of Dvexu. "Thank you."

In the next second, Dvexu grabbed the guy's head and said, "Hold still."

Dread and terror covered the guy's face; he panicked and asked, "Yes… sir, what is it? What should I do?"

Dvexu ignored him. He raised one of his tentacles and carved a large mark deeply into the guy's forehead.

The guy pushed wildly to break Dvexu's grip but didn't succeed. He hollered in pain while blood ran down his face.

Screaming and crying erupted from the pedestrians on the sidewalk; people were taken aback when they saw the guy get hurt, a mixture of shock and horror on their faces. Some stepped back in fear; others tensed up. Many weren't sure what had happened, and murmurs flew around.

"That's cruel! How can he do that?"

"This isn't the first time. A month ago, a guy was beaten up in OIIIzoi for no reason."

"And they keep raising taxes!"

"We can't let the Gattis do whatever they want!"

Meanwhile, Dvexu let go of the guy after he finished. "How is that? Do you like it?" he laughed hard. "You won't forget my gift to you."

The guy's wife trembled as she burst into faint sobs, her face white and terrified. She put down the baby and tried to help her husband. The baby was crying louder and louder.

Taenc looked annoyed. He muttered under his breath; his eyes darted around, as if searching for anything that would make the crying stop. The next second, he stole the baby with one of his tentacles, swinging hard.

The wife screamed in fear while keeping her eyes on the baby. "Please… please don't harm her," she cried uncontrollably.

The crowd had got into a state of intense agitation.

Things could go out of control, Don thought, frowning slightly. He must do something.

Just then, Shana stepped out of the vehicle to take a look, and Dvexu happened to turn his face around, a rough and scaly face that was full of marks.

Shana froze. "That figure… that face…" she stared hard and murmured.

"Shana," said Don, taking her hand to calm her.

"You know his name?" she then questioned sharply, her voice cracking.

"That's Dvexu, the Head of NIISS Guard," Don replied heavily.

"*He* killed my parents," said Shana, trembling slightly. "I remember him better than I thought. I can't believe we run into him again."

"I knew why you asked. I was there," said Don quietly. He kept holding her hand and tried to comfort her. "I remember."

"Dvexu and his NIISS guards seek blood with a passion," said Lei, looking at her sympathetically.

Shana reached for her laser gun.

Don shook his head immediately. It wouldn't do any good if she acted impulsively. Dvexu was heavily guarded, wearing armor, and had the fast heal ability. Also, his tentacles had enhanced functions, which increased his perception of his surroundings.

So Don grabbed Shana's shoulders, looked into her eyes, and said, "Let's see if we can save the baby today. For Dvexu, we need to find a better opportunity. Trust me."

The corners of Shana's eyes turned red. She swallowed and then nodded with difficulty.

By then, more and more people had gotten off their vehicles. "Remember the Alien War and the Red Purge? We cannot tolerate their violence anymore!" a voice shouted.

Some people started to push the NIISS guards around them; others threw shoes and stones. The guards readied their guns, and it looked like they would open fire on the crowd at any minute.

"What do we do?" Shana asked. "How can we save the baby?"

Don thought about it for a second and said decisively and clearly, "Let's try this — I'll handle Taenc. I'm going to find a good spot and give him a shot with the death bullet. After I fire, he may release the baby or somehow throw her away.

Shana, you go blend in with the crowd and get close to the baby. Try to catch her and leave with the mother immediately."

"Understood," said Shana.

"Now, Lei and Steve, please direct people to leave and ask them to cooperate. This place will be in turmoil. We don't want to see people stampede or, worse, get shot down by NIISS. You're going to save a lot of lives."

"Yes, sir!" they answered together.

"Is there anything I can do?" asked Eio eagerly.

"I do have an important task for you," said Don. "Use your Senset to alert Jack and Geoffrey. They're at B-2 waiting for us. Explain the situation. Let them know we need help. At a minimum, I'll need a ride back. I can send them my exact location later. After you're done, regroup with Lei and Steve."

"Got it," said Eio.

"Can I trust you on this?" asked Don seriously.

"Yes, you can," Eio replied. "I know what to do."

"Good. Stay alive. Let's rendezvous at B-2."

At these words, Don quickly moved to one side of the bridge and hid behind a lane divider. By then, Lei and Steve had disappeared out of sight, and Shana had got to her position. The attention of the crowd was all drawn to Taenc, and nobody noticed him. Great. He drew his pistol and chambered a round, the special 5.7x28mm Andro made for him.

Don wished he had tested if the death bullet could work the magic Yang told him. However, he hadn't had a chance to use it on any enhanced NIISS guards until now. But even if the bullet was just a regular one, the shock and damage from it should be able to force Taenc to release the baby.

Please work, Don thought. There would be no chance for a second shot. Once he fired, he'd expose himself immediately, and the NIISS guards would be alerted. He knew he must succeed with one shot if he wanted to save anybody.

Don watched the swinging rhythm of Taenc's tentacle, timing each full swing at just over a second.

He took aim and took a deep breath.

Ok, three, two, one!

He pulled the trigger in one steady motion.

Peng! Taenc was shot in the neck. His face twisted, and his limbs gave a jerk out of reflex. With a shriek, he let go of the baby and coiled in pain. Close to him, Shana quickly caught the falling baby and wrapped her well in a bundle.

Chaos erupted at once with the sound of the gunshot.

"Fight for freedom!" someone shouted. Some people grabbed the guns from the NIISS guards while others tried to push away the barriers to leave.

Don knew he must get away as soon as possible, no matter the result. Without delay, he went straight to the edge of the bridge, climbed over the rail, and swung to hide underneath a large crossbeam.

He heard noises above, pushing, yelling, and screaming from dumbfounded and scared people. He wished he could see if Shana had left with the baby, but there was no time for that.

Don moved onto the arching support frame and sat himself steadily. Below him was the steepest valley, five to six kilometers deep at least. He couldn't even see the bottom of it through the sand haze. A weak mind would have fainted, but he didn't survive this far without a strong mind.

Don took off his jacket, revealing the uniform beneath, then checked his gear. Yes, he had a small, compressed parachute on his back. In fact, he always had it with his uniform. Now he needed to convert his uniform into a tri-wing wingsuit.

He unzipped the side pocket on his left arm and pulled out a chambered fabric, its edge lined with a zipper. He quickly secured the fabric by zipping it to the side of his torso.

He repeated the process. Once finished, he had three individual wings: two stretched between each arm and his torso and one between his legs. The added surface area would create a significant increase in lift.

Don had trained extensively with Jack for aircraft drop skydiving, as well as wingsuit BASE-jumps. This wouldn't be difficult for him.

With an irrevocable leap, he plunged into free fall. Gravity would accelerate him, generating the necessary airspeed for the wingsuit to provide lift.

When the wind burned his face, the accumulated acceleration was sufficient. Don then spread his arms and legs at the precise moment. Within a split second, an intake filled the suit's baffled chambers with air, turning them rigid. Don adjusted his body position and glided down to the west side of the bridge as fast as he could.

In the meanwhile, Dvexu heard the gunshot. He glared in the direction where Don had been and dashed over.

"Get out of my way. You big morons." Dvexu fired his Wkeye energy gun to clear the way. The fearful crowd quickly let him through; some would have been hit if they had ducked a second later.

When Dvexu got to the lane divider, he caught the scent of strong gunpowder. He stopped, looked back to where Taenc stood, and knew that he had found the shooting spot.

Dvexu was enraged. "Someone dared… to open fire right in front of me," he yelled. "Guards, search!"

Immediately, a dozen NIISS guards rushed over.

"A trained gunman," Dvexu told them furiously, "very likely one of those resistance rebels, someone I've been chasing down."

"The gunman mustn't have gone far," one of the guards suggested. "The odds are low that he would go into Gatti cities."

"Right," Dvexu looked around and immediately ruled out those ordinary faces. Then he rushed towards the direction of the human settlements, with his tentacle carefully sampling the air. But he didn't detect any more of the gunpowder smell.

Quickly, he turned around to search in the opposite direction. Still nothing.

"It's impossible the gunman's gone. But where is he?" asked the guard behind him.

"He may not have left at all," Dvexu replied as he had the sudden realization of another possibility. "There is a perfect place to hide since both ends of the bridge are heavily guarded… I know it!"

In a great hurry, Dvexu dashed back to the shooting spot and got to the edge of the bridge. Holding on to the rail with his tentacles, he lowered his body and extended his arm downward, his gun in hand. Without looking, Dvexu raked the underneath of the bridge with rapid fire.

However, there wasn't a single scream.

Dvexu peeked below. "No one is here," he yelled in disbelief. Then he climbed down and examined it more closely with his tentacle sniffing around. He found a trace of the same gunpowder smell.

"So, I've been right," he told his guards while scanning the area in a frenzy. "The gunman was here, but he's gone, and where?"

Just then, Taenc wobbled close to the edge of the bridge, trying to hold on to something. It seemed that he was losing control of his limbs since he kept shaking violently. A minute later, with one surprising twist, he threw himself off the bridge.

Dvexu saw Taenc falling.

"Idiot," he sneered. "One dumb guard isn't worth my time."

But then, all of a sudden, Dvexu saw a black dot gliding down at an incredible speed. It was not an aircraft. "The gunman has jumped off the bridge!" he called out.

"No way you're escaping from me." Dvexu then raised his Wkeye gun and fired many shots angrily. "HHex, get to me right now!" He sent a command to his cruiser parked at the north end of the bridge. Within a couple minutes, HHex zoomed toward Dvexu, then hovered in the air for him.

Meanwhile, Don heard the rumbling sound of Dvexu's cruiser firing up as the murky ground came at him fast. He must land quickly and hide, he thought. He needed only three more minutes.

The altitude was low enough. Don deployed his parachute. Six hundred meters… Three hundred meters…

Don came down in a controlled landing as he rushed to a stop. Then he quickly stripped off the parachute, ran at top speed, and found a good place to hide.

Before long, Dvexu had got down to the bottom of the valley in his ship; he searched quickly and found the parachute. He shot the parachute into pieces and then set HHex to cruise in the vicinity. But he didn't see the gunman.

"Turn on the Bio-heat detectors," Dvexu ordered his guards. "I'm positive he hasn't gone too far."

However, the sand haze clouded the detectors and gave him excessive background clutter. Nevertheless, Dvexu shot madly at every small blob of signals, which just aroused more dust. The detectors told him that he had got nothing.

"No human can climb out of the valley that fast," Dvexu declared. "I'll find him, even if I have to turn every rock upside down." So, he parked HHex on a relatively flat surface and called for reinforcement.

Five hours passed.

The NIISS guards got nothing. It was getting dark in the valley.

What Dvexu didn't know was that Don had been on the move since the shooting stopped. Before more NIISS guards reached the parachute site, Don was far away.

Don knew that he was seen flying down from the bridge. When he thought about which direction to go, he believed the seemingly dangerous place would be the safest.

He decided to go back toward the bottom of the bridge.

Don moved as fast as he could on his way back. When he was close, he even picked up the body of Taenc. It would be bad if the Gattis found out about their new weapon. Besides, Dr. Yang would love to analyze the effect of their first death bullet.

Don dragged the body with him, passed under the bridge, and continued east for hours until he couldn't go any further. Then he sent his location and asked Jack to be stealthy. Human stealth technology couldn't make aircraft completely invisible to Gatti's detection. But Dvexu wouldn't anticipate anything like that, because NIISS believed all human military forces were destroyed long ago.

Within fifteen minutes, Jack and Geoffrey had flown the Guardian — their multirole aircraft — over. For a short minute, Geoffrey steadied the aircraft above Don.

"Come on," said Jack, throwing down ropes from an open door. Don fastened himself and the body to the ropes.

"Hold on tight!" Jack pulled them up, and he took Don's hand. After that, Geoffrey made a sharp turn and disappeared into the night.

* * *

In the meanwhile, Shana had caught the baby nice and safe. She bundled her securely and carried her on the back. Luckily, the NIISS guards either tried to see what happened to Taenc or tried to stop the riot. They didn't pay her attention.

Shana then gave a hand to the mother in shock. "Hurry up, come with me," she said firmly in a low voice. The woman looked into her eyes and nodded. Shana led the mother through the crowd, and then they ran as fast as they could. Quickly they went down the pedestrian exit and got into the local streets. They made several turns through a market and ran past many street blocks until they were out of breath. Then they stopped and hid behind a tea station.

"Are you Ok?" asked Shana.

"I can't go any further," the mother replied, panting, "and my baby needs feeding."

"Let's take a break then," Shana said. She carefully took the baby off her back and placed her into the mother's arms. "There you go."

The baby hadn't cried along the way, and she looked calm, with a slight smile playing on her lips.

The mother rocked her baby gently. She looked rather pale at first, but after a while her face had more color to it. She gave Shana a weak smile and said, "Thank you."

"You're welcome," Shana replied warmly. "Where do you live? We need to keep going and get as far as we can. Those

NIISS guards will come looking for us once they see that their team lead is dead. We cannot risk being found."

"We live in Crestmont, west of Redland," the mother replied.

"That's quite far from here. We need a Rover," Shana said.

"Ok. You lead the way."

Shana nodded. After two hours of running and walking, they finally got to a self-service Rover rental and drove off. However, Shana soon received a message from Brian saying that all main roads down south were blocked by NIISS guards.

"What should I do?" Shana asked herself, worried. It was just her now, and she had to make a decision.

Midzor wasn't far away from where they were. They could get some food and water and continue south later.

"How about we go to Midzor?" said Shana. "It's close, and we may find a place to rest for the night."

"Ok," the mother agreed. "You decide. I'll go with you."

It was getting dark, and they arrived at Midzor completely exhausted. Shana had thought about where she could go on the way. With no Wake members close by, Last Lamp Tavern was probably the best choice to stay for the night. Shana knew Laurelynn was a kind woman at heart; hopefully, she would let them stay. Even if she refused, she was not likely to turn them over to NIISS.

After making up her mind, Shana went to the tavern and knocked on the back door.

"Who is there?" Laurelynn sounded alert. After a while, she opened the door slightly and peeked at them.

"Shana, what are you doing here? What happened?" Then Laurelynn turned to look at the mother suspiciously and asked, "Who is this?"

"Laurelynn, could you please let us in?" Shana whispered. "The NIISS guards are after us."

Laurelynn's face turned glum when she heard the word NIISS. She stood behind the door, frozen with fear, her hands shaking slightly. Moments later, she opened the door without any more questions. She put a finger on her lips to hush them and showed the same wine cellar to the mother.

After that, Laurelynn wanted to speak to Shana alone. She took Shana to another room and shut the door behind them.

"It's better you stay separate in case the NIISS guards come again," said Laurelynn, looking cautious. "Now I need to know who I've helped and how much trouble I'm in."

"The mother and her family are just innocent people," Shana explained breathlessly. "They tried to cross TTado Bridge but had trouble with their passes. The father was hurt by NIISS, and it turned into a riot this afternoon. I want to help them. We're only staying for one night. Is that Ok?"

Laurelynn didn't say anything for a moment.

"I'm sorry, Laurelynn. I have no one else close by," Shana pleaded.

"Tell me the truth," Laurelynn then demanded, her voice suddenly turning cold. "Are you two in the resistance?"

"Two?" At first, Shana wasn't sure what Laurelynn meant by two, but soon realized she was talking about Don.

"Yes, we are," Shana replied honestly. "How did you know?"

"I knew it since the first time I met you," Laurelynn said with a quiet, solemn look. "The NIISS guards just searched every place in this town an hour ago. They said an armed gunman shot their team lead, and a woman escaped with a baby. The nerve of you!"

"We can leave if this is too much for you…"

"To where? You just said you had nowhere else to go," Laurelynn said. "You can stay. No need to thank me. You saved me from my trouble once, and now we're even."

After that, Laurelynn drew a long breath and let it out slowly. Then she turned off the lights and said, "Just keep quiet. I'll go give the mother something to eat, as well as pillows and blankets."

Shana nodded. She sat in the corner of the room, trying to rest, but she couldn't feel at ease. Where was Don? Was he safe? She wondered. Sometimes Don joked about how he could turn impossible into possible, and that was the best she could hope for now.

When Laurelynn returned minutes later, she walked over to Shana with measured steps and then sat down by her side. "Want to tell me how you got into the resistance?" she asked, her eyes now clear and calm. She seemed to have overcome her fear and ready for whatever came next.

"You really want to hear?" asked Shana.

Laurelynn nodded and said, "This is what best friends do, right?"

Shana held her own arms as an intense pain shocked her body at once. "Have you heard of the Red Purge?" she began in a suppressed, small voice.

Laurelynn gasped. "The Red Purge?" she repeated blankly. "Oh, my goodness. You mean — that was more than one Mars Year ago, right?"

Shana dropped her head as the nightmare rushed back to her. Whenever she touched it, her heart clenched. The pain was so suffocating that she never thought she could talk about it. But this time, she decided maybe she could tell her story in a calm way.

"Do you know Waterford?" she continued, "it was my hometown, a little more than a hundred kilometers east of SIIKwari."

"I've heard about it," said Laurelynn, nodding.

"Waterford was a good-sized city. Once there was a large population of humans living there," Shana said darkly. "It was destroyed by Gattis in one day to root out human resistance."

"Is there really water there?" asked Laurelynn.

"Yes. Waterford was next to Utopia Planitia," replied Shana, "that place has a large amount of underground water. Human pioneers built the city there for that reason."

She took a deep breath and continued, "I grew up in a happy family. My parents ran a clinic. I still remember the three of us eating late dinners together after the clinic closed, exhausted but laughing about the smallest things." She smiled at the thought.

"Beautiful memories," said Laurelynn, "I have no doubt about that."

It had all changed that night. Shana told her how the NIISS guards bombed the city, searched her house, killed her parents, and burned the place.

Laurelynn covered her mouth in shock. "Oh, dear, I'm so sorry to hear that," she said a moment later, giving Shana a hug.

"After that, Waterford is pretty much in ruins," Shana murmured; her body trembled involuntarily.

"Cry all you want."

Shana didn't cry.

Laurelynn held both of her hands and said, "But I'm so glad you survived. And you're here with me. Stay strong. I know you are."

Shana nodded.

After a while, Laurelynn seemed to think of something else. She leaned forward and asked curiously, "Wait, who's your life savior? I guess — it was him? Don brought you out of that rubble?"

"Yes, it was Don," Shana replied quietly. "And I've stayed at the resistance since." A small sigh escaped her lips, and a weight seemed to lift from her shoulders. She couldn't believe how much better she felt after having someone to talk to.

"You're a brave girl. It's going to be Ok," said Laurelynn, patting her back.

Soon, it was time for them to go to sleep. "I'll stay with you tonight," said Laurelynn after she made a bed for her. "Sleep tight."

Shana lay on the most comfortable bed with lots of pillows to cuddle. But she tossed and turned, and her thoughts about Don wouldn't stop. It had been many hours, and she hadn't heard from him. On the other hand, Eio, Lei, and Steve had already sent her their safe message. They had done an excellent job and regrouped at B-2.

Had Don gotten out safely?

Shana couldn't call him; he might still need to maintain radio silence. All she could do was wait. Don had gotten himself into dangerous situations numerous times, and in one way or another, he managed to stay alive. Did he make it this time? She wondered, dreading the thought of anything happening to him.

Shana's mind raced with these thoughts, then she heard Laurelynn humming in a low voice. Apparently, Laurelynn couldn't sleep either. It must have been a tough day for her, too.

The tune Laurelynn was singing sounded familiar, and she sang well.

To Shana, Laurelynn was never a dull woman. She was full of life, even in the hardest times. Shana opened her eyes and sang along.

"A touching song, don't you think?" Laurelynn said, looking at the ceiling. "All Old People know this song by heart. They said it was created by an unknown artist, who used to sing in restaurants."

"It's called *Going Home*, right?" said Shana, remembering its name. "Our commander loves to play it with his guitar, and we all sing along."

Going Home

I can still see the beautiful moon around you,
From my small window.
But I can only hear the waves of oceans,
And the chirps from misty mountains,
In my dreams.
Dear Earth,
Are we looking at each other in tears?

Oh, when the spring flowers blossom once more,
My returning footsteps will grace your floor.
When the summer rains splash once more,
My eager spirit will knock on your door.

I can still feel your warm hand holding mine,
A gentle comfort, a love divine.
But I can only touch your face in a photo,
A cherished memory, from long ago.

Oh, when the autumn leaves dance once more,
I'm going home to what I adore.
When the winds of winter sing once more,
My faithful heart will reach your core.

And they continued their singing and bedtime chitchat until it was late.

After midnight, Shana received a message from Don. He said Jack and Geoffrey had picked him up, and he was out of the valley. After reading the message many times, Shana felt greatly relieved and fell into a sound sleep.

The next day, Shana and the mother were ready to leave. Laurelynn provided them with enough food and water for their trip, and she came to see them off at the door.

"I cannot thank you enough for your help," said Shana.

The mother gave Laurelynn a deep bow while holding the baby in her arms. She said many thanks and added at the end, "I won't tell anybody about you and your friend."

"Great, that's going to help all of us," replied Laurelynn, giving her a smile. "Have you heard from your husband? Is everything alright?"

"Yes. My husband said he's safe, and he's in hiding," the mother said, smiling. "He told me where to meet him."

"That's great. Come for a drink next time," said Laurelynn, waving goodbye.

"Sure," replied Shana. The mother thanked Laurelynn again before they headed out, and then they set off south.

Chapter 15
The Council Meeting

The night was as dark as usual outside Base-2, and there wasn't much sound. It was almost midnight, and most Wake members were fast asleep except Yang and Eio.

Yang was too excited to sleep that night. He had long waited for samples to study the genome composition of the enhanced NIISS Guards, plus the effect of death bullets on them. Now he had what he wished for.

Since Don brought back the body of the NIISS team lead Taenc, Yang had been busy setting up experiments in his lab at Base-2, where he ran secret tests for the Wake.

It was as bright as daylight in the lab, and Yang dared not delay a minute. He had to process and preserve some samples as soon as possible.

First, he got some samples for genomic sequencing; next, he isolated many different types of tissues for establishing Gatti cell lines; then, he put all the samples into rapid freezing. After Yang finished all that tissue harvesting, he allowed his fingers a minute's rest and then moved on to the last task.

"I'm going to deal with the area where he was shot now," he told Eio by his side.

With that, Yang changed out his exam gloves, getting forceps in his left hand and a pair of fine scissors in his right. He separated out layers of scale skin, muscles, and bones from the wound and then exposed a group of nerves. Then he tried to isolate the nerves without damaging the cells.

"Keep still. Keep still here…" Yang murmured while he worked.

"Are you talking to the dead body?" asked Eio, peeking curiously, arms crossed. His chin pointed to Taenc lying on the experiment table.

"No, I'm talking to my hands," said Yang. "You know how hard it was to get the body? Don, Jack, and Geoffrey risked their lives to smuggle it back to the base. I need to act fast, and I certainly don't want my shaking hands to ruin it."

"Am I bothering you if I just watch you work?" asked Eio, his eyes wide open.

"Not at all. I always love to share," said Yang enthusiastically. "You know what's even better? Let's work together. Can you help me with this dissection?"

"Of course," said Eio.

And they kept busy until the first light of dawn crept into the lab. Yang found his eyes drooping despite his best efforts to keep them open. He had to pause to stretch his arms and rub his eyes.

Just then, Don burst into the lab and asked eagerly, "How is it going?"

"I haven't had time to complete all my experiments, but it looks like the magic bullet has worked." Yang gave Don a short answer. Then he yawned before he could continue, "I guess you aimed for his weak spot. So, part of his central nerves was disrupted, and his muscles got paralyzed."

"You're right," said Don, "and?"

"And most importantly, I saw a lot of damage and tissue death around the wound. The toxin has shut off the regeneration of his cells. Therefore, their speedy repair mechanism should have been blocked," Yang concluded, feeling a sense of pride and accomplishment.

"So, we've succeeded?" said Don, a smile spreading across his face. "Thank you, Dr. Yang. This means a lot on the battlefield."

While they were talking excitedly, the door of the lab burst open again, and Andro dashed in. "There you are," he said as he caught his breath, "I came right after I heard about the riot."

Yang and Don were delighted to see Andro. Both of them gave him a tight hug. Don explained what happened on the bridge, and Yang couldn't wait to tell him all about the bullets he had made.

"So, it has worked?" Andro asked, his eyes widened with amazement.

"Yes," Yang exclaimed.

"This means we finally have some advantage against the NIISS guards with superpowers," Don added.

"Awesome, I'm such a genius," said Andro in smug satisfaction. "What a great achievement!"

"Yeah, you're the damn best," Yang said, amused.

"Would you please use the rest of the Thallium to make us more bullets?" Don asked seriously. "The sooner, the better. Is that Ok?"

"No problem," Andro nodded firmly. "I'll let you know when I'm done."

Don and Andro's energy was electrifying. In that moment, Yang felt his spirits soar and his weariness dissipate. He knew they were going to do great things together.

* * *

Three days after the riot on TTado Bridge, a lot of people living in Midzor and Redland organized a protest. They paraded through City OIIIzoi, holding up the slogan "AUTONOMY," and they repeated the six goals.

Protests were widespread a week later. In Redland and other human settlements, people surrounded the NIISS stations and demanded the guards leave their towns.

NIISS guards refused, of course, and they opened fire to shoot the protestors at multiple sites. In east Redland, a Rover blocking the NIISS station entrance was hit, and it exploded in the middle of the road. The driver was killed on the spot. Buildings and vehicles were burned; the air was thick with smoke. Debris and broken glass littered the ground, and the streets turned into ruins. Many protestors were injured. On the sidewalks of Exlon Street, a woman was knocked down when she tried to walk across the rubble, and she fell into a pool of blood.

Amosirx was watching the news when he received an urgent call for a council meeting. Immediately, he got ready to go, and his son Tlagiss helped him to start his cruiser.

"Father, the unknown substance we found a month ago…" Tlagiss said, "do you want to bring it up in the council meeting?"

"No. The council must be overwhelmed by the protests at the moment," Amosirx replied.

"I know. But you said Superior ordered you to find a solution for bigger wormholes," said Tlagiss carefully, "and the unknown substance could be the key to solving the problem."

Amosirx thought for a moment and didn't answer right away.

"This new discovery is going to help you, isn't it?" Tlagiss added. "Don't you think Superior and Icus will be happy to hear about it?"

"Yes. That's exactly why we need to be one hundred percent sure before I report. Otherwise, I'll face Superior's tough grilling," Amosirx said, giving his son a meaningful look. "Keep it a secret for now. We still want to do more studies on it, and you should work hard while I'm away."

"Got it."

Amosirx then jumped into his cruiser and headed out.

Michael received the council meeting call at the same time. He knew it wouldn't be an ordinary meeting, so he asked John to start his Rover at once, and they drove to OIIIzoi in a hurry.

On their way, news kept coming in.

Michael heard that the number of human deaths had risen to hundreds, over half of which occurred near the NIISS stations. The Gattis took some losses too. Two of their large stations had been burnt down; five NIISS guards were dead, and a dozen vehicles were destroyed.

"How could it happen?" said John nervously.

"Don't know," Michael groaned. "I don't like this at all."

When they arrived, Michael rushed to the Central Hall. However, he regretted coming into the meeting the moment he sat down in his seat.

What was he thinking? Being a hero was never one of his life goals, yet there he was.

Michael had a feeling it was going to be a bloodbath that day. What else could it possibly be? Protestors went wild; conflicts between humans and Gattis kept rising. He could have pretended to be missing.

While Michael waited, he had to take deep breaths and drum his fists on his legs to stay calm.

Before long, Icus walked straight to his post. Without sitting down, he pressed both hands on the table and began.

"We all know why we are holding this emergency meeting today. Look at the protests, burning, and death of humans and NIISS guards," Icus said as he pointed out the continuing news to the council members. "What is the best way to deal with this problem?"

"NIISS guards have already been deployed at the protest sites," Dvexu answered plainly. "I have ordered them to open fire."

"So I have heard. But we are here to discuss a plan to prevent things from getting worse," Icus emphasized. "What else can we do?"

Michael lowered his head and dared not to make a sound.

"How about a negotiation? Do we want to set a day to talk to them?" Icus then suggested.

"A negotiation? Are you kidding me?" Dvexu laughed. "There is no need to talk to humans anymore after we have established and flourished. Who still wants to talk?"

Dvexu then answered his own question sarcastically, "Oh, right, only you."

Zullom held back a laugh and straightened his arms. He said, "Icus, as you wish, we can ask everybody's opinion, and then we can do a majority vote on negotiation — or not. Let's start from the left side of the table. Dvexu?"

Dvexu replied lazily without looking up, "If you ask me, I say humans are taking advantage of our patience. And the best way to deal with them? Kill them all."

"Be sensible, Dvexu!" Icus snapped. "Not everything is about killing. At least not yet!"

"I am not kidding," Dvexu continued. "Seriously, remember the war and the Red Purge? Let's do it again and make it grander. A bombing campaign can be followed by ground sweep operations. All protesters and underground rebels will be destroyed, civilians, too, if they get in the way. It will keep them quiet for a couple of years."

"I also object to a negotiation," said Zullom. "I agree with Dvexu. There is far too much tolerance from our side."

Dvexu got excited upon hearing that. He stood up from his chair and said, "Finally, here comes some thrills. It has been so boring."

For a while, there was just silence after Dvexu expressed his opinion.

Michael shuddered at the words. As far as he knew, over five thousand people died in the battles of the Alien War. Two major human cities were burned to the ground. Humans on Mars were defeated and surrendered in just three days. After that, there were no armed human forces against the Gatti rule anymore.

Icus disagreed, "Killing only breeds more killing. Although I have to admit the short-term effectiveness of a blood purge, we also need long-term solutions. I want to bring order to this solar system, not just destruction. Anyone agrees to negotiate?"

No one spoke.

"Amosirx? Jyvesi?" asked Icus, looking at the two. "I hope to hear your support."

"I decline to vote," they said together, and then each of them quickly gave some reasons for the abstention.

"Icus, I trust you know what to do. You cannot delay it any longer," said Zullom, pressing on. "And I warn you, do not sympathize with humans."

"What do you think, Michael?" asked Icus.

“Me?” Michael almost collapsed when he heard his name. He didn’t know why Icus asked him. Obviously, he had no voting right, and he didn’t want to be caught in their fight. He cleared his throat nervously and mumbled, “Well, yes… We’ll cooperate. I’ll see to it. Yes —”

“Icus, humans have made you soft over the years,” Zullom said, cutting Michael off. “Perhaps you should let me lead this operation.”

“No, and no,” Icus refused flatly and ignored Zullom.

“Two votes for elimination against one,” Zullom concluded. “If Amosirx and Jyvesi don’t change their minds right now, Dvexu, you may begin.”

“All units, get ready for an airstrike,” Dvexu laughed and gave his command immediately. “Fireworks are about to happen in Redland. How I look forward to enjoying it.”

The more Icus heard, the more annoyed he became. He was sure Zullom and Dvexu intended to undermine his power. His efforts to fight for peace in the meeting had been in vain. It was useless for him to stay.

Just when Icus was looking for a chance to leave, his assistant Kyinn came close, connected their tentacles, and sent him a private message.

A break was exactly what Icus needed. “Excuse me,” he said and swiftly exited the meeting. Once he stepped into a quiet room, he saw it was an important communication from GIIxb Lab regarding a status update for his Nucleus Transform Program.

Icus had been trying to bring this peaceful transformation to the planet, and it seemed to have worked. But the progress was slow, which had given his rival brothers reasons to question his abilities. He really needed some good news now.

With that in mind, he quickly went through the lengthy report and noted major progress, which made him feel considerably better.

When he got to the end, there was a special note:

“Your friend came to visit us by himself, and he was tested,” the summary of the note read. “Per your previous instructions, he has been released back into his environment. So far, he has not returned for a follow-up…"

"At last!" Icus exclaimed in surprise. Once, he had thought all was lost.

"… Everything goes well as we expected. As of now, his genes are being activated since he has come of age. You should see the full results in less than two Mars Years. Details of the tests below:

Blood work…
Gene sequencing…
Genetic material composition…
Basic physical level I…
Brain function evaluation level I…"

Icus skimmed through the detailed numbers and got to the bottom of the note.

There were some future action items for him to fill out. Icus wrote, "Continue to study him and understand him in the next encounter if he returns. Plus, send me a record of his visit. I want to know what he said and what he was thinking."

Icus then sent his reply to GIIxb Lab and closed out the communication with a smile.

When he returned to the meeting room half an hour later, Dark Spiral and many Gatti fighters had already arrived above the city of Redland and other human towns. Live feeds streamed onto the main display, showing intense energy beams flashing. The whole sky was as bright as if there was continuous lightning.

A confirmation video was brought back to the council shortly after. The streets were then as empty as possible. All the noises and thousands of protestors had gone.

"Mission accomplished," said Dvexu, looking quite satisfied with himself. "If there are any protestors left after this, a full-scale ground operation can begin tomorrow in all human towns."

"Great. End of meeting," Zullom announced immediately.

Amosirx and Jyvesi rose to leave. Icus followed them, heading for the door, but before he could step into the hallway, Zullom moved swiftly to intercept him, a mocking grin spreading across his face.

"Seen the confirmation video?" Zullom said airily. "Your favorite puppets are dead. Mind you, Father has asked you to get things under control."

Icus stared back at Zullom and replied, "Things *are* under control."

"You're kidding me. It's only a little over a year since the Red Purge, and the rebels are happily running around. You call this under control?" Zullom sneered. He circled Icus slowly, a dangerous glint in his eyes. "You know Father's patience has a limit."

"I know what I am doing. As for the rebels, you should ask Dvexu," Icus replied indifferently. He looked straight ahead and ignored Zullom's threat.

"Father will decide whether you meet his expectations or not," Zullom said. "When is the plan to embark on Earth? Is that under control, too?"

"Within one or two years," Icus replied. "We are waiting for Amosirx to build our interplanetary warships. You know how fast that goes. Amosirx is finishing up the first batch."

"A timeline, finally. I will take your word for it," said Zullom, his face twisting into a smile, and he seemed to be satisfied for the time being. "Meet Father at the Communication Tower this afternoon. Answer to him yourself."

After that, Zullom walked towards the exit with his parting words, "Good luck with that. I know you're going to need it."

Icus fought back his anger. He turned to see Zullom off, his face unmoved.

Soon, it was time for him to depart. "I'm going to the Communication Tower," he told Kyinn. "I need to clear my mind, and I'll just go by myself."

Kyinn had Icus's CoEEi cruiser ready. Icus hopped on it and left for the tower. As its engines roared, CoEEi crossed the Martian sky. Icus was certainly leaving his frustrations behind him at lightning speed. He pulled a lever to bring the ship to a higher altitude and headed west.

Icus reached the Olympus Mons region later in the day. After he parked his ship, he rose via the skylift to the top of the tower. Then he entered the communication room and stood in the center.

"Operator, prepare for data transmission and live call," said Icus.

"Yes." The operator got to work at once.

Soon, a tiny dot appeared in midair above Icus. Seconds later, the dot grew bigger into a sphere silently.

Since he arrived at Mars, four years had passed, and Amosirx hadn't made any progress in increasing the size or duration of a stable wormhole. But Icus knew live calls were sufficient for Superior to shout across his hundreds of solar systems. He needed to be ready for that.

Icus waited for the glowing sphere to stabilize, and he called when the connection was made, "Superior, System Architect Icus greets you."

Images from the other side flickered onto the screen. Icus saw his father's awful face, and not surprisingly, his high council was there behind him. Those council members would be there for important issues. They must have been questioning his ability to execute the plan.

"Zullom has informed me that you have difficulties carrying out your transformation. Therefore, the plan to conquer Earth has been delayed. Is that true?" Superior's icy, bleak voice came through.

"That is not true," said Icus.

His father continued, raising his voice, "I think we agreed upon a course of action in our last communication. Do you remember?"

"Yes. I remember," replied Icus, remaining calm.

"Then where is my armada?" Superior shouted.

Icus could feel his father's anger across the galaxy. He resisted his instinct to take a step back. The operator in the communication room trembled and dared not make a sound.

"Do you know I have to open this energy-expensive channel just to remind you?"

"I know," said Icus hastily, trying to defend himself. "Please let me explain. For the interplanetary warships, Mars does not have all the resources we need. After a lot of exploration, we chose to mine an asteroid belt. Jyvesi has built a mining platform there. It is a remarkable achievement. Since then, we have been working day and night to build a fleet of warships. The first batch is finishing up as we speak."

There was a moment of silence after his words.

Icus then added quickly, "I have done everything as I promised. We are almost there."

"You said the same thing a year ago," Superior retorted, "and your solar year is four times as long as mine. You should have taken over Earth by now."

Icus sensed a storm was gathering on the other side. He needed to fight his way out. "Superior, I understand Zullom and Dvexu prefer a simple, direct approach," he argued. "They want to set sail to Earth tomorrow and destroy all its defenses. But that is not the most effective way to conquer."

Superior turned to talk to the council members behind him, so Icus continued boldly, "Unless we can wipe out all humans in one blast, which is beyond our current capability, they will grow back. Dvexu and Zullom, for example, have *not* been able to eliminate the resistance on Mars."

"The resistance?" asked Superior, sounding confused. "Dvexu said he had killed them all, did he not?"

"Not entirely. Dvexu bombed their cities twice, and again today. He arrested and killed many. But the rebels keep coming back. The same thing happened to the previous planet that I worked on. That is why I said it's not the most effective way. Isn't it better if we can avoid violence and killing?"

Superior remained silent.

Icus grew more confident as he spoke. He reiterated a point he had communicated to Superior long ago, but Superior seemed to have conveniently forgotten:

"I prefer penetration instead. We change them by altering their minds. Make them think in the same way as we do, and in the end, turn them into our own."

"Our own…" Superior paused a moment and asked, "Is your technology going to work on the humans? Zullom has expressed doubt on that."

"Yes. I am certain." Icus then explained patiently, "GIIxb Lab has made a major breakthrough, and we've just confirmed developmental milestones. We analyzed data from ongoing experiments, and the results are very encouraging. The technical details are in the Nucleus Transform Report, which I'm submitting to you right now."

Superior stared at him in silence.

Icus had made his arguments before, but not as clear or compelling as today. Recent progress from the Lab was great, which gave him hard evidence to push his idea further.

The council members murmured as they searched the incoming data for Icus's submission. They quickly reviewed it, then debated its likelihood of success.

"Father, please, you know why I've requested the program. You have supported me," Icus carefully reminded him. "Please give me some time to complete it. We have penetrated thirty-five percent of their population on Mars and ten percent on Earth. Within a year, we'll see the results of the transformation on a massive scale. If it doesn't work, I'll be the first one to board the warships to Earth."

Superior thought for a moment and said, "It took you more than three local years. Do you realize it is a *very* long time? It could turn out to be another three years, knowing you…"

"It will not delay this time. I guarantee it with my life," Icus swore.

"I will give you just one more year. You need to take over Earth by that time. If you fail, I do not want to see you again. I have plenty of sons. Your brother Zullom can replace you. This is my final decision," Superior said, and then he ended the connection.

"Yes, Superior."

Icus stood at the same spot, going over the entire conversation in his mind. Minutes later, he walked out of the tower, still preoccupied with his father's words. Slowly, he made his way back to his ship. As he looked at Olympus Mons, the highest mountain in the solar system, he decided to make a stop there before returning to his mansion.

Icus boarded his ship, started the engines, and ascended higher and higher toward the mountaintop. He then landed near the circular surface of the volcano's caldera.

The sunset from that vantage point was breathtaking, with the mountain itself scattering the red light.

Icus stepped out, contemplating the land of red below him. Boundless mountain slopes extended from his feet, stretching out as far as the eye could see. The color was his favorite. The deep orange-red reminded him of the passion of fire.

Far away in the west, strong winds formed vast, swirling whirlpools. The howling sound came rushing in and then faded away. Icus watched the winds shape the sand dunes. "The enormous power of nature, amazing," he murmured to himself.

At that moment, Earth was rising gradually in the sky — the blue planet he knew he was going to conquer.

He was serious when he said the first batch of warships could sail to Earth soon. He looked east toward Haxxilic, where the warships were being built, and almost thought he could hear the low hum of the machines.

Icus never acted without a backup plan. In fact, everything had been well considered. He had already ordered Dvexu to check out the military power and defense layout on Earth. He would lead the attack if the Nucleus Transform proved to be a disappointment, even though he hoped not.

Besides, the report from GIIxb Lab had given him confidence that the transformation would work. He would conquer both Mars and Earth in his own way. It shouldn't be too long before Earth became just another in his collection of planets.

Either way, he would not fail. On this mood-boosting thought, Icus let out a long whistle. The sound was fierce and powerful, and he had the whole universe as his audience.

* * *

Michael didn't speak on his way back to the south, and John just drove in silence. As they entered the Redland streets, they saw many shops had been smashed, and shattered glass was everywhere. A lot of burnt-down houses stood empty, as people had chosen to hide out in the wild, too afraid to go home. Dozens of bodies lay on the ground, and several Rovers were burning. It was a horrible scene.

"John, you know, I shouldn't have gone to the meeting," Michael finally said. "I don't want this job anymore. It's time we should consider finding ourselves a way out."

"This is so bad," John said.

"I feel horrible… Dvexu ordered Dark Spiral to kill. Thousands of people died," said Michael blankly. "Today's death… I'd have made no difference, no difference…"

"Are there going to be more attacks?" John asked carefully.

"Dvexu says yes if there're still protestors."

What Michael didn't know was that the death toll could have been worse if not for the Wake.

Right before the airstrike in Redland, Don and his squad team blended into the protest parade. When Dark Spiral appeared in the distance, Don recognized the imminent danger at once. He directed people to evacuate, and his team members helped many to take cover. Shana came to join them after she sent the mother home.

In fact, Jack had activated the same emergency rescue plan in all human towns, and that helped a lot. Jack assigned the seven squads to protest sites, as well as plazas, town centers, and major roads. After the airstrike, they helped the injured people and carried them to hospitals.

When Don and Shana finished their tasks in the late evening, they were exhausted. On their way back to Base-H,

Don noticed that some people were digging a large pit. Piles of black bags, in the hundreds, lay randomly around. On the bags, Don saw white labels with scribbled writing.

It took him a while to recognize those were names of people on the labels — dead people. So, the pit was… a mass grave, and the bags were body bags.

"This is a lot of death in one day," said Shana, a melancholic sigh escaping her lips. "Each one a life cut short."

"I know," Don said as he took Shana's hand, and they got into the home base with heavy hearts.

By then, a lot of members had returned for the day. All the seven squad leaders and other key members were there, too. Jack turned off the news video stream and looked at all of them.

"We've seen the situation out there," Jack said grimly. "The casualties are immense."

"I've done my best, but still… many people have died today," Don said heavily.

"What happened today was cruel and tragic," said Jack. "But it is *not* different from what had happened before."

"Yeah, the protestors won't get what they want," said Don darkly. "If there's anything we've learned from the past, the NIISS guards do not hesitate to use weapons. Civilians can be attacked in our city and towns."

"Right, in case there are more NIISS attacks tomorrow, our priority is still assisting people in evacuation," Jack continued. "Guide them to safe places, make them aware of the trouble areas. Understood?"

"Yes, Chief!"

"You've done a great job. Let's call it a day. Go and have some rest," said Jack, giving each of them a good pat on the back. Then he added, "Squad team leaders, please stay for a discussion."

While the others were leaving, Jack paced the room slowly, deep in thought. Don had a feeling that he was deciding something significant.

Sure enough, Jack twisted his eyebrows together and began shortly after, “I’m afraid that we’re on the brink of a large-scale war, a war that is inevitable —”

Geoffrey jumped off his chair and interrupted, “Hell, yes! If war is what they want, we are not afraid of fighting.”

Jack gave Geoffrey a solemn look and said, “I knew that’s what you were going to say. Don’t get too excited yet.”

“A war is a matter of life and death. I don’t take it lightly,” Jack then continued. “But if we do nothing, it’ll soon be the end of all of us. So, I want to go on the offensive. I want to wage war.”

“Let’s do it!” Don shouted, looking determinedly at Jack. All the others agreed simultaneously.

“Great,” said Jack decisively. “First, we’ll need strategic plans, and we’ll discuss them starting tonight.”

Chapter 16
The Coming War

Soon, it had been a month since the airstrike, and the NIISS guards cracked down hard on more protests. It was a whole tragic mess everywhere, just like the Red Purge happening again. Gradually, all the protests went quiet.

Don went out to protect people during the daytime, and at night he joined other squad leaders to discuss different strategies and make battle plans.

After weeks of discussion, Jack called them together to review the plans and finalize who would carry them out. Jack didn't forget to invite his old friend Andro, and Don knew Andro would be a great help if he was interested.

The meeting was held in the conference room on a crisp morning. After everyone arrived, Jack began passionately, "In the past few days, we've pooled our ideas and held extensive discussions. Now, here is our final decision — we will coordinate assaults at three Gatti locations within the space of two days..."

Everyone in the room held their breath; Don's heart quickened its beat in excitement.

Jack then brought up a hologram map of Mars and pointed to the three locations: Haxxilic, SIIKwari, and South Pole. "The three places form a triangle on the globe," he said. "Our primary target is inside Haxxilic city, the hub of their arms factories. We've always known that war machinery is built there, and this time, our intel has pinpointed the exact location of a central arsenal. This arsenal, with its vast collection of weapons and military equipment, will be our target, and we're going to destroy it."

"What does their defense look like?" Andro asked.

"That's the key question," Jack replied thoughtfully. "Haxxilic has the toughest defense. If we hit it directly, we'll be met with heavy fire. Not only that, the NIISS guards headquartered in SIIKwari will come to their aid. We could be trapped and attacked from two sides. On the other hand, South Pole, deep in the middle of human settlements, has the weakest defense."

Andro nodded in agreement.

"Brian will try to hack into their network and sabotage their warning system," Jack continued, "but I don't want to rely entirely on that. Therefore, we plan to attack South Pole first, which will create a distraction. We then launch a second diversionary attack on SIIKwari, aiming at the NIISS headquarters. By then, they should be focusing on the trouble we present them. That's when we send our best to Haxxilic."

"Risky, but brilliant." Andro applauded after hearing out the plan.

"Indeed," said Jack. Then he announced, "After lots of heated arguments, we've decided that Don and Sachin will lead the 6th and 7th squads to Haxxilic. Fletcher and I will lead the 1st and 2nd squads to SIIKwari. Geoffrey and Terence will lead the 3rd and 4th squads to South Pole, and the 5th squad will remain at the bases to keep an eye on potential threats."

Jack then looked at Andro hopefully and said, "Andro, you're welcome to participate."

Andro felt his chin and replied, "I'm only here to deliver the finished death bullets." But moments later, he added, "Let me think about it — just don't count on me."

In the meanwhile, Shana decided to check on Nelson and Cohen and see whether they had found a way for Eio to go home. It'd be best for Eio to leave before the outbreak of war.

One morning, she visited their lab while Jack, Don, and the others were in their meetings.

Nelson gave her a warm welcome and said, "Come on in. We've got something to show you." Cohen then led the way towards their main research bay, his eyes sparkling with enthusiasm as he motioned for her to follow.

Upon entering, Shana saw the whole floor was full of specialized tools and gleaming hardware components. Clusters of interfacing computers hummed, and a dense network of wiring snaked across every surface. When she looked up, she almost bumped her head on a sturdy, cuboid frame, and several more identical frames stood arrayed on heavy-duty work platforms across the room.

"What are these?" asked Shana curiously as she took a closer look.

"These will become the hull of our prototype hyper vehicle," Cohen replied proudly. "Eio is supposed to guide them into the 4-D space and assemble them there. I've made them according to his instructions."

"And those will become the heart of the Hyper-V," said Nelson, pointing to some oddly shaped engine parts sitting in the middle of the floor. Each part was made of numerous metal tubes and shone brightly.

"I know this one," said Shana when she recognized the Cube-Energy Exchanger.

"You're right. The C-Cube is already in there," Cohen smiled. "It'll provide the energy needed for the vehicle to operate."

"This is great," Shana exclaimed with joy. "When did you guys build all these? Why didn't you tell me?"

"We've just finished the parts," said Nelson, grinning.

"Right, there was nothing to tell you until now," Eio added.

Shana then looked at Eio and asked a little nervously, "Are you going to fly home in this Hyper-V soon? I'm not ready to say goodbye to you yet."

"We don't even know if it works," Eio replied. "We've struggled, and I had to help Nelson here and there." Then he told Shana briefly about their knowledge implantation experiment.

"You did that? Unbelievable," Shana said. Then she looked at Nelson critically, assessing if he was any different.

"I tell you, it's phenomenal!" Nelson met her gaze and said in excitement. "In the past month, there have been sparks, no, fireworks exploding in my head. I feel activated… unblocked. I can see Eio's world. I feel like one of them!"

"Is Nelson over-stimulated?" Shana asked suspiciously, questioning Eio with her eyes.

"Dunno," Eio mumbled. "Shana, you've come at the right time," he then added quickly, as if trying to redirect her attention from their unauthorized experiment. "Today we're going to test out the vehicle for the first time. Welcome to the big show."

"Oh yeah, let's start now," Cohen said excitedly. "Nelson, you got it?"

"Yes." Nelson took a leaf out of a box and put it down on a workbench. "One leaf from Dr. Yang's greenhouse," he said. "Note that it's fresh and green. Eio, please go ahead."

"Now I'm going to move the parts into 4-D space and see if I can do the assembly there," said Eio.

Shana and the other two stared tensely as Eio began his work. The parts in the room suddenly moved a little. Their shapes also seemed to change a bit. It looked like they were contracting in size, and then they gradually shrank to a point before vanishing completely.

"Eio, how is it going?" asked Nelson moments later. But Eio didn't answer. He had shut his eyes and seemed to put his focus elsewhere. After a while, he shifted out of view altogether.

Shana looked at Nelson and asked uneasily, "Is Eio using his eyes and hands in the 4-D space now?"

"I guess so. We'll wait and see," replied Nelson, turning his head to look at the leaf.

They waited for a long time.

Then it happened in a flash. Before Shana could believe her eyes, something — a point — emerged in front of them in midair. It expanded and grew into a cuboid structure that she could still recognize.

"It's the Hyper-V," Cohen exclaimed.

The vehicle was then suspended above them, and a door on its underside opened. Shana gazed in awe as an unseen force lifted the leaf into the air, pulling it directly toward the open door. Seconds later, the vehicle disappeared together with the leaf, leaving only an empty bench.

"We can specify an object's location, and the Hyper-V can pick it up with pinpoint accuracy," Cohen explained to her.

"Yes!" Nelson shouted. "Eio must have done it. He's going home."

Cohen and Nelson high-fived, then embraced, and they seemed electrified for the following ten minutes.

Before long, something came out of nothing again. The cuboid Hyper-V reappeared, and it dropped the leaf back down to the bench. To their surprise, however, the leaf had turned brown and wilted.

"What the hell?" Cohen cried out. "The leaf should remain green. Is there something wrong with the lifting process?"

Just then, Eio came back into view again and opened his eyes. He went to lie down on the bench, looking exhausted and a little shocked. "The assembly has gone through," he said, casting a dull gaze at the ceiling. "But the leaf was cooked. There are so many errors. Looks like I'm not going home anytime soon."

"What's wrong, Eio?" asked Nelson, looking confused. "Where should we start troubleshooting?"

"I don't know. I need to think," replied Eio in frustration.

Shana said encouragingly, "At least the Hyper-V went somewhere for a little while? You guys are the most brilliant brains. You can figure it out sooner or later."

The guys fell silent at her words, and they just sat there, deep in thought. Then all of them received a message from Jack:

Come join the biggest assembly of the Wake in years!

See you tomorrow at noon.

"Most likely, Jack will give a pep talk for war," said Shana. Nelson looked at the others and said, "Ok, let's keep working until noon tomorrow."

* * *

The next day, before the assembly began, Don and Brian went to look for Shana. Don wanted to let her know that his team was going to Haxxilic. As he rounded a corner and stepped into the hallway, he spotted her in the common area.

From a distance, Don saw her playing a game with Eio, and they were arguing about something. She complained that Eio was a naughty boy and never played fair, and Eio just imitated her and laughed. Somehow their constant babbling made Don smile, and he felt a rare moment of lightness and peacefulness.

When Brian was about to walk over, Don put a hand on his shoulder to stop him. So he and Brian just stood there and watched the two play. At that moment, he truly wished for her a happy life without a single worry.

Don had been fighting for the Wake, for the greater good, and for the future of all — at least he'd like to believe that. He had been fearless and always charging forward, and he hadn't thought about what'd happen if he failed.

But now, the imminent war had given him something to worry about. What if something bad happened to Shana in the battles? What if she was gone forever?

Don became preoccupied with that thought.

Before long, Shana seemed to notice someone there and turned around.

"Hey, Don, Brian," she greeted them with a smile.

Don gave a small nod in response. He tried to find a way to bring up the topic with her, but his mouth had gone dry, and he just swallowed.

"Is something bothering you?" she asked, glancing at Don's face.

"No, nothing," Don replied, trying to sound lighthearted and relaxed. "I'm just thinking… if you and Eio can stay out this time, it'll be the best."

"So, it is decided?" Shana asked anxiously, stepping closer to study his eyes. "I've been living on my nerves for the entire time of the meetings. It's torture not knowing what you're going to do."

"Yes, it's decided that Sachin and I will lead the Haxxilic attack," Don replied as simply as he could.

"Then why can't I go with you? I'm on your team," Shana complained. Her face turned gloomy, and she looked greatly disappointed.

"It's the most dangerous one, and we can't take care of you," Don replied quietly, avoiding her eyes.

"I don't need to be taken care of. I want to fight side by side with you," said Shana, her lower lip quivering, and she seemed really upset. "I knew you were going to say something like that."

"Shana doesn't want to stay at home and do nothing," said Eio supportively. "She hates waiting the most, and I respect her decision."

"Let me help you, no matter how small," Shana then pleaded, her voice barely above a whisper.

"Shana, please…" Don said, and then he noticed the corners of her eyes had turned red. Feeling flustered, he wondered what he should do. Jack would lead the SIIKwari attack, which was a relatively easy mission among the three. So he said, "If you insist, Jack is going to SIIKwari. He could use your help…"

Shana offered no immediate response, her gaze fixed on him. There was a moment of silence.

"Why don't you sit down?" Brian said, bringing Shana a chair. After she sat down, Brian sat by her side and said quietly, "Listen to Don. He has his reasons."

Don tried to find some comforting words to say but failed. He turned to Eio instead and said, "Eio, I'm sorry we haven't found your friends or a way for you to go home. It's best for you to stay safe."

"I know," Eio grunted.

Don then peeked at Shana. She stared back at him and bit her lips. Eventually, she said, "Eio, you stay. I'll go with Jack's team."

"Good, thank you," Don mumbled, feeling greatly relieved. "Let's go to the assembly together."

Soon the home base became crowded. Hundreds of members arrived to join the assembly; some even came a long way from Flat Rock and Crestmont. Andro was there, too. They squeezed into the conference room and stood so tightly that no one could easily move, and there was a murmur of excitement.

When it was time, Jack stepped forward to the center of the room, and everyone fell silent.

"I believe we should strike back," Jack cleared his throat and began his frank, hard-hitting speech.

Immediately, a spark flared among the members.

"We've been challenged by Gattis, the intelligent beings said to be stronger and more advanced than us," Jack continued. "It's a challenge for all mankind. Yet, many still believe their leader Icus's pledge of peace. Since the Alien War, we have become numb. It is widely assumed that after our government's surrender, we can live our lives in the same way as before.

"That assumption proves wrong. Right now, our world faces annihilation. We cannot and must not pretend that things can continue as they are. The Gattis have pushed us into a corner, and now we must choose — we give in, and we die, or we fight, and we may live!"

Many yelled after Jack's words.

"It's now or never!"

"For humanity!"

"I say fight!" Don shouted in high spirits.

Jack then took a flag from Brian, who had been holding it by his side.

"This is our flag of the Wake!" Jack bellowed, raising it high. On the flag, a red *W*, shaped like an eagle, took flight on a blue fabric.

"I'll fight till my last breath. Are you with me?" Jack called.

"Yes! Yes!" The room erupted with answers as loud as a fighter jet's rumbling. "Yes!" Some members slapped the tables; others stomped their feet. Many went wild.

"Now or never!" Terence and Geoffrey yelled.

Jack looked thrilled upon hearing them; his eyes sparkled with enthusiasm. "It's going to be tougher going forward," he said, "but we're more resilient when it's tougher. I don't want to wait until I'm old and grey."

"You're already old and grey," Andro laughed. "But you can surely do serious damage to the NIISS guards. I believe in you."

Lei patted Steve's shoulder and said, "I've wanted to do this since we came back from JIIson."

"Me too," Steve replied. "I was afraid you guys would say it was not the right time yet."

Shana asked Brian, "I didn't know we have a flag. Where did you get it?"

"I designed it and made it just before today's assembly," Brian answered proudly. "Do you like it?"

"Yes, I sure do," Shana replied.

Jack waited a couple minutes for the voices to quiet down and said, "We will go on the offensive, and there will be sacrifices. It's completely voluntary. If you're not ready, you can leave the meeting." He looked around and searched the faces of everyone. Nobody moved. The time had come when enough was enough.

"I want to do this," Don said loudly.

"Great!" Jack exclaimed. "It's been weeks in the planning. We have our primary target and who will lead which attack. *Now* report to your squad leader and submit your name if you want in."

"What do we do?" Nelson looked at Cohen and Yang and then turned to ask Jack. "We don't want to be left out."

"You'll provide your expert opinion," replied Jack, beaming at the scientists. "Brian will stay at the home base to coordinate the three attacks. So, help him make decisions and stay ahead of any problems. We depend on you."

"Eio, you stay with them," Jack added as he winked at Eio. "You can help a lot, too, you know."

After that, the Wake members split into three groups in separate rooms. Many surrounded their squad leaders to put down their names. Dimitri from the 5th squad made a request to switch tasks to the Haxxilic team.

Half an hour later, Don and 6th squad leader Sachin started a headcount. "Lei, Steve, Jayden, Thomas, Dimitri…"

When finished, Don said, "I'm grateful to get lots of names here. We have people from the 6th and 7th squads plus Dimitri. He has asked to join as well."

"Now, everyone, please take your seats," Sachin said, beaming. "Let's hear Don present the details of the battle plan."

Just then, Andro came into the room and tapped on Eio's shoulder. "Hey," Andro said, smiling. "I heard you were quite helpful in the TTado Bridge rescue."

"I certainly was," replied Eio, crossing his arms in a smug gesture.

"Mind if I sit here?" asked Andro, and he sat down beside Eio in the back row.

Don began to speak after everyone settled in. Although Andro sat casually, with his hands behind his head and legs on the table, he had a look of interest on his face, and his eyes were fixed on Don as he talked.

At the end of the presentation, Brian walked over to Andro and offered him a Senset once again. "Take one, just in case," said Brian.

"All right." Andro didn't refuse this time.

Don saw that. He looked toward Andro and asked, "Are you joining us? I know you never like to be an official member of the Wake, but you're most welcome."

"Break my neck? No, thanks," replied Andro, lowering his legs to stand up. "I intend to live a long, healthy life and enjoy the beauty of the universe. I'm just checking out how much mess you're going to make."

"Fine, suit yourself," said Don.

Andro thought for a moment and added, "I can consider hosting a celebration party for you when you come back."

"I look forward to that," Don replied with a smile. Andro had been a free spirit. It'd be nice to keep it that way.

"Good luck," Andro said. "I'm gonna say hi to Shana before I head out."

Shana was studying the map of SIIKwari when Andro stopped by. "How have you been?" he asked.

"I'm doing well. Thank you." She nodded slightly.

"I heard you joined Jack's team," Andro said, a faint worry clouding his eyes.

"Yeah, Don wants me there," Shana replied with a bitter smile. Just then, she noticed Andro was wearing a necklace. "Hey, is that new? I haven't seen it before."

"Yep, it's a special gift," Andro replied brightly, lowering his head to appreciate its unusual style.

Shana's eyes widened in surprise, then she smiled. "Oh…" she said, casting him a meaningful look. "Do tell."

Surprisingly, Andro lowered his eyes, shying away from her direct gaze, and hesitated.

"It isn't like you," Shana commented. "You've always been open about your romance and adventure."

"I'll tell you when it's time," he replied with a grin.

"Ok…" she said, still looking at him curiously.

"Take care, Shana," Andro said as he leaned close and held her shoulders gently. "Don't get hurt. I can't bear to think of that. See you next time."

"See you." Shana waved, and then Andro left swiftly.

The assembly ended in the late afternoon. Most members had got their tasks and left for the day. Shana stayed behind to clean up after the meeting. She stacked the chairs neatly, wiped down the tables, and swept the floor clean.

When she opened the door to check whether the security system was properly engaged, she was surprised to see Dimitri standing out there in the rays of the setting sun. He gazed into the distance, frowning slightly, absorbed in thought.

The moment he saw her, he turned and walked straight toward her. Then he took a deep breath and looked into her eyes a bit nervously.

What was going on? Shana wondered. He had been confident and active just now in the meeting.

“Hey, Dimitri, how is it going? Can I help you with anything?” she asked softly, searching his face for clues.

“Shana, the Haxxilic mission is extremely difficult. Please don’t go,” he said earnestly.

“Don’t worry. My name is not on Don’s list.”

“Not on the list?” Dimitri repeated, looking quite confused. “So, you’re not going with Don’s team?”

“No. He doesn’t want me to risk my life,” she replied simply. “Don’t you guys want the same thing from me?”

Dimitri’s mouth fell open, and his eyes grew wide with surprise, but he became relaxed moments later. “So, Don has talked to you,” he said, “I see… that’s actually great.”

Yet in the next second, he dropped his jaw when Shana said, “I’m going with Jack instead.”

“No, Shana,” he pleaded at once, “please don’t join any missions. It’s too dangerous. It’s a man’s job. I know you’ve trained with Jack, but the chance that you can come back safely is slim.”

“Don said the same thing,” replied Shana curtly, feeling impatient. “I really don’t want to hear that again. Isn’t it everyone’s duty? Besides, it’s not the first time I’ve gone out with you guys.”

“This time, it’s war. I can’t — I can’t risk losing you,” said Dimitri, his words tumbling out in a rush and his voice growing increasingly emotional.

“Don’t try to talk me out of this,” said Shana with determination. “I want to help. This’s something I want to do. We’ve put fear behind us since we swore to join the Wake, haven’t we?”

“I know you’ve made up your mind.” He inhaled deeply and then let out a sigh. “But do you know I just switched to Don’s team because I thought you would be there? I want to protect you, Shana… I lo… I like you.”

It sounded like he was going to use the word love but chickened out. Shana suddenly understood. However, she just thought of him as an old friend. She looked at him hesitantly, wondering how she could politely refuse.

Dimitri then went on hastily, as if worrying that she might interrupt, and he wouldn't get to finish, "Shana, you're so beautiful and so kind. I've liked you longer than I knew. Remember you used to walk by my place on your way to school? I'd wait faithfully by the window at eight every morning, and then I just walked behind you. Seeing you would make my day. Once, I went to your clinic just to get a shot so that I could talk to you —"

"You did?" said Shana, recalling vaguely. "I remember…"

His face lit up when she said she remembered.

"You don't have to go to war, Shana," Dimitri continued, looking at her face. "We can leave and have a normal life like other people. I can make you happy."

"Thank you, Dimitri…" Shana paused a little and said, "but —"

"You don't have to answer me right now," Dimitri said, quickly stopping her from finishing, as though he'd still have a chance, as long as she didn't say it out loud. "I know what your thank you means, but I'm willing to wait."

"If you choose to stay in the Wake, I'll be there for you. At least let me go with you to SIIKwari," he continued. "Please."

"Dimitri," Shana said, feeling increasingly uneasy, "since you've already signed up for Haxxilic, can you stick to it?"

Then she realized Don might lose people because of her, so she added anxiously, "Don needs you more than I do. And… and we cannot succeed without you…"

"So, it's about him, right?" Suddenly Dimitri questioned hotly, his voice tinged with frustration and jealousy. He stared into her eyes for a while, and then he exhaled and said, "Alright, if that's what you want…"

Shana avoided his gaze, feeling embarrassed.

"May I?" Unexpectedly, Dimitri drew near, his face inches from hers, and it looked like he was about to kiss her on the forehead.

Shana was a little shocked. Her instincts took over, and she stepped back.

Dimitri ended up only placed his hand behind her head and gently touched her hair. Then he took a deep breath and looked away awkwardly.

"Just think about it, Shana. After all this, leave with me. I'll give you a better life." At these words, he turned away and left.

Shana watched him go, different thoughts crossing her mind like waves. She knew she couldn't reciprocate his feelings. But at least he had the courage… She wished she had the same courage to express her love for Don.

* * *

The preparation for the battles began early in month twenty-four, the last month of the Martian year. All squad leaders and their teams started to tally their weapon inventory and check their supplies. Geoffrey and Terence geared up for South Pole, and Jack joined their first team meeting one night.

"Your target is the South Pole Water Treatment Facility," Jack told them. "It belonged to us. Humans built this plant years ago, but the Gattis took it from us during the Alien War. The South Pole ice cap is a critical resource, providing everyday water usage for the southern hemisphere. Many of our towns depend on it, but it's currently under the Gatti's control. We'll try to take it back, even just for a brief while."

"That'll be great. I can't wait to see their faces when we take it," Wei from Terence's team yelled.

"I have no doubt it'll be a huge boost to our morale. But remember the purpose of this is to create a distraction for our main mission," Jack emphasized.

"Their air defense is tight," said Geoffrey, who had done his research. "It's impossible for us to attack from the air without heavy casualties. But they won't expect us to come from underwater, because it's frozen most of the time."

"We swim in?" Wei asked in surprise. His black eyes widened, and his eyebrows shot up.

"Yes. It's mid-summer in the south," Terence explained as he pointed to a hologram map and drew a circle on it, "within this circle, midnight sun occurs — the sun stays above the horizon for a whole day, like polar days on Earth.

"It's been the warmest summer in recent years. Parts of the ice have receded, and water passages have formed around the facility —"

"The perfect timing for us," Jack interjected. "And the water passages are where we'll go in."

Geoffrey and Terence nodded in confirmation. A buzz of anticipation rippled through the team members.

Geoffrey then brought up another map and said, "This's the layout of the facility before the Gattis took it over. Brian hacked into our old government system a week ago and found it for us. It could be a bit out of date, but I believe the Gattis have kept its main structures."

All the team members then took a good look at the map.

The facility was on top of the permanent ice cap. Around it, there were twelve water intake pipes, spreading out in all directions. Then, the intake pipes merged into six tunnels. These tunnels went up to the top, and they were connected to pump stations that kept water coming in.

"Clear enough," said Jack.

"Water from the ice melt is then pumped into this pretreatment sedimentation reservoir," Geoffrey added, pointing to the map. "After that, these are the main water treatment filters, and these are the storage places for fresh, clean water."

"Look here," Terence went on after Geoffrey, "our exit points are close to the end of the tunnels, before the pump stations. The lids designed for maintenance can be opened from the inside.

"Two NIISS teams are guarding the facility. Their two barracks are on each side of the oval storage cylinders, here and here. Their cruise ships are next to the east barrack. Our goal is to take out the NIISS ships and barracks and avoid damaging the facility."

"That's a good plan," Jack concluded enthusiastically.

"Four of us will spearhead our mission," said Terence. "Other than Geoffrey and me, we need two more people who can swim and have good stamina. The remaining members will join the backup team, ready to land once we've weakened their defenses."

Jack looked at all the team members solemnly and said, "It's dangerous, even deadly, and you may not come home. But if any of you want to have some fun swimming, let me know."

Immediately, more than a dozen members raised their hands. "I want to do it," said Wei eagerly.

Geoffrey and Terence looked at their qualifications carefully and then chose Ethan and Wei from the 3rd and 4th squads.

"Jack, what do you think?" asked Terence. "Ethan and Wei are young and tough, and they've proven themselves in previous missions."

"I have a good feeling about them," Jack replied. "Terence, I know you and Geoffrey are veterans with good judgment. Ethan and Wei can be your strong support. I can trust the four of you. This is it."

So it was decided.

Geoffrey looked at Ethan and Wei seriously and said, "The first battle is critical. We must succeed. And you'll need training. Are you ready?"

"Hell yes, I've been waiting for this moment all my life," said Terence excitedly.

"Not asking you," Geoffrey chuckled. "You know who I'm talking to."

"I'm more than ready," Wei replied without the slightest hesitation. Ethan nodded.

Jack beamed at them and said, "Your bravery has always moved me. I'm grateful that I never have to fight alone. Let's begin."

"Sure. To go into the water passages, we'll dive," said Terence, starting to talk about the basics and risks of scuba diving since he was an expert in that field.

"Unfortunately, we don't have a large body of ice water to train with, but Brian has designed a simulator that provides a realistic imitation of the South Pole environment," Terence continued, handing each of them a device. "Wear it, and you'll feel like you're in water. Try to swim towards your target. This is how we'll practice in the coming weeks."

While the four were doing their ice diving lessons, Jack and Don helped them to get their equipment ready. They shipped their stuff to Black Mountain, a mining town with a small human population. Base-7, the southernmost outpost of the Wake, was located there.

Weeks later, Jack and Don got together with the team of four in the meeting room of Base-7. The room was filled with ice-diving equipment, and everything was well organized. Don showed them the impressive array of gear and supplies they had obtained:

Underwater propellers, micro inertial navigation systems, full-face masks, and underwater ultrasonic communication were neatly laid out. Also included were scuba air cylinders — one primary and one secondary for each of them — along with regulators and gauges. To their right, they had cube-operated thermo dry suits, stabilizer jackets BCD, harnesses, fins, and headlights. To their left, they had explosives, plus something special from Brian — a tiny interfacing computer to Gatti's devices.

"Look at all the professional gear," Geoffrey exclaimed. "Navigation, comms, and high-pressure air supply, not something you can easily find on Mars."

"You're damn right," Terence smiled. "Navigation system is from Cohen. Many others are from my own collection. I've triple-checked the equipment and made sure all of us know how to use it."

"Most of the time, we won't need to deep dive," Terence then reminded them. "Just remember to breathe continuously, use gas management skills and buoyancy control skills."

"Got it," said Ethan.

Geoffrey then said, "Jack has gone through the details with each of us twice already. I trust you know what to do even in your sleep, correct?"

"Yes, sir! First, we get into the water passages, and then, we swim in from the intake pipes," Wei replied as he highlighted the key points.

"Then we blow them up, and we are done." Ethan summed it up well enough.

"Great," said Geoffrey.

Jack added, "The backup team will stand by at the shore. They'll come to take over the facility if you succeed, or come to save your asses if you run into trouble."

"Understood!"

"Perfect. Stay alive," said Jack as he put a hand on each of their shoulders. "Geoffrey, Terence, in an emergency, act as you see fit. No need to wait for me."

After that, Jack thanked Don for helping out. "Don, this is where you and I part then," he said thoughtfully. "Each of us has some final preparations to do for SIIKwari and Haxxilic. Your mission is the most dangerous, but I know you can do it."

"Thank you for trusting me," Don replied seriously.

"Of course. You have perfect aim and always carry out our plans flawlessly," Jack said as he looked at Don with encouraging eyes. "I trust you'll live up to my expectations, and I wish you great success."

Don stood straight and swore, "I will do my utmost, Chief."

Chapter 17
The Tri-Battle: South Pole

Mars Year thirteen, month one, day two

"Today is the day the battles begin," said Terence. "We leave B-7 now."

With that, the group of four men got ready for their extraordinary mission in the early morning chill of Black Mountain. They were going to dive and swim through ice water to the pole. The distance would be over a hundred kilometers, and they estimated they would need hours of swimming to get to the Water Treatment Facility.

"How do you feel?" Geoffrey asked Terence as the four of them loaded their Rover with equipment and supplies.

"Excellent," said Terence. "You know, once I swam across the English Channel and broke the world record at that time. This should be easy for me. We'll bring good news to Jack."

"I'm feeling fantastic," Ethan said.

"Same here," Wei chimed in.

The rising sun cast a soft glow over their confident faces. Terence grinned as he looked toward the horizon.

Soon they drove out of the base and headed south. There were few inhabitants along the way. The air grew colder and colder, and a thin layer of snow began to coat the red dust and sand. Four hours later, they arrived at the water's edge of the South Pole. Icebergs stretched out before them, imposing and grand.

Ethan checked the coordinates and said, "Destination confirmed. Here we are!"

It was mid-summer, but the air was freezing. Geoffrey found a nice flat surface, a backlit spot under a small hill, and parked their Rover there, taking shelter from the cold wind.

Then they dragged their heavy equipment out of the Rover. Terence said, "Did you know, before the Gatti's planet transformation, every inch of this place was perma frozen? The permanent ice cap has become smaller since Mars got warmer."

"I know. The dry ice has all sublimed," Ethan replied. "I've done my research too. That's more than ten Mars Years ago."

"Good for you," Terence smiled.

None of them had traveled to this far end of the planet before. They went to the waterfront and stood mere feet away, gazing at the boundless expanse of water. The streams from the ice melt were as calm as a mirror. They knew millions of lives depended on this water.

"I've never appreciated the volume of water this much," said Wei. "I was born on Mars, and I'm used to bottled water and algae ponds."

"Yep. Even our recent training was done virtually," said Terence. "I'm excited to have something this magnificent to test myself in."

"This is bigger than I thought. I was thinking more of a lake," said Ethan, "and the scenery is so unexpectedly beautiful."

"Yeah. It's fascinating," Geoffrey replied. "We should come camping here next time. No mission involved."

"I'd love that, camping." Ethan and Wei exchanged a smile.

"Totally agree. We should name this place," said Terence. "How about White Sea for the water in front of us and Red Sand Beach for where we stand?"

"This isn't a sea," Wei argued.

"Well, it's big enough for me."

"Fine."

"Nice name."

They all agreed quickly. None of them was the rhetorical type anyway.

Terence then went out scouting. He saw spotless snow scattered on the reddish open land. Near the shore, small ice cubes glittered like crystals, while further out, colossal white icebergs, tinged with a faint blue, were bathed in the sunlight. Each iceberg took a unique shape; many looked like they had been carved by a master sculptor, with sharp angles and smooth curves, and the expanse of ice and water stretched limitlessly into the horizon.

Gazing out at the sea, Terence was struck by its immense and awe-inspiring scale. He stood there for a time, absorbing the stark beauty of the frozen landscape, before he went back to the others.

"All I can find are some things like lichens, moss, and algae," he said. "No bushes, no animals, and no enemies."

"Good to know," said Geoffrey. "Ethan and Wei have set up a tent. Come sit down and have lunch. Let's eat, rest for an hour and then begin. Nutrition Mix tastes bad, but it's good for your strength."

Upon hearing the Mix, Terence let out a disappointed groan.

"The Mix again?" said Ethan.

"On top of that, Shana has sent some beef jerky for us," Geoffrey added quickly.

"Really?" Terence's mood improved instantly.

"This is a feast," said Ethan excitedly, his eyes bright and shining.

"Indeed, imported from Earth," said Geoffrey. "Dig in."

"Taste of home. I'm moved to tears," Terence exclaimed. He took a large piece and a big bite, grinning.

They shared and chewed the beef jerky, and then each of them drank up three bags of the Mix.

After that, Terence took out four water bottles and passed them on.

"Here, drink," he said as he opened and drank from the bottle.

Ethan passed the water to Wei and then to Geoffrey.

"Tastes good," said Geoffrey after he took a gulp. "To freedom!"

All four of them cheered as they drank it off.

When lunch was done, Geoffrey brought up the hologram map again.

"Let's review our paths," he said. "Our scientists have studied the topography as well as the depths and currents of the water passages. They identify these possible channels to get close. Among them, the ones in front of us are the most practical according to recent satellite data, because less ice may block the way."

Geoffrey highlighted the paths and said, "We'll start together and then split into two groups at this point here. Then we go on two separate routes so that we'll end up in two different water intake pipes, lowering the risks."

"Ethan, you're coming with me." Geoffrey looked toward Ethan, who nodded.

"As planned."

"We're going to take Route A. It's a bit longer than Route B through the dotted line over here," said Geoffrey, pointing to the map. "And we'll come out of the tunnel farther away from the barracks. It'll be safer, and we're less likely to get detected."

"Terence, you're going with Wei." Geoffrey then looked toward Terence and double-checked with him.

"Yes, I am. But I could even go by myself," said Terence casually. He peeked at Wei while crossing his arms over his chest. "Just don't slow me down."

Geoffrey then continued, "Great. You two will take Route B. It's shorter and faster. The two of you can carry half the explosives. If we don't lose them all on the way, each of us will have enough for the barracks and cruise ships.

"When we're close to the facility, we'll get into the water intake pipes, swim up the tunnels, and come out before the pump stations. The NIISS guards will have a big surprise from us in their sleep."

Geoffrey went through the use of equipment and weapons again as he ran his fingers down the prep list. “And the last one, how do you feel about the weather, Terence?” he asked.

Terence looked out toward the desolate and vastly wild place.

When they first arrived, there was only a light wind, and the reflection of the icebergs stood quietly in the water. But just an hour later, their tent was fluttering in the howling wind.

Terence knew the weather at South Pole changed rapidly, and it was hard to predict. The forecast said the wind would be 15 km/h when they set out, and the light wind would last until the next afternoon, which should be suitable for them.

However, the wind speed had already picked up and become a headwind for them. It might pose a problem.

Still, Terence felt rather calm. He said, “Not my favorite weather for swimming, but hey, I used to train for the Olympics — men’s marathon 10 km swimming. This is a piece of cake to me.”

“That was years ago,” Geoffrey reminded him instantly. “And now you’re, what? Close to fifty? Besides, you didn’t even win a medal.”

Ethan and Wei turned to look at Terence with curious eyes.

Terence didn’t know Geoffrey remembered his story so well. He shifted a little in his spot, feeling slightly embarrassed. “I would’ve gotten a medal if I could’ve participated in the game one more time,” he replied a moment later. “I was only a fraction of a second behind, and I wasn’t feeling my best that day. Wait until I tell you about my last swim after this mission. Fifteen hours of unassisted swimming was just a warm-up for me.”

“Mind you, we’re going to bring a lot of weight in freezing temperature,” said Geoffrey. “I like to be careful.”

“Could be a problem for you, but not gonna stop me,” Terence replied. He was ready for his life’s biggest challenge, and he felt a fire had lit up in his heart again.

It was time for them to act then. After one hour of rest and observation, Geoffrey gave the go to head out in the afternoon.

As they dressed up and packed their gear, 75 km/h gusts of wind raged.

"There will be no better time," said Terence determinedly. "We can't wait for the wind to stop. Besides, it may not matter that much once we submerge."

After they suited up, they gave each other a hug and then walked into the water.

They walked against the icy wind for more than twenty minutes. The water got deeper gradually, and blocks of floating ice clogged the surface.

"Now we dive," said Terence. With a splash, he charged forward and led the way.

Wei struggled a bit with his propeller and buoyancy at first but soon kept up.

"Call me if anything happens. Otherwise, save your breath, and your air will last longer," Terence said. He tested his underwater comm link to the others, especially his buddy Wei.

"Roger," Wei confirmed. "You've taught me well."

As they embarked on the treacherous journey, Terence used the inertial navigation system to keep track of their speed and heading. After swimming thirty kilometers, they reached the point where they were to diverge.

Geoffrey directed, "Gentlemen, we split up here and swim the rest of our way in two groups. Let's show our strength today."

"Stay alive," Terence said. "Stay tuned." After that, he and Wei disappeared underwater.

Geoffrey and Ethan took their route. However, they were met with strong katabatic winds right away. The wind was blowing persistently against them, and it had gone from 75 km/h on Red Sand Beach to 100 km/h further into the route. The wind generated rapid surface currents, and their path was filled with ice blocks that were pushed out with the water.

If it went on like that, they would be delayed by wind-driven currents and pack ice coming their way.

"I'm a little worried," said Geoffrey.

Indeed, things didn't go so well. An hour later, when they checked their location again, they hadn't moved as far as planned.

"I wonder if we need to send Terence an update," Geoffrey told Ethan, "Terence must be out of range for our underwater comm now, and I'll have to surface to use Senset, since radio waves do not travel well through water."

Ethan became anxious. "What do we do now?" he asked.

"Let's go deeper to avoid the ice," Geoffrey replied as he dived. "Keep moving, and we'll see how it goes."

Ethan nodded and followed closely behind. However, he cramped suddenly; his muscles clenched. Ethan panicked and gasped for air.

"Geoffrey," he cried out. "I've got cramps in my legs!"

Geoffrey turned around and swam back to Ethan's side as fast as he could and halted their propellers.

"Keep breathing. Just breathe!" Geoffrey held onto his shoulders and yelled. Ethan grimaced in agony, struggling to stretch his legs as they twitched uncontrollably.

Moments later, Ethan calmed down a little, but his first stage regulator got frozen just then. "I've got a free flow!" he called out nervously.

Geoffrey had sharp eyes and swift hands. He noticed it soon enough and shouted, "Let me try shutting it off and see if I can switch to a spare." He fumbled with the handwheel on the cylinder, but it was so stuck that he couldn't turn it off.

"Dang it!" Geoffrey cursed.

The two of them had no other choice but to surface and climb onto an ice floe. Ethan was still trembling slightly after serious distress.

"I'm sorry. I don't know why I got cramps," Ethan cried, his face strained. "I took Ox-100 long ago, you know, the oxygen-carrying organelle, and I should have more energy than average guys. I'm so sorry."

"Hey, it's not your fault," Geoffrey said. "Maybe you're just tired. Fatigue can do real damage."

"Why did my regulator freeze? I believe Terence said all the equipment is cold-water rated?" Ethan still couldn't understand.

"Yes. Terence did say that, and we've taken extra precautions," replied Geoffrey. "But you breathed heavily just a moment ago. I guess the flow rate increased, and the malfunction happened because of that."

Geoffrey then sent Terence and the backup team a brief message about what happened. "Ethan, I've asked for someone to come pick you up," he said.

"Is that necessary?" Ethan argued. "Just give me some time. I can recover. My secondary cylinder still has enough air."

"No. I don't think so. I'll go on myself once you're safe," Geoffrey insisted. "Don't worry. The rest of us can get the job done."

* * *

Terence and Wei swam silently, navigating into an area with lots of icebergs. Their inertial navigation system indicated they had roughly an hour left until their destination. They had no idea what had happened to the other two. The message wouldn't reach them until they surfaced and turned on their Sensets.

Terence just focused on finding his way through those icebergs and kept moving. Visibility near the icebergs was very poor. The ice-melting process generated many bubbles. He couldn't see clearly, even in the midnight sun, with his headlight on.

To him, the real danger was the turning icebergs in summer. The undersides of the icebergs were constantly eroded by water. They could turn upside down violently and then turn again when the balance was lost. This cycle would go on until the icebergs completely melted.

He needed to be extra careful when approaching those icebergs. It was like walking under a building that was collapsing.

"Slow down and stay close," Terence told Wei.

"Roger," Wei replied, "I'm watching your movements so I know what to do next."

Suddenly, Terence noticed a sound. It was a short, brittle fracturing sound emitted by a nearby iceberg that was dissolving. Just when he was going to issue a warning, he heard Wei yelling from behind.

"Oh! No!"

A massive iceberg behind them was turning over. Terence felt a powerful downward swirl pulling him in, and he quickly swam away out of reflex.

When he looked back, the iceberg's underside was flipping. It was slow but horrible. Wei couldn't escape in time; he was thrown off balance, tossed around, and dragged down.

Terence heard him scream anxiously, "Run for yourself! Run!"

Just then, another huge wave hit Wei, and he vanished from sight.

As soon as the wave subsided, Terence swam back desperately, but the area was empty.

"Wei, come in. Wei!"

There was no answer. Terence swam as fast as he could, circling the area twice, but found no trace of him. Wei might have been swept far away.

"No, no, this didn't just happen," Terence muttered, a surge of anger rising within him. He hated himself for not being able to do anything. He just watched Wei disappear.

Terence kept calling and searching, and he waited for a long while, but there was still no answer. Somehow in his heart, he believed Wei was still alive. But he couldn't use the life sign tracker to locate him since radio signals didn't work well underwater.

Terence had to surface to deliver the bad news to Geoffrey and request help from the backup team to search. Just then, he received the incoming message from Geoffrey:

"There was an accident. Ethan got injured, and I'll continue once Ethan is picked up. How is it going on your side?"

"This is very helpful," Terence murmured.

"I must keep calm and carry on," he told himself. So, after he spoke with the backup team, he turned forward and swam toward their destination.

In silence, Terence swam for another hour. When he checked the navigation system again, he had arrived.

He should be able to see the water intake pipe now, but he was met with solid ice walls. He swam around, yet there was still no pipe opening.

Feeling confused, Terence slowed down and surfaced again. Turning on his Senset, he used radio signals to correct the inertial navigation system for his location. Still, he got the same result.

"I wonder why? I need to get Brian," he said to himself.

Terence called Brian, who had been on standby since the beginning of the mission. "All I see are solid ice walls. Where is the water intake pipe?" Terence asked. "Any error in the facility layout?"

Brian responded at once, "I've checked your location. You should have arrived at the right place. But you don't see an intake pipe? Can you try going deeper? I'll talk to the others and see what may be wrong."

"Again, very helpful," Terence grumbled, letting out a sigh. His first air cylinder was used up, and he took it off. He decided not to wait. He was already behind schedule. It was almost 10 PM, and they were supposed to get to the facility an hour ago.

For the next hour, Terence searched for the pipe in vain. He swam back and forth and also explored various depths. There seemed to be nothing else but ice walls within the five-kilometer radius he covered.

He felt tired and worried; his mind was grasped by the endless cold and silence around him. Although he was wearing the thermo dry suit, the chill kept deepening.

No, he needed to rest a bit to concentrate, he decided.

He ascended to the surface again and hung onto an ice floe. There was no new message from Brian, so he just stared at the facility layout and tried to think.

Nothing came to his mind.

The sun was lying at a low angle to the surface at the moment, and Terence just gazed at the ice cap. It looked so close to him, but how could he find the pipe that went up there?

Droplets from slowly melting icebergs continued to fall from the top into the water. Drip, drip, drip, that was the only sound that reminded him time was flowing. Right in front of him, steep ice walls were hundreds of meters high, full of blue cracks, and they were like frozen castles towering above him.

"It's all me now. I'm the last man standing. I cannot fail," Terence thought out loud. He was always eager to excel. Returning empty-handed was simply unacceptable to him.

"This is the final swim." At these words, his strength was replenished, and he jumped back into the water.

After Terence cleared his mind, a vague but continuous rumbling sound came to his attention. He stopped and listened, forcing his ears to notice anything unusual. Something was going on ahead of him, and the closer he swam, the louder the rumbling sound became. It must lead somewhere. This thought gave his limbs a boost.

Faster! He told himself.

An idea popped into his mind. It could be the sound of water flowing into an intake pipe. He could be close.

To his delight, indeed, he found a hole in the ice wall. There was no other way, so he pushed against the surrounding ice to widen the narrow opening, and then he squeezed into the hole carefully, minding those ice bumps above him. He gave the top of the hole a little push, it felt stable enough, and he dared to move inside a bit more.

On the floor, he found something half buried in ice. It felt warm.

A heater.

Suddenly, Terence understood. The heater must be used to keep water liquid and flowing, especially during winter times. The heater was the reason that the hole had formed through the ice walls.

So, he was observant, and he was right. The back of the ice hole was connected to the intake pipe. Brian couldn't have foreseen this — the mouth of the pipe had been covered by ice walls, only leaving a hole outside. Hard to blame him.

In ecstasy, Terence went out and sent Brian and Geoffrey a short message to explain the situation. "Geoffrey, in case you run into the same problem…" he said. "Now you'll see from a world champion how it's done."

Then Terence went back into the hole. Upon entering the pipe, he sped up. Soon he reached a larger rising tunnel with water rushing in.

"Here I am! In I go!" Terence shot up like a black carp riding a wave. His heart beat faster as he got closer. He was not too late after all.

The last part of the tunnel was level, and Terence knew he must have gotten onto the top of the ice cap. Water was rushing through him to the pump station, and it was totally dark inside.

"Ok, Ok." He turned his headlight to the max and searched for the lid that opened to the outside. It should be right on the ceiling of the tunnel.

He found it. But he couldn't push it open, no matter how much strength he used.

In his frustration, he pushed it again and again, but nothing happened.

"To hell with this."

What should he do? Turn back and exit the tunnel? He simply would not accept that.

"No. I'm not coming this far for nothing. Come on!" Terence told his weakening arms to do one more push.

The lid didn't move.

After a while, Terence stood there alone and almost cried.

Then he heard somebody calling his name. It sounded noisy and far away. Was he hallucinating? Minutes later, he felt something touch his shoulder, and that almost freaked him out. He gave a sudden jerk of his head and made out the outline of a person.

It was Wei! Terence couldn't believe his eyes. But it was him.

"Aren't you a dead man?" said Terence.

Wei gave him a tight hug and told him eagerly, "A swirl pulled me in, and I collided with an iceberg. I became unconscious for a while but woke up before my air ran out. Luckily my propeller was still tethered to me. So I got to the surface, and Brian told me where to find you."

"I'm so glad you're Ok. Why didn't you call me earlier?"

"I did, but I guess I was out of range with the ultrasonic comm. And then there's a lot of noise here."

"You've saved the day, man. You've saved the day." cried Terence. "Now help me get us out."

They then pushed the lid together with all their strength, and it moved. They climbed out quickly.

"At last!" said Wei.

"We don't have much time, and it's just the two of us," Terence said. "You go straight to the east barrack and cruise ships to set up your bombs. Ping me when you're done."

"Yes, sir!"

"I'll go to the control room first before I go to the west barrack."

"The important task you need to do for Brian?" asked Wei.

"Yes, I need to plug in the interfacing computer Brian gave me. Let's go." Then they split up and got to work.

Terence hurried toward the control room, scanning the surroundings as he approached. Luckily, no Gattis were found there. He quickly disabled the surveillance before entering. No one was inside, either. All the machines were humming, their indicator lights flashing occasionally to signal normal status. Everything seemed to be fully automated.

"Hey, dude. Tell me where to plug in your device," Terence called Brian over video stream. "I'm showing you a panorama view right now. Your stuff better work — because it almost cost four lives to get here."

On the other side, Brian, Eio, and the scientists all sat in front of computer screens. They waved their hands frantically and cheered, looking exhilarated to see that he had gotten in.

“Great! I can see it,” Brian exclaimed, staring hard at the stacked-up equipment and controllers in the video.

Terence showed Brian all the machines in the room. Most appeared to come from the original human design except for one central piece, which seemed to be a Gatti addition.

“Go to the middle section — yes, yes, that Gatti thing, the water tank —” said Brian. “Please put me closer.”

“Ok.”

Terence stood over the water tank and saw an irregularly shaped grey panel and its wiring submerged in the water. The whole thing was like a coral reef in an aquarium, and the tank was connected to the sedimentation reservoir outside by several tubes.

Terence looked closer at the grey panel. It was made of some dull-looking Gatti material. The surface was porous and rough to the touch. But it was weird that there were no visible buttons or switches.

It had to be the control device, he thought. Because it was the only thing that the Gattis had added on top of the human machinery, and it was like none other.

“Is this the Gatti system you’re looking for?” Terence called again. “I don’t see any ports you can interface with.”

“Weird. I can see movements — tiny air bubbles coming out of the panel in the tank…” Brian replied. “It seems to be a live thing. Terence, do you think you have five minutes? I need to ask Yang.” Immediately Brian turned to talk to Yang next to him.

“Hurry up! Damn it. I may not have five minutes,” Terence said as he glanced at the door vigilantly and listened to any sound outside.

“Is this thing alive?” asked Brian.

Yang studied what he saw carefully and said, “I think you’re right. It looks like live material.”

“Perhaps a hybrid of living organisms and a chip — something that can interact with the environment and give responses,” Yang added quickly as he continued his thought process. “I tend to think of it as a smart self-regulated system, automated by the living organisms themselves…

"We can achieve something like this if we integrate our biosensors and a computer chip —"

Brian interrupted him anxiously, "We're running out of time. Give me an idea how to crack it!"

"Come on! Apply your ten thousand IQ. The two of you!" Terence urged.

"The first step of the water treatment must be toxin detection," Yang reasoned. "Although snow is made of fresh water, it'll contain some pollutants from the air or ground, and the melted ice water can pick up toxic chemicals from Martian soil…"

"So? Tick tock, tick tock, think, think, think!" Terence said.

"Therefore, the living organisms may be detecting toxins in the water," said Yang, pulling his hair, thinking hard. "And then the system will process that information and decide how to remove the toxins dynamically… We can try to overload the system…"

Suddenly, Yang exclaimed, "Tell me if there're calibration solutions nearby. Look for test tubes around you."

Terence turned around and indeed saw a row of tubes labeled with different names of chemical solutions. He showed Yang the labels one by one.

"Take the one labeled PCLT and dump it into the tank!" said Yang. "We don't have time to try all the chemicals. Just take that one. If I can only place one bet, that's it."

Terence quickly emptied the whole tube of PCLT into the tank.

"PCLT is a toxic chemical harmful to almost all life," Yang explained while all of them watched for any changes. "So there must be a function in the system to detect its concentration."

A minute later, bubbles rose to the tank's surface, and a layer of white foam was spreading. The foam carried small, yellowish flecks; some organisms seemed to have perished.

The control circuit must have been disconnected somewhere. Because at the same time, a monitor flashed a warning in Gattish:

"PCLT out of range…

"PCLT out of range…

"Request for manual adjustment…"

To Terence's surprise, the grey panel rose completely out of the tank for investigation, revealing a hidden hardware interface.

The overloading had worked!

"You just found a backdoor into the Gatti system," said Brian; his jaw dropped as he looked at Yang in total astonishment.

"This must be it." Without waiting for Brian's instruction, Terence found a port that fit Brian's device, plugged it in, and started uploading the remote access program.

"Please work…" Brian murmured while staring at it nervously.

"Thirty seconds remaining," said Terence, peeking at the status bar. He began to bounce on the balls of his feet, overjoyed at finishing the first job he'd come to do.

"Done, done, done!" Terence yelled shortly after.

Brian's screen switched to Gattish instantly. "This means you're in?" asked Yang, looking at Brian in disbelief.

"Yes," Brian exclaimed.

"Ok, next!" Terence raced towards his last stop. The water treatment system had just issued a warning. It wouldn't be long before the NIISS guards found out they had visitors. He needed to hurry up.

While en route, Wei's voice came through: "All set! Need help? If not, let me know when you're ready, and I can press the button. Meet you out there in the freezing water."

"Roger!" Terence was glad to hear Wei had already set the explosives in place. He passed the oval storage cylinders and arrived at the west barrack, pulling out his bombs.

Right at that moment, however, an alarm went off. He heard noises and heavy footsteps behind him. He was found. More than ten NIISS guards ran toward him.

"Get him!" one of the guards shouted.

They surrounded Terence at once. But he was not going to let them catch him or stop what he was going to do.

“Wei, detonate now!” he called out loudly.

Then, with a smile, Terence pressed the bombs tight against the wall of the barrack and hit the button.

In Terence’s heart, he was still the same Olympic athlete from thirty years ago. It was a hell of a marathon he just swam, not too bad for a world record, and he had already gotten his medal.

A deafening explosion consumed everything.

“Are you safe? Terence, where are you?” Wei called out, his voice strained with panic as Terence’s life signal disappeared.

In the meanwhile, Ethan had returned to the shore. Geoffrey just reached the foot of the ice cap and learned from Brian that Terence had been to the control room. They all heard the explosion sound. It must have happened. Geoffrey tried to call Terence at once but got no answer.

Then they received a message from Wei:

“Terence and I have done it. Now he swims among the stars.”

A mixed feeling of shock and sorrow swarmed in their hearts. Ethan dropped to his knees in disbelief, and then he bowed his heads and cried.

“Backup team, it’s your turn to land,” Geoffrey gave his order. After that, nobody spoke, and the wind finally stopped.

The White Sea under the clear sky was calm again. For a moment, that looked like eternity.

Chapter 18
The Tri-Battle: SIIKwari

Since Shana decided to join the SIIKwari team, she received intense flight training from Jack. Jack made sure she got as many flight hours as possible over a month.

In the meantime, Fletcher and Ian from the 2nd squad worked hard to get their fighter jets ready in Flat Rock. Dimitri had identified a nice spot in advance, and he went there to set up a camp for them. Light-Heat Camouflage was put in place to avoid Gatti detection.

Three days before the South Pole mission began, Jack came back from Black Mountain. He and Shana went to join Fletcher, Ian, and Dimitri.

Two fighter jets — the Storm-Petrels — were parked in a hidden building close to Cohen and Andro's workstation. Once the NIISS forces rushed to retake South Pole, the team would fly the Storm-Petrels and kick off the second deceptive attack.

On the second day of their arrival, Jack could hardly wait to get out of hiding. They had been doing nothing else but examining the fighter jets and weapons, plus going over the plan again and again. Fletcher and Ian, on NIISS watch, got bored with the flat background noise signals on their monitors.

Jack paced around the camp restlessly, and he kept telling them it would only take less than an hour to fly to SIIKwari.

Dimitri, on the contrary, seemed to savor every moment before the first gunshot of the war. He watched over Shana's shoulder as they double-checked supplies, his hands ready to help her lift heavy items. When they sat together during meals, he was quick to enliven their conversation with easy jokes.

Later that afternoon, before leaving for his Haxxilic mission, Dimitri sought a moment alone with her. "I could have left the first day after I was done," he said, staring into her eyes with intensity, "but I wanted to spend more time with you…"

Shana remembered what he had said about giving her a simple, happy life, and she didn't have the heart to refuse him before their parting. "I just hope everyone can return safely," she replied, her gaze meeting his with deep sincerity. Though her feelings weren't what he hoped for, she wished him, and all of them, the best.

The second night began to fall shortly after. Jack grumbled, "Shana, can you ask Eio to speed up time? Is he capable of such thing?"

"Why, Jack? I feel that time is going too fast," said Dimitri with a soft chuckle. "We should make it go slower."

"Don't be anxious, gentlemen," said Shana. She went over to them and placed a hand on each of their shoulders. "I can ask Eio, just out of curiosity. But you two need to come to an agreement first."

"Only one more day to go," Jack continued, a thrill of anticipation in his voice, "Geoffrey and Terence will head out the day after tomorrow, and we'll fly to SIIKwari under stealth and make a feint at our enemy's face."

"I know how important this is to you," Shana replied, looking at him with calm resolve. "I'm as ready as you, Chief."

Jack then turned to Dimitri and said, "Thank you for helping out here. Shana said you planned to return to the Haxxilic team tonight. Is that right?"

"Yes. I'm already packed. In fact, I should leave now," Dimitri replied plainly as he gathered his stuff.

Jack and Shana gave him a hug to see him off. Dimitri took Shana's hands lightly and said, "I'll come back to you as soon as I can."

After that, he looked at Jack and said, "Chief, I'm counting on you to take care of our angel. Please don't make me regret it."

“Don’t worry. I’ll protect Shana with my life,” Jack replied, his gaze unwavering, his voice a low, resolute vow.

Dimitri nodded solemnly.

“I don’t need protection. I can take care of myself,” Shana complained, feeling slightly annoyed. She knew they meant well, but this constant need to protect her was starting to get on her nerves. “I’m no longer the little girl who just joined the Wake. I know what I’m doing.”

“No, you don’t need us,” Dimitri replied softly. “But we all care too much.”

Then he gave her a last tender look and left.

Finally, three long days passed. Their ground forces, including scouts, headed out to SIIKwari in the morning while Geoffrey and Terence headed out to South Pole. Shana, Jack, Fletcher and Ian were on standby after nightfall, fully dressed in their uniform.

Jack stared into his Senset while they waited anxiously, and they waited the whole night. It was seven tense hours. In the middle of it, Brian told them Terence was delayed, and they were two hours behind.

After midnight, Shana almost jumped when a short, high-pitched beep sounded.

“Is that it?” Fletcher asked eagerly.

The beep came again following three long flashes and two quick flashes.

“Yes, that’s it. That’s the message from Geoffrey,” said Jack, smiling. But after he read the message, he stood frozen, his face overcast with sadness.

Geoffrey just informed them they had succeeded but lost Terence.

A deep silence settled over the camp after they learned what had happened. The air was heavy with a sense of loss and mourning.

“Terence was truly one of the bravest men I ever met,” said Jack.

A profound sorrow filled Shana’s heart; she trembled as she struggled to hold back tears. Fletcher and Ian came over to comfort her, and they hugged each other tightly.

"We must carry on," Jack said after a long silence. "Now we wait for Brian to give us an update."

Brian called a few hours later. "I can't believe Terence is gone, right after I talked to him," he said, his voice low and somber. "How I wish I could have helped him earlier, when he was stuck…"

"Don't blame yourself. None of us could have known," Jack replied, "and it can't be changed now."

"Right, I decided to take full advantage of the backdoor we've discovered," said Brian. "I studied their algorithm and found similar backdoors in the systems of SIIKwari and Haxxilic, apparently by the same design. I've installed more remote access programs there. Now I can bypass their security settings and override their surveillance."

"Really?" said Shana, her spirits picking up.

"Yes," Brian replied with quiet confidence. "Once I give my command, the remote agents will disable their warnings and display constant normal information."

"Great. This'll make the attacks much easier," said Jack.

"I could perhaps make NIISS blind for three hours," Brian added.

"Good job," Jack replied. "We plan to fake an attack, but this is even better. Three hours are more than enough for a round trip. We're going to use it well, hopefully buying more time for the Haxxilic team."

* * *

In the meanwhile, far away in SIIKwari, Dvexu received his bad news.

"This is South Pole station reporting! This is South Pole station reporting! We are hit. We are hit!"

"Calm down," said Dvexu, sitting in the NIISS headquarters at leisure. "What is the situation?"

"Rebel forces are trying to land!"

"How did this happen?" Dvexu asked in disbelief. "Don't we have two cruisers and over one hundred NIISS guards stationed at the pole?"

"The cruisers have been blown up, and the two barracks are destroyed," the Gatti on the other side shouted in panic. "Most of the guards are dead. The rest of us cannot fight them off and they are going to take control of the station!"

When Dvexu heard that, he became utterly mad. He jumped out of his seat abruptly, grabbed his gun on the table, and strode back and forth. Then he called his teams to set their course to South Pole and prepare for an all-out war.

In the afternoon, a massive fleet took flight. Dark Spiral led the way, carrying more than a hundred fighters. Four cruisers followed, and Dvexu sat in his HHex.

"I will finish my job once and for all," said Dvexu as the ships formed a great wedge and moved towards the south.

Jack's ground scouts had been observing the NIISS guards and their ships, down to the smallest details. The movement of a hundred ships wasn't hard to notice.

Soon Shana saw Brian's channel lit up. "Dark Spiral sighted. It's up in the air with their main force," said Brian excitedly. "It's heading south as we expected. I'll kickstart my program once they cross the thirty degrees south latitude."

Jack jumped to his feet upon hearing that. "Way to go," he shouted. "It's our turn. Let's board the fighters."

The four of them rushed out of the camp. Fletcher and Ian hopped on one of the Storm-Petrels, Shana sat with Jack in another, and they waited.

Just then, Don's message arrived. "Sachin and I are ready. We'll set out simultaneously with you guys," he said.

"Roger."

"Stay alive, Shana," Don added moments later.

Ever since Shana became a field member, Don would always say the same words each time they were in for a rough ride. It had become an encouragement and a habit.

"Stay alive, Don," Shana replied. A surge of warmth spread through her, and she felt as though he was right by her side.

Brian called forty-five minutes later, "Dark Spiral has gone far enough. Activating remote agents…"

"Great. Put on your flight helmets. Let's go!" Jack called passionately. He fired up the six engines of the Storm-Petrel, pulled the throttle, and engaged at maximum speed.

"Remember, most likely, you'll have a three-hour safe window before they find out and kill the agents," Brian reminded them.

"Understood," Jack replied. "SIIKwari mission now begins."

Fifty minutes later, when they arrived above SIIKwari, they didn't seem to be detected. No NIISS ships took off to intercept them. Shana knew that their stealth technology could only provide some protection against Gatti detection, so Brian's trick must have worked.

"I have a suggestion," Fletcher said, "why don't we do some real damage? I know this is not in the original plan, but I don't want to waste such a great opportunity."

"Approved! Let's crush them!" Jack replied as he headed straight to a main building structure.

"Brilliant!" Fletcher shouted as he followed Jack and zoomed forward.

"Let's take their Command Center," Jack said, "Shana, ready?"

"Missiles armed," Shana replied.

"Send the babies out!"

At those words, Shana hit the button and launched two missiles toward the Command Center.

"The Gattis have left some of their fighters behind," Ian said thrillingly. "I spot at least twenty of them on the ground."

"Let's take them out," said Fletcher. Immediately, Ian launched another two missiles and inflicted serious damage on the NIISS force. Ian screamed, "Time to engage more targets!"

However, soon after Dark Spiral passed Hellas Planitia, Dvexu noticed something. He dashed forward to check the status of SIIKwari, his eyes fixed on the non-responding headquarters system. "Something is wrong," he murmured, scowling at the screen.

"Stop!" he yelled seconds later, raising his arm to pause his cruiser abruptly. "Turn around. I need to return to SIIKwari."

"What's going on?" his pilot asked in disbelief. "Are we going back now?"

Dvexu didn't bother to explain. He glared murderously in the direction of Redland for a few seconds, then decided that Dark Spiral would continue south, while he took five of his elite fighters to double back.

Dvexu and his fighters rushed back to SIIKwari in no time.

Before Jack and Fletcher could decide on the next target, Shana suddenly saw several high-power energy beams shooting toward them at light speed.

"Someone is behind us," she cried out, almost not believing her eyes. "Who is that?"

"Their Command Center has been damaged by us," Fletcher replied. "Their remaining ships shouldn't have flown up so fast."

"Whoever he is, he's vicious," Jack shouted. "We need to get out of here!"

Jack pulled the jet up to a higher altitude and sped away.

At the same time, Brian's channel flashed. "It's Dvexu's HHex!" Brian shouted, "he and part of his fleet have abandoned their route, and they're back! He might've figured out what we're trying to do. Retreat as fast as you can!"

But it was too late. They had been spotted. HHex was only minutes away, and the five NIISS fighters were coming up to intercept them.

"Get out of their locking!" Jack shouted out to Fletcher. "Try to lose them off your six!"

"Understood! Fletcher out."

The Storm-Petrel was an incredible fighter jet in terms of its speed, maneuverability, and climb. But the NIISS elite fighters had more powerful engines.

Before Jack and Shana could make significant headway, Dvexu's HHex was coming close on their tail, and energy beams were chasing them nonstop.

"You are not going to run away from me," Dvexu cursed. "Death awaits you."

Fletcher and Ian's situation was even worse since they lagged behind.

SIIKwari's terrain was flat; there were no mountains or other natural barriers for them to take cover. And they couldn't outrun their enemy.

Ian cried, "They're going to flank us, and we could get burned any minute!"

"I'm going to turn around and engage the enemy ships head-on," said Fletcher determinedly.

The Storm-Petrel was slower than Gatti fighters, but it could turn in a much tighter circle. There was a slight chance Fletcher could out-turn them.

"Want a dog fight, bastards?" Fletcher yelled and fired all their weapons at the three NIISS fighters surrounding them.

But still, they were outnumbered. Minutes later, Fletcher's Storm-Petrel was hit by multiple energy beams; holes were burning through the metal hull. In the end, it exploded in midair with several enormous balls of fire, its parts scattering everywhere.

Shana saw the explosion on her screen. Pain grew rapidly inside her. But there wasn't even time for sorrow because their own jet was being attacked from two different directions.

Jack pulled its head up sharply and tried to break out of siege again. However, two NIISS fighters and HHex caught up shortly.

"We've lost two engines. And the right wing is damaged!" Shana cried.

Looking at what was left of the wing, Jack knitted his eyebrows into a straight line.

"Shana, we'll have to eject," he said. "Go in separate directions once on the ground. Connect with our scouts to get help."

"Understood. Meet you at B-5," Shana confirmed. Base-5 was their emergency assembly point according to the plan.

"Now!" Jack shouted.

In the same second, Shana pulled the ejection handle to drive herself out. With the huge sound of a blast and heavy smoke, her seat shot out of the cockpit, and the wind roared past her.

Jack pulled the Storm-Petrel into a final vertical climb, so it was almost higher than HHex. The next second, he opened fire fiercely at HHex from very close, and then he set a course to crash into it.

The Storm-Petrel dived abruptly, running straight to Dvexu. Jack ejected himself at the last minute.

“An astonishing act of pure guts, but useless,” Dvexu sneered as the Storm-Petrel’s wing almost scratched his windows. He fired the energy cannons at once, shot the Storm-Petrel into rubbish, and sent it crashing to the ground.

“Do not let anyone escape!” barked Dvexu. “I want them, dead or alive!”

Immediately, the NIISS fighters dived to follow the two ejected seats. Energy beams shot down toward Shana and Jack relentlessly.

As Shana dropped straight down, explosions and flames rumbled above her head.

Her parachute deployed but it caught fire from the energy beams. It burned fast and collapsed at once.

Shana almost had a free fall. She hit her right arm when she landed too fast. But she didn’t have time to look at it. A NIISS fighter had tailed her and continued to fire.

“Take cover!” Jack told Shana in his Senset as he dropped into the northern fringes of SIIKwari city. However, she could not hear him. Her helmet and Senset were lost during the fall.

Shana struggled to get up, ran as fast as she could, and got inside a building. Energy beams shattered the windows of the building and kept passing through. She crouched down and stayed still until the shooting paused. Then she ran again to the exit and sneaked into the next and then another building. Luckily the buildings seemed to have been evacuated because of their bombing earlier, and there were no Gattis around.

As Shana expected, HHex soon landed. Dvexu and hundreds of NIISS guards rushed out to search for them. The sound of their footsteps couldn't be more than three hundred meters away. Knowing Dvexu, the exact vicious monster he was, he wouldn't give them any chance.

"Humans, show yourself and surrender," Dvexu shouted and then laughed madly. "I have this area sealed. You cannot hide for long. We will blast you out starting right here."

Strong lights then flashed not too far away. Dvexu had ordered his troops to sweep the area with energy guns inch by inch.

Shana thought hard about what to do. She needed to call for help, and if she got caught… she wanted to record some last words to Don.

At that moment, she found out her Senset had been lost.

She slumped onto the floor and broke out in a cold sweat. Was there anything else she could do?

Then she couldn't help but think about the years she'd fought alongside Don — all the hard times and enemies they'd faced together, and all the moments her heart had fluttered when near him. Her only regret was not letting him know earlier.

Why didn't she tell him how she felt? Those words sounded easy in her mind, but to say them out loud was something more intimidating than those approaching Gattis…

Suddenly, she heard voices and footsteps passing by in a rush. All the NIISS guards were moving west. No one came close to where she was hiding. That was strange. What happened? Did they find Jack?

She had no more time to think. This was a good chance to break out of the siege. She wouldn't be able to help anyone if she got caught. She ran north as fast as her legs could carry her until she was out of the city, out of breath, and crumbled to the ground.

Night had fallen; pitch-black darkness surrounded her. Only then did she realize that her broken right arm was hurting badly. And she was dying to know how Jack was doing.

Jack's leg was shot badly during the fall. He gritted his teeth as blood flowed freely from the wound. He limped to hide behind a bush of Black FrIxes, and then he sat down, pressed hard on his arteries to stop the bleeding, and then found something to wrap up the wound.

Jack heard the NIISS guards. Their voices were getting closer as he sat. He heard Dvexu's threat and saw flashes of light not so far away.

Dvexu's extreme sense of smell would soon lead him to find the trace of blood on the ground. Hiding was of no use in this case. Even if Jack could move to a fresh location, Dvexu would be able to detect him kilometers away.

"There's still something I can do," Jack said to himself. "At least I'll give Shana a better chance to escape."

Jack made up his mind. He then gathered the mini bombs he'd brought and hid them in good places, forming a circle around him. Once finished, he told Shana in his Senset, "Please get away as far as you can. I'll miss you." Then he sent a message to the home base, asking them to keep going. After that, he stood silently in the center of the circle, tall and still.

Dvexu emerged with his dozens of NIISS guards only minutes later. At the sight of him, Dvexu paused and signaled his guards to stop.

"Check him out," Dvexu told one of his guards.

The guard recognized him at once. "It's Jackson Huntsman! The top one on our wanted list. The leader of the resistance."

"Oh…" Dvexu laughed, "my futile search for rebel leaders has ended by sheer luck?"

Jack stood straight and stared at Dvexu fearlessly.

"He's not afraid of death," the guard said, "and the only possible explanation — this is a trap."

Dvexu began to hesitate, shifting his weight from one foot to the other. He squinted his eyes as if considering his next move. And they just stared at each other for a few minutes.

"Come on," said Jack. "Why so shy?"

"You're surrounded," Dvexu sneered. "If I were you, I'd be worried."

Just then, another guard approached rapidly and reported, "No other rebels nearby."

"In any case, it's impossible for me to lose," said Dvexu, raising his left hand to signal two of his guards. "Get him alive!"

Explosions came when the two guards stepped on the bombs. Dirt and rocks were blown up high.

At the same time, Jack opened fire at Dvexu and all the NIISS guards around him.

Dvexu didn't hesitate to fire back. He took a step back from the flame and smoke, firing his Wkeye gun frantically.

Jack got hit multiple times, wet spots of blood dotting his uniform, yet he kept his head high and his eyes wide open. None of the NIISS guards dared to get any closer for a moment.

"Shoot with all you've got. We won't be falling down!" Jack shouted out with his last strength.

Dvexu sent one more energy bullet to Jack's chest, two to each of his legs. Jack crumbled down.

"Now you fall. Humans should have more respect for the law of nature." Dvexu let out a little laugh full of disdain and then secured his weapon back onto his back. "You, stay here and search for more of them," he ordered his guards. "I'll report this to Icus myself."

Then he left for his HHex.

Upon hearing the explosion and continuous gunshots, Shana turned to look back in the direction of SIIKwari. She watched the burst of energy beams and the glare until they were gone, and the sky was dark again. Suddenly she realized that was the reason the siege was lifted.

Jack must have led the enemy away; he sacrificed himself to protect her. Shana felt a great sense of loss, like a part of her had been ripped away. Jack had been a coach, a mentor, but most importantly, a father to her since she joined the Wake. And now he was gone, just like that.

Tears poured down her face quietly, and she sat on the ground for a long time, immersed in grief.

The night grew colder and colder before she knew it, and it must be late.

"Jack, rest in peace now. We'll carry on," she swore solemnly and continued her path north to Base-5.

B-5 was an unmanned base inside Gatti territory, roughly one hundred kilometers from where Shana was. That was the shortest route. She was sure that now their attack was exposed, all the major roads would be watched closely. The alternative was to go through the wild trails, which would add another hundred kilometers. She needed about two days to get there by walking. Still, it was manageable since she had three days' supply of dry food and some water on her.

Shana had lost her Senset and couldn't call for any help. She had to get to B-5 as soon as possible. She moved fast on the first day while her energy was high. When night fell, she hid and tried to rest, but she grieved for Jack, Fletcher, and Ian and couldn't get much sleep.

By the second day, the simple medicine she brought with her ran out. Her broken arm was swelling and hurting. She gritted her teeth and commanded herself to keep going.

With half the way still ahead, she tried to think about the food, water, and medical supplies she'd find once she got to the base, and of course, the radio comm she'd be able to use. She was hoping to hear Don's voice soon enough. The battle of Haxxilic should have ended by then. Was he safe?

As dusk fell on the second day, Shana reached Base-5. "There it is," she said to herself. She was so relieved when the top part of the safe house came into sight. It was a plain and unattractive underground house, just like any home one would see for early human residences. There was a faded yellow ribbon tied to its door, their secret code.

She edged closer, hid behind a hill, and looked for any suspicious signs that the base might have been compromised, a habit she had learned from Jack. In a good thirty minutes, nobody appeared near the house.

She checked her surroundings again, then hopped out and hurried to open the door to the house. It seemed to be empty; there was no sign of life inside.

However, when Shana climbed down into the underground room, she saw the place had been searched. Closets were open, and drawers were turned upside down. Supplies and electronic devices were all smashed and scattered around. It was a mess.

But the most terrible thing was… she heard voices and footsteps. Gattis were coming. She took a quick look and climbed into an air duct that led to the ground.

Two NIISS guards returned to collect the supplies that they had dumped on the floor.

"No!" Shana cried inside, peeking through the filter of the air duct. In desperation, she saw them picking up all she needed.

Her two-day walk had been in vain. Yet she could do nothing but hold her breath and wait for her escape. This was too bad… maybe just getting out of here without being caught was all she could hope for.

Finally, the NIISS guards left, and it looked like nobody would come again after a long while. Shana climbed down quietly. All the medical supplies, Cubes, and communication devices were gone. She only found some scraps of food in the corners and ate them.

The next closest base would be Base-6, which was located southeast across the border and quite far away. Shana wondered if she could still walk there. Even if she could, there's a chance that Base-6 was compromised, too.

On that thought, Shana felt a chill down her back. Her arm hurt, and she knew the inflammation was going to last for a while without medicine. On top of that, she had only one day of supplies left.

She had been out of contact with others for two days. What happened in those two days? What was the reason that Base-5 was exposed? A dreadful thought crossed her mind. Did they fail? Where was Don now? Was he still alive?

* * *

Three days before the South Pole mission

Don had come back from Black Mountain. He needed to do some final preparations before heading out to Haxxilic.

He and Sachin had trained fifty men and got them ready in Base-2. They performed a thorough pre-flight check for their two multirole aircraft — the Guardians. They would fly in stealth mode to the armament factory hub, and their target would be the central arsenal. They knew the walls of the arsenal were made of special reinforced material. Ordinary human weapons couldn't penetrate it. So they planned to land, sneak inside the arsenal, and destroy it from within.

Two days later, Dimitri came back from Flat Rock and reported to Don. Immediately, Don asked him to join the other members to complete last-minute assignments.

Don made sure that everything and every member was perfectly ready. At the end of the last day, before he went to bed, he went through all the possible scenarios and their corresponding actions in his head.

His mind was unusually clear after that. He felt the mounting pressure from the significant risk they were going to take, and he couldn't fall asleep.

As the clock ticked on, Don became aware of a fresh growing pain in his body. At first, it was just a twinge on his back, a slight discomfort that he could just ignore. But the pain seemed to intensify at times, and then it quickly spread through his whole body. Dr. Yang once said that his muscles might have been stimulated in a certain way by the treatment he took, and there was probably no better explanation than that. He just hoped that the pain wouldn't get worse on the battlefield.

He only drifted into a restless sleep after midnight, and Aria came to visit him again.

A couple of months ago, she came occasionally when Don had sleepless nights. These days Aria seemed to come more often. It was like she had become a reliable old friend, and Don had given her a key to his mind.

She was finishing up her work that night, another of her house cleaning part-time jobs. The floors were vacuumed, the windows were polished, and the rooms were tidy. The solar panels were also dusted, and the Rovers had been charged.

On her way out, she raised her head to look at the twinkling stars. Back on Earth, on those hot summer nights, she used to lie on a piece of cool rock with her mom and gaze into the sky. She was little then; she couldn't have imagined coming this far to Mars.

Who would have thought?

Now the stars looked the same, and yet she had changed so much…

While she was driving home, music came into her mind, and she started to sing.

It was an oddly familiar tune. Don must have heard it somewhere. It sounded like *Going Home*, the song that Jack and Geoffrey liked to sing.

Don reminded himself to try talking to her in his dreams. That could be a way to communicate with her.

"Aria, I'm going on a dangerous mission," he said, concentrating on this one thought. "If you need my help, please let me know now, or you'll have to wait until I'm back. If I'm lucky enough, I'll be back."

She seemed to hear him, for she turned to look at him and waved goodbye.

Chapter 19
The Tri-Battle: Haxxilic

Brian called Don and Sachin after Dark Spiral had gone far enough, "I've kicked off my remote agents. Everything looks good to go."

Don and Sachin were already waiting inside the two Guardians, ready to take off. Each of them took twenty-five men, all in full combat gear. Their submachine guns were equipped with the special death bullets Andro made. Once getting Brian's signal to proceed, Don flew the aircraft up, side by side with Sachin.

The sun had already dipped below the horizon when they reached Haxxilic forty minutes later. Haxxilic was a typical Gatti city. Instead of massive grids of night lights, its streets were only dotted with sporadic solar lamps. They flew past a large area of factory buildings rising from the hillsides, their rooftops lined with curved metal structures that clawed at the sky.

It looked like Brian had done an excellent job. The Gatti's early warning was down, and the Guardians' arrival hadn't triggered any alarms.

Not surprisingly, Don saw the central arsenal was built inside a cave under a hill. Several NIISS teams were guarding it, and their barracks were located to its east. If they wanted to get to the arsenal, they must cross a bridge connecting it to the barracks.

Soon the Guardians landed. Don and Sachin were the first to rush out, and they led the way. Dimitri, Jayden, Thomas, and the others followed in the middle, while Lei and Steve secured the rear. They sneaked toward the bridge. By the time they reached its east end, the last light had faded, and night had fallen.

Don turned on his night vision and fired several shots at the two orange-red shadows in front of the bridge.

The two NIISS guards cried out and fell to the ground, twitching and kicking. Their fall caused a commotion immediately.

"Humans are here!" one of the guards yelled.

Dimitri lunged forward, knocked him down, and silenced him.

More NIISS guards came on the bridge. Don opened fire continuously as he moved. Lei and Steve shot some of them off the bridge and sent more rolling and crawling on the ground.

In the meantime, Sachin's men broke into each of the barracks. They surprised the enemy and made good use of their death bullets. The bullets proved to be highly effective. Most of the guards couldn't put up a fight, and only some of them escaped.

"We are being attacked!" a Gatti shouted.

"Get your weapons!"

The escaped NIISS guards bolted out of the barracks like black shadows, trying to fight back. Sachin and the others waiting outside got into a fierce fight with them. For a moment, high-intensity energy beams flashed in the night, and they were met with heavy gunfire.

The NIISS teams were totally unprepared, and Sachin's men defeated them after a brief struggle. Sachin made sure the Gatti cruisers parked on their tarmac were destroyed as well. The last one of the NIISS guards sprawled on the ground, too scared to move. Sachin gave him a quick shot in the head.

After twenty minutes, the energy beams, voices, and gunfire died down.

Don dashed across the bridge and arrived at the gate of the arsenal. Jayden and Thomas followed, carrying the explosives.

"Brian, I'm in front of a heavy black gate," Don called, "can you try to open it up from your end?"

"Let me see…" Brian said.

Don could hear Brian tapping his fingers swiftly across the keyboard, and then the gate slid open slowly. "You did it! Thank you very much!" Don shouted in exhilaration.

"Yes!" Brian exclaimed. "Remember, you have roughly a two-hour safe window left."

"Understood," replied Don. "Lei and Steve, hold the gate." Then he ran in with Dimitri, Jayden, Thomas, and the others.

"I can't believe the gate just opened without a glitch," said Dimitri.

Don nodded; indeed, it had been almost too easy, leaving him with a slight unease. Then he noticed that the arsenal was much more complex than he had anticipated. It was a labyrinth, and they had to check the chambers one by one. It looked like it would take them a while to locate the main storage area.

"Let's move quickly," he said.

However, before they could cover much distance, they all received Brian's update — Dvexu had returned to SIIKwari unexpectedly.

"Jack's team is fighting a brutal battle with HHex and five NIISS fighters," Brian cried out. "Their situation could get worse very fast!"

"What do we do now? We've just started," asked Dimitri, panic-stricken. "Now I really regret that I didn't go with Shana."

Don didn't answer right away, his pulse racing. Jack and Shana were well-loved. He dreaded to think what would happen to them. True, in Brian's update, he mentioned that he had requested support from their ground members, but they were less experienced.

"I knew something like this would happen," Dimitri murmured to himself while Don hesitated. "I cared too much about what Shana wanted to agree with her during the planning."

Don's chest tightened and he couldn't decide. Beads of sweat began to form on his forehead as a wave of anxiety washed over him. He only knew he couldn't abandon the Haxxilic mission.

“I need to go *now* to help Shana,” Dimitri broke their silence moments later. He said it out loud, word by word, his fists clenched. “None of these matters to me anymore. I just hope she can stay alive until I reach her.”

Don didn’t need an explanation. He, too, knew every second could mean the difference between life and death. He looked seriously into Dimitri’s eyes and said, “Go save them. Take one of the Guardians and remember to turn on the stealth mode.”

Dimitri nodded. Without any more words, he rushed out towards the exit.

Immediately, Don had a lot to worry about. Once the Haxxilic mission concluded and they needed to return, the remaining Guardian couldn’t hold all of them. Moments later, he announced a change of plan: most of his men would retreat with Sachin after they were done, and he would lead the rest of them to fall back by land.

After that, Don scanned through the place anxiously, trying to get things done as soon as possible, and then Sachin brought him the most surprising good news.

“The bird-shaped Rhea is emerging from the low sky of the south!”

“What?” Don couldn’t believe his ear. At the same time, he received a message from Andro, and he exclaimed after reading it, “Andro has come to help us. We can all fly back!”

A wave of elation swept over everyone as their situation improved quickly. Sachin gave Andro directions after he landed. Andro rushed into the arsenal, wearing the Senset Brian gave him.

“Good to see you, man. I thought you wouldn’t come.” Don gave him a tight hug as Andro came up and clapped him firmly on the shoulder. Although Don had prepared to go on even if it was just himself, Andro’s arrival was certainly cheering after the heavy news of SIIKwari.

“I thought I wouldn’t,” Andro said lightly. “But Brian told me that the NIISS system is down, and I can fly my Rhea over without being detected.”

“Smart thinking,” Don replied.

"Besides, this looks like a huge adventure," Andro added while looking around at the chambers with great interest, "how can I miss the fun? I can get a chance to see their advanced weapons."

"You'll have your share of fun for sure," said Don quickly. "Now, come help me."

Andro joined him to locate the weapons, his chatter a steady background hum as they worked. Together, they identified two chambers packed with energy guns and high-power cannons.

Don marked the chambers so that the others could place bombs, and Andro continued jokingly, "Also, I realize I may need to save your ass again. You see, the world's not as fun without you."

"You've got that right," replied Don. He gave an involuntary smile, and then both laughed.

When they reached the west end of the arsenal, they found another large chamber filled with all types of weapons. Don saw small portable arms, as well as others that looked like some sort of missiles with a variety of warheads.

"I wonder if this is a particle beam weapon," said Andro, pointing to a long, polished cylinder mounted on a gimbal.

"Could be," Don grunted. "But we can't take it back home."

"Oh, the Wkeye guns! These are easy to carry," Andro said, his eyes lighting up as he spotted them in a corner, and then he gladly took one for his own use.

Jayden and Thomas came up after hearing Andro, and each of them took a handful.

Minutes later, they finished deploying the explosives.

"We're almost done here," Don told Sachin, who was watching outside. "What's the situation on your side?"

"One of us is severely injured. Another eight were hit by stray energy bullets. I've asked them to fall back to the Guardian. The rest of us are still holding the bridge for you," Sachin replied calmly. "But you need to hurry up. We've made a loud noise, and their ground reinforcement should be coming."

“Got it,” Don replied. “Please take everybody out there to the Guardian now and retreat immediately. The remainder of us can leave with Andro.”

“Roger. Stay alive,” said Sachin, and he was quick on the move.

“We’re right on time,” Don then notified Lei and Steve at the gate, “should be out in five minutes. You can leave first with Sachin.”

“Great. But I want to stay behind and leave with you,” Lei replied with determination. “Right,” Steve echoed.

* * *

Earlier in the evening, the sun was sinking fast from the windows of Icus’s mansion in OIIIzoi. Icus was pondering upon a galaxy map in his study room up in the high tower. He carefully labeled more stars with potentially habitable planets and marked down their distance from the current solar system.

It was time for him to expand his Nucleus Transform Program on Earth. After he conquered Earth, he would use both Mars and Earth as his relay planets for his next target.

Just when Icus was focusing on his work, a sudden uproar came from the lower floors.

Moments later, Kyinn and several NIISS guards rushed into his study room. The guard in the front muttered in a disturbed tone, “The South Pole station is attacked.”

“I already know,” Icus replied impatiently. “Dvexu informed me this morning. He said he would take care of it.”

“Humans have certainly gone too far this time,” said Kyinn. “After the attack, there will be no more peace, even if you fight for it. How stupid they are.”

Icus ignored Kyinn’s comment and asked immediately, “What is the damage? Do you have an update?”

“No, we don’t. The South Pole station is still not responding,” another NIISS guard replied in a panic.

“Then leave me alone,” Icus said testily. He made a fist to close out the galaxy map in anger.

An hour later, another urgent message popped up in front of him. "Brother, bad news. We are attacked again. SIIKwari got bombed!" Dvexu's voice came through as his face image emerged and flickered. "But the good news is — I've shot down the rebel fighters and killed their leader. I'm on my way to report to you now."

"So we are caught cold and unprepared? This is totally unacceptable!" Icus shouted. "You better have a good explanation." He then looked out of the windows, puzzling over the situation.

Dvexu arrived in half an hour, and he had picked up Zullom on his way.

"Sorry, Icus. I've come a little late," said Dvexu, showing a rare good manner.

"You know you could be accused of dereliction of duty," Icus said harshly. "Superior will not be so happy to hear it."

"Sorry… anyway, I was heading out to South Pole, then I noticed something weird," Dvexu continued. "The SIIKwari link was not responding. How strange. There could be another attack. So I reversed course to check it out. Then aha! Two annoying suicidal rebel aircraft were trying to attack our headquarters."

"And then?" asked Icus.

"I shot them down. And guess what? I caught the rebel leader, Jackson Huntsman! Certainly, he was then killed by me. Nobody fools me," Dvexu concluded, a smug on his face. "I have stemmed the rebels and saved SIIKwari from more damage."

"Is that so?" said Icus, unmoved by the report. He was lost in thought for a minute or two.

Dvexu nodded and looked excited again. "It's actually good that the rebels revealed themselves," he said. "We will wipe them out today, once and for all. I've ordered more than a hundred ships to retake South Pole, and we should hear good news from them any minute."

But Icus was still thinking. The whole thing was obviously not so simple. He needed to anticipate his enemy's next move.

He turned to Zullom and asked, “What do you make of all this? Do they look like synchronized operations?”

Before Zullom could answer, however, Icus suddenly realized something. “We need to go to Haxxilic now!” he said. “We don’t know if they have discovered our armada there. We need to make sure.”

“Agreed,” said Zullom.

“Dvexu, call your remaining fleet in SIIKwari,” Icus added as he rushed down the high tower. He must check out the warship hangar in Haxxilic himself.

Icus raced to Dvexu’s cruiser with his two brothers; other senior NIISS guards followed in a hurry.

Soon HHex rose out at lightning speed. Its engines rumbled across the city of OIIIzoi.

* * *

Don did one last check before he turned to the exit of the arsenal. Right then and there, he noticed something.

“Wait… look here,” Don called out to Andro, pointing at a power distribution diagram on the wall of a chamber. It showed more than sixty percent of total power went into an unknown section. When Don approached the section’s entrance, he found another heavy black gate, locked tight.

Andro checked on the walls around the gate. “Don, I think you’re right,” he said. “There are indeed strong power lines going inside there, leading to something.”

Immediately, Don called Brian over video stream. “Brian, do you know what’s on the other side? Can you try to open it?” he asked, hoping Brian could do magic one more time.

“No, I can’t,” Brian replied after a moment. “That area is not even shown on the map I can obtain. A higher security level must have been set for that.”

Don had a strong urge to figure out what was inside. Jayden and Thomas also came over to examine the gate, and they noticed an access lock.

“Look here,” said Jayden. “A lock!”

Don saw mysterious symbols written on the lock. Undoubtedly an authorization code would be required to open the gate. "Anyone recognize these symbols?" he asked. "They don't look like the Gatti language characters we often see."

Andro took a look and then shook his head. Don showed the symbols to Brian on the other side. It might be possible to decipher the code if they could first get an understanding.

Brian showed them to Eio by his side.

"I've seen those somewhere. Let me search the Gatti literature I once loaded," Eio said. He closed his eyes quickly and then opened them again. "The symbols are Gatti genetic material markings."

Eio got it quick enough while Yang was coming over. "The passcode must contain these symbols," said Brian, his brow furrowed in concentration. "But I don't know how many symbols we'll need."

"Try the length of their genetic encoding," Yang suggested at once.

"What is the length?"

"Six," Yang replied without thinking. "I've done many experiments on that project myself."

"With a length of six and twenty-four symbols to choose from, I could try a brute-force hack," said Brian. "But I need roughly three seconds to try each permutation with repetition, and… that'll be years, theoretically, unless we have some hints —"

"I'm sure we don't have enough time," said Don.

"And it could be more or less than six symbols. So much could go wrong," said Eio. "I don't like the odds you're facing."

"And we don't know if we'd trigger any automatic defense programs if we hack it," Andro added.

"Or other countermeasures." Don had to admit.

Right at that moment, something popped up on Brian's screen, and he cried out, "A group of NIISS ships is flying toward you from SIIKwari. Fall back now! You have probably less than thirty minutes."

Lei's voice also sounded in their Sensets, "Our scouts have seen their ground reinforcement coming. We need to leave now!"

All of them exchanged a final look except Andro.

"I may have seen the symbols somewhere," Andro said suddenly, scratching his head. "They look oddly familiar."

Don eyed him curiously and asked, "Where in the world have you seen — ?" But then he stopped right there and exclaimed, "On your necklace!"

"What?" Both Jayden and Thomas turned to stare at Andro.

"You're right, Don," Andro exclaimed. He took his necklace off and brought it close to the access lock. "Let's see if the symbols can indeed match."

Unexpectedly, the necklace gave out a shimmering light. A low beeping followed. Then the access lock was activated, and the gate clicked open.

It was unbelievable. They all laid their eyes on Andro, but it was not the time to ask him to explain. Besides, Andro looked as bewildered and uncertain as everyone else.

Don pulled Andro and the others aside as another huge chamber was revealed behind the gate. Don waited until he was sure that no auto-defense program was triggered from within.

Inside the chamber, an extensive floor appeared in front of them.

Don saw something enormous casting obscure shadows on the floor. Rows of dim red lights hung on the gigantic arched ceiling, and the red lights were flashing occasionally, like the blinking eyes of half-sleeping monsters.

"Can we go now?" said Thomas. "I have no desire to linger."

"Jayden, Thomas, you lead the others out first," said Don decisively. "Andro, please go with them." Don didn't want to involve the others. It was neck or nothing, and it wasn't in the original plan.

"Don, I wish to stay," Jayden said. But Don shook his head. Thomas grabbed Jayden and hurried off with the others.

Turning his flashlight on, Don entered. He raised his head high, staring hard.

Andro didn't leave. He followed Don inside and looked around. "I don't take your orders," he said casually when Don shot him a disapproval look.

Don said nothing; Andro could be as bullheaded as himself at times.

Seconds later, Don could tell what was inside, since his eyes were then adjusted to the darkness in the chamber. He had gotten a real prize, he realized — the whole place was a final assembly hangar for warships, the size of at least a hundred thousand square meters.

Right in front of him, a work platform stretched out. It looked like three sections of a warship's body needed to be joined together. Around each section, an enormous spherical tooling jig had been positioned. Along its orbital railways, over a dozen robots hung, seemingly able to move freely and work in parallel, each dedicated to a specific task. Besides the warship sections, Don spotted stabilizers, engine pylons, and weapon bays, all waiting for installation. A complete build-up sequence seemed poised to begin.

"Impressive," Andro exclaimed as he climbed up one of the accommodation ladders to admire it. "The whole thing seems to be fully automated."

Don noticed that the hangar hosted at least fifteen such warships in the installation process. To his right, another five ships had already been completed, ready for run-up and flight testing. The entire production facility looked highly advanced and streamlined.

Don's heart pounded, and his blood was up. So, the Gattis had been building their armada. Peace with them, or even a meager existence under their rule, had always been an illusion. He now knew for sure.

There was no turning back after he saw all this. He must do something.

Don then caught sight of a testing station. He rushed over, fumbled with the panel, and managed to turn on the power.

"Andro, come help me!" he shouted.

Andro came running, and they succeeded in opening the system, revealing the first few layers of non-critical information. They saw technical specifications, including crew number, Cube capacity, speed, range, and armament. "The ships have interplanetary range," said Don after he glanced through the specs.

"Here. The navigation system," said Andro, who found a data feed module to pass information to each of the warships' brains. In the data feed, there were maps with layouts of roads, airports, natural resources, cities, and their populations.

"These are the maps of Earth," Don exclaimed. As he was afraid, the destination of these warships was Earth, and the Gattis had collected a lot of information they needed.

After that, they couldn't get further into the Gatti system without access authorization. Nevertheless, it was enough. That was all Don needed to know.

"Do you think we can hijack one of these?" said Andro, studying the ships with great interest. "Maybe we can hack into the warships' brains?"

"Try the necklace again," Don suggested.

Andro tried. "Not working," he said.

Don guessed their luck had run out.

There was only one option left then: he had to destroy these warships. This discovery was far bigger than he had ever anticipated; the energy weapons they'd found earlier were nothing compared to what lay before them. If he succeeded, he could derail the Gatti's invasion of Earth and buy humanity precious time to prepare. Yet, a bitter truth remained: he and Andro should have retreated long ago. If only they had thirty more minutes…

"Andro, help me get all the explosives we have left!" said Don, springing into action.

Just then, Lei's voice sounded again, "Hurry up! NIISS will overwhelm this place in ten minutes. Steve and I won't be able to hold them off for long!"

"Leave now!" Steve shouted.

"Roger!" Don replied, his heart pumping to its fastest. "Andro, time for you to go! Lei and Steve, meet with the others at Rhea now! Andro will take you to safety."

During the planning, he and Jack had simulated many scenarios, but no way they could have foreseen this. Don was willing to risk his own life, and the arsenal could well be where he was going to end, but there was no need for others to suffer the same fate.

Don said a silent goodbye to Andro with his eyes, leaving no room for argument this time.

"Why just me?" asked Andro.

"Please, they can't leave without you. Besides, you didn't sign up for this. I cannot risk any damage to your prized face," Don forced a joke, "got nothing to make up for that, you know."

"You do realize that," Andro gave a short chuckle, "and you've finally learned from me how to crack a joke."

"Just go. Get back to your ship and sneak out!" Don urged.

"What about you?"

"Can I get out alive?" Don knew the answer was most likely no, but he tried to relax his tone and said, "That depends on how lucky I am, right? You'll see soon enough."

There was no other sensible choice.

Andro hesitated a second and said, "I'll think of a way to help you. Don't die before that."

"I'm counting on you," replied Don.

Andro gave him a grim last look and hastened off.

At once, Don dashed to plant the explosives where they'd deliver the deadliest blow. When he finished, he heard gunshots, screams, and fighting at the entrance. After setting a timer and watching the countdown begin, he walked out of the arsenal and stood tall in the middle of the bridge.

A troop of NIISS guards blocked his way. They halted one hundred meters away the moment they spotted him.

Don found Lei and Steve's faces in a pool of blood. Their bodies were lying among dozens of dead NIISS guards. They didn't leave without him; they had fought to their last breath. Don's heart burned with grief.

In no time, six NIISS fighters appeared in the sky. The rumbling noises were deafening. Dust and debris swirled up from under his feet, and everything was waving wildly in the unparalleled wind.

There was no doubt that energy beams were going to rain down like a storm. By then, Don couldn't care less about his own life; he didn't even bother to guard against the guns and cannons pointing at him. He worried whether Andro and the others had gone far enough.

"My name is Don!" he shouted. If he could draw the enemy's attention…

"Look here! We are the Wake!" Don continued to bellow at his top volume. He pulled out Brian's flag from his pocket and waved it in his hand. On a blue fabric, a red eagle shaped like a large *W* took flight in the dark night.

"The blue is ocean, the color of our home planet. The red is blood, the price for freedom."

Don clearly remembered that was how Brian had explained it at the assembly. What a smart guy Brian was, he thought, and he was glad that they had done it together.

Just after he uttered his first words, three fighters came to hover above him, casting searchlights so bright that he couldn't open his eyes.

Don and his flag drew all the attention of the NIISS. He was simply waiting for heavy fire, but there was a moment of odd silence.

Minutes later, Dvexu's HHex appeared from behind. Other fighters immediately cleared the way for it to come close and then flanked it in formation.

Icus and his two brothers stood at the front of the flight deck. They saw a large visual of Don's image pop up on their screens.

"All guns and cannons charged. How do you want us to proceed?" asked a NIISS guard, looking toward Dvexu for permission to open fire. "Just finish him here?"

But Icus raised a hand to stop the guard.

"Why not?" said Dvexu, eyeing Icus curiously. "Do you recognize him?"

“I do,” Icus replied as he looked down upon Don, his voice emotionless as ever. “He’s one of my early experiment subjects. I know that from the report of GIIxb Lab.”

“Oh…” Dvexu murmured, a thin smile forming. “If he’s yours, Icus, we might as well see what he does under pressure.”

Don didn’t know what was going on. He thought to himself, “Hell, if I die, I die in a fire. I need to make sure the others have enough time.”

Then he continued to yell, “What are you waiting for? I’m not going to beg. We’ll never bend our knees to your rule, and we’ll protect our home!”

“This is really what you look like —” Icus finally spoke. His coarse voice passed over, as chilling as Mar’s northern winter. “A juggling clown.”

“Destruction, is that all you are capable of?” Icus continued slowly and confidently as if he didn’t think Don would turn anything around. “Is it not in human nature to sit down and have a conversation?”

“I’m sick of your pretenses!” Don replied angrily, his voice fierce. “Look at this blood-soaked ground. I’ll only sit down to negotiate when I point a gun to your head.”

Dvexu went to the windows and looked down at the piles of dead bodies, his mouth curling in disdain, and he said, “You think it’ll make a difference killing one or two of us? Your kind will lose, little by little, until there’s nothing left.”

Zullom wore a look of impatience. “Wound him,” he gave the order. “I have zero interest in this war of words.” Zullom then took a quick peek at Icus and added, “but keep him alive.”

Four NIISS guards on the ground closed in cautiously, each holding a high-power gun. They took up positions behind the bridge’s pillars, two guards on each side. Then they fired four energy bullets simultaneously, aiming at Don’s legs.

The bullets hit Don; severe pain shocked his balance. He crashed down fast, but he held his head high. On the last day of his life, he felt a profound satisfaction, knowing that he would take out their entire fleet.

"Enough?" Zullom asked Dvexu.

"More!" Dvexu shouted.

"Surrender! This nonsense will soon be over," Icus cut in. "Or suffer the consequences."

That was it. Don saw the explosion timer had counted down to ten seconds, and he shouted out his last words, "You have lost! Today, and as of now, I can die with a laugh!"

Right then and there…

Boom!

With a ground-shaking sound, the assembly hangar blew up. Hot waves of flame rushed out from its roof. The same was happening to the arsenal.

Dvexu quickly pulled HHex to a safe distance.

"Impossible!" Icus yelled.

At the same time, Zullom darted towards the windows of the flight deck, terror-stricken. "How did he find out…?"

The whole structure of the hangar began to collapse part after part. Broken pieces of warships were flying around among dust and ashes. Thick smoke rose like a sandstorm, breaking through the sky.

Don calmly waited for the explosion to consume him. However, something appeared above him suddenly. A machine? It certainly had a weird shape. The next second, the machine expanded rapidly, and a door swung open. Don couldn't see clearly, but he felt a strong force pulling him towards its center.

Don wasn't sure what was going on, but he had no fear because it couldn't be worse than the explosion. While he wondered what it was, Eio's voice sounded in his Senset in time.

"Listen, Don, if you trust me, do exactly as I say."

"Eio, where are you? Aren't you at the base?"

"I've come to Nelson's lab after Andro told us about you," replied Eio. "We've directed a Hyper-V to your location, and it should get you out of there. Stay right where you are!"

"A what?" Don couldn't understand what Eio just said. He guessed Eio was talking about the strange thing above him.

Before he could fully register what was happening, he was lifted into the air.

"No time to explain. Now!"

That was the last thing Don heard from Eio. The next second, he was submerged by waves of an unknown matter. He gasped for air, but air wasn't there. He felt suffocated, like a person drowning in the ocean. He believed his eyes could still see, yet there was nothing to be seen. He tried to look harder, but the NIISS ships and the bridge were certainly gone. He couldn't hear anything either; it was as if someone had shut off the volume of the noisy world and left him alone.

Don lost all his senses and became unconscious.

"What's that?" asked Icus in disbelief. "I do not understand. He didn't seem to have done anything special, yet he's disappearing into a machine."

"Whatever that is!" Dvexu roared. "Do not let him escape!"

Energy beams poured down towards the machine like a thunderstorm, but they became null and void the moment they hit an invisible barrier, as if some shield was protecting the machine. Seconds later, Don and that machine vanished altogether.

Everything around the arsenal was erased by a final explosion.

"I cannot believe it," Icus said, narrowing his eyes as he watched. "Something beyond our space-time has happened. But how is that possible? Humans cannot have mastered some advanced technology."

"You should have gotten him earlier," said Dvexu, his face contorting with fury, his nostrils flared. He smashed his fist down on the control panel and then turned to leave.

"I hope this is not what you've planned in your sick mind," Zullom snapped, casting a malicious look at Icus. "Losing all our ships in one night! This will really get us killed by Father's wrath." Then he stormed out of the flight deck following Dvexu, their heavy footsteps echoing through the place.

Chapter 20
The Lost Angel

"I need to go. I can't stay sleeping here…"

Don struggled to open his eyes but fell asleep again. There were voices screaming, calling his name, vague but familiar, as if from another world.

When Don finally woke up, he was surrounded by a crowd of people. The comforting sound of their chatter filled the air. Looking around, he saw Andro, Yang, Brian, and others. He was still alive. It was not a dream.

"Welcome back, Don," said Brian, smiling at him.

"Welcome back!" Geoffrey and Wei yelled as they burst in.

With some effort, Don nodded. It took him a while to find his voice, and he asked, "Where am I?"

"At our temporary campsite west of Midzor. You're safe," said Yang, feeling Don's forehead. "The fever is gone."

Don got anxious at once. He blurted out, "No! We need to move. It's too close to OIIIzoi. NIISS will come looking for us."

"Relax, they already did. You've been sleeping for ten days," Geoffrey kindly told him. "The worst is over. Their search has become less intensive."

"Ten days? Why, what happened?" Don tried to get out of bed, but dizziness hit him as the room kept spinning around him. Then a sudden, severe pain in his legs reminded him of his last moments in Haxxilic. He shook his head, trying to recall his memories. He was shot… the explosions… and a machine took him. Don remembered it was like suffocation inside, and he lost consciousness. But was that even real?

"Four energy bullets hit your legs. You need to rest," said Brian, putting him back into bed.

"So, it's been ten days since the battle of Haxxilic, and I survived?" Don asked. It was still too good to be true to him.

"No, it's been fifteen days. You spent five days trapped in the 4-D space and another ten unconscious." A familiar voice came from behind the crowd. It was Eio.

"There was a malfunction," Eio continued, "I couldn't cross the Hyper-V back into your universe right away. But fortunately, I solved that problem in time."

"What do you mean… five days… trapped in the Hyper-V?" Don asked. When Eio talked about 4-D space, Don often felt bewildered, as if he were struggling to decipher an impossible frequency — especially back when they first met. After all these months, the static was finally clearing, but he wanted to make sure he'd heard it correctly.

"You got a ride from the hyper vehicle," said Eio, weaving through the crowd to reach the front, and he kept bouncing up and down, looking as relieved and overjoyed as the others. "You were outside this universe for the initial five days. But worry not. Your five days aren't too long in the higher dimension. You survived."

"Outside this universe?" Don repeated, his brow furrowing in concentration, for he knew he'd need extra brain power to comprehend what Eio was going to say.

"Yes, consider yourself lucky. I had no idea if it'd work, but that was the only thing we had at the time," Eio said, sparkles in his eyes. "Remember the C-Cube we got from Ghalf? We built a Hyper-V to utilize its energy so I could travel through 4-D space and go home. But at the last minute, I decided to use it to save you."

"You guys made it work?" Don asked, his eyes widened with awe.

"Right, Nelson and Cohen built the parts, and I assembled it," Eio replied. "After assembly, the machine you saw was only its cross-section. You were lifted into a different space-time inside one of its 3-D faces. And then you were lowered back into this universe, exactly the way you were, wounds and all."

"A question just came into my mind," Yang interjected. "Does Don have to return here? Can he go into your universe instead?"

"You guys are 3-D beings. Your visit to the higher dimension can only be temporary," Eio replied. "If it were me, I should be able to go through 4-D space and go home."

Just then, Nelson burst in, yelling from behind, "I've told them many times. The Hyper-V was my idea. I made it work. I worked very hard for nearly two hundred days and nights, non-stop, to figure out the underlying math and physics."

While Nelson waved his arms in excitement, Cohen rushed in and added, "I built the actual vehicle. I've made history."

"A brilliant success," said Don, turning his head to look at Nelson and Cohen. "Thank you so much."

Cohen then showed Don a picture of the Hyper-V before it was assembled. "Look, this baby was the size of a whole room," he said. "It can do a pickup at a precise location. For example, Eio gave it your location from your life sign tracker, and the Hyper-V appeared right where you were on the bridge —"

"I played the most important part in this," Eio interrupted Cohen. "Of course, Nelson failed so many times, and he only succeeded after I pulled some strings in his brain. Therefore, you need to thank *me*, in particular."

"Thank you, Eio," Don said sincerely. He was still processing what he had just learned. It sounded like science and technology far ahead of his time. Yet, there was no other way he could have escaped.

"Why didn't you use it to go home, Eio?" Don asked, a sudden realization dawning on him.

"Like I said, I wasn't sure if it would work," Eio admitted. "We failed terribly, and you were the guinea pig. Now I wish I had put more trust into human engineering."

"So, you lost your precious opportunity?"

"Yeah, the C-Cube had already been used many times during testing, and retrieving you depleted it completely," Eio mumbled and let out a sigh. “I need another C-Cube. How can I get one?”

Don knew the C-Cube was hard to come by, and they wouldn’t know how to create one any time soon. He placed a hand on Eio’s shoulder and said again earnestly, “Thank you. Trust me, we’ll do our best to get another C-Cube and send you home.”

Eio nodded.

After a while, Don remembered something else and asked, “The rest of the South Pole team has returned?”

“Yes. We retreated in time before Dark Spiral showed up,” said Geoffrey.

“And what happened to Jack?” asked Don. Brian didn’t provide him with more updates when he was in the arsenal, and it didn’t sound like Jack also got a pickup from the Hyper-V.

There was a moment of silence.

“Old J has left us,” Andro then calmly broke the news to Don.

So he had lost Jack. Don felt a burning, prickling sensation in his eyes.

Jack had taken him in from the homeless shelter and given him a home, teaching him everything he knew. Although Don understood that there would be no victory without sacrifices, this was still a great grief.

He wanted to cry, but his throat was so obstructed that he could make no sound. For others, the pain might have gradually subsided over the days, but Don knew he would need time to work through his loss and sorrow.

Geoffrey added, “We found his body two kilometers away from the crashed Storm-Petrel. From the look of it, Jack drew the attention of a dozen NIISS guards and killed a few of them before he died.”

“There must be something that can still be salvaged,” Don blurted out. “Where is Shana? Is she Ok?”

Why didn’t he think of her earlier? He wondered.

Andro and Geoffrey exchanged a cautious look. They were hesitating as if trying to choose the right words.

"You found her body?" Don asked breathlessly.

Eio shook his head. The others remained silent.

"Don, she may be gone," Andro said at last.

"May be... gone...?" Don opened his mouth rather painfully, his heart sinking.

"You know, the two Storm-Petrels were hit," said Geoffrey. "Fletcher and Ian were in one of them when it exploded. Jack and Shana were ejected, yet none of us has heard from her."

"I went with your people to search the entire place for her," Andro added, "but only found her smashed Senset and a burnt parachute. Nothing else."

Geoffrey told Don that the search continued for more than ten days. In the first couple of days, everyone had their hearts in their throats, hoping Shana could be found or magically return to one of their bases. However, there was no sign of her, nor any news.

Their hope diminished with every passing day. By day fifteen, they didn't even dare to mention her name. Although nobody wanted to accept it, they had to consider Shana might not be coming back.

"No. I'm not going to take it just like that. I'll go look for her," said Don. For the first time, he felt denial and anger.

"Please try, but we've really done it as thoroughly as possible," Brian swore. "Andro and I didn't even sleep. We searched inch by inch over the past fifteen days. Eio and I also tried to break into the NIISS system again to see whether they had any information. We didn't succeed."

Andro and Eio nodded. Andro said, "It's... likely that she's no longer with us."

"We're sorry. We're as sad as you are."

Their sympathizing faces hurt him.

Don knew they had done their best, but he refused to give up. He must do something. "I'll search again myself," he said, determined to see it with his own eyes. "I won't stop until I see her body."

Don found it incredibly difficult, but he managed to pull himself up and said, "I leave in an hour."

"What? What about your legs?" said Yang. "I don't think you can —"

"I've been in bed for ten days. That's enough rest," Don replied with grim determination. "Brian, give me packs of painkillers and the Mix."

He swallowed the pills Brian brought him. Then he pushed with his arms to get off the bed and commanded himself to eat. He sat for a while for the dizziness to go away, and then he stood up to leave.

"I'll go with you," Brian said. "We can take two Rovers to search faster."

Don nodded, and they headed out to SIIKwari in the afternoon.

* * *

As they traveled, Don tried to think about the places where Shana could be. He then remembered Dimitri, who went to Shana's rescue!

"Where is Dimitri? Has he found anything?" Don called Brian tensely.

"The Guardian was hit and crashed. Dimitri has gone missing," Brian delivered the astonishing news. "His Senset signal was last seen near SIIKwari, and we haven't received any transmissions. He might have been captured by NIISS, or he's dead."

Don's heart dropped to his stomach. He couldn't believe it.

"I've changed the encryption of our communication and taken care of the Light-Heat Camouflage devices," said Brian, sounding worried. Then he quickly briefed Don on other events they hadn't had time to cover earlier. "B-5, their assembly point, was raided by NIISS. It looked like a random incident, though, since all the other bases are fine. It doesn't seem like our information has been given away."

"Anyway, Geoffrey has ordered the members not to return to the bases anytime soon. We've mostly been camping out,"

Brian added. "Let's pray that Dimitri and our angel will be fine."

So, Dimitri also faced grim odds, Don thought, but at least it was comforting to know that Brian had taken responsibility without being asked.

They arrived north of SIIKwari in the late evening. Brian sent Don the locations of the Storm-Petrel's crash site and where Shana's parachute was found.

They parked their Rovers far out in the wild and snuck into the city.

Don saw several NIISS guards cleaning up the street. He overheard their conversations; it sounded like NIISS had checked everything thoroughly, and they didn't seem to have Shana or any valuable information about her.

After the NIISS guards left, Don rushed to the crash site. The main body of the Storm-Petrel had been removed, but parts of the broken hull and fallen debris were still scattered across the ground. He went north from there and found traces of a burned parachute. As he knelt to examine the debris, worries and anxiety flooded his mind.

Don told himself to calm down and tried to think about what Shana would do. Chances were, she had headed north towards Base-5 as planned.

"Let's split up from here, Brian," Don said, having made his decision. "I'll drive to search north and east, and you'll take south and west."

"Got it," Brian replied.

Not surprisingly, Don didn't find her around SIIKwari that first night. He believed NIISS must have done the same, because they had made their job easy by turning many buildings into rubble.

Then he searched in a bigger radius towards Base-5. It was likely that Shana had hidden somewhere if she wasn't captured. He studied the terrain on the map, planning a grid search for every possible corner, cave, and gully, then spent the day going through them frantically.

One day quickly passed since their arrival. Don reached Base-5 by dusk, and he had exhausted all the likely places.

There was still nothing. Nothing from Brian either. If Shana had reached the base before NIISS, she should have called for help. What happened?

Don didn't rest. His arms and legs began to go numb, but he refused to stop. He couldn't waste her chance of survival.

"Shana, please stay alive! Please, let me find you," he cried inside, yet there was only silent darkness surrounding him.

Don's fatigue gradually turned into a great fear as he went on. Had he really lost Shana? Would it be different if he'd left with Dimitri? Could he really afford the what-ifs regarding the warships?

The second night fell, and the two pale Mars moons shone coldly above his Rover. Don felt he was losing his grip on reality. He couldn't remember which areas he had already covered or where he had searched more thoroughly. For a while, he was just wandering randomly, praying for a miracle.

In the end, he parked his Rover, and he didn't pay much attention to where his legs were taking him. He walked hopelessly until almost dawn, and he arrived at a desolate valley. In the distance, he could see the remains of what must have been a great city. The once-grand buildings were now reduced to crumbled walls and broken pillars, factories lay in ruins, and the empty streets were covered with sand and dust.

Don rushed down the valley, and he noticed some lichens pushing out of broken street slabs, struggling to grow. The color was bright green, so strikingly resilient among all the Black FrIxes on his way, and that gave him comfort somehow — a glimpse of hope in his desperate hours.

Don was quite sure that he was all alone then. The NIISS guards wouldn't stay in this place of no value, so he called out loud for Shana.

His voice echoed through the empty streets, met only by the rustling sounds of unseen animals running away.

"Shana! Shana… please, if you hear me…"

After racing down a main street, he turned into a forgotten neighborhood and soon found himself at a dead end. Mottled walls and broken old houses were all that remained. He turned back and fixed his eyes on the street sign that was almost beyond recognition. It read *Stargaze Av.* in English.

Why did it look so familiar? He must have seen it before. Don tried his best to recall, but where?

A gust of icy wind swept his face and cleared his mind. Suddenly, he realized this was the place where Shana's old family house was, from before the night of the Red Purge, before she joined the Wake. The city ruin was once Waterford, a prosperous human settlement.

"Is it possible — ? Yes! This must be it!"

Why hadn't he thought of it earlier? Shana's old house in Waterford was not too far away from Base-5. She could have easily come here, Don thought. It was a natural place to hide out. Waterford had been wiped off the map after the Red Purge; otherwise, he would have remembered it sooner.

Don just couldn't believe the frame of the house was still standing. He'd thought it was completely shattered. He hurried to the front door, his heart racing, and then he quickly lifted aside some fallen blocks in his way.

"Shana, are you here?" Don called out her name and waited. But to his great disappointment, no one answered from inside the house.

"Shana? Shana!"

He went further and looked around quickly, but he didn't see any signs of life.

"Shana!" he cried louder. "Please…"

Don looked everywhere and called her name for some time. There was no response.

If she was not here, where else could she go? Don wondered, racking his brain for other possibilities. But nothing came to mind. Only horror grew, reminding him of what everyone had said: she was gone, forever. Don slumped to the floor, buried his face in his arms, and let out a long cry.

Just then, a clacking sound came from nowhere, barely audible. Was it a stone hitting another? Don sat up at once and looked around.

Was it his imagination?

Tat-Tat. It came again! The sound was coming from below, and it had a rhythm. Animals were unlikely to make such sounds. Don searched the floor carefully. He pushed away bricks and wiped off dirt with his hands. Then he stopped at a corner.

There was a metal ring at his feet. Yes! A door! An entrance to what seemed like a basement. His heart was racing again. With a yank, he lifted the door and revealed some stairs going lower. He ran down. It wasn't as dark as he thought since there were two small windows on the wall. There were some cabinets and bags as well, perhaps used as storage.

Then he saw a figure in the morning mist, a silhouette he couldn't be more familiar with.

His heart missed a beat as he rushed forward. With great happiness, he uttered a suppressed cry of joy, "Shana, is that you?"

Shana turned her head slightly.

Just then, the first light of sunrise passed through the open door and ended the long night. Another day had come.

"This is not an illusion… It's really you, Don?" she murmured in a voice that was almost inaudible, and she stared hard as if to make sure it was him. Then she struggled to say more, but seemed too weak to get any other words out.

Don noticed that she had gone extremely thin and pale, losing all her glow over the past days. He couldn't bear to see she had suffered. Tears rose to his eyes. "Shana, I'm so sorry. I've come so late." He almost cried, his voice broken.

Then he felt her face and her hands. Her breathing was good, and the uniform was still working to keep her warm. Her pulse was weak but continuous. Don let out a deep breath, a breath he hadn't realized he was holding. Feeling greatly relieved, he couldn't help but smile, and he'd never felt so happy before.

"I have some food with me," he said, helping her to straighten her back against the wall. Then he rummaged in his backpack for food and water. He wished he had something better, but he only packed Nutrition Mix and water before he left.

"Here, are you able to take a sip?" asked Don, holding a bottle of water for her.

Shana lowered her head to slowly sip some water, then the Mix. After a while, some color returned to her face, and she looked slightly better.

She gave him a smile. "I have so much to tell you and so much to ask," she said, reaching out to hold his hand. "Where should I begin?

"My Senset was lost. I was out of food and water after leaving B-5. NIISS guards were everywhere. I had to hide out here. In the basement, I was lucky to find some canned food, bottled water, and medicine from long ago.

"The guards searched the area. I didn't get any chance to escape. My only hope was that someone would come. You'd come to rescue me. I knew you would…

"But if I were to die, my old house is a good place. It's the place where I was born, where we first met…"

"I'm here now," said Don. "You'll be fine."

"I ran out of the last stale food and water on day nine," Shana continued. "I thought about going out, but it'd be impossible to pass the guards without help. At first, I slept most of the time, trying to conserve energy, but then I felt a creeping cold, as if my soul was leaving my body. I worried I'd soon fall asleep and never wake up…

"When I heard you calling my name earlier, it took almost all my strength to make that sound with a stone."

"How lucky I am," Shana said, leaning forward onto Don's shoulder. "This is the happiest day of my life. I thought I wouldn't be able to see you again."

"You're Ok now. You're going to be fine," Don repeated.

Shana paused to draw breath and then opened her mouth to continue, "Don, there's something important that I always wanted to tell you…"

But she looked weary after saying so much, her voice low and tired. Don gently shushed her, "Shh… save your strength, just rest. You're safe now. You can always tell me later."

"Ok, Don… hold me," she murmured.

Don opened his arms, pulling her into a tight embrace as if, in that way, she wouldn't slip away again.

"I'm here. Close your eyes. I'm here."

Then she fell asleep.

It was rather quiet. Don only heard the breathing of Shana and himself.

On the wall, he saw some marks on a chart that she had made for herself. It must be something she used to count the days that she spent in the basement. The earlier writings were vigorous and clear, the last ones weak and shaky.

He looked at her thin face; her bones were showing, and her eyes were deeply set. It pained him to see that her body felt so light, and her hands were so cold. He gently closed his fingers around hers.

He couldn't bear to think of the terror if he had failed her, or if he had come a day too late.

Don had only himself to blame. Shana was just a regular girl; she never had to get into the Wake. If he hadn't taken her in a year ago, she would be a doctor living a far more peaceful life. And what a great doctor she would have been. He had no doubt about that.

Or, even better, if the Wake hadn't reached out to her parents for help on the night of the Red Purge, if he hadn't hidden in her place, the NIISS guards might not have come searching. She would have been spared all the pain of losing her parents.

At the thought of that, tears ran down his face. Don hoped he could do something to make it up to her. He didn't care much about his own life when he was on the bridge in Haxxilic. If the situation arose again, he'd make the same decision to trade his life to stop the Gatti's warships. But Shana was different; she deserved better.

"I won't let you get hurt anymore," Don whispered. "I won't."

He pulled her closer to his chest.

The day grew brighter. A ray of sunlight crept through the small windows and moved slowly to illuminate her face. Her thick eyelashes fluttered, and she turned her head slightly in sleep. Just like that, they sat until almost noon.

Don had enjoyed the happiest hours of his life. He called Brian, asking him to steer his Rover to where they were so they could carry Shana back to their campsite.

When they got back, all the members at the campsite came out to welcome them.

"Don really brought you back!" said Geoffrey, shaking her hand. "We almost thought we wouldn't see you again."

"I'm so glad you're Ok!" Eio exclaimed.

"Come here and let me look at you," said Andro.

Everyone gave her a warm hug in turn.

"It feels so good to be home," Shana said as she greeted each of them.

Then she embraced Eio tightly, pressing his head against her own forehead, and said, "I love you, and I've missed you."

In the end, she turned to Don and said, "You're truly my hero."

A few days later, when Shana had recovered from her weight loss, Don, Brian, Eio, and the others told her what happened in Haxxilic, including Lei and Steve's sacrifice.

She listened quietly. Tears welled up in her eyes, and she brushed them away as they continued.

Don then told her how Dimitri had left Haxxilic early to help her but was still missing.

"He did?" asked Shana in surprise. "And no one has heard from him ever since?"

"No. But we haven't given up," said Don, trying to comfort her. "See? You've come back to us. Maybe we'll find him tomorrow."

Then Shana told Eio and the others everything there was to tell: how Jack protected her till his last moment, how she went to Base-5 in vain and ran out of everything, and how she hid in her old house until Don came to her rescue.

"I feel as tense as if I'd been through it with you," said Eio, looking at her intently. "And I have something to share with you, too." Then he proudly filled her in on the details of Don's pickup.

"When did you guys solve the wilted leaf problem?" asked Shana curiously.

"Hush… don't mention it," Eio whispered, glancing back before he continued. "Nelson and Cohen aren't here, right? I burned one of their devices and caused a fire when testing my modification ideas. Now they're not very happy with me."

Shana's mouth opened into an 'O' while Eio winked at her.

"Thank you so much for saving Don," Shana said, and she kissed Eio on his broad forehead. "Have I told you I love you?"

"Yes, you have. Don't nag."

"All right, all right," she said. "Why didn't you use the vehicle to go home?"

"Because I'd be sad if he was gone," Eio said as he glanced at Don, his eyes twinkling. "I don't want to be sad."

Don smiled. Eio's answer was surprisingly heartwarming.

* * *

A funeral was held two weeks later. A lot of people came. They all had a memory to share about Jack, Terence, Lei, Steve, Fletcher, Ian, and the others.

They had chosen a place to bury Jack. Jack once said that he wanted a spot where he could see the rise of Earth, and he'd gotten his wish.

It was a cool afternoon. The Wake members gathered, and they waited quietly to show their respect. Don was asked to deliver a eulogy since he had been chosen as the new Chief Commander.

After everyone settled, Don began, feeling the weight of the moment, "I know it is hard to accept that our dearest friends, Jack and the others, have left us. Jackson Huntsman was our commander, a mentor, and a frontline soldier. He created the resistance, trained many of us, and saved many lives. Personally, he helped me out of the homeless shelter, and he was like a father to me since.

“Terence joined the Wake as the twelfth member, believing he was needed. He had a strong will, a true strength, and he never gave up his pursuit of great achievements…

“Fletcher and Ian would be the first ones to the action. Lei and Steve — they worked hard, and they were devoted to their duties. All of them fought NIISS until the last moment of their lives…

“In the last words Jack sent back to the home base, he said, ‘All life has an end one day, but I am not afraid because you will carry on.’ ”

Don had to pause there because his eyes went wet. He took a deep breath and relaxed his shoulders before he could go on.

“And yes, the entire lifework Jack devoted himself to — the Wake, us — will keep fighting for the future of mankind. Trust me, our courage will not be exhausted, our enemy will not succeed, and we will march on until we are free. And we will remember our heroes.”

Everyone stood in silent grief. Brian rubbed his face, his eyes filled with tears, and it looked like he was about to cry, too.

At last, Don said, “Thank you for standing with me, brothers.”

He looked at the people clustered around him, then over their shoulders toward Shana standing behind in the last row. She met his gaze with calm and clear eyes. In that moment, he was simply grateful to have her by his side once more.

He added, “And thank you, our angel of the Wake.”

Chapter 21
The Face

A month later, the Wake members gradually resumed their normal activities. Shana felt the lingering echoes of her ordeal fading. Her body had regained its strength, and a steadiness began to return to her spirit.

"I'm calling for a celebration," Andro declared one day. "I said something about a party before the battles, and I never forget my promise for fun."

"A party is exactly what we need," Geoffrey chimed in, and many others agreed readily.

"I can help with that," Shana gladly offered. Don gave a nod. With that decided, she and Brian spent the better part of a day looking for a suitable location. A week later, a party was held at a campsite outside Redland.

Laurelynn was also invited, and she brought five cases of wine. Shana prepared a spread of light refreshments. Everyone was pleased to see the good wine and delicious food.

Andro popped a wine bottle as Shana set up the food table, and the party started in the morning. By noon, the camp was alive with people, laughter, and the clinking of glasses. Shana talked casually with Brian and Andro at the makeshift bar as she waited for Don's arrival.

The moment he showed up, a burst of applause and shouting broke out from the tables.

"Come on, Don, here is your bottle," said Brian. "Drink up!"

"Cheers!" Nelson and Cohen called out to him over the noise of the camp. Yang was drinking deeply from his cup.

"We've succeeded!" Geoffrey yelled. "We've caused severe damage to the Gatti's military power."

"Yeah. We've crushed their plan to invade Earth," Sachin agreed.

Don simply raised a cup and said, "To the journey ahead!"

The cheers became louder from the crowd. Jayden, Ethan, and many others came up to give Don a big hug.

"Congratulations," Jayden said with a grin, and many others chimed in. "You're now the Chief Commander. We're going to call you Chief."

Andro handed Don a package and said, "Here, a gift from me. It's a new blade I've made for you."

"Thank you so much, Andro," said Don as he took the package. "I really appreciate it."

"But don't expect me to join you or call you Chief," Andro continued frankly. "You're still Don to me."

"Right," Don agreed with a smile. "Just call me Don."

Shana watched the guys from nearby as they chatted and laughed with one another. Their faces looked more relaxed than they had in weeks. Everyone seemed to be making the most of the brief calm, she thought, even though they all knew the victory was only a temporary reprieve before the enemy struck back again. Still, they needed a moment like this.

"Shana, do we have more dipping sauce?" Just then, Jayden's voice pulled her out of her thoughts.

"Yeah, give me a second," she replied, remembering the extra sauce left in the kitchen. As she went back to get it, she spotted Eio walking ahead of her, apparently going to the same place.

At the kitchen door, Eio paused for a moment before peeking in, as though making sure nobody was there, then he sneaked in quickly. Without making any sound, he extended his hand, long and thin, up the counter and got a cookie. Before he put it into his mouth, he glanced back.

Shana was right there, looking at him with questioning eyes. Eio was so startled that he almost dropped the cookie.

"Just one," she said flatly. "You need to stay healthy before we get another C-Cube and send you home."

Eio nodded as he swallowed down the cookie.

"Besides, you can get energy from radiation now," she added, "you don't need to eat technically."

"True, but I love cookies. So tasty," Eio replied. Then he ran away, apparently not interested in a lengthy lesson.

Shana thought about the C-Cube for a moment, wondering where they might find another, before retrieving the sauce and heading back to the food table.

Minutes later, Laurelynn came over and gave her a hug. "It's so good to see you!" she said.

"Good to see you too," Shana replied. "I can't thank you enough for your help during the riot. Let me know if I can return your favor."

"We're best friends now. There's no need for formality," said Laurelynn, holding Shana's hands and smiling warmly. "But if you insist, I do want one thing from you."

"Anything I'm capable of," Shana replied seriously.

"What do you think I want?" Laurelynn laughed. "I want to be your bridesmaid."

"What?" Shana gasped, her hand flying to her chest. She couldn't believe what she had just heard. Laurelynn's abrupt thought made her heart skip a beat. Heat crept into her face before she could stop it. It was as if everyone knew her feelings for Don but the man himself.

"What are you talking about? I… I'm so far from that," Shana stuttered. Then she asked uncertainly, "Do you think he even likes me? You must have met more guys than I do and know them better."

"How could he not like you?" Laurelynn asserted. "There're no other girls in your bloody business, yes? You're kind and strong, loving and brave. You're supportive and in charge of yourself at the same time."

Shana was amazed that Laurelynn could say so many good things about her in one breath. "Are you sure?" she asked. "Why do I feel like you're talking about yourself?"

"I was talking about *you*, of course," Laurelynn said, giving her an impossible look. "The first thing people know about me is that I'm beautiful."

Shana saw the difference instantly, and both of them laughed at that.

"I haven't even had a chance to tell him my feelings," Shana then said in a low voice.

"Oh… I can certainly help you with that," said Laurelynn with a wicked smile. She then pulled Shana closer and whispered in her ear, "I have an idea… seduce him tonight…"

* * *

At the end of the party, Shana decided to take Laurelynn's advice and go bold for once. She calculated how long it would take to prepare dinner and asked Don to meet her at her place in the evening.

Then she hurried back to her two-story home in east Redland. It was a nice house Don had helped her move into after her parents passed away. But she had only been back there a few times since she joined the Wake. More often, she just stayed at her compartment in the home base.

Upon entering, she unpacked two bags of groceries she had bought on the way and then glanced at the clock. It was already late afternoon. There wasn't a lot of time left, but it should be enough. She quickly threw on her kitchen clothes: a simple graphic T-shirt and her old blue jeans. Then she tied her hair up into a short ponytail and got started.

Half an hour later, several dishes were already cooking. "Should be enough for a romantic dinner for two," Shana thought while looking at them, feeling proud of herself. She cleaned up the dinner table in the meantime and polished the kitchen utensils and cutlery to shine. Utensils had become antiques anyway since most people only needed the straw that came with the Mix.

She then pulled a bottle of red wine out of her bag, a gift from Laurelynn.

"French Bordeaux, imported from Earth, to celebrate becoming a woman," Laurelynn had said, smiling broadly, and she'd seemed more excited than Shana herself. "Very expensive," she'd added. "Don't waste it. Remember, try not to use your brain."

Shana could see her winking. On that thought, she felt her heart beating faster. It was thumping so loudly that she could hear it herself, and her face became hot.

"Shana… Shana!"

Just when she was dwelling in her imagination, she heard Don calling her name. Never in her life was she so panicked to hear his voice.

"Oh, my goodness." She dropped the wine bottle onto the table and hurried toward the front deck, almost tripping over a chair on her way.

Just then, a Rover eased to a stop in front of her house, and there Don was. He hopped off the vehicle and waved at her.

"What time is it now? Am I getting it wrong?" cried Shana. She felt weakness in her knees as if her strength had left her, and she had to lean onto the railing for support.

Don looked up at her, his mouth slightly open, and he seemed rather puzzled by her strange reactions. He glanced at his Senset and replied, "Five minutes past four. Why? What's the matter?"

Shana wished she could vanish into the ground. "You're two hours early!" she said. Now she had no time to finish cooking, set the table with candles, or shower and change into her evening dress. Even worse, she smelled of food and was covered in sweat.

"Please come again later," she pleaded in a faint voice. "I'm not ready yet."

"It's Ok. I needed to send a document to the United Nations and let them know about the three battles," said Don, sprinting up the stairs already. "I finished that, and I come to help you."

Shana showed him in and said, "You're an extremely punctual person. I was counting on that. You could have… talked to Eio, for example."

Don gave her an "I'm already here" smile, then he set his backpack in the corner and left his shoes outside.

"Everything here is quite simple…" Shana said quickly as he looked around the house.

"But warm and comfortable," Don finished for her. "I didn't know you've made your home such a nice place." He then looked at pictures of Shana and her parents — cooking together, traveling around, and celebrating birthdays…

"Sleepover parties," he said a moment later, his eyes fixed on one of the pictures. "I don't remember ever going to a birthday party, or staying the night at a friend's house."

"You're very welcome to stay tonight," Shana summoned her strength to say it out, her cheeks feeling warm, and then she quickly changed the subject. "I haven't been home for a long while. Everything is covered in dust. Could you please help me with some cleaning?"

"Sure." Don rolled up his sleeves and fixed the place at a fantastic speed. He scrubbed the countertop as well as the windows. He vacuumed the floor, took out the trash, and even cleaned the garage. Shana stole glances at him as he worked, captivated by the unexpected charm in his serious expression.

When dinner was ready, Shana laid plates, knives, forks, and spoons; Don opened the wine bottle. They made a toast to the incredibly tranquil night that rarely occurred. Their life in the Wake was full of tough days and restless nights. It was truly blissful that they could find one night to enjoy their dinner together.

Shana told him small, amusing stories about herself; Don just listened and smiled. After cups of wine and some warm and tasty food, she noticed that he yawned and struggled to lift his eyelids, and he seemed barely able to keep up the conversation.

"Are you feeling Ok, Don?" Shana reached out to hold his hand, wondering if it was time to carry out Laurelynn's plan on this special occasion.

"I'm fine, probably drank too much. Not much of a drinker, only found out today…"

"Can you wait here for five minutes? I want to show you something."

"What is it?"

"A surprise," she said softly.

"Ok…"

Shana hurried to her closet and quickly undressed. She was going to put on her special attire.

"Show him what you look like in lingerie," Laurelynn had said. "Choose lively colors."

Shana remembered her suggestive eyes and her advice on style. Laurelynn liked vibrant colors; she wore a different bright dress each time Shana saw her. Naturally, Shana's day-to-day whites, blues, and blacks were heavily criticized by her.

The red underwear or the more revealing mesh beige? Shana battled fiercely in her mind. Red was hardly her color since she never knew how to wear something that eye-catching. On the other hand, the mesh was desperate… After some long minutes, a voice screamed in her head, "Just pick one, hurry up!"

Shana finally put on the red and loosened up her hair. Then she sprayed on some perfume, applied lipstick, and looked into the mirror. A new girl looked back at her, her lips scarlet.

"Great, I've just become someone else. It certainly makes things easier," Shana said to herself. Feeling the need to keep up her courage, she tried an inviting smile. "Ok, this is going to work."

When she finally came out of her closet door, her heart pounded wildly.

Was this really the night? Shana wondered.

However, to her great disappointment, she found Don half-sitting, half-lying on the sofa, eyes closed. She inhaled deeply and called out his name, "Hey, Don."

There was no response, only the soft sound of his breathing. Shana took his hands and held them gently.

"Hey… hey, Don."

Nothing.

She leaned over and touched his face.

It was unbelievable. He was really fast asleep.

She went to her knees beside the sofa and watched him, and then she ran her fingers gently through his jet-black hair.

"How could you do this to me?" she murmured. "Do you know how much I have to say to you?"

Then she let out a sigh. At least this was the night she could look at him all she wanted, and she could never get enough of that.

Phobos crossed the sky quickly. Soon it was time for bed. Shana changed back into her blue uniform. Since Don and Cohen gave her the uniform, she often slept dressed in it so that she could jump up and go at any time. The whole idea of sexy sleepwear made her feel awkwardly uncomfortable.

She laid Don's head down, lifted his legs onto the sofa, and tucked him in a blanket. After that, she gathered some pillows for herself to cuddle up on the floor by his side.

She then turned off the light, leaving only a lamp. The night light illuminated his relaxed body, but his expression was contemplative and solemn as usual.

"Why are you still knitting your brows in your sleep? What's in your dreams?" Shana asked as she tried to smooth out his light eyebrows with her fingers. Did the world finally offer a moment of peace for this man? she wondered.

* * *

Outside, the night was cold and still. Aria arrived alone at the foot of a hill. The paved way before her wound up among steep rocks, lit by rows of pulsing lights that flashed ahead of her before quickly vanishing into the dark behind. As she climbed, glimpses of a white mansion surfaced between the jagged silhouettes of the rocks.

She'd taken this job to perform at the residence of an eminent Gatti figure. Her roommate, May, had told her it was a rare opportunity, and the payment would be generous.

When Aria reached the towering gate, she heard waterfalls somewhere in the darkness and glanced around uneasily. But no one was there. A faint tightness settled in her chest.

"Hello?" she called tentatively.

Sensing her presence, a virtual guide bearing the appearance of a Gatti appeared.

"State your name," a voice commanded.

"Aria Flowers," she replied.

Several sensors scanned her biometric signatures instantly, and her face image was recorded. After a brief mechanical whir, the gate slid open automatically.

"Welcome, Aria. I'm expecting you."

The virtual guide flashed an arrow, directing her forward. She was led into an elevator that ascended soundlessly to the mansion's highest level. When the doors opened, a long corridor stretched ahead toward a colossal room at the far end.

Aria stepped forward uncertainly. The ceiling above the room was a transparent dome. The starry sky was right above her, Jupiter hanging like a pale banded orb while the Milky Way stretched across the dark. Beneath it all, she felt so small and far away from everything.

Down below, she could see all the night lights of City OIIIzoi. The sound of water she'd heard earlier came from two waterfalls on each side of the mansion, tumbling down into the black depths of Valles Marineris. Across the valley, strings of vehicle lights blinked faintly on TTado Bridge.

This place was an enormous display of status and excess, Aria thought, and she couldn't shake the feeling that she didn't belong, until she saw that the entire floor was dedicated to music playing.

The owner seemed to love music. Rare and unknown instruments stood throughout the expansive room: a narrow metal tube resembling a wind instrument, its end opening into a flared bell, a cannon-shaped drum mounted upon a vessel, and a ten-string harp wired into a flag rising from the base of a warship… Some others were massive and heavy-looking, and she wondered if they could even produce sounds audible to humans.

A grand piano rested near the eastern edge of the room. Its surface was etched with ornate patterns, its ebony finish dark and reflective in the dim light. The ivory white and jet black keys looked familiar and inviting. Under the curved board, the delicate strings waited in silence.

It must be a collectible brought from Earth, Aria thought, and she stood there for a long while, unable to ignore the growing weight of the room's stillness.

Yet no one appeared.

Just a few touches, she thought. It should be the piano she was meant to play tonight. If she could only hear its tone for a moment…

What should she play? She closed her eyes. Perhaps the piano sonata she had been working on since the beginning of her journey.

Her fingers touched the keys, and a crisp sound flooded the room. She was amazed at how beautiful it came out. The first movement opened with a four-note motif, bright and eager. It carried the warmth of sunrise and the memory of her younger self boarding the space shuttle for the first time.

The second movement slowed into quieter rhythms. She walked through long days and sleepless nights, tracing the changes of the four seasons with a subdued melancholy. It reminded her of life on Mars — the hardships, the loneliness. Home now felt impossibly far away in the darkness.

Was darkness the true color of eternity? she wondered.

In the meanwhile, unnoticed by her, a tall black figure emerged silently from the corridor. The piano melody had drawn his attention, and he advanced without a sound, stopping far behind her so as not to waver the music.

Aria went for the final movement. The opening theme returned. Then the dense and continuous notes led to a series of crescendos, like all the beauty of the cosmos gathered into one fleeting moment. At last, the sonata ended in a thunderous coda.

When she finished, she suddenly saw an obscure shadow in the reflection of the piano. She gasped and turned around sharply from the bench.

The dark figure came closer as she straightened up in haste.

She dropped her head low and mumbled, “I… I’m so sorry, sir. I didn’t mean to… I should have asked…”

Compared to the incredible music earlier, now there was a long moment of unbearable silence.

“What is its name?” he finally asked.

It took Aria a while to realize that he referred to the sonata she had just played.

“No… no name, I mean… it’s a piece I’m writing — I haven’t given it a name yet,” Aria replied, shaking slightly; her voice was so low that it was almost inaudible.

“A nice piece,” he said casually. “Light and darkness, repetition and change, survival and evolution, just like our marvelous world.”

She calmed down a little after hearing his comments.

“Show me your hands.”

Aria held out her open palms. He grabbed her hands, turned them over, and stroked them slightly. “Nice hands,” he observed, “fair skin, delicate fingers.”

She quickly withdrew her hands and dared not to look at him.

“You play well. Don’t stop. Now do it again,” he continued, his gaze fixing on her body.

Aria sat back at the piano. An inexplicable sense of unease welled up inside her. She shouldn’t have come, she thought, and she couldn’t shake the feeling that his eyes were still moving back and forth over her body. The hairs on the back of her neck stood up. She shivered, and the tune came out jumping and missing beats.

Just then, a pair of stiff, coarse arms came to seize her from behind. He twined his arms around her waist and her neck. His tentacles caught hold of the rest of her body, tight as iron, and began to tear off her clothes.

Aria’s fingers dropped dead. Fear flooded her.

“Please, let go!” She felt the end of his tentacles clinging to her skin, and then she became acutely conscious of a strange sucking motion.

“Stop!” she shouted in panic, trying to break his clamp.

"Stop… I can't breathe!" Aria struggled to break free. She pushed, hit, and bit hard again and again.

Suddenly, he pulled her hair madly and hit her head against the piano; blood ran off her face like red tears. She could not help but let out a loud scream.

She fought the tremendous pressure with all her strength until her limbs gave out. Pain crushed against her ribs as if they were about to break, and then she passed out, but he went on…

Long hours passed.

His roar grew lower, and the violent moves slowed. The chill air brought back some of her senses. The pain made her feel like dying as things came back into focus, and she had bruises all over her body.

Don was enraged at what he saw in his dream. He clenched his fists and bellowed, "Who is he?"

"Show me his face!"

As if his voice was heard, Aria's eyes widened for a moment, and then she turned around and stared.

A pair of cold, indifferent eyes stared back at him.

It was the face of System Architect Icus.

CONTINUE THE JOURNEY!

Man on Mars: Invasion of the Mind
(Book 2)

Available Now

https://www.amazon.com/dp/B0FVS5YN55

X. Quinn loves science since she's a child. She dreamed about becoming an astronomer, or a doctor who can cure all the disease in the world… Growing up, she earned a Master's degree in molecular medicine and becomes a life scientist. She's done basic research and has several scientific publications in biomedical journals. Inspired by the COVID-19 pandemic, she put her passion for science and fantasy into the novel, Man on Mars: The Wake, the first one in the trilogy.

She lives on Earth.

Dear Reader,

I want to hear what you think! I'd really appreciate it if you could leave me a review or rating. Thank you very much for your support!

Follow me on Facebook, Tiktok, or Goodreads to stay tuned for future book releases of the Man on Mars trilogy and promotions:

https://www.facebook.com/profile.php?id=61582167116185

https://www.tiktok.com/@qqsauieoh19

https://www.goodreads.com/author/show/22108015.X_Quinn

Happy reading!

www.ingramcontent.com/pod-product-compliance
Lightning Source LLC
Chambersburg PA
CBHW030352310726
48979CB00001B/277

* 9 7 8 1 7 3 7 8 5 6 4 1 2 *